THE EGO MAKERS

BOOKS BY DONALD EVERETT AXINN

POETRY

Sliding down the Wind

The Hawk's Dream and Other Poems

Against Gravity

The Colors of Infinity

Dawn Patrol

The Latest Illusion

FICTION

Spin

The Ego Makers

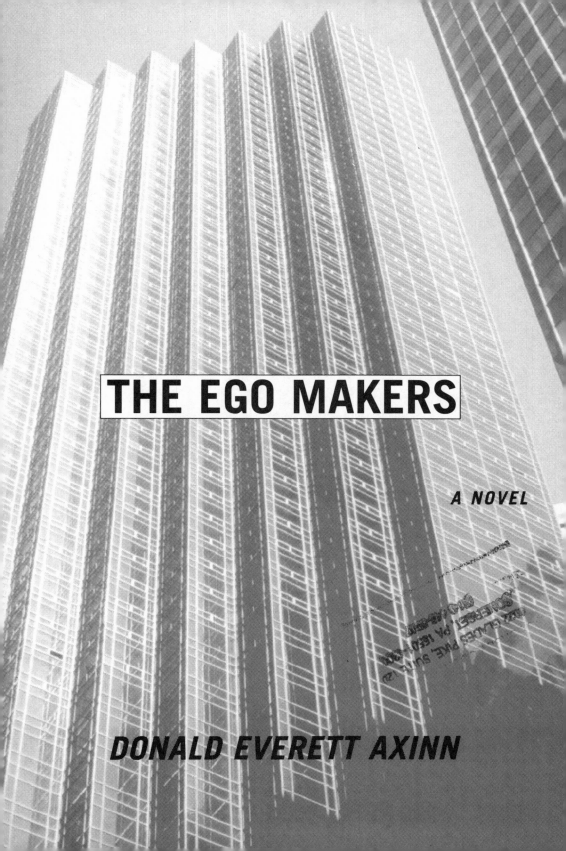

THE EGO MAKERS

A NOVEL

DONALD EVERETT AXINN

FIRST EDITION

This is a work of fiction. Names, places, characters, and incidents are either the products of the author's imagination or are used fictitiously.

Library of Congress Cataloging-in-Publication Data

Axinn, Donald E.
        The ego makers / Donald Everett Axinn.—1st ed.
              p.   cm.
        ISBN 1-55970-336-9 (hc)
              1. Corporations—Corrupt practices—United States—Fiction. 2. Businessmen—United States—Psychology—Fiction. 3. Brothers—United States—Fiction. I. Title
        PS3551.X5E37   1996
        813'.54—dc20   95-53073

Published in the United States by Arcade Publishing, Inc., New York
Distributed by Little, Brown and Company

10 9 8 7 6 5 4 3 2 1

Designed by API

BP

PRINTED IN THE UNITED STATES OF AMERICA

This book is dedicated to the memory of my parents, Ann and Mike, who introduced me to a world of awe and excitement, one filled with almost endless possibilities.

And to my best brother, Calvin, for encouraging me to create the relationship between Henry and Steven as I have, which is nothing like ours.

And to my wife, Joan: I'm grateful for her patience, criticism, support, love, and friendship.

Is not this great Babylon, that I have built?

DANIEL 4:30

ACKNOWLEDGMENTS

In creating this story, I was helped with the legal aspects by several sharp attorneys: the real Steve Apthaker, Sam Yedid, and that student of human nature: Joan Axinn.

Technical information regarding real estate transactions for the period were critiqued by the real Frank Sullivan; Ken Katzman reviewed the tax aspects and implications. The flying actions and events were verified by three professional pilots: Craig Sampson, Greg Galuso, and Neal Almond. The Sicilian spoken in the 1940s was furnished by my Italian "teacher," Jo Geluso. And, thanks again to Roger Straus III.

I am grateful to my assistants Tina Rogovin and Dianne Francis for their hard work, suggestions, and patience.

AUTHOR'S NOTE

During the 1980s, real estate developers in New York could do little wrong. Demand for space was strong, rents kept going up, and the banks battled with one another to provide the loans. Real estate resembled a runaway stock market. There was, however, one crucial difference: stocks and bonds can be bought and sold on the spot; new buildings take years to plan, finance, erect, and lease.

The real estate crisis and the savings and loan debacle almost brought the country to its knees. Many developers failed and are gone; some survived the collapse. The excesses that caused the crisis are still very much present, disguised perhaps, but there.

The characters in this novel are based upon actual people and events from those tumultous days. But I would remind readers that this is a work of fiction, and that any absolute identification between real people and events and those portrayed here could be a mistake.

Part 1

You are what your deep, driving desire is.
As your desire is, so is your will.
As your will is, so is your deed.
As your deed is, so is your destiny.

Brihadaranyaka Upanishad
IV.4.5

"*T*HEY *what?*" I shouted into the phone. "They won't sign the lease? Damn it, Steve, we agreed to every one of their demands, including that additional two months' rent concession! Sonofabitch! And that on top of a year's free rent!" My fingers grabbed the top sheet of notes from the thick folder marked "Standard General Corporation" and crunched it into a ball. "What's Hollick doing about it?"

"How should I know what our hotshot broker is doing?" I heard Steve sigh. "They said they were genuinely sorry, but they're renewing with their present landlord. Gave me some lamebrained excuse about a board member's golf chum bragging about a fantastic lease he had just signed. So this clown calls Jordan, and naturally Jordan starts checking around. No way he's going to stand up to the board for our deal. Not with the lousy profits they've projected for next year."

For a few seconds, silence stretched between us.

"These bastards assured us we were done negotiating. Didn't you remind them of that?" I stood up, as if ready to spring, or start round ten.

"Another problem, little brother," Steve said, ignoring my question. "Yedid, their current landlord, has matched our price. And he said he'd take over any existing leases they had with us or anyone else. Where the hell is he getting the dough? I told them not to fall for that bait-and-switch game. I said we couldn't improve on our offer or give them a lower rent, but that we'd try to come up with a good answer. Henry, I had to say something." He sounded less than convincing.

I pounded the desk with my right hand. The phone, which I was balancing precariously between my shoulder and head, slipped loose. I caught it in midair. I should have gone in myself. Steve was too fucking passive. Panics in a crisis. And in 1989, developing commercial office buildings was no longer a slam-dunk.

Inwardly I was seething, but went on coolly, as if responding to bad weather information from an aviation weather briefer. "Can you get in to see Jordan? No, wait. What about Phelan? As chairman, he could order Jordan to close the deal with us, and also square it with the board."

"Henry, be realistic. You know Phelan's getting ready to retire. He won't rock the boat. Besides, Jordan would really get pissed off if I went over his head."

"Look, Steve, Phelan dislikes Jordan, right? Hates his guts, in fact. Wasn't really his man for president. They pressured him into it. Phelan would like a way to get even."

"You don't know that. Suppose you're wrong?" That sounded familiar, like the gotcha or catch-22 Steve used whenever he had the chance.

"What the hell do we have to lose? Turn lemons into lemonade. You know as well as I do, if we don't close this deal, Federated Bank will pull the chain. We're on the note personally."

"I am certainly aware of that!" Steve said. "You didn't have to add another project in Montvale! Or buy that land in Greenwich." Another swipe. "You never goddamn listen to me, do you?"

"This isn't the time, Steve, or the place. Let's focus on trying to close the lease with Standard General. Unfortunately, I gave out some of the work, believing . . ." I didn't finish; he wouldn't be receptive to the details.

"Great! You'd better undo any commitments, because this deal doesn't look like it's going down," he said tightly. "I'll talk to Jordan. Tell him he can't make that other deal."

"That's not the way. Stay put, I'll be there in less than an hour."

"Traffic," Steve said. "You stay put. I can handle this."

Maybe he could. It wasn't that Steve didn't have talent. He just didn't have the drive to finish the job. No killer instinct.

"Look," I said, "you know my relationship with Phelan. All those dinners and golf games. I'll come in by air."

"You'd better think about selling that helicopter, Henry," Steve said. "The toys and goodies go first."

"If I had listened to you, Steve baby, we'd still be piddling around doing shitty general contracting. Dad wanted us to make this company into one of the big players. Well, we have." I glanced at my watch. "We've been through recessions before, and came out stronger. Remember '82? I was right about starting those buildings on spec." I took a deep breath. "Look, Steve, let's not fight, all right?"

Roslyn, Long Island, 1951

Roslyn Village's park sloped down gradually between two hills, the terrain rolling gently like a great English lawn. A small stream, the remnant of an ancient river, terminated at Hempstead Harbor. In colonial days a gristmill harnessed the waterpower. A century or more later, that building had been restored on Northern Boulevard, Route 25A, the single east-west road through town. Above the lake several man-made ponds had been created, with benches around them. The park was filled with fine oaks and beech, willows and maples, pines and hawthorns. Footbridges spanned the stream that flowed into a small lake, at the end of which was the gristmill. Swans inhabited the lake, their nests carefully hidden in the cattails. Mallards, blacks, and a few Pekin ducks could be heard chattering away in the large pond that had a path surrounding it. The Canada geese thrived so well many gave up migrating.

Jake and Barbara Martin loaded Steven and Henry into their Olds station wagon for the day's adventure. It was a crisp October day, the sky a sharp, lively blue. Barbara was in great spirits. "My three men," she trilled, humming, as they turned north down Roslyn Road from Horace Harding Boulevard.

The boys played contentedly in the backseat; Steve kneaded his Play-Doh and Henry divided his time between his drawing book, stroking the back of his father's head, and watching cars and buildings. "Beat that one, Daddy." It sounded more like a command than a request.

They arrived at the park, carrying or dragging — depending upon who had what — the ingredients for the picnic. Barbara placed various containers — plates, glasses, and napkins — on a picnic table and then spread a blanket on the ground. "Cold pasta, bologna and provolone sandwiches. But you have to eat your carrots and celery, or else no dessert." When she looked away, Henry shoved the carrots and celery into his pocket.

"Mommy," Steven announced, "I'm not eating mine if he doesn't eat his." Henry stared at Steven then hit him on the back and ran from the table, Steven in pursuit, his parents observing the scene.

A frustrated Steven returned shortly. "He stinks. He stinks! I hate him!"

"Steven," his father said, "Henry shouldn't have hidden the carrots in his pocket. But he hit you because you tattled on him. Isn't that right?" Jake rose and turned to look for Henry.

"Yes, but it all started because Henry wasn't doing what I told him to," said Barbara.

"Okay, you're right. You find Henry. Steven and I will feed the ducks," Jake said.

They walked down the slope, where they found Henry busily grandstanding for a little girl. "Look," he announced, "I'm not afraid." He leapt from one large rock to another, then to the ground, rolling over in a somersault.

"C'mon, showoff," his father yelled, "over to the pond. The ducks are waiting for us!" Henry bounced up, began to run, but turned and waved back at the little girl.

At the pond's edge, they all held pieces of bread in their hands. Ducks swam toward them, assembling for the feast. The geese remained nearby, cautious but ready to pick up scraps. The boys laughed and shouted as they threw the bread, the scramble now including several obstreperous gulls.

Henry stood on one foot, balancing himself, and tossed pieces as if he were shooting basketballs. He was unaware of his gracefulness, but it did not escape his father's attention. Steven glanced up, saw his father's grin of approval, ran over to Henry, and shoved him. Henry landed in the pond, up to his hips. Swiftly, he grabbed for Steven's legs, caught one, and pulled him in.

"Stop that, Henry!" his mother yelled. "Jake, pull them out!"

When they were lifted, dripping, onto the grass, Henry slugged his brother, who hit him back. Jake pulled them apart. "Enough of that! Don't make me have to take off my belt!"

Barbara ran down to the pond and cuddled Steven in her arms. "I think we should just go home," she said, on the verge of tears.

"What about me, Mommy?" Henry said, pouting. "Why do you always take care of him?" But his mother was still rocking Steven, who was whimpering. Henry compressed his lips, slapped his hand against his leg, turned, and ran toward the car.

Barbara stood up, leaving Steven wrapped in the picnic blanket. As she and Jake gathered up the half-eaten picnic, she turned to him and said quietly, "It's only going to get worse. We have to do something."

"All kids fight when they're young. They'll get closer later on, you'll see." Jake looked at Barbara, hoping to find if not agreement at least understanding. But he found neither.

"I hope so," she said, shaking her head. "They are so different . . . so very different."

I hung up, slipped on my jacket, which was tailor-made and fit perfectly. At six-one and 175 pounds, I worked hard to keep fit. I was forty-four and aware the lines in my boyish face had deepened, but I also knew it enhanced my appeal. My hair was still thick and soft. Hints of gray seemed washed in like the frost on the edges of leaves in late fall; it only enhanced the image of a dashing young — well, not quite that young — tycoon.

I flipped on the intercom. "Dianne, ask Craig to get the bird ready for a hop into Manhattan. I'll be there in fifteen, no, ah, twelve minutes. Oh, and Dianne, call MacDougall at the bank. He's in Melville today. Tell him I have to cancel. No, wait. Ask him if he can make it tomorrow or Thursday. And change anything else I have scheduled."

"Fine, Mr. Martin," she said with a lilt in her voice. "I'll make

Mr. MacDougall feel it'll be the best lunch he'll ever have. Your tennis club?"

"No, Glen Pointe. The atmosphere at the golf club is more toney. Thanks, Dianne."

Instead of waiting for the elevator, I raced down the five flights of stairs. The first call I would make from my car would be to John Phelan. I didn't want Dianne to set up an appointment; Tina, Phelan's assistant, would probably turn her down. But I knew I had charmed Tina Schrager often enough, and this was payoff time. As I unlocked my car I glanced up to check the weather.

Experienced pilots analyze the conditions they have to contend with, and years of practice make the habit instinctive. That morning, the sun was draped with thick gauze, following the forecast for heavy humidity and lousy visibility for this late-May day.

I quickly closed the car door. I decided the weather shouldn't present any problems for my Jet Ranger. Glad it's not the thirtieth, I thought, with a shiver. Never fly on the thirtieth. That was the day Clancy was killed.

I called Phelan on my cellular phone and told Tina it was critical that I see him. She said he was tied up, but she would tell him.

The second call was back to my brother. "Steve, I forgot one thing. Jerry Hollick has to get more involved. Johnson and Amoruso are among the biggest brokers in the business. And Hollick's commission is damn near three million bucks. Tell him we'll improve the payout, fifty percent on occupancy, the balance in twelve months." That should get him to move his ass, I thought. Probably sharing some of it with Jordan. I could care less.

"You're forgetting something, kiddo," Steve said. "Hollick's also the broker for our competitors. Gets his commission either way. A lease extension with those guys is a helluva lot easier for him than making a new deal with us. Plus their attorneys were Yale classmates. 'Nuff said."

"C'mon, Steve, that's 'twosies.' First we have to get them off that other deal. For Chrissake, don't always be so damn negative. Besides, Hollick's commission with us is larger. He knows that. Oh, never mind, I'll call him myself from the chopper." I waited for a response, which didn't come. "I'm sorry about what I just said.

It's just that we'll be in deep shit if we don't get Three-Fifty-Five leased."

"You don't have to remind me," Steve replied coldly. "Ten thousand bucks a day. A huge drain on our cash flow. Ari collared me yesterday, by the way. With all our other vacancies plus the land we're carrying, he doesn't know where the hell to get the money to cover the deficit. Oh, I might as well mention, he added that you're not keeping him informed." Another jab in the ribs.

"Steve, you know I'm involved in a million things. Like settling refinancings. The Montvale III building. Hey, are you guys working with or against me?" I decided to stop beating the moribund horse. "Listen, I have to go. I'm pulling in to the heliport. Will you pick me up in the city?"

"Better get yourself a cab," Steve said curtly. "I'll do what I can here."

Let him win the small ones, I thought. I jumped out of the car at the heliport entrance, saw the blades of my helicopter rotating slowly, and waved to my pilot, Craig Sampson. I dashed into the waiting room and tossed my keys to the receptionist. "Sorry, I have an emergency. Would you ask one of the guys to park my car?"

"No problem, Mr. Martin." Shirley Dennison's red hair curved artfully around her face and shoulders, which showed through her sheer pink blouse. When she got up from behind the counter and walked across the lobby or down the hall, which she did fairly often, the eyes of every man in the area followed her. She had hinted to me more than once that she wouldn't mind hitching a chopper ride with me. That would be very nice, was my first thought. But I suspected she was trouble. One of the pilots mentioned that she got a particular charge pursuing married men, then dropping them after they had left their wives.

A lineman held the door to the helicopter. Double white arrows ran the length of the fuselage, ending with attractive script letters forming "The Martin Companies." The logo was displayed next to the name: double triangles with crossed arrows that formed an X. Beneath was, "Form Follows Function," and "Founded 1946."

Thick haze dirtied up the sky and enveloped the heliport,

banished the sunlight. I took the right seat and donned a headset, looked down and scrutinized my boots. That morning I had put on my lizard pair, handmade for me in El Paso. My lucky boots. I relaxed a little.

"We all set, Craig?" I asked into the voice-actuated intercom.

Craig Sampson was born in Madrid, the son of a State Department military attaché. He was short, lean, and a year or two older than I was. He had served as a lieutenant colonel in Vietnam, been shot down twice, and awarded almost every medal they could think of. A gash ran from his left ear across his cheek all the way to his chin. The plastic surgeons had done as much as they could, but it was still very pronounced. It was known he had gotten it when he had tried to escape. Sampson had a dry sense of humor except when he was flying. Then he was all business. Craig had logged thousands of helicopter and jet hours, had been with IBM, but came to us when they tried to push him into early retirement.

"Don't like the oil pressure, Henry. It drops thirty or forty pounds, then comes back up. We checked the level and all the hose connections but didn't find any leaks." I knew Sampson personally examined any work performed by the mechanics. "Be better if we drove in."

"Craig, I gotta get to the city. I mean, fast."

I searched Sampson's face. I wanted him to insist on grounding the bird, hoping in spite of my macho behavior that he would try to overrule me. Engine trouble, real or imagined, scares the shit out of me. So does bad weather. But no one was going to find that out.

"Look, Henry, you pay me to fly with you and be responsible for your aircraft. I don't shy away from weather or anything else unless I think it's necessary." He glanced at the gauges. "Make a deal with you, boss. We go, but if I see anything I don't like, it's a fast one-eighty back here or wherever we have to put her down. No ifs, ands, or buts," he added with military authority.

"Agreed, Colonel. You handle the radios."

The air was thick and ugly. No wind to blow it away.

"I don't like taking off in this stuff," Sampson growled.

"I don't care. I have to be in Manhattan pronto!" Sampson gave me a dirty look and shook his head. In a testy voice he advised the traffic in and around the heliport that we were departing to the west, while I twisted and raised the collective, causing the craft to rise into the northwest wind. The sleek, midnight-blue helicopter, its nose slightly down, moved rapidly up and forward in the direction of the Manhattan skyline. Sampson's eyes were fixed on the oil pressure gauge. I also checked for any fluctuation of the needles.

It normally took about seventeen minutes to the Sixtieth Street Heliport, but today the flight controllers needed to vector us, so that would add several minutes.

"LaGuardia Approach Control, Jet Ranger 2285 Whiskey, nine to the southeast. Sixtieth Street Heliport with information Kilo." Sampson's professionalism was evident in his crisp, clear tone.

"Roger, 85 Whiskey, squawk 4247 and ident." Sampson set the numbers into the transponder and idented. Since planes were landing on Runway 4 at LaGuardia, the controller directed us to a heading of 260 degrees and an altitude of six hundred feet.

The next five minutes were uneventful, despite the haze obscuring our visibility. When we were over Long Island City, we both noticed a sudden drop in the oil pressure.

"Yes, I see it, Craig," I said as calmly as I could. "What do you think?" Good God, I thought, is this going to be it?

"We're closer to Sixtieth than LaGuardia," Sampson said in a voice so untroubled you would have thought he had just awakened from a pleasant nap.

"If it quits over the East River, we're in the drink," I responded, aware of the tightness in my voice. "Otherwise, we can put it down almost anywhere. I like my baths warm. Maybe we'd better land."

"We go to Sixtieth Street. Smarter. Only four minutes away." He paused. "We'll climb as high as possible. Maybe three minutes." He pressed the transmit button on his stick as he pointed in the same direction we were headed. But we couldn't get much above six hundred feet or we'd lose all visibility. I tried to remain calm, but I could feel my heart thumping like a big drum. Like it had thumped so often back in Vietnam. Some of my buddies and I were in Vung Tan on a couple of days of R & R. We were drinking pretty good and went to a palm reader for a few laughs. *"Air, fire, water,"* the old crone had intoned. *"You will die by air!"* Was the witch's crystal-ball prediction finally coming true?

Beaufort, South Carolina, 1967

Cherry Point jet school. Hotshot Henry, fresh with his fighter-pilot wings. Best in his squadron. Best in the whole damn school! I loved flying jets, screaming into the wild blue yonder.

I earned my wings, and was assigned to the jet school. One well-oiled night, on a dare delivered at the bar in the officer's club, I wagered Kevin Clancy that I, Henry Sabatini Martin, would, but that Clancy would not, fly under a particular concrete bridge. It was a small two-lane span that joined the mainland and one of the barrier beaches.

"C'mon, Martin," cut in one of the other pilots, Neal Almond, who wasn't quite as sloshed as we were, "you guys are talking nuts. That bridge is no Golden Gate. Too damn low, like maybe 100 feet over the water. And they'll can you as soon as you land, which you won't because you'd be a fucking dead twenty-two-year-old mackerel. Sober up, tiger." He pointed at me. "You're a pain in the ass, Martin, but we tolerate you only because you bring around those foxy women."

"I mean it, Clancy," I slurred, paying no attention to Almond, "one hundred bucks, one for each foot. Put up or shut up!" Clancy nodded. I liked and respected Kevin. He was black and raised in Chicago. He excelled in high school, had received a Navy scholarship to Dartmouth and qualified for flight school. We met the first day and hung out together. A lot of teasing and drinking.

"You're on," he slurred.

"Okay," I said. "No problem. We'll fly under the radar."

Three days later, at the end of a practice flight, our two planes were screaming along the beach at five hundred feet, an interesting altitude at 450 knots. I wiggled my wings, maintaining radio silence, and circled tightly over the concrete bridge. I didn't notice any cars, only a single shrimp boat traversing the wide channel.

I pulled back on the throttle and popped the speed breaks to slow the jet to 200 knots, to better view the objective. Damn, that's one small bridge, I thought. That arch is pretty low to the water. Fuck it, I can make it, and ol' horseless Clancy will definitely freak out. I'll show those birdheads what flying's all about.

I smiled, turned quickly to see Clancy flying in a wide circle, then dropped the gear to slow my aircraft even further. "This has to be just right," I whispered, "level wings, steady altitude and pitch, power just above stall speed. Checklist complete. Watch and scan, scan and watch!"

I made one practice pass over the bridge, turned back, and thought I saw the men on the shrimp boat gaping up at me. I circled to make a second run. A stiff crosswind was blowing from the north, evident from the small foaming whitecaps and streaky lines the wind was writing on the water. I lined the bridge up and dropped down to fifty feet over the channel. "Okay, okay, okay," I murmured, "nice. Just above stall speed. Watch, watch! Easy, e-a-s-y. Okay. Slowly. Just take it through, baby. Yeah! You are the best. The best!"

My plane slid along on the flight path as if guided by invisible wires, only twenty feet or so above the water. The blast of the jet engine carved a sluice into the surface. I flew under the bridge with approximate equal distance and leeway on all four sides. I screamed, forgot all about the radar, and pointed my aircraft straight up into a double victory roll. I found Clancy, flew side-by-side, and gestured with my hand, Alphonse to Gaston. Clancy gave me the finger and dropped down for a practice run. The men on the boat seemed mesmerized. They continued heading toward the bridge instead of turning around and away from the next moment of truth.

Clancy made a wide sweep over the small marsh islands. As he came in over the channel, the plane's exhaust also created a rounded groove in the water, like the wake of a powerboat. I slowed down even further, to try to get a better view. Clancy's jet was underneath me, slightly to my right. It seemed to me he was too high. The way to execute the maneuver was to set his height above the water early, so that only minor adjustments would be required. The boat was beginning to get in the way. What the hell is the matter with those guys? Get out of there! "Hey, Clancy," I said over the discreet frequency we had decided to use, "you need more room. Wait till those clowns move away." I listened and watched the jet approach the bridge. "Clancy!"

"Shut up, I'm busy," came his answer. Fifty yards away Clancy flew an abbreviated S-turn to avoid the boat. I could only guess what his exact *configuration was in relation to the water and the bridge's arch when he entered.*

In the miniseconds that followed, I first saw white smoke rising from under the bridge, then the jet coming out, banking sharply, the outer portion of its left wing shorn. The right wing dipped into the water, flinging the plane into a crazy-looking cartwheel. It continued on its undisciplined course, the momentum of approximately 150 knots air speed propelling it madly until it ended up on its back on an island marsh, enveloped in steam. There was no explosion or fire.

"Oh, God, no! No, no," I whispered, head down for a few seconds. I circled the wreckage and noticed cars now stopping on the bridge. The shrimp boat's wake became larger as it crossed under the bridge and headed rapidly to the smoking jet. I kept circling. "Beaufort Approach, Marine 2874, Mayday, Mayday! One of . . . Lieutenant Clancy . . ." I couldn't finish.

"Marine 2874. Beaufort Approach. Report situation!"

When local rescue teams arrived, it took them two hours to extricate Clancy's body. Apparently he did not die instantly, but shortly after the shrimp boat arrived. I landed at the base and was immediately confined to quarters. The other pilots were ordered not to discuss anything among themselves or to visit me until the military court convened. The body was dispatched to Clancy's parents in Chicago, who made a special request that I be permitted to attend the funeral. I had expected the Clancys would want me charged with at least involuntary manslaughter, but they were religious Baptists who attributed the incident to their son's bad judgment and not to my instigation. Their request was rejected, as was one by my father that he be allowed to visit me.

Four days after the accident, Major Palmer Spenadel, our commanding officer, summoned me to his office. A third-generation Annapolis graduate, Spenadel was all spit and polish, but under the military veneer an okay guy.

"We debated for quite a while whether we should send you up for a court-martial. You should be sentenced to hard labor at a military prison. However, there's a war going on, and the Marines have spent a great deal of money on you, Lieutenant," Spenadel said acidly. "You are hereby put on probation and your pay suspended. You are ordered to report immediately to Camp Pendleton for infantry training. Normal officer's privi-

leges, including longevity, will be suspended for one year. Your record will so indicate." Major Spenadel paused and stared hard at me. "In layman's language, Martin, because what you did was presumably not premeditated, I argued against the court-martial. If we weren't involved in the Vietnam conflict, I can tell you it would have been very different."

He walked to the window. A squadron of planes was flying noisily overhead. "We need our pilots to be confident, even a little arrogant," he said. "Many of us have broken a rule or two in our flying careers. But you got a man killed, no matter how much you may regret it now. Not to mention the loss of a several-million-dollar aircraft. We don't give second chances in Marine Air for that."

He turned to face me. I was staring straight ahead. "Martin, do something right in Vietnam. You owe it to Clancy. And his family. That is all, Lieutenant." I saluted sharply, which was returned by the major. There was no handshake.

"LaGuardia Approach, 85 Whiskey." The controller responded. "85 Whiskey has a drop in oil pressure, requesting direct Sixtieth Street."

"85 Whiskey, you declaring an emergency?" That was the question the controller by law had to ask.

"Negative. Just want the shortest route possible as a precaution." Sampson knew all the red tape we'd have to go through if we declared an emergency. Besides, if we did have engine failure, it might not make any difference.

"Approved, 85 Whiskey. Keep me advised."

Craig reset the Loran for Sixtieth Street and flew on that heading. Both our eyes were focused on the critical pressure indicator. As pilots, we had both experienced emergencies or near-emergencies. Even though most of us would never admit it, it was reassuring to have a second pilot present.

We crossed the East River right next to the Queensborough Bridge.

"You're a good girl," I whispered. "Not much farther. Daddy's going to take care of you, get you something very special. For now, just behave."

"She's okay," said Craig. "Pressure's holding. About two more minutes. Damn lucky, Martin. Next time I'm not listening to you," he said coldly, staring at me. "We should never have left."

"C'mon, Craig, smile. We weren't in any real danger." A broad grin spread across my face. "Not really."

"Of course we were," Sampson snapped. "We both could have been killed. Look, Martin, I don't fool around. I could lose all my licenses. . . . I don't have your millions," he added.

That was unnecessary, I thought. But what good would my millions have been if the chopper had crashed? I welcomed Sampson's candor. I respected him greatly, even though I viewed him as a man with limited goals. What the hell, I often said to myself, not too many guys have the drive to make it big.

"Yes, sir, Colonel," I responded as we began to shut down the engine. He had made a perfect landing, right on top of the triangular mark, following the hand signals given by the blue-overall-clad lineswoman, who guided us to a landing position. "Sorry to have insisted. Promise I won't do it again. There's a real emergency with the Standard General deal."

I grabbed my coat and attaché case from the rear seat and opened the door. "Can't tell how long I'll be. Dianne will call you at Operations. Or I will." I smiled and put out my hand. "You were there for me today, Craig. Thanks, I won't forget it," I yelled, as I ran toward a waiting taxi.

2

IN the taxi, I tried to compose my thoughts and focus on exactly what was happening. I had come too far to lose this lease now. Other deals had presented obstacles, and over the years I had closed damn near every one of them. All the big ones, anyway. Competing developers, brokers, prospective tenants, bankers, mortgage lenders, and especially opposing attorneys. I had beaten the best of them.

Still, an uneasiness had begun to permeate the office building market. Recently *Barron's* and *Business Week* had carried articles about the growing supply of space. A few economists expressed concern regarding what they believed were excessive loan portfolios that banks and insurance companies carried with developers.

I paid attention to what they were saying. I remembered all too well the big recession in the '70s when some developers got caught with buildings they couldn't rent. That didn't happen to me then, and I had been careful to analyze the various factors before deciding to go ahead with my new office structure.

I thought back to the early '80s and the go-go years of the Reagan era. Developers put up more and more buildings on spec, certain they would rent, assuming each lease would be at a higher number than the last one. Financial institutions went on a spree, falling all over one another to make loans. Owners took advantage of the loose-money environment and heavily refinanced their existing buildings. Hell, I did, too. The additional funds made possible new purchases of land for suburban office parks and also projects, like my 355 gem in Manhattan. I was even able to put some money into the stock and bond markets.

To keep up with the latest trends, I attended seminars and lectures on real estate finance. I particularly liked listening to Asmund Faerevaag, a top Citicorp economist, whose analyses and prognostications over the years were generally accurate. He warned that when mortgages became too high in relation to the equity and value of buildings, they inevitably become riskier investments. In a downturn, when vacancies are greater and cash flows negative, property owners find it difficult to make mortgage payments, particularly if the payments are higher due to larger mortgages. It was simple arithmetic, but how many professionals refused to listen?

When I decided to start 355 in 1987, I weighed the risks carefully. For one thing, our overall portfolio had only a 4 percent vacancy. I didn't like the fact that it would take as long as three years from the initial shovel in the ground to getting the last tenant in and closing the permanent mortgage. No one could predict how good or bad the economy would be that far ahead. Everyone agreed that our Park Avenue location was one of the very best in the Midtown area, and a market study I commissioned indicated demand should remain strong. The banks from whom I needed a building loan mortgage felt comfortable with the study. After extensive negotiations, I concluded the loan with Federated and a permanent take-out mortgage with Teachers Insurance.

Three-Fifty-Five manifested exactly the architectural style I had always admired: towering vertical lines of limestone alternated with indented windows, making the structure at once dramatic yet classic, functional yet appealing, elegant yet simple. To make it unique, portions of the facade were designed to look like slabs of different widths applied against each other. This building was one of a kind, and I was the guy who created it.

What also made me confident was the strong interest by Standard General, along with the Eady Corporation, Seaver Network, Allison Communications, as well as smaller prospects. Despite those rumblings about overbuilding, I sensed my timing was good.

In the past couple of weeks, the whole market was buzzing

about the pending lease for the entire building with Standard General. An invitation came from Washington. Steve barged into my office.

"What do you mean," he said indignantly, "you're going to the Senate Foreign Affairs dinner. Why didn't the invitation include me? That money you give is *our* money."

"I don't know why Senator Dole called me. Maybe because I know him."

"That helps get us recognition, but Dole said we were mentioned during a committee hearing, and it developed from there. Besides, I'm the guy who goes to all those functions."

He turned and slammed the door as he left.

Investment bankers had called: Morgan Stanley, Goldman Sachs, and Dillon Read. Venture capitalists Jim Seymour, Christopher Griffin, and Jeremiah Hartnett, among others.

But the call I most cherished was the one from the mayor the previous Wednesday. Dianne buzzed, and in hushed tones, as if afraid my caller might hear her, said, "It's the Mayor for you, Mr. Martin."

"The mayor of what? Jericho?"

"Of New *York*," she whispered.

I picked up the phone. Probably one of the mayor's flunkies.

"Henry . . ." I recognized his nasal tone immediately. No flunky. Hizzoner. Himself. "Henry, your people have just given us a grand tour of Three-Fifty-Five. Congratulations! It's a gem. A real gem. I'd like to discuss a formal ribbon-cutting ceremony sometime later this month. I know it's short notice, but we can whip up something terrific. Bring in both senators from Washington. What do you say?"

I only wished the mayor could see my grin. "Great idea," I said. "When would you like to meet?"

We set up a date for the following week. When I set the phone back on its cradle I felt my ego growing bigger by the minute. "Jesus, Henry, you *have* arrived," I heard myself saying. I couldn't remember when I'd felt so on top of the world. Well, maybe the night I spent with Michael Allen a couple of months ago.

Allen — Michael Allen III — was a senior partner at Lazard

Frères. He had invited me to dinner in their corporate "house." Again, Steve had not been invited. On purpose, I presumed. On the way there, I reminded myself that the invitation was no accident. Damn right I should have dinner with Allen. A few years back, players like Allen wouldn't have given me the time of day. Act like you belong, I kept telling myself. You do this all the time. Stay with him. On his level. No matter what, no excuses.

Imagine this: a meticulously restored Colonial house located on Wall Street. These guys had taken one of the original, lower Manhattan pre-Revolutionary houses and placed it on top of their forty-story office building. What a photo story that would have made. But Lazard's whole style was understated. Sorry, ladies and gentlemen. No publicity. No article in the *New York Times* or the *Wall Street Journal*. No photo section in *Architectural Digest* or *House and Garden*.

An attractive Stepford-type young woman in a historically accurate recreation of a Pilgrim dress had conducted me from Executive Reception into a small, private elevator to the top floor. I entered through the front door of the house. The decor was perfect Early American. Allen was sitting on the sofa, another period piece from Revolutionary times, I was sure. He put aside some folders and rose to greet me. We were both trustees of the Museum of Modern Art, and on museum matters had for several years taken aggressive positions on finances and acquisitions at meetings. We were usually in the minority, but we had often been persuasive enough to win over the other more conservative trustees. Both of us were in line to become chairman — Allen first, no doubt, with me as vice-chairman before succeeding him. I knew nothing about contemporary art and cared about it even less. But I'd worked my ass off to become a trustee, and it was already paying off.

Allen was short and wiry, with black hair and fair skin. And his eyes, as dark as his hair, fixed you as if you were the total object of his attention. Nothing escaped his notice or memory. His pinstriped suit was impeccably tailored, and he wore, as always, a crisp white shirt with French cuffs. His trademark, a red handkerchief, sat neatly in his breast pocket. Mike traveled continually and was consultant to a number of foreign governments. In the Nixon administration, he had been an assistant secretary of the Treasury and then deputy secretary of commerce under President Ford.

"What country did you buy or sell on this trip?" I asked as we shook hands.

"Can't remember, there have been so many," he replied, smiling. "I think we bought England. Or was it France? Scotch on the rocks, if I remember correctly, Henry? Some fifty-year-old single malt. MacDoughton's. It's really better neat."

"Sounds good," I said. He sat in a chair, I on the sofa, which I noticed made me lower than Allen. A clever Lazard device? I was six inches taller than Allen, yet in our respective positions he towered above me. "I never imagined a place like this could still exist," I continued. "Thanks for inviting me. Priscilla okay? And how are the twins?"

"All fine. Dean and Townsend are graduating this year. Both Phi Beta Kappa. And it's also my thirtieth and Dad's fifty-fifth reunion. We're going to have a major celebration." His pride was evident. I knew him to be a good family man, and devoted father. Nine on a scale of ten. Which made me what, a one?

"What's next for them after Princeton?"

He pondered my question. "Both have been accepted at several medical schools, including Harvard and Yale. They say they'll split up, but I know them. They'll end up at the same place. They always do." He nodded to the waitress to set the drinks down. Allen seemed far less restrained than usual. "Fascinating to watch them. Ever since they began to walk and talk they've functioned better together than alone. It's as if their two minds doubled their capacities. Priscilla and I used to be concerned about their interdependency, but we long ago stopped trying to separate them."

"What will happen when one of them wants to get married and the other hasn't found Miss Right yet?" Was I getting too personal?

Allen laughed. "An interesting thought," he said. Then, "Say, enough about my sons." He lifted his glass. "Here's to you and your brilliant coup."

"I assume you're referring to Three-Fifty-Five," I said, hoping to imply I had more than one coup up my sleeve. "Thanks, we're just about to consummate a lease on the whole building." I had planned everything so carefully, strategized how I would respond to any hurdle Standard General might come up with. No, it wasn't signed, but I firmly believed it was a done deal.

"Everyone in your industry is saying that it's one of the most skillful transactions in years. You've outwitted your competition." Allen smiled, sharing the victor's triumph. "You could stop after this one, but that doesn't seem to be your style. You're quite young, Henry. What, forty-four? There are worlds out there just waiting to be conquered. At least we're inclined to think so."

He was obviously probing, but I decided not to respond. It was flattering, and great fun to be entertained by one of the business world's heavy hitters. I knew his purpose in inviting me would be revealed in due course. The Pilgrim lady entered, curtsied (not just the costume was out of fashion), and announced that dinner was served. "We'll be a few more minutes," Allen said, and poured me a second scotch. It was the smoothest I ever remembered, blessed with a flavor those Scots had obviously kept secret from their envious brethren.

We chatted about the state of our fair city, and the economic conditions both regionally and nationally. I began wondering when Mike would get to the point. Lazard never wasted an evening without a purpose. Patience, Henry. In the fullness of time.

We made our way into a small but cozy dining room. I kept feeling I had stepped back two hundred years, and I was about to share a meal with one of the signers of the Constitution. The appetizer was Coquilles Saint-Jacques, followed by a crown of lamb, done to perfection, with new potatoes and asparagus served al dente. The corn muffins were warm and delicious. The linens were spanking, the silver sparkling white, the service impeccable.

I had to remind myself of where I was, especially after an '82 white Corton Montrachet, followed by a '69 red burgundy, Nuit St. Georges, its bouquet superb. I declined sweet potato pie, a traditional dessert in Colonial days, but said yes to a twentieth-century espresso.

"What I want to discuss is not a typical Lazard deal," Allen said as we finished the feast. I knew the point had come. "We have a partners' investment account. Well, actually, several. Depending on the investment." He looked squarely at me, and despite the pleasant wine buzz, I concentrated on his every word. "What I recommended to my senior partners at our last meeting," Allen said, "was a sizable involvement with The Martin Companies. With *you*, Henry." Allen was the kind of man who would gauge my reaction before continuing.

"I really don't know what to say. I'm honored, of course."

"You've proven you possess a high level of competence, Henry. But more important to us than any deal is people we invest in, how trustworthy they are. Their integrity, their probity." He smiled. "You couldn't have known it, but you were subjected to a very thorough investigation. We checked every place you lived, your friends and acquaintances, records at prep school, college, the military. The report covered your relationships, past as well as current. By the way, I'm the only one who has read it. I'm telling you this — and perhaps I shouldn't — because, all things considered, you're exactly the man we want to get involved with."

A compliment, sure, but holy shit, what didn't he know? I kept my voice level: "You had no right to investigate me without my permission."

"Understand something, Henry," he said in reassuring tones, as if he had anticipated my reaction. "I'm being completely open with you because I want you to know. I didn't have to tell you. Investigations like that must be made. If we're going to get deeply involved with someone, it's essential we know exactly whom we're dealing with. I apologize, but not really. I couldn't ask you first. If the report had come out less than sterling, there would have been no need to go any further."

I supposed I could understand that. But hell, I didn't want the whole goddamned world to know the details of my private life. I wondered about the "sterling" part. Clearly Allen had missed a few of the darker details — or maybe he didn't want to mention them. Professionally, I'd give myself an A to A+. But personally — I had to admit I did not rank very high.

"Let me add, Henry, I make no judgments about a man's personal behavior or habits," Allen said, as though reading my mind. "What interests me is whether he's a straight-shooter. Will he act coolly in a crisis? You meet both criteria." He lifted his glass — he was now serving a delightful Beaume de Venise — took a sip, and said, "Henry, I'm really terribly sorry about Nancy. It must have been a very difficult period."

My ex-wife, Nancy. Nancy MacAllister. The memory of her slow, agonizing final months brought back a flood of emotions and, I suspect, a flush to my face that Allen couldn't fail to notice. Hell, if that bothered him, then I wouldn't want to be involved with the guy.

"We tried everything the doctors recommended," I said. "Everything. And then some."

Allen left the room to take a phone call. His remark about Nancy made me realize to what degree I had been forcing myself not to think about her death. The worst was that she was only thirty-seven, and she died alone, without me. Feeling so helpless while she withered away, wasted by the cancer. For the first time in my life, I had been unable to keep something I desperately wanted to keep.

What made her death so wrenching was that I believed, until the very end, that there might have been time, time to reestablish our relationship, time to share intimacies I had not previously been able to share. I had married Nancy because I believed she would be my counterpart, the woman with whom I could share my hopes, anxieties, and fears. No, it wasn't Hollywood romantic. Nan was very sweet, perhaps a little naïve at times. She loved me in ways that other women hadn't. I also felt some guilt because, despite all my efforts, I couldn't completely stop fooling around after we were married. We never did become as close as I had hoped and wanted. After four years, we divorced. As much Nancy's idea as mine. She told me she realized it was a mistake. I wasn't a villain; we just weren't right for each other. The divorce was amicable, and we remained friendly. I regretted I didn't have more insight.

Allen returned, led me back into the living room, and poured me some very old brandy. "What I'm offering you is this," he said when we were seated. "A partnership, with you receiving thirty-three percent. You would be responsible for overhead costs. We'll furnish the capital, say fifty million to start and another tranche of fifty million when the first is well invested. You create income properties.

We've concluded that New York is overdeveloped, or soon will be. We like other cities, like Atlanta, San Francisco, Seattle. We also believe that the future will be in the underdeveloped countries: Mexico, Central, South America. Plus the Pacific Rim nations, Malaysia, Korea, maybe Thailand. No one can break into Japan, so we can't go there."

"You've forgotten Yemen," I quipped, "not to mention Bulgaria and Morocco."

"With your new building leased to Standard General," he went on, ignoring my remarks, "you'll have considerably reduced your vacancies. The balance of space you'll lease. You'll make it happen. That's your style."

"I still own a considerable amount of vacant land in Montvale and Heightstown, New Jersey, and in Newburgh and Greenwich. Also a little in Florida and Vermont. Would these properties be included in the partnership?"

"No," he said quickly. "We're not sanguine about the New York Metropolitan area. And that goes for Boston and Chicago, too. It used to be that Washington was thought to be recession-proof, the assumption being that government never stops expanding. But now it's our contention that for the time being the whole Washington area is overbuilt."

I declined more brandy. My head was already spinning, both from the alcohol — which was considerably more than I usually imbibed — and from Allen's proposal. I wanted to explore another possibility, although the one he had outlined was certainly appealing. Except that I would lose my independence. Making a giant out of my company was appealing, but the prospect of losing control was not.

"What you describe, Mike — even though it's sketchy — sounds very interesting, but there may be another way to accomplish what we both seem to want — raising funds in the capital markets. Do you think my company could go public? Either conventionally or as a real estate investment trust?"

"REITs are too limiting," Mike said, shaking his head. "I gave considerable thought to that idea. We could take you public. We'd take a large position in your company." He smiled. "But we wanted something different for our personal accounts. When a company is public, it's forever having to answer to the SEC, all the regulators, and to stockholders. It's quite a nuisance. Staying private has its advantages."

It was true. I would have even less freedom if The Martin Companies were public. Unlikely that I would be the largest stockholder. I wouldn't settle for anything less than being listed on the New York Stock Exchange. Public, I might not be able to maintain full control. Yet, were Lazard my partner, I would have even less.

"I've given you a lot to mull over, Henry," he said, as if sensing my thoughts. "Finalize the Standard General lease. We'll have lunch afterward and continue our explorations." As if by magic, another Pilgrim-clad woman appeared to conduct us down to our limos.

Outside, he added, "I'm sure you know that one of Lazard's essential requirements is absolute discretion. It's important that all this remain completely confidential."

"I understand, Mike. For me, too. I really appreciate your interest. It's quite a compliment."

"Yes" — he smiled — "it is." No false modesty there. "We'll talk soon, Henry."

Partners. Would Allen be a good one? God knows. Steve and I were brothers, and he sure wasn't your ideal partner. Dad had always warned us about partners. "Stay away from them, boys," he had told Steve and me on countless occasions. "They start out okay, but if you begin having problems and they're supplying the money, you could lose everything. Like that!" He snapped his fingers. Both hands. He liked doing that. "It's not worth it, believe me." When we reminded him how good he always said his partnership had been with Uncle Joe, he would respond that that was very different because they had started out from scratch. However different their backgrounds, they had grown up together in the same neighborhood, with similar values. Jake and Joe. Joe and Jake . . .

New Hyde Park, 1939

After he graduated, Jake Martin, who with a civil engineering degree aspired to better, couldn't land the right job. In those days, just finding work was considered success. Finally, Jake found a day laborer's job with Prestige Construction, a struggling Long Island builder. There he met Joe Sabatini, a young Italian with whom he immediately struck up a friendship.

Over a beer at Bernie's Beer Joint on Hempstead Turnpike, Jake turned to Joe and said: "Haven't you had enough of this stupid job? Bust our asses to take home a few lousy bucks? Times are getting better, Joe. That damn war in Europe's going to bring in a lot of work for this country, you'll see. What say we start our own construction company?"

"You crazy?"

"No, I'm serious!"

Then Joe broke out laughing, and put his hand on Jake's shoulder. "You know, you dumb walyone, I've been thinking the same damn thing."

There was something animal-like about Joe, something primitive and basic. His hands hung down at his sides like big mitts except when he reacted instinctively to something he didn't like, at which point they balled up into menacing fists. He was five foot eleven inches, with a build like a Mack truck, had an olive complexion, deep blue eyes, and dirty blond hair that was rarely combed. His ears stuck out a little too far from a craggy face. A large roman nose bespoke his Italian ancestry. In a fight, you wanted Joe on your side. But despite his rugged appearance, he was essentially a gentleman, strong principled, and slow to anger. His speech was rough and raw, but he possessed a keen analytical mind. Like his sister, he was constantly struggling to bridge Sicily, where he was born, and the new world to which he had come when he was one year old.

Because of Jake's features and dark hair, he was sometimes taken to be Joe's Italian partner, an impression strengthened by his ability to mimic a Sicilian accent. Blond, blue-eyed Joe often sprinkled Yiddish expressions into his conversations, further compounding the confusion. The two friends loved confusing crusty bankers, unenlightened prospects, and even longtime clients and subcontractors. They often left stuffy meetings where they had pulled off their ethnic ploy in a state of near hysteria, roaring with laughter like two bad schoolboys.

But that bond suddenly deteriorated when Joe's sister Barbara made the mistake of falling in love with Jake Martin. Working together was one thing; marrying — if that was the outcome — quite another. Slumbering prejudices slowly began to turn the families against each other. Martin-

Sabatini, which had been a rising star on Long Island, seemed jeopardized by the turn of events.

Sal Sabatini, Joe's father, had brought his family to America in 1915, but was still unsure of himself in his new country. He had just enough education to read and write, but he was still uncomfortable in English, which he spoke haltingly with a heavy Sicilian accent. Sal's work as a mason was physically demanding, but he put in long days without complaint, happy after the Depression to have a steady job. At five-nine, he didn't appear as strong as he was. His coloring was dark, his hair jet black. A two-inch scar over one eyebrow, the result of a fight, never healed properly; Sal had disdained a doctor's stitches, which gave him the look of an ex-boxer. In his family, though, he was the archetype of the Old World patrone: *he held strong opinions and was anything but progressive. In America, new ideas, especially about behavior, were rejected out of hand.*

One early morning over breakfast, Salvatore turned to his daughter. "I watch you last night. The boy who belongs to the car you getta out of, in front of Coletti's house, he was Jake, right?"

Barbara looked at her father without expression and didn't respond. Angela, her mother, stopped eating, and Joe suddenly pushed his chair noisily back from the white porcelain-topped table. He remained seated, his hands gripping the edge of the table.

"I tell you he's notta come here again!" Sal roared. "He's a nice-a boy, un bell' giovane, *he's Joey's partner.* Ma *no Jew!" Sal looked over at his wife.*

"What the hell are you doing, Barbara?" Joe shouted, standing now, his face red, his fists balled. "You're still seeing Jake? You promised!"

Barbara looked helplessly from her brother to her father. "I got nothing against Jake," Joe continued, calming slightly, "but in our family, you marry an Italian."

Barbara stood up and stared hard at her brother across the table. "We're in America, Joe, not Sicily!" she said icily, and strode out of the kitchen. In the doorway, she paused and turned. "Jake is the sweetest, most wonderful man I've ever met." She ran upstairs and slammed her bedroom door. Sal followed her to the bottom of the stairs.

"No Jew, in mi famiglia!*" Sal bellowed up after her. "You hear me!" He glanced over to Angela, who nodded in agreement. But her face revealed pain.*

Joe pulled open the kitchen door, ran down the sidewalk to his car, jumped in and roared off, tires squealing. He guessed Jake would be at the construction site. Their company was building on Fourth Street in Mineola. Yes, there he was. Bastard!

"Hey, Jake. Get in! I want to talk to you," Joe yelled through the window of his '36 Oldsmobile coupe, his voice controlled but his hands still trembling. He drove six blocks to Willis Avenue near the train station, pulled the car sharply over to the curb, and turned off the motor. The August heat was unbearable. Today it was supposed to top a hundred degrees.

"Apparently the whole fucking world knew you were seeing Barbara." He nervously lit a cigarette. "You out to wreck our company?"

"Joe, I never had a brother," Jake replied. "Or even a friend like you. Barbara and I never expected it'd go this far. We all know the problems. Not to mention for the kids we might have." Jake pulled a pack of Chesterfields from his pocket and tapped out a cigarette.

"Who said anything about getting married? Barbara won't never get my father's permission. Mine neither, for that matter. In Italian families, that's the rule." He inhaled deeply. "And you damn well know it."

Jake ignored Joe's remark. "The thing is, we are finally starting to make it in business, Joe. But down at the Reserves the brass're starting to speed up our training. Tougher drills. New equipment and weapons."

"You're probably right. Jesus, Jake, just think of it, me going off to fight against Italians! Screwy world. So, you see it's no time to get married."

A portly policeman sauntered over to them, twirling a billy club menacingly. "You boyos waiting for someone?" he asked with strong traces of an Irish accent.

"No law against conversing, is there, Officer?" Jake asked.

"Don't use fancy words with me, bucko. We've had a couple of break-ins around here. You guys look like you could be from the city." He waited for an answer.

Joe started to respond but Jake, sensing Joe's temperature rising, grabbed his arm and cut in. "We're putting up a building a couple of blocks from here. Over on Fourth Street. Have to talk over some business."

Apparently reassured, the policeman nodded. Joe started the car and pulled away from the curb. "Where does that dumb palooka get off?" He shook his head. "Give 'em a blue uniform and they think they own the goddamn place."

He parked across the street from the site.

"So" — Jake glanced over at his partner — "where does that leave us?"

"So smarten up," Joe said. "We got enough problems. Whyn't you both cool off?" Without waiting for an answer, Joe got out and strode onto the building site.

3

I DECIDED the taxi wouldn't make the corner light for at least two more red-green cycles, so I thrust ten dollars at the driver, opened the door on the traffic side, heard the driver screaming at my back, "Hey! You tryin' to get yourself killed?" and dashed the three blocks to Standard General's headquarters building on Park and Fifty-fourth.

Originally a family-owned enterprise dealing mostly in tobacco and food products, Standard General had been taken over in one of the early leveraged buyouts, in 1979, by the aggressive but highly respected Wall Street investment banking firm of Leo A. Guthart Partners. Standard General's highly touted management, headed by John Calbraith Phelan, Jr., had been recruited and installed by its new owners.

Under Phelan's brilliant leadership, S.G. had proceeded to buy up Rogers & Straus Boat Corporation, a successful, cash-rich shipping company, the Bradford Group, an old-line financial services firm, and then more recently Nelson Computer. When the leveraged buyout originally took place, Standard General's stock backed off, but quickly rebounded after their later acquisitions. Before the move by Singer, it had traded between $12 and $16, but currently was at a new high of $38. Some brokers, Tallulah & Zimroth, for one, reclassified it as a hold, because it was selling at a P/E ratio of twenty-four. Others, such as Dolman and DeVore, continued to recommend it as a buy.

The Standard General building was sheathed in gray glass that alternated with layers of black granite — sleekly modern yet solidly institutional. Like old wealth in Tiffany garb. The structure had been deemed one of the best examples of post–Second World War architecture, not only because it rose elegantly through several nondescript structures in the surrounding landscape, but also because its designer had endowed it with graceful horizontals offset by circles both on the top and bottom portions of the structure. The balance between the two motifs was aesthetically pleasing, enough so that the judges Morgan and Zahra awarded it the 1976 First Prize for Design. They wrote that the building represented "in its immediate environment, a sensitivity to postmodern simplicity that imparts aesthetic responsibility while encompassing the utilization of natural forms." And something about spatial relationships and controlled motions.

I waved to one of the security women, who, I was pleased to see, recognized me, dashed to the bank of elevators, and pressed the button for EXECUTIVE OFFICES. There the receptionist informed me my brother was waiting in conference room F.

I strode down the hall and glimpsed Steve through the glass windows. Louis XVI chairs were positioned around a highly polished cherry conference table, which stood on a handsome, dark-red Persian rug. The setting always reminded me of an elegant home in the Hyde Park section of London. At one end of the room was a sideboard upon which were two thermoses, black for regular coffee, white for decaf. A red thermos contained hot water for tea. On the opposite wall hung a large-scale map of North and South America, on which the company's operational sites were indicated by colored pins. A remote-operated movie screen was concealed in the ceiling.

A young secretary, immaculately dressed in a navy blue suit and white blouse, came over and, with a practiced smile, asked if I would like some coffee. "Regular, please." After she had filled an elegant china cup and left, I shut the door.

"What the hell's going on, Steve? I couldn't get through to you from the taxi on my cell phone."

"I haven't a clue," he replied, shaking his head. "Maybe you can figure it out." He sat back in his chair and rubbed his chin that same way he always had since we were kids. "Something's fishy. I can't get a straight answer from anyone. Everybody's as tight-lipped as a bull's ass in fly-time." He looked at me knowingly. "Time for Henry Martin to perform his magic. Charm them into changing their minds."

I shot a glance at Steve. "I want you to tell me exactly who said what. Or, more accurately, who didn't say what." I began pacing the room.

"Well, both Phelan and Jordan. 'In meetings and couldn't be disturbed.' That bullshit. Even the secretaries couldn't hide their smiles." He turned, and said in a tone that was sincere, "I guess it's up to you, Hen."

I stopped pacing and looked at Steve. I could never recognize the "striking" similarity people always talked about. To me we looked entirely different. He had inherited the Sabatini build; I, the Martins'. Steve, no more than five-nine, weighed almost as much as I did at six-one. He had never been athletic, so his stockiness was not the healthy kind. What was left of his hair hung long in the back, which I thought looked silly, as did his mustache. Steve suffered from a serious lack of self-esteem. When he was uncomfortable, he had a terrible habit of coughing and asking you to repeat what you had just said. Drove me nuts. Still, Steve dressed with great care. I gave him good marks for that. At college — Duke — he did well in the sciences but poorly in arts and literature. Mother insisted it was due to the rugged courses he took, but there was a tacit acceptance in the family that Steve never had the all-round smarts I did. Barbara and Jake Martin had always been careful to make any comparisons between us as subtle as they could while Steve and I were growing up. But we both knew how they felt. The point was, we had very little in common. I didn't blame Steve for being Mom's pet. Probably because I was happy to be Father's. I did respect Steve's attention to the details of our business, and his sharp abilities in math. He brought in our first computers and streamlined a number of our methods and practices.

"Before I sit down with Phelan," I said, "who may turn me over to Jordan, I want to be damn sure of our numbers, so we'd better review them. Carefully, because this may be our last shot." I was almost tempted to bum a cigarette, but remembered the vow made years ago that after Vietnam I would be done with butts of any kind. I pulled out the princely chair across from Steve and sat down.

"Spread sheets. The last projections we made," I said as I opened my briefcase and pulled out one of the several folders that Dianne had marked "Standard General — 355 Park Avenue." A second line said "COST SHEETS/REVISIONS." I had underlined the last word in red. "Have yours? Okay, site first," I said as he found the page.

"Before we begin, Steve, remember this is still a spec building, so we don't have to renovate, just the tenant fit-up. Comes out of the mortgage, not our pockets."

"You said that the last time, Henry. The bank limited us because the tenant fit-up was too fancy. We had to finance the balance our-selves. Why the hell do you always have this habit of trying to make everything come out the way you want?"

I didn't respond. We had to focus on this situation.

"And before you mention it, we can't reduce the cost of the site. Don't even suggest it," Steve snapped. "You paid a couple of million bucks too much, Henry. You just had to have it, didn't you?"

"I'm not going to debate this with you again," I said. "I admit it was at the top of the market, but you know damn well that the car-dinal rule is not the price paid for a site but what can be done with it. Also, three hundred thousand square feet — a larger building than we expected, and I might say, hoped for. I did a helluva job with the planning board. Our cost put us in line with Mark Hamer's outfit and the others. They bought their sites years before we did, at much lower prices." I stared at Steve and smiled — smugly, I suspected. "But those clowns had to carry their sites for years, which made their costs end up the same as ours."

"You're whitewashing reality," he said. "The market's gone shitty. Nobody's doing spec buildings these days. Land has dropped in value and price."

"Negative, Steve. No one could have predicted the market. And you know that. Federated's appraisers gave the site a higher value than the purchase price, so what are you bitching about?"

He shook his head. "You just go on your merry way. Get in a jam, and charm your way out. Well, I don't like situations where I have to depend on your luck!"

I bristled. "This isn't the time or place for a fight," I said. "In case you haven't noticed, we have a crisis on our hands."

"You know why, little brother? Because I can never get your goddamn attention. And if I do, you don't listen." He paused, as if making up his mind about pursuing the fight, then gave a major sigh, like a balloon losing air. "Oh hell, we'd better get back to the cost sheets."

"Okay, so we can't reduce the cost of the site. But," I added, "maybe we can reduce some of its carrying costs."

"You're wrong. You know that interest has to be capitalized. They stopped letting developers write it off years ago."

"Well, if I can get the bank to reduce the interest rate, that'll lower our cost a little. Then we can reduce the rent, right?" I looked across the table.

"C'mon, Henry, you haven't gotten the bank to do that."

"No, but I'm sure I can. Then we can pass it on as a reduction in the rent," I said.

"Not until you get it firmed up with the bank," he countered.

I stood up and began to pace. "We can also find savings in construction and overhead."

"Show me, kid," Steve cut in. "Flash cards, hyperbole, the whole bit. Your specialty. No one in New York is any better at it than you." His sarcasm nipped like ice flakes flung in your face by a winter blizzard. It stung, but I was used to it.

"You're too cynical, Steve. I'm trying to create a solution here, and all you seem to care about is shooting holes in everything I come up with."

"Because that's your typical defense," he shot back. "You rationalize when you fabricate revisions. If I don't watch you, you'll cut the rent from fifty dollars a square foot. No way," he added decisively.

"I actually quoted them forty-six-fifty."

"You what? Henry! You never told me that. Hey, Henry, I'm your partner, remember?"

"Sorry, there wasn't time. Hollick got hold of me last night and said the deal was ours at forty-six dollars. We still have room."

"The hell we do."

"We'd be further apart at fifty dollars," I said. "Anyway, it's academic because we're still too high, even for a new building. By the way, how do we know he's not bullshitting us? Remember the Nucci and Forte deal? The brokers tried to set us up with those phony quotes."

"Maybe we should hang tough," Steve said as he rose from his chair.

"We can't. Jordan and Phelan wouldn't be avoiding us. I'd have gotten the word that if we reduced the rent down to Yedid's, they'd sign with us. Except," I added, "my instinct tells me someone in that law firm is pulling big strings."

"I thought Phelan was your buddy."

"He is. Hey, where the hell's Hollick? Probably grabbed some cute secretary and is screwing her brains out. The guy's insatiable." I loosened my tie. "I'll call him after my meeting, try to find out what the hell he knows. Damn brokers. All some of them want to do is introduce you to a prospect. If the lease gets signed, they're right there with that big commission invoice." I stared at the rug. "Trouble is, Hollick represents other developers as well as us. The information he provides isn't always accurate."

"Anyway," Steve said.

"Anyway," I echoed, "let's look at construction."

"Wait a minute," he sputtered. "We disagree about how to handle the carrying charges."

"No, you made your point," I said.

He nodded. "But don't try to take the depreciation on the building as a way to reduce costs. For Christ's sake, Henry, that would be playing games." He was fuming. "Kid someone else, not me."

"Tax credits are important, Steve. We need to use them, especially because the building is up, and we don't have any tenants. I'll check with Ari later. And Grubin."

Steve pushed his chair back. "All right, construction."

I quickly pulled another folder out of my briefcase and continued before he could think of more things to criticize. "Lucien Cattai's contracted to build the shell for twenty-four million. Eighty bucks a square foot. Right? Add thirty a square foot Standard negotiated to finish their interior space. That makes a hundred-ten, okay?" I looked up.

"I know where you're going, but we can't be sure," Steve said. "Remember Montvale III? After that we decided not to get a general contractor to build the tenant finishes. Also, this job is too big for our crews. It'd be a mistake."

"No, it wouldn't. Think about it. Lucien has to put in a four to five percent profit that we don't need to include. That's one savings right there. Maybe we can get Michael Gordon out of retirement for this job. He buys aggressively, even though he sometimes squeezes the subs too much." Steve shook his head, but I went on. "Even if we don't do it ourselves, we're sure to save ten to fifteen percent. Lucien always comes in high, and when he's finished, it's always less."

"Too big a chance, little brother. There's no assurance that prices won't go up. Just one more way to get hurt."

"For Chrissake, stop calling me 'little brother,'" I snarled, no longer trying to hide my growing irritation. "This is a risk-reward business. If we're going to save this deal, we have to take some risks. Calculated risks." I stood up. "Even if I make assumptions you don't like, using them is a lot better than continuing to carry the building vacant. Who's going to rent three hundred thousand feet in one shot? Most of the current requirements are in the fifty to hundred thousand square foot range — max — and that means it'll take a lot more time."

"Very convincing," Steve said, sarcasm oozing. "Save it for your women."

"Am I right, or not? I am," I said, not waiting for an answer. "Look, it's obvious. We stay vacant and the overhead skyrockets. Money never recovered. All right, next," I said, putting the "CONSTRUCTION" folder aside. I pulled out "OVERHEAD."

The first sheet was a printout, containing all the components. Steve began with the first item, R. E. Brokerage. "Hollick gets five percent a year for ten years, that's fifty percent of the first year's rent. What did we agree to?"

"When the deal was at fifty dollars a foot, we agreed on that commission for the full ten-year rental, no credit for the concession," I said. "If we can get them to cut their number from $7.5 million — Jesus, that's outrageous! We have to get it lower. In my next life, I'm coming back as a broker. Or one of those $300- to $400-an-hour attorneys who keeps the clock running. Bastards!" I was tempted to interject my old joke that I really wanted to return as a brassiere, but Steve had heard it too often.

"Maybe we could have reduced the commission before, but not the way things stand now," I said, reconsidering. "Can't touch it. We need Hollick to help us, and he certainly won't if we try to play around with his fee."

Interest was the next item, broken up into two parts: Construction Mortgage and Site and Other Loans. Steve handled this category. "Obviously with the building up, bank interest on construction is fixed except for changes in the prime rate," he said. "No way of knowing the duration. With this building, we have to assume twelve to eighteen months from the time the shell is finished until a tenant or tenants are in and paying. It's eight months already. We'd better not touch that." I could tell he liked his analysis.

"Maybe we can," I suggested. "If we sign Standard General, we can give them occupancy, say, in six to seven months. That means a savings of three to four months, which translates into big bucks, like . . ." I began to punch numbers into my calculator.

"No, Henry. You didn't allow enough time for the lease execution. And seven months to finish the tenant work is too fucking tight for a job this big. Computer rooms, elaborate cafeteria, gym, and so forth. Their attorneys are going to drag it out. Those guys can't justify their fees unless they pull apart every clause."

"They've already reviewed it," I said.

"Sure, but the game only begins when their client agrees to go ahead. You know that. Cal is not the problem, never has been. It's the Standard bunch. And Yedid will do everything he can to get them to drag their asses, hoping it will kill the negotiations with us."

"True, Steve. I'm assuming we can get Phelan to move the lease along. But on second thought, they're in no hurry. Their present lease expires in January."

"Yeah," said Steve, "and I found out Yedid has no tenants to re-place them. He's going to keep them as long as he can. And another thing. Standard's a public company. No one's going to do anything that might result in criticism. Did you know one of Yedid's attorneys from Ellison and Pearce sits on the board?"

Yes, of course I knew, but didn't acknowledge it. "We have to take the risk," I said. "If we adjust the vacancy period, even three months, not five, we save . . ." I looked down at my calculator.

"Henry, why do you keep playing these goddamn games? You want me to agree just so you can get the result you want. Forget it!" He slammed his folder shut.

I shook my head. "Stop for one bloody fucking minute!" I stood and leaned across the table. "Even if the rent is lower, we'll have to take it!" I stopped for dramatic effect. "Partner," I said, "we don't close this lease, our asses are out there twisting in the wind. You said so yourself. Everything's tightening up — credit, leasing, every-thing. You know the saying, 'In a recession, take any rents you can get because tomorrow they'll be lower.' "

Steve seemed ready to capitulate. I was going to do what I had to regardless of what he thought. I was the only one who could save the deal. That's the way it had always been. Nothing was going to change the pattern.

"All right, Henry, you win. It's in your great, big capable hands. Close it with Phelan. We've got enough of an investment in that relationship."

I have, I thought. *I'm* the one who's spent endless hours creating that relationship. "Okay, I'll try," I said. "But something's not ring-ing right. What's changed and why." Let him know I wasn't taking anything for granted. And he shouldn't, either.

I shoved the folders into the briefcase and locked it shut. Steve followed me out of the room. When we got to the end of the long carpeted hall at the bank of elevators, he pressed "Down." The ex-ecutive offices were one flight up, reached by an elegant, curved stairway.

4

*E*VERYBODY knew the story of John Calbraith Phelan, Jr. He was a legend in his own time. Chairman and CEO of the Standard General Corporation, he was one of the highest paid, most respected and envied corporate leaders in America. You knew his story even if you weren't a colleague or peer.

Born in the Bronx, Phelan was the oldest of eleven children. His father, when he wasn't drinking, was a steamfitter. Which meant that he didn't fit a whole lot of steam. His mother, an iron-willed woman, was increasingly bedridden with pleurisy. It became apparent that young Jack, at fifteen, would have to substitute for the father as the family's breadwinner. His brothers and sisters helped with part-time jobs.

"Johnny, I know you to be the Lord's answer to all that has befallen us," his mother would say whenever she sensed the burden of their survival to be almost more than her son could manage. Then she would say, "Now, here, John Calbraith, rest yourself. You're only a boy. Tonight I've made your favorite meal. A good piece of meat, you know, some fine potatoes, and a nice sweet pie to top it all off."

Two jobs, sometimes three. But Phelan did manage to finish high school as well as organize a number of local service businesses. He convinced a few schoolmates and his two younger brothers to join him. The brothers had no choice. J.C.P. Enterprises, he called himself. The services ran from delivering drugstore prescriptions, and food, both Chinese and Irish, to driving those who would pay the cost, which was no more than going themselves by taxi. He began modestly and afforded great attention to details. He made phone calls, wrote thank-you letters to customers, canvassed extensively for business. After six months, he was known to most of the community, particularly the Irish. He borrowed as much as he could in order to pay the bills promptly and keep up the pressure to generate the lowest possible costs. It was apparent that he possessed excellent business sense, which quickly translated into growing profits.

Three years after graduating from high school, on a hot Monday morning the last week of August, Phelan walked into the office of the dean of the Columbia School of Business, Dr. Frank L. Sullivan, Jr. He was met by the dean's assistant, Dede Houghton, who had served Sullivan for the past fourteen years. An older woman whose children had graduated from Columbia College, she was reputed to be particularly effective in helping the dean with his relationships with the provost and president.

"I know I don't have an appointment with him, ma'am, but I'll be pleased to wait until he can see me," Phelan said, with just enough of an accent and winsomeness to break down anyone's resistance.

Young man," Mrs. Houghton said politely but firmly, "you don't seem to understand. You want the dean of admissions. That's . . ."

"Beggin' your pardon, ma'am, I really need to see this man. I can wait. It'll be all right." His smile was infectious.

"That's just not possible. The school year has just begun, and Dean Sullivan has more appointments and meetings than he can handle. I'd like to fit you in, but at best I don't think it could be for several days." She was trying.

"If I'm not botherin' you, ma'am, I'll just sit quietly here and wait. It's real important I talk to him. He is the only one. He is," he concluded.

She was charmed, but she couldn't help wondering if he had finished his sentence. "He is . . . what? God?"

Dr. Sullivan's office door opened and closed twenty-eight times that morning. John counted them. The dean, who at first didn't notice the young man, could hardly ignore him when he rose each time and said politely, "Good morning, sir," whenever the dean came out to greet or say good-bye to his visitors. By late that morning, Sullivan called in his assistant.

Frank Sullivan was starting to thicken around the middle. At fifty, standing six foot three, he was slightly hunched over and limped a little, the result of football injuries playing end for Cornell. His nose was ski-jump thin and his eyes a trifle watery. He had never married and worked long, hard hours, which was plainly written on his face. He complained about academe but wouldn't have changed his life one bit. He suffered fools badly, tried to act tough but was in reality a pussycat. "All right, Mrs. Houghton, now who is he?" She told him as much as there was to tell, and with that handed him a note that said, "Begging your pardon in advance, sir, it is most critical that I have a moment to speak with you. My name is John Calbraith Phelan, Jr., and I am convinced I should be enrolled immediately. Respectfully yours, J.C.P., Jr." It was typed carefully on his business stationery.

"You see, sir," Phelan said when he was finally ushered into the dean's office, "it seems so very clear that my talents for doing business are evident in my already considerable experience." He smiled and looked fixedly at the dean, whose face betrayed no expression. "It stands to reason then, don't you think, sir, that were this lad to get the magnificent education offered by your great school, that he could do even better? And of course, later on, he'll be in a position to contribute monies to worthwhile charities, universities like this one, and to people who can't make do for themselves for one reason or another, the way it was with my own family. As an example. And I was thinking that —"

Dean Sullivan finally cut him off. "Hold on, young man. You're not trying to bribe me, are you? You talk very rapidly. Slow down. Let's get a few things straight, shall we?" Sullivan walked to his window and closed the blind to temper the heat, for it was sweltering, the temperature hovering near 100. "First, the academic year has already begun. Second, only the very top college graduates can matriculate here. And last but surely not least, for the most part, I stay out of decisions regarding admissions." He got to his feet, to indicate the interview was over. "Young man, I admire your determination, but you'll have to apply like everyone else." He smiled. "By the way, what was your undergraduate college?"

Phelan, who was sitting on the edge of his seat, shook his head. "That's just it, Dean Sullivan. What I had in mind was combining the undergraduate and graduate schools. Together. I know that's not the way it's regularly done, but I'm sure you'll agree it's important I get through rapidly."

The dean's expression was shocked. "You mean you haven't finished college? I'm sorry, Mr. Phelan, but I'm afraid I can't help you. You must be a college graduate, or at the least a gifted senior. What have you been doing? Oh, yes, your businesses." He started toward the door.

"There wasn't the chance, sir," said Phelan, his voice rising. "John Calbraith Phelan, Jr., didn't get the opportunity. You see, when you're responsible for putting food on the table for ten younger ones, when your father doesn't work and your mother can only work a little because she's sick, you don't have much time, sir."

Dean Sullivan, who had retreated to his high-backed leather chair, sat down slowly. "There wouldn't be any chance you'd be making this up, would there, John Phelan? We Irish do have the gift of gab." He twirled a pencil nervously between his fingers. "And pretty vivid imaginations, too."

"We do that," Phelan said. "But every bit of this is true. Every word. And in a way, sir, my business experience has been an education."

Phelan slumped in his chair, his head drooping. He sighed audibly, but said nothing. Sullivan peered at him. "Still, what you're requesting is inconceivable," he grumbled. "I have never heard anything quite like it."

"Yes, sir. You're absolutely right," Phelan agreed.

"The university has certain rules and regulations that exist for very good reasons," Sullivan continued. Phelan remained frozen, his face intent, eyes on the dean's.

"I haven't even seen your high school transcript. It had better be excellent."

Phelan nodded. "It is, sir."

"You'd better write me a couple of pages about your business activities. We'll see if you can write decent sentences. I certainly know you can express yourself."

There was a moment of silence. Then, "All right, John Phelan, I may give you a chance to prove yourself. Subject to the approval of the provost and other deans, I will get you started." Phelan jumped up from his chair. "Now, hold on, young man, you'd better understand what that means — what it is that is expected of you. There'll be five subjects the first year: four in Columbia College and the last one here. Now listen carefully. If you do not maintain at least a 3.0 average, you're out. No ifs, ands, or buts. No excuses. Is that understood?"

Phelan rose and started pumping the dean's hand. "You'll not regret it, Dean Sullivan. You surely won't."

"And what about the cost of this education, Mr. Phelan? How do you expect to pay for it?" The expression on the young man's face gave him the answer. He sighed. "All right, we'll try to get you financial aid. How will your family manage without you?"

"I've got that all figured out, sir. I've been training me two brothers and me other chums. I've got everything organized, so all I need to do is read their daily reports, meet with them for a half hour or so, then make adjustments. It'll work good, sir."

"Mr. Phelan," Dean Sullivan said with an unrestrained smile, "if you're going to become someone in the business world — and I rather suspect you will—you'd better straighten out that language of yours. It's not 'me' tasks. It's 'my' tasks. Not 'work good,' 'work well.' "

Phelan nodded, then broke into a broad grin himself. "I'll work on it, sir. I'll make you this solemn promise" — he took a deep breath — "I will do you proud, sir. Indeed. You and this magnificent school." He reached for the dean's hand and pumped it again. "There's not a bloody thing that'll prevent that, sir. My entire future and those around me is the thing at stake."

Phelan proved as good as his promise. His academic advisor planned liberal arts courses that included American literature, history, philosophy, Spanish, and fine arts. Phelan enjoyed them and did well, telling his professors on occasion that he never imagined learning could be so stimulating. He was a good student, although he did engage in numerous arguments with his business school professors, especially disagreements about the practical applications in the case studies. But he handled himself with restraint, and never alienated his teachers, who were not unaware of his background and the double load he was carrying. Five years after his meeting with Dean Sullivan, John Phelan graduated third in the class of 1950 at Columbia.

The balance of his storied career can be surmised. After graduation, his businesses now in the hands of his brothers, Phelan was hired by IBM in 1950 to train first in marketing and then in sales. He began to set records for sales of mainframe computers, but felt the tug of the Korean War. "You know, Mom, I didn't do any service in the big war. I believe I'm to do some now." She reminded him that not only was he just eighteen when the Second World War ended, but he was supporting the family. "Well, yes, but the boys can take over. It's going to be the Navy. I'm to report to officer candidate school in Newport, Rhode Island, next week. Oh, Mom, don't look that way. This country has done wonderful things for the Phelans. We can give a little back."

When he was discharged in 1953, United Computer Corporation made Phelan a very attractive offer. A few days after his twenty-ninth birthday, John Phelan was promoted to vice president, in charge of North American sales. His next job was as sales manager for Europe and the Near East. IBM then enticed him to return, put him in charge of marketing, and made him a senior vice president. When he was not elected to the board eight years later, Phelan left IBM. He took a presidency of a middle-size corporation. Several years later, he was offered the presidencies of several major companies and settled on the hot, rising Standard General Corporation. Now, decades later, Phelan was at the pinnacle of his powers.

I first met Jack Phelan at a major fund-raising affair held in Central Park by the Nature Conservancy for the "Last Great Places." I liked him immediately, respected his self-assurance and style, as well as his political savvy. I made it my practice to attend other benefits where I would see him occasionally, as well as at the Marco Polo Club, a private dining facility in the Waldorf Hotel, and also downtown at the Players Club. I became a friend of his, and he introduced me to other executives whose names I carefully wrote down as soon as I could. I followed his company closely and decided it might be in the market for office space in the Midtown area, where we were then contemplating 355 Park.

Phelan had his own style of managing, which was unconventional in many respects. But he did get results. I asked him about it one day at the Lotos Club, where I was also a member. I had invited him to lunch to begin to negotiate the 355 transaction.

The Lotos was on Sixty-sixth Street off Fifth Avenue. Its membership included businessmen and women, retirees, and old money. It had been a private mansion years earlier, and its ambiance was elegant. The spiral staircase off the subtle but tasteful entrance was venerable and dignified. It led up to a large, high-ceilinged sitting room, across from the formal dining room, where some read newspapers or engaged in small talk. One flight down from the first floor was a grill room, which was less formal, but the food was superb. This dining facility was warm and charming, with round oak tables, checkered tablecloths, stained-glass windows lighted nicely from behind, and a tile floor.

"You see, Henry, all those CEOs and would-be top executives, those men," Phelan pontificated, stopping to nibble his appetizer of smoked salmon, "think that intimidation is the best way to get results. But what they're really doing is exercising power. They love power, worship it, would trade their wives and girlfriends for it. Power gives them their opportunity to rewrite the rules." He raised his glass of white wine to his lips and tasted it. "This is quite good. What is it?"

"A Meursault, '82. I thought you'd like it." I smiled. The waiter, a man I had tipped well over the years, hovered nearby and appeared as if magically to refill Phelan's glass. I wanted Jack Phelan to remember this lunch. I was practicing what was needed to gain full acceptance by the right people.

"But they're mistaken about how they use power," Phelan went on. He scrutinized my face, saw that I was concentrating on what he was saying. Of course, I had the good sense to make the food secondary to the conversation — or in this case, the instruction.

"You'd think that people in top business positions would feel secure," Phelan went on, "but I assure you many do not. They issue orders and mandate change to validate their authority and lessen their insecurity. Wield power indiscriminately . . . and often stupidly. They've got it all wrong," he said. "You don't alienate your competitors on your way up. If they receive the top job and not you, they'll be after your scalp. And you don't know that you wouldn't be content being *numero dos*." He smiled.

Phelan had a wonderful way of exposing an essential truth, making clear something that was often obscure.

The waiter cleared the remnants of our appetizers, and deftly replaced them with our main course: sautéed blue-clawed crabs for Phelan; calf's liver for me.

"I've learned from many different men, Henry. Disraeli, Charlemagne, Caesar — or in our era — John D. Rockefeller, Churchill, Truman, Mellon, Ford, both Roosevelts. Even the not-so-greats, men like Hoover, Estes Kefauver, even Nixon. I've studied the philosophers, social scientists, great writers. Machiavelli, Tolstoy, Nietzsche. A brilliant Englishman, Christopher Caudwell." I was having trouble figuring out how all those people related to his musings on power.

"I'll tell you something else," he said between bites. "I had a commander on my aircraft carrier, during those pretty awesome days in the Korean War. I was a junior air intelligence officer. This Annapolis man, a full commander, a big redheaded Irishman named James Duffy, took a shine to me. He would take me aside when he could and carefully explain his plans. Bright fellow. Now heads one of my divisions.

" 'When you show your men you respect them,' Duffy used to say, 'they always bust their butts for you. Everyone has to function as part of a team. Get them to want to kill themselves for you. Never forget to make them feel they've contributed to the creation of the plan. You rarely issue orders, even though you have the power.'

"We were so damn proud of what we accomplished," Phelan said, "determining what were the most significant air strikes. We lost men and planes because we had to send them not only long distances but then to face flak and enemy fighters. Terrible days and nights. But wonderful, too. We stank for days, had just enough time to eat and an hour of sleep here and there.

"Duffy taught me a lot about power," Phelan continued. "I

served under some I wouldn't give you two cents for. Idiots. Power crazy."

Phelan was enjoying his monologue, which could have been overbearing but somehow was not. I listened attentively, not wanting to interrupt his flow.

"It's truly impressive how your particular management style has taken Standard General far beyond what Wall Street projected for volume and profits this year," I said. It probably sounded obsequious, but I meant it.

"The last *three* years," he corrected. "You, Henry. A real leader in the real estate investment field. All those buildings."

"I had a CO in the Marines like your Commander Duffy. Got one now, my helicopter pilot, Craig Sampson. He keeps me on the straight and level."

"What about your brother? Isn't he your partner?"

I shrugged, surprised he had asked about Steve. "I suppose I was always the one who led. What I mean is, Steve's comfortable executing. He's better at that. We own equally, the way Dad wanted it. I'm satisfied, and I believe Steve is, too."

That didn't seem to convince Phelan. "Are you sure?" He didn't wait for my reply. "Didn't he end up marrying the woman you were with for some years?" He watched my face carefully.

How the hell did he know that? Oh, right, a former intelligence officer. "Yes," I said slowly, "but I can assure you it's never been a problem for any of us."

He sipped his steaming coffee "Being a dedicated realist is essential for top leaders," Phelan said at the door as he was about to climb into his limousine. "I'm sure you're right," he said. "About your brother. Otherwise, you could wind up with big trouble."

He eyed me as if looking for a reaction. I made sure there was none.

5

PHELAN had been expecting me. When I entered his inner suite, he peered at me fixedly, then motioned for us to move into the private sitting area adjacent to his office. The room was tastefully English: two tan, smooth-leather couches faced each other, separated by a mottled brown granite coffee table. A round conference table was set to one side, surrounded by wonderfully ornate chairs, the bottoms of the two front legs carved onto eagles' talons over round balls. They stood on a handsome thick Persian rug, which was laid over an equally thick beige carpeting. The feeling it gave was of elegance as well as careful organization. The only things that seemed inconsistent were the paintings on two of the walls. Then I remembered Phelan told me he had a son who painted.

"Nice to see you, Henry," Phelan said, extending his hand. But instead of inviting me to sit down, he turned and walked over to the window that spanned the full length of his sitting area, and stood there, his back to me. I joined him and looked at the toy panorama below. Office buildings towered like children's blocks; miniature streets were clogged with tiny buses and cars. Pedestrians appeared like ants, slow-moving, programmed by some ageless instinct. Central Park spread its green rectangle to the north, the East River visible to the right through gaps between the buildings. Queens ran farther to the east, distinctly flatter. Several airliners played follow-the-leader as they made their approaches to LaGuardia. They turned into long base legs and then on final to the runway.

As often as I had looked out onto scenes like this one, I remained impressed. I didn't have much time to muse about my life in general, but in the seconds before he began to talk I remembered feeling I was at the top of everything, exactly where I had always wanted to be.

"So, what can I do for you, Henry?" His tone was tight and remote, I thought. Bad sign. I hoped I was wrong.

I cleared my throat. "Jack, I can't understand what's holding up the final execution of the new lease. Everyone's in full agreement on all the open items. The attorneys can quickly settle any remaining differences in language. I'm sure you know I made an even further concession in the rent."

He turned to me and put his hand on my shoulder. "Let's sit down, my boy," he urged. "Something I want to share with you. But I must have your word you'll not discuss it with anyone. Including your brother." I nodded.

Phelan rang for Tina Schrager, who came in with a tray of both regular and decaf coffee, and hot water with choices for teas. English biscuits and scones were carefully assembled in circles on a brightly colored Spode plate. "What may I serve you, gentlemen?" she asked pleasantly. She continued to smile as she poured whatever it was we had requested. I didn't give a damn what I was drinking.

"Henry, I'm afraid your lease has been caught in a struggle, one over which I do not have my usual control." What the hell did that mean? "As you know," he continued, "I've announced I was planning to retire, but I've become uncomfortable with that decision because the board would in all probability appoint Jordan to succeed me. I misjudged that man. He turned out to be a lousy manager, and an even worse president. He'd make a disastrous CEO. The only way I can prevent that — and remember I own a significant amount of both common and preferred stock — is to stay on. Even though Jordan has some backing, the majority of the board votes are, without question, mine. Before I'm through, he'll be out of here."

"I understand, Jack, but what does that have to do with my lease?"

"Robert Ellington Prince — you know who he is — sits on our

board and quite a few others. He's all right except when he gets priggish, after he's been with his Princeton or his Harvard Business School pals."

He took a sip of coffee, then went on. "Jordan has been buttering him up. So he decides — Parker, that is — that he's an expert real estate negotiator, a maven, and spouts off about a 200,000 square-foot lease he's just concluded for his own company. Supposedly the rent ended up fifteen to twenty percent lower, plus additional tenant work, and — get this — the deal included a twenty percent piece of the equity! So Jordan, out to make himself a hero, goes to Yedid, our present landlord, sits his people down, and tells them that if they drop the rent significantly, we might reconsider staying in their building." Phelan glanced at me, waiting for a reaction. I decided to remain silent, because I knew there was more.

"It's a package, I suppose. Jordan saves us lots of dollars and makes a big impression on the board; and Parker gets his ego boosted." He hesitated. "Jordan would remind me of Machiavelli except he's a rank amateur. His mistake was he didn't figure on me staying on."

"Don't you have the power to finalize the lease with me?" I knew the answer, but I wanted him to spell it out.

"Your lease can't be my main priority right now." Phelan stood and faced the window. "I have to let Jordan win that one. We're into a power struggle. I'm playing more than one card. It's most unfortunate, Henry, it really is. And I'm sorry, but that's the way it is. We're extending our present lease." Phelan turned to look at me. "At the next board meeting — I will have it all worked out in advance — there'll be no surprises, except for Mr. Jordan. At one time this Irish lad from the Bronx was a pretty good gutter fighter.

"The board will urge me to sign a new three-year contract, maybe five years, with an option to terminate after three. When and if I do exercise the option, I will be provided with a rather large golden parachute. I've already discussed my idea with a few key board members. They're sure Parker and his faction will go along. Frankly, no matter what Jordan would like to believe, Parker could care less about him."

"I never could connect with Jordan," I said. "He always makes me feel he has more than one agenda. The one we might be talking about and the other he keeps to himself."

"Mr. Martin," Phelan said with a bit of his old Irish accent and with a broad smile, "don't we all?" He sat down next to me and patted my knee paternally. "Do you really believe that even in the most intimate of conversations, the various parties let on how they actually feel?"

Screw the lesson. My deal was in a flat spin, an inevitable crash, a foregone conclusion. Jesus Christ. No tenant. The bank will pounce on me like an angry lioness. I had to do something. This was my last chance.

"Jack, you have an incredible way of cutting to the absolute essence. I've got something to tell you. It's private." I took a deep breath. "My companies — well, you know how bad real estate has become. Too much space available. Rents dropping. Tenants demanding more expensive improvements, and so forth. What's exacerbating the situation more this time than during the last recession is the intransigence of the banks. Both the commercial and long-term lenders."

"I'm fully aware of it," he responded. "I sit on the board of First Trust. We're very concerned about outstanding loans. The situation with Donald Trump has everyone's attention. He seems to have gotten himself heavily overcommitted. But he's very clever, and has an incredibly strong self-image. The examiners, state and federal, are all over us demanding that we increase reserves for bad debts. And threaten foreclosures if developers don't reduce or pay off their loans."

He glanced at his watch and walked over to an intercom. "Tina, tell Steve Aptheker to start the meeting. I'll be another ten minutes. Oh, and remind him that all division heads must present their quarterly reports by, ah, the eighth. I will not tolerate slippage."

"Yes, sir," she responded. "And please don't forget there are some important calls before your luncheon. Senator Flowers called. His AA sent a fax. The senator would like to talk to you about your suggestions regarding his amendment before he leaves Washington. Oh," she added, "your trip to Denver?"

"Yes, thanks. I'll use the Gulfstream out of Teterboro. Bob Osinski reported that the Citation's down for some work."

He turned to me. "We're going to spend the weekend with my daughter Jamie in Aspen. I bought a place so we could all use it. My two granddaughters are exactly the right age. Wonderful kids!" His tone changed: "Henry, this situation should not be too great a surprise to you. Developers are a greedy bunch. Each one has an ego bigger than the next. When times are good, they jump in with too many projects. As though they can't help themselves. There's an old Irish expression, 'You can't put your rear end into more than one wedding.' Actually, I think it's Jewish."

I stood up and shook my head. I had positioned us so well. Projections, careful planning. Now all those downside risks were crashing in all at once. I looked at a portion of Central Park, which suddenly seemed shaped like an albatross.

Then I remembered something I had learned a long time ago about selling: a smart salesman has a better chance of landing an order if he acts as if he doesn't need it. "I've been through recessions before," I said. "Despite all the problems, we're stronger now than we've ever been — experience, depth, credit, staying power."

"You said you had something to confide, but you sound like everything is dandy," Phelan said. He offered more coffee, but I declined.

"The impact of losing this lease could be serious," I said. "There are other prospects out there, but it could take months to close another deal. . . ." I was asking him to help me, but I didn't want to appear as if I were desperate.

"I'd like to help you, but your lease is dead for the reasons I've just outlined. Look," he went on, "another company, one I've been trying to acquire, may need space. But we won't know that until after the acquisition. I've mandated tight space projections throughout the divisions. No exceptions."

He walked me to the door, his hand on my shoulder. "The top man always has to set the example, Henry. You know that. I promise to keep these eyes open. Let you know if any of my friends are in the market." He extended his hand. "Call me next week and tell me how you're doing. I've always liked and admired you. Learn from others. In this case excesses, like Trump's. You're a bit arrogant, but a real driver." He looked at me squarely. "Unlike most men, you and I are unwilling to be deterred from our goals. No matter what the obstacles. Others drop out on their climbs up their Matterhorns. Not us. In the genes, Henry. Plus environment and training."

"I'm sure you're right," I said.

"But, my young friend, be obstinate and you become an ostrich. Get your tail bitten off. At times you will be the only one who believes you'll make it. I know, Henry, I've been there."

As I walked down the long hall toward the bank of elevators, it occurred to me that Jack Phelan had ended with a warning couched in a compliment. But what he hadn't given me was what I needed most: the lease with Standard General.

I passed the executive stairway and reached the end of the hall before I realized I had completely passed the bank of elevators. It surprised me I had been so absent-minded. It annoyed me. I was supposed to take problems in stride, not be completely fazed by them. I retraced my steps and took an elevator down to the first floor.

Earlier, I had called Charles, my chauffeur, and told him to wait for me outside. I exited the building in a daze, found my limo parked at the entrance. I said to Charles, "We'll stay here a few minutes." Inside, I slid the privacy window closed. I had to assess the significance of my meeting with Phelan.

I glanced at my watch. 4:35 P.M. Squash with Daniel Spear at 5:00. Should I cancel? No. I'm going to take him today. Then call Karen. God, it's been ten days. Far too long. How had I let so much time slide by without seeing her? Sometimes, Martin, you're not as sharp as you think you are.

6

I SLUMPED down deep in the seat and closed my eyes. Thoughts and images raced through my mind like railroad trains bearing down on each other from opposite directions. One, Standard General; the other, Federated, the bank. Me in the middle, caught on the tracks. Phelan, the engineer on the first, a death mask, smiling. MacDougall, the banker, on the other. He's got this horrific expression. Steve watching, grinning. And Jordan with the Standard General directors in the stands. They're all conversing, paying no attention to the trains and me. I put up a hand in each direction for them to stop, but they don't.

I'm lying there, waiting for the crash. MacDougall stands over me: "I told you I'd extend the loans and finance the tenant work when you got the lease signed. But you didn't do it, did you?" He points at me. His words are almost drowned out by the roar of the oncoming trains. I open my eyes.

Months earlier, I advised MacDougall that at some point I would obtain a mortgage commitment from a permanent lender, like an insurance company or some large pension fund. With a tenant as strong as S.G. it would have been easy. Maybe mortgage out, which meant eliminate any permanent investment.

I had assured MacDougall that all but the loose ends were tied up, that we expected execution copies within days. Every major open item had been resolved. The entire real estate market had been talking about this deal. Calls had come in from all over. Henry Sabatini Martin was king of the fucking hill! No, could have been. Damn. There must be, there had to be a way to save this deal. I knew how good it was: a ten-year lease with a big Triple-A company with a net worth of approximately $600 million. The rent was acceptable for the first five years — $46.50 a square foot, and there was a yearly increase of 2.5 percent. In the sixth year the rent would go up by 12.5 percent. With the debt service fixed and the tenant covering increases in the operating expenses and taxes, our net cash income should double. Our only additional investment would be in five years, for repainting, new carpeting, and minor repairs. We had already plugged those costs as reserves into our expense budgets.

A sweet deal. Standard General renting the whole building. It achieved my goal and provided options. We could milk the building for income. That income would be tax-sheltered to a large extent because of depreciation. The building would also appreciate in value over the years. Or, sell it now at a multiple of its cash flow. We'd have to pay the capital gains taxes, federal and New York State, and the "Cuomo Tax," but we'd still make a huge profit. Or trade this building for another one, utilizing the device of a tax-free 1031 exchange. The idea was ingenious. As long as the debt in both buildings matched closely, it would work taxwise. Forty-five days to locate an exchange property and 180 days more to close title, enough time for the due diligence: the examination of the structure and the leases, any environmental problems. Also an exploration for financing and anything else that might have an effect on the value.

Ah, you're fucking dreaming, Henry. Face it, will you? You're dead, man. No, no, you're not. Find some way to close the lease with S.G. Get Phelan to change his mind. Maybe do something to S.G.'s current building. Or mine. But what? You wouldn't stoop that low. At least, I hope not. No one's powerful enough to limit an earthquake to one block. Play with the wiring. Better, circulate a rumor about Legionnaire's disease? I needed to clear my head.

I opened the privacy window. "Charles, I'm going to walk."

He got out and opened my door. "Yes, sir. Five o'clock at the

Club. And sir, I fixed those plumbing and electrical problems at your place." I nodded, then began to walk briskly. Charles followed ten yards behind.

The office buildings stood as straight as giant soldiers. Clean and rectangular. But I knew they were actually Trojan horses. Like the CEOs in them. Polite but ruthless. Beneath the Brooks Brothers suits they were feral animals, ready to rip one another apart at the first opportunity. Watch your back and your jugular. Pinstriped hypocrites. Good guys belong in classrooms and on farms. Flying airliners. Collecting salaries. C'mon, Henry, you know better.

I looked down Park and saw the Regency Hotel. Big deal lunches. Larry Fineman, Herbert Rose, Donald Trump, top bankers and brokers. I remember that unforgettable night at the Regency when I'd come back from Juarez, divorce in hand. Karen and I had a sumptuous dinner brought up to our suite. Never finished it. She left around eleven. I slept as if there were no tomorrow.

The buildings towering around me suddenly appeared completely uninteresting. Even the Seagram building, which had been unique in its day. There is a way to create an interesting facade and avoid drearily similar bands of windows and metal sheathing. It might cost a little more to design steel with curves, recesses, and indentations, but not that much more. And the payoff is in higher rental income. Look at the entrances — almost all are boring. Developers are so cost crazy, they limit their architects. It doesn't take much more to make them distinctive. David Heyman and his sons achieved it. They had some graphic designer put mounds and sitting areas outside his building, and left the ceilings exposed. They painted the steel beams and ductwork in exciting colors. They also had the lobby receptionists wear different outfits every week. Smart. They rented fast, I remember David telling me.

Color and texture. Use them creatively and you'll have a structure corporate real estate managers and CEOs go for. Except sometimes it makes no difference, I was beginning to realize. Not to Jack Phelan. Or Standard General.

I forced myself to think of something else. Like when I used to fly my friend's Second World War biplane, the Pete Jones/Boeing Stearman. Really fun plane. It won prizes for restoration at air shows.

Just then a striking woman in a filmy summer dress breezed by. I swear she gave me a smile.

I love the way women dress in warm weather. More of them to look at, more to appreciate. Fewer layers to divest. Hey, I'm no different than any American male.

Joyce, my sister-in-law. Now there's a fantastic-looking woman. Joyce Stokke, Norwegian parents. Minnesota family and upbringing. Tall, willowy, very blond and very fair. Scrubbed. Moves with exquisite coordination. Almost a perfect body, athletic, naturally coordinated. Mole on her face she decided not to take off. Scandinavian blue eyes, fierce, they hold you while you fantasize about her. They almost close when she laughs. Her hands are the most beautiful I've ever held; she tends to put a hand, with those long, perfect fingers, on your arm when she talks to you. Kisses on the mouth when she's saying good-bye. Knows how attractive she is and uses it. Sometimes commits herself too soon, as she did with me. She was naive , but now quite sophisticated. Very bright, formerly a model, then a stewardess, now an attorney.

I met her on an American Airlines flight and couldn't take my eyes off her. Immediately wanted to drag her off. Anywhere, even into the lav. Took a couple of months to get her to bed. I wanted to love her as much as she said she loved me. I did love her. But not enough. Maybe I strung her along too long. She ended up marrying Steve. Yes, brother Steve. I couldn't believe it when Joyce told me.

"How can you possibly be happy with him?" I had asked. "It makes no sense."

"It's no longer any business of yours," she said, more than a little testily. "When I was involved with you, you had yourself a woman who was a lot more confused than she is now. And dependent. Looking for a perfect daddy. I thought you were him."

I grinned. Don't know why I did. Anyway, Joyce smacked me hard on the cheek. Then on the other side. I deserved it, but I was convinced she wouldn't be able to stay away from me.

Once, long before we broke up, I asked Joyce whether women responded the same way as men. How do they react when they meet someone they find attractive, assuming both are available or want to be? Her answer was a long explanation about the difference between male and female chemistry. Yes, I remember saying, of course we're different, amen to that. Yes, I know women respond to strength and stability, affection and gentleness. And a man's genuine interest in them. A women assesses whether or not he will be a good provider.

I told her that premise tended to be pretty old-fashioned. "Damn right!" Joyce exclaimed. "You sometimes see a beautiful woman with a dumpy guy, or vice versa. The reason is simple because, for those two, the fit works." She patted me on the arm. "What really counts is there — the trust, the respect, the friendship. They don't see the facade any longer. That's when the relationship becomes the best. But let's face it, Henry, every one of us is flawed."

"Yeah, blind is blind and beauty is in the eye of the . . ." She placed her hand over my mouth. She held my face in her hands and gave me a long, deep kiss.

"You know, Joyce, most guys need and want love and affection. Sex is important, but not everything. And women, today's professional women, seem to want gratification. They aren't necessarily interested in commitment." I liked scoring a point with her. When I did, she softened up like a cat, tender and warm.

"Nonsense!" she said. "Deep down the so-called modern woman is not all that different from her mother or grandmother." She was beginning to sound like the lawyer she was. "She's talked herself into believing she thinks and responds the same as a man. But it's really only because men are not marrying as young as they used to, if at all. And anyway, half the men around here are gay."

I opened my mouth, but Joyce was in high gear and high dudgeon. "Men are making out better than ever because of women's lib. They shack up with Ms. Terrific for three, four, five years, whatever. Then he's thirty-four, she's now thirty, not quite as attractive as she was in her twenties, right? So, when Joe Shithead finally gets ready to tie the knot, he finds some twenty-five-year-old. Bingo, goodbye make-believe wifey, her chances of marriage and family severely diminished."

"Okay, okay, maybe you're right," I said. Joyce looked at me incredulously. "I mean it, you're right. Really."

Of all the women I had ever known, Joyce was by far the sexiest. I absolutely lost myself with her.

It was like that with us. Magnets. Maybe the problem had been being together too long in the state I just described. Whose problem? Mine, I'm sure.

I was stirred from my reverie by a screeching of brakes and then the sound of metal against metal. It looked as if a cab had tried to make a right turn from the left lane. Typical Manhattan. Collision. Crash. Me. Caught between two trains. Just my imagination. Bad dream. I can prevent that from happening in real life. I can. I will.

Did I really believe that? Did I really believe that modern women were not all that different from their mothers and grandmothers? Joyce no different from my mother? From dear, sweet Barbara, the perfect wife and mother who never aspired to anything beyond loving and serving her husband?

7

THE squash game with Daniel Spear . . . Christ, I can't think of playing him. Maybe cancel. No, too late. Body and mind do affect each other. The better my conditioning, the better my ability to think clearly.

Spear, a high-stakes, high-profile real estate developer, was also originally from Long Island and, like me, had inherited a small construction company and then built it into an empire bigger than mine. Unlike me, however, he loved the limelight and employed not one but three full-time PR people. Self-centered and self-indulgent, he tried hard to appear classy, but his rough spots kept showing through. He'd been married twice, once to a woman who paraded as a Hungarian countess but who had about the same amount of blue blood as Daniel did. When he ditched her, the press had a heyday, as the "countess" kept feeding the press juicy stories about their marital life and his private avarice. He — whom the press had dubbed "The Daniel" (which he relished) — retaliated by marrying a ditsy model who was the spitting image of the countess. *She* retaliated by "writing" a novel whose seedy protagonist was a thinly veiled portrait of her ex-beloved.

The Daniel was compulsive about his physical conditioning. He wasn't bad-looking, touched up his hair, and recently had had cosmetic surgery he didn't want anyone to find out about. I did, and teased him, but assured him I'd keep it to myself.

The pompous bastard, I thought. Can just see him smirking when he hears about my losing the Standard General lease. Funny how your so-called friends love it when problems descend on you like fiends from a nightmare. Revel in your humiliation. Even more in your floundering. I'd love to beat his ass into the floorboards.

I've never let anyone know when I've felt insecure. That I didn't belong up there with the big guys. Didn't always know whether what I was pursuing was worthy. But I did understand charm. Learned it at a very early age. Except nothing I ever did seemed to please my mother. Why do guys like Allen and Phelan seem to have it all together? Study them. Reflect on the conversations with Phelan.

God, it's competitive as hell out there. Bring home the meat. We all fight for it. Supposed to. No different from the cavemen. Only now we wear pinstriped suits and smile at our enemies before bashing their heads in. Oh, sorry, is that your brain on the floor? Nature. Darwin. Knew that early on, didn't you, Henry? You're an aggressive sonofabitch, aren't you? But still have those damn doubts. Never disclose 'em, Henry. Reach the top. And stay there, but that's even harder. Phelan said that.

Hasn't always been easy or pretty, has it? You broke out and ran with the wind. You weren't like Steven. What kind of a mother was she, trying to straitjacket me? Mom cared, but she favored Steven. I was a bother to her. Trusted her when I was little. Where the hell did it get me?

Dad always told me I had what it takes. But his warning was that to succeed unethically wasn't succeeding, it was failing. Okay, so my ethics aren't perfect. No one else's are, either.

C'mon, Henry. Analyze it. Like in flying. Say I've lost my radios. Or clear ice is forming on my wings. In seconds it could impede the airflow that provides lift from the wings, drag instead from the extra weight of ice. Good-bye, Charlie. Where's the out? Declare an emergency if necessary, but get the hell out of there. Request or demand a different altitude from air traffic control. Screw the metaphors. Explore all the choices. Check how they stack up to the planned projections and pursue the strategic plan.

You have the luxury to make some decisions over time; with

others, the first one has to be right. No second chance. Flying solely on instruments.

I remember that deadline to close a permanent mortgage, one that I sorely needed. At the eleventh hour, the mortgagee's attorney said he wasn't satisfied with the Phase I Environmental Report and wanted an update. If the mortgage didn't close, a chain of negative events would be triggered. "Sure," I told Cal, my attorney, "we can get the report revised, but it'll take ten days or a week at best. The commitment expires on Friday." He advised that the bank was adamant.

"Okay, let me get in touch with Bob Goodman. See what he can do." Bob had been our mortgage broker for years. I liked Bob and respected his experience. We played golf once in a while and went to charity dinners together. My bank would start to wonder if a delay in replacing their building loan with a permanent mortgage was unavoidable or whether the permanent was in jeopardy.

"Bob, what the hell are they trying to do, kill the deal?"

"Hang on, Henry. I just got off the phone with Greg Geluso, the lender's rep on this deal. They'll extend the closing for two weeks, but they want interest paid from the original date."

"But we didn't cause the delay, they did. They took their goddamn time approving all the documents. Why should we be penalized? Their attorneys only care about keeping the meter running. . . . Would it help if I flew down to Atlanta?"

"No, Henry. Absolutely not." I heard him sigh. "You know they've bought the money as of the closing date. They'll stop the clock on the attorney's fees. You want the mortgage, you'll pay interest from Friday." We both knew I had no other choice.

"What about splitting it?" I asked. "More than two grand a day, including Saturdays and Sundays. That's a lot of dough."

"Forget it. They could have also made you pay amortization."

"Shit. Next time we get ourselves another outfit. These guys are killers!"

"My dear Henry," he had said in a didactic tone, "let me remind you the market is completely different from what it was even six months ago." I owed Bob a lot. When I started creating income properties, he was very helpful, teaching me about the complexities of mortgages. I listened as he went on: "Most of the insurance companies and pension funds are out completely. This mortgage commitment was by far the best I could get from any institution. We're lucky to have it at all."

Bob was right. We've always had cycles. Like the weather: magnificent blue skies or lousy freezing rain. At least there was a solution, though it was expensive. That mortgage wouldn't be lost. I could absorb the extra costs. In a transaction amounting to tens of millions, $20,000 or $30,000 was insignificant.

If I lost a prospective tenant during periods of strong demand, there was always another. Perhaps the rent would have to be a smidgen lower, but at least I'd end up with a lease. The permanent loan would also be lower, but the deal would still work.

The situation with Standard General was different. I had assumed the S.G. lease was locked up. Bad mistake. Should have had a backup. But if I had, S.G. might have concluded I was working another company against them. Then they would probably have considered other buildings, not to be caught short. So, I was screwed. Not by design, but screwed nevertheless.

I played squash at the Javelin Club on West Fifty-sixth Street. It fashioned itself after the Ivy League clubs on Forty-fourth Street, except that Javelin's members were self-made. Most were graduates of state colleges and universities. A few, like me, had graduated from private colleges. They really aspired to be the social equals of their old-line brethren on Forty-fourth.

Both "A" and "B" teams were in the squash league; no victory was sweeter than beating Harvard-Princeton-Yale. You'd think our members, most second- or third-generation Irish, Italian, and Jewish, plus a sprinkling from Scandinavia, the other Americas, and the Balkans, might have accepted their heritage. Been proud of it. But most of them tried, if not to bury it, then at least not to expose it. Not that they were ashamed. They simply possessed an unspoken but undeniable inferiority complex vis-à-vis the downtown crowd.

My fellow members weren't just satisfied with trying to beat everyone on the courts, they wanted to win at everything. A few had married upper-class women from the Upper East Side, Westchester, New Jersey, and southern Connecticut. Love was not always their primary motivation. In any case, Javelin members were fierce competitors. Maybe I have it wrong about the Ivy League crowd; if you dig a little, I suppose only a few are descended from the *Mayflower*. I'll bet a sweet hundred some of those so-called swells have indentured service in their background.

Spear was a typical Javelin member. He was unstoppable, beating up on his business competitors as often as he could. Also a wild stallion, intent on taking away any alpha male's harem. He chased women, early and often. His line — he would call it his charm — was something to behold. Being married didn't seem to make any difference to him. "Need variety, Martin," he would say. "Only doing what I was designed for. We're male animals, you know." Spear was famous for his clichés.

"Dan," I said as I was lacing up my sneakers, "one of these days some broad's going to get to you. She'll get you to divorce again, marry her, have a baby or two. Then when you're old and tired, she'll not only have your money, but some young stud to keep her satisfied."

He ignored my remark. "Always coming, pal, never going. I know where to draw the line."

"That why you've been married only twice?" I said, laughing, though I knew my question would irk him.

"Don't like the trip, don't come along, I tell them from the start," Spear said. "Ten years is max. Maybe five. They can get tired of me, too. More fun with something fresh."

"That's fine in theory," I said, "but what about all that alimony each time?" I said it too quickly and hit his not-so-funny bone.

"That's none of your goddamn business." He turned to his locker and took out his racquet. "Going to whip your ass today for sure, pal," he said with a grin, his calm returning.

"Ready when you are, old buddy," I said. I really didn't like him. Probably because I recognized some of me in him.

He took the first game. Handily. Like a pro beating an amateur into the ground. I think I got eight points. The second game went to 22–all. Why was I so tired? Spear was four years older and had put on a little weight, but he moved around the court like a cat. I thought I had him a few times, slams into the corners. He got most of them back for winners.

"Whatsamatter, Martin?" Spear asked. "Lost your youth and beauty?" He had just broken my serve for the game.

"The next game, I'll give you five points," I said as we began again. I won the first four points, but after that he was off to the races. He took the next ten in a row. The final score was 21 to 9.

"Another one?" he asked, a grin carved on his face. "A thousand bucks says you don't beat me. I'll even give you two-to-one."

"Think I've had enough. Nice playing," I said, trying to be a good loser. I was thinking of telling him about what had happened to me earlier, that my mind was not on the game, but decided not to. Sour grapes. Besides, he'd hear soon enough.

I showered, standing under the hot water for several minutes, wanting to ease the tightness, get that conversation with Phelan off my mind. Phelan was okay; he only did what he had to. It was the meeting I had to have with MacDougall. First, I needed to assess with Steve and Ari the full financial impact of losing the lease. Here was Steve's big chance to give me the business. MacDougall was going to be one unhappy banker. And I would be the object of his anger.

8

I RETURNED Steve's call from my limo. He was out, so I paged him on his beeper. "Why didn't you call me?" he asked. "I am your partner, after all."

I hesitated, then: "Phelan told me Standard General closed with Yedid."

"You're joking! You said you'd convince him to sign with us." My brother was frightened.

"An internal problem. With Jordan. We're the sacrificial lamb. Nothing Phelan can do." Saying those words etched even deeper the gravity of the situation. They had biblical finality. "Look, Steve, first thing tomorrow, you, Ari, and I will sit down and review the whole goddamn situation. Our options."

"Tomorrow's Friday. Joyce and I have been invited for the weekend to her parents' place in the Thousand Islands. We're supposed to leave early."

And I was going to meet Karen in half an hour in my enchanted hideaway in the Village. We got together occasionally, so the relationship would retain a nice edge.

"Oh," I said. "I think it's pretty important, don't you?"

"What's important, my going away for the weekend or meeting with you?" How I loved Steve's sarcasm. I decided to ignore it. I had to focus on what to do next. Once in a while Steve and Ari came up with creative ideas on their own; and I could bounce mine off them.

"Up to you," I said. "Ari and I can meet without you. But if I don't make a date with MacDougall first thing Monday morning, he's liable to hear the good news through the grapevine. It's not going to be a cakewalk."

"I'm in as deep as you, Henry." He paused. "All right, I'll delay leaving. By the way, do you happen to know where Joyce is? She said something about a meeting, but didn't say where."

"How the hell should I know where your wife is?"

"Well, you do have all those foundation and museum meetings with her. I thought there might be one today."

"No," I said. "Anyway, we're on different committees."

"Where will you be later, little brother? In case I have to talk to you about something."

"I'm having dinner with a new date." That wasn't true, but I didn't want him knowing about Karen. Then I added, "If it can't wait, you can reach me on my beeper. Otherwise, eight-thirty to-morrow morning?" He agreed to the time. "I'll call Ari and let him know."

I hung up and directed Charles to drop me off at my townhouse on East End Avenue and Seventy-third. I'd take a cab downtown to meet Karen at my other place on Bleecker Street. We generally preferred to meet there.

Karen Viscomi personified today's modern career woman: in-dependent, ambitious, talented. A little conflicted about not having children. Karen was thirty-three, and in great shape. She could have modeled. She was also a natural athlete. Very self-assured, she was an attorney, on a fast track with the district attorney's office. Her mother was a prominent pediatrician, her father a trial lawyer. In that family, all the children were professionals. Two brothers were phy-sicians and the third was an astrophysicist. Karen had recently been divorced from a Delta Airlines captain.

Soft, brown eyes, large and searching; thin face and high cheek-bones. Perhaps the only defect on an otherwise stunning face was a slightly crooked nose. She rejected cosmetic surgery. Karen combed her auburn hair down the middle, swept it over her ears, or sometimes tied it in a bun. I had noticed her right away at the Uptown Racquet-ball Club. She didn't move, she flowed. After my last ladyfriend gave me the heave-ho because I wouldn't get serious, Karen became the center of my attention.

I had bought the townhouse after Nancy and I divorced. A great bachelor's pad. Spectacular view of the East River, ships forever in motion: tugs, pleasure craft, sailboats, Circle Liners carrying tourists around Manhattan, even Navy and Coast Guard ships, frigates, and patrol vessels. I loved watching airliners fly their patterns into LaGuardia. Viewing a sunrise. I chose not to live nearer the office on Long Island but in Manhattan. Only blocks to the heliport on Sixtieth Street and near the entrance to the East River Drive on Sixty-fourth. Close to Midtown, restaurants, and the theater district.

I never used Charles when I went to meet Karen at my loft in the Village. I trusted him completely, but there was no reason he should be privy to my love life.

"Ask what happened to me today," she said with a twinkle.

"What's this, time for another Karen Viscomi show-and-tell?"

She rose, put her arms around my neck, and pressed her body against mine. She was wearing a multicolored warm-up suit. I began to melt.

"Since you insist, I'll tell you," she continued, ignoring my question. "No, wait, Henry. One would think you'd been without a woman for years." She pushed me away. "Sit down, I want to share this with you." Karen sparkled. I sat on the sofa and pulled her onto my lap. "Henry, I won't be able to concentrate if you do that. Henry . . . please." She held my hands and turned her face to mine.

"You know the case, where those bums beat up a storekeeper when he wouldn't give them money? Claimed they had acted in self-defense after he brandished a gun. I mean, it's so damn obvious!" She was excited, as if she had won an important medal. Fact was, if I'd been the judge, I'd have thrown those guys in the slammer for ten years.

"The D.A. told me to take the lead on this case. He'd probably stop by the court. The problem is, the mob has money to hire the best lawyers. Anyway, I get the third guy, this palooka, on the stand. If I can get my witness to forget himself and his fear of the gang, maybe he'll hand it to us. As a matter of fact, we already had pretty convincing proof."

Karen had already indicated what the outcome would be, but I knew I'd have to hear the details.

"So, I begin slowly, trying to make him relax. Then I give 'big boy' a wink, and he grins back at me like some carnival clown. 'Mr. Thompson,' I ask sweetly, 'let's talk about intent, shall we? When you saw the two defendants from where you were in the back, when they didn't see you, wasn't it possible you thought they were trying to get Mr. Koeppel to pay them for protection?'

" 'Ah, well . . .'

"I winked at him again. 'Please, Mr. Thompson, I really need your help. They weren't really there to purchase something, were they? They wanted his money, right?' And Thompson shakes his head like a donkey in his stall. 'Isn't that correct, Mr. Thompson?' And he blurts, 'Yes!' That did it. The defense tried everything, but the judge supported us. It looks as if we got the bastards." She kissed me sweetly on the mouth and placed my hand on her breast. "Aren't you proud of me, Henry?"

I nodded and ran my lips across her neck slowly up to her ear.

"What did you bring us to eat?" she asked.

"Little Italy's best pizza. And Amstel Light. Plus a large veggie salad. But it'll have to wait. What I want right now, my little one, is you."

I swung us down flat on the couch and kicked off my shoes. I was on my back, Karen on top. Our lips brushed. Kiss one. Better to follow.

She stopped abruptly. "Your reaction to what I just told you is underwhelming, Henry."

"Reproaches later, Karen. I think you're a very effective attorney."

I brought my mouth to hers, but before our lips met she rolled off onto the floor, stood up, looked down at me, and said, "You're a great salesman, Henry. But you have a convenient way of forgetting that I too want certain things out of this relationship." She went over to the counter and opened the pizza box. "And . . ."

"And what?" Karen wasn't always honest with me. Little lies I had caught her in. Like forgetting to let me know she was dating other men.

"We never go to the theater. And last fall, I wanted you to take me to the U.S. Open. You never would."

"You should make me take you," I said. She looked at me oddly. "And I am genuinely pleased you were good in court." I went over to her, stood behind her, pressed against her, ran my hands down her body, slowly over her thighs. She had torn off a piece of pizza and bit off the pointed end. She turned and gave me a look.

"I'm hungry, too, honey," I said. "But food comes second. I'm sure you don't want to hear about an abominable day in the life of Henry Sabatini Martin." I must have looked as pained as I was feeling.

She softened. "I'm sorry," she said. She took my hand and led me to the couch. "You don't usually complain, Henry. Tell me about it later." She told me to stand and close my eyes. She kissed me lightly, provocatively. She undid my tie and unbuttoned my shirt, moving her fingers across my chest as she slowly removed my shirt.

For me the lovemaking was no good. I went through the motions, and I think she enjoyed it, but all I could think about was the S.G. lease. Karen had to have sensed it. We showered and dressed in near silence. We ate a few pieces of cold pizza, washing them down with beer. The salad lay wilting in its bowl.

"Maybe a good night's sleep is what you need," Karen said. "I've got to dash. You can call me tomorrow in the office. I should be back from court late in the day."

I went to the window and watched her hailing a cab. I stood there a while, then turned back to the apartment door.

I kicked it hard, then slammed the door with both fists. "Goddamn it!" I grabbed an empty bottle of Amstel from the coffee table and flung it at the lamp. It hit the shade dead-center, both lamp and bottle caught for a second in a slow-motion dance before crashing to the floor in a hundred pieces. "Fucking Christ!" I screamed. I stood there, shaking, then dropped to the couch, face down, sobbing.

The last time I had cried was during the endless days before Nancy died. Before our divorce, Nancy had tried to convince me several times we should have a child. She was well into her thirties and felt her biological clock ticking. After we were separated, her gynecologist had discovered melanoma during a routine exam. All those years as a kid on Atlantic Beach, that glowing tan, those freckles, that could have been a warning. But who in their teens and twenties ever has such thoughts? I cried not only because I realized how much I had neglected her during our years together, but because now she would never, thanks to me, have the baby she wanted so badly. But, I kept telling myself that Fate or God or whatever never meant us to have a child. One more Henry Sabatini Martin rationalization.

Some months after our divorce, I heard about her. At this point, the melanoma seemed under control, but later on it metastasized with frightful swiftness. A friend of a friend had dated her. He had done or said something she didn't like, so she dumped him. Summarily, no second chance. I never imagined she could be that strong-minded. Later, I saw her playing tennis at her club with some guy. She was laughing and seemed to be having a great time. I did miss her that day. And I was jealous.

About a year later, Nancy died. Her funeral service was in the elegant Episcopal cathedral in Garden City where we had been married. I swore to myself I would display no emotion. Her father and one brother showed great restraint, but her mother and younger brother broke down several times during the service. Her mother and I held hands. When she began to sob, I did, too.

None of us wanted to witness the cremation. We went back to her parents' big Victorian house on Fourth Street, set primly among huge oaks, beeches, and willows. The next day, I picked up the urn and, together with her father and brothers, scattered the ashes over the sands of Atlantic Beach, as Nancy had requested.

I liked the MacAllisters: I admired their stability and equanimity. Emotions were almost always kept under control, rather than all over the place like the Sabatinis and Martins. They seemed to have it together. All of them. Nancy's father, a top executive with Prudential Life, had graduated from Colgate and had an MBA from Wharton. He had met his wife, Gladys, on a visit to Smith College, then saw her again when she was a bridesmaid at the marriage of one of his college roommates. They seemed an ideal couple, though once or twice I did pick up on a few incompatibilities.

Nancy's two brothers teased her and adored her. Jay, the older, was an engineer designing jet aircraft for Grumman. Calvert was a flight instructor at Farmingdale. He and I had lots in common. Although I got along well with her parents, I knew her father had expressed concern about our relationship. Once, when we first began to date, I was sitting in the living room with Gladys waiting for Nan to finish dressing.

"It looks like you two are beginning to see a lot of each other, Henry," she said with a smile. "What I'm trying to say is, our Nancy is pretty important to us."

"Your daughter is very special to me, too, Gladys," I said. "I get along better with her than I ever have with anyone else. In every way." I hoped that would reassure her.

"Please don't misunderstand me, Henry. I'm not trying to interfere. Just a mother's interest."

I nodded. They say if a man wants to know how a woman will turn out when she gets older, take a close look at her mother. Gladys was still a knockout.

After the funeral, I tried as best I could to comfort my in-laws. And they me. Brother Jay poured me a second Dewar's. I thanked him, then slipped away through the sunporch, out the French doors, across the brick patio, and through the formal gardens to a huge ash tree in the corner of the property.

I sat down on the swing that hung from a thick lower branch. I imagined Nancy here as a child, pushing her feet higher and higher, feeling free as she arched her body with the swinging motions of the pendulum.

That spring day in the Garden City Hotel where we first met she was sitting in the lobby, obviously waiting for someone. A girl, I hoped. She caught my eye immediately. Her long flowing blond hair. She was willowy and fresh. Prim, scrubbed, and athletic. Her eyes, already wrinkled from smiling, were blue-green, with a few touches of brown. And the purest skin I had ever seen. I wanted to stroke it. I was there to meet someone from European-American Bank.

It didn't take long to strike up a conversation with her. When she rose to greet her friend — female, I was pleased to see — I had a chance to look her over head to toe. Even lovelier than when seated. I managed to overhear that they were going to play tennis after lunch at the Casino Club across the street. During lunch with my banker,

I had trouble concentrating. I hurried through it with the speed of a teenage boy parked in lovers' lane. Declining coffee, I glanced at my watch, murmured something about being late, and almost ran to the Casino. I went to their court and sat down, saying nothing. It had the desired effect.

"Are you a coach?" she finally asked during one of the change-overs. "It's difficult to concentrate with you watching us."

"I was hoping it would be. I want to sign you up for Forest Hills." She laughed. "I'll make a deal with you. I'll go away if you'll have dinner with me tonight."

She laughed again. A full, hearty laugh that tripped up and down the scales. "Oh, I couldn't. I don't know anything about you. But I see you're not the passive type."

"Henry Martin. Henry Sabatini Martin. I'll fill in the details over dinner." I had a huge, probably silly smile on my face, both hands turned up in mock supplication.

"I'm not sure if . . ."

"Let me call you later."

"Nancy MacAllister. Five-five-five, nine-three-nine-zero."

Nancy was in her late twenties and was, or seemed, unaffected, and a little naive. So I moved cautiously. Everything we did was fun; I phoned her using a variety of foreign accents, sent letters, unexpected gifts, went dancing, to art shows, ballets, and concerts, ate exotic food in Manhattan, put the top down with the air conditioning on in her convertible during nice summer days. I did not attempt to get her into bed. Actually, she was the one who said to me one night, "Henry. Oh, Henry, please make love to me." Now that's great strategy, Henry, my boy!

She worked in an office building in Jericho, an assistant marketing director for Weybridge Publishing Company. She enjoyed her job, and was told she had a solid future with them. Friday afternoons, in good weather, we'd play tennis at her club or mine; afterward, we'd often have dinner with her family. On occasion, I'd have the MacAllisters to my club. Two or three times, I included my parents.

Nan radiated. I felt very comfortable and totally at peace with her. The more time we spent together, the better it got. If there was one thing that bothered me, it was her complete lack of interest in world events, national politics, or the economy. But she was very astute and sophisticated about the arts. And had a real talent for painting. Watercolors, especially. Collages, too, that were highly original.

One weekend, we flew out to Nantucket. Over a huge bucket of steamed clams and beer in an out-of-the-way restaurant on the water, I leaned over and whispered, "Hey, young lady, look out or you're going to turn into a clam. But before you do, how about getting married?" She dropped the steamer she was holding. Before she could say anything, I carefully put a napkin in her lap and told her to open it. Inside was a blue ring case.

"Yes," she said, before opening the case. "Oh, yes, Henry. A thousand times, yes!"

I studied her for a moment. "Nancy, you have the most beautiful face on the face of the earth," I said. "I'll be the best husband they ever created."

We were married in that same cathedral. Protestants, Catholics, and Jews assembled as if for an ecumenical conference. Nan and I were on cloud nine. I had every intention we would stay that way forever.

What a difference a generation makes! Neither my parents nor Nancy's had ever raised a murmur about *our* intermarriage. I thought suddenly of all my parents' tribulations when they made the mistake of falling in love.

"This is lousy, Barb. I mean, it really stinks." They were having hamburgers and Cokes in a White Castle on Jericho Turnpike in New Hyde Park. Barbara met him there after his Army Reserves training meeting. She looked scrubbed and pert in her pleated skirt, sweater, and saddle shoes; Jake trim and fit in his officer's uniform. "Can't even go over together to your house or mine," Jake growled. "Like we're criminals or something, sneaking around." He waved an arm, accidentally knocking over the bottle of ketchup, which broke on the tile floor, spilling its contents over a wide area. A disgruntled waiter shuffled over, mop in hand. "For Chrissake, watch what you're doing," he said. Then, seeing Jake's uniform: "Sorry, sir," he said. Jake realized it was one of the men in his platoon.

"They won't listen," Barbara was saying. "My father won't even let me

bring it up. Mom keeps reminding me that in Italian families the father always has the last say." She reached across the table and took Jake's hand. "Jake, what are we going to do?" Her look was imploring; tears were forming in the corners of her eyes.

"Here's what," Jake said, squeezing her hand. "Next Saturday, you tell them you're staying over at a girlfriend's. We leave early, drive down to Maryland, and get married."

She managed a smile. "Jake," she said. "Dear, dear Jake . . . I couldn't. They'd never forgive me. Ever."

"Yes they would. So would my mother. She's just as worried as your parents. But if you want to wait . . ."

"No," Barbara said, smiling broadly, "I accept! Let's do it. Let's elope. Yes, elope!" Jake got up, and moved over to Barbara's side of the table, put his arm around her, and kissed her. A long kiss. Minutes. Maybe hours. Several people at nearby tables began clapping, but the young couple didn't seem to hear or care.

On a Friday afternoon two weeks later, Salvatore Sabatini walked into his home and was greeted in his dining room by his wife and daughter. And Jacob Martin.

"Hey, what'sa he doing here?" he asked belligerently. "Barbara, I told you, he's notta to come here!"

"Poppa, please. We want your blessing." She was standing, her hands open. "Jake's going on active duty very soon. I know it's not what you wanted for me, but Jake's a wonderful man. I love him, Poppa. With all my heart. Please, Poppa, we want to get married." Her voice was breaking; tears were streaming down her face. Next to her, Jake stood at attention.

Sal glanced over at his wife, who was looking at the floor, then back at his daughter. "I tell you — no, no, no, no! Notta my daughter in mi casa!" *With that, he marched to the stairs, walked up two steps, and said, "He's notta to come here anymore,* mi sendisti?" *He stomped up the stairs and went into his bedroom, slamming the door behind him. Barbara turned to Jake, collapsed into his arms, and began to sob. Angela sat, saying nothing, shaking her head.*

"Momma, talk to him. We're going to get married even if he —" She stopped, gazed into Jake's eyes, and then said quietly, "Momma, you're not

to tell Poppa. We eloped last weekend. Please forgive me for not telling you. I was afraid."

"Oh," Angela said slowly, "oh." She started to get to her feet, fell back on her chair for several seconds. Finally, she stood up and faced the window. "You think I didn't know this might happen," she said as she went over to Barbara. "This is not a good thing." She looked up, as if searching for help. Then, "But you're my sweet, wonderful daughter, my baby girl. I want you always to be happy." She held Barbara's face. "He's not Sicilian, but . . . the thing is, you are already married!" She embraced both of them, then stepped back. "Poppa should never know of our little secret. I'll try to work on him to come around. Joey, he won't approve, either. Maybe not as bad, he being Jake's friend." She pushed them toward the front door. "A little time . . . later, a real wedding . . ."

"Momma . . ."

"You heard me. A real wedding. Just like in Sicily, with a priest . . ."

"And a rabbi . . ." Barbara said.

"Oh, God! I don't know, I just don't know. . . . But I'll try." She paused, "I don't know how long. Poppa must say yes. I must make him say yes!"

"Mrs. Sabatini," Jake cut in. "You should know my mother's going to be very upset, too. Especially when I tell her our children will not be brought up Jewish. Or Catholic, for that matter. Barb and I have already settled that question."

"Oh," Angela said. "Oh, oh, oh . . . Not Catholic." She gave a deep sigh. "But I'll try. I'll try."

But Angela could not get Sal to agree. Arguments were the order of the day in the Sabatini household. One afternoon Jake drove Joe to Jones Beach. "Joe, you're not going to like this, but —"

"But what? You took another job without checking with me first?" They were walking on the boardwalk. The gulls were screeching overhead, their raucous cries spoiling the peacefulness of the afternoon. The sky was a perfect blue, a few puffy clouds drifting east.

Jake stopped, turned to face his partner. His friend. "Look, Joe, it's time I told you." He took a deep breath. "Barb and I eloped. A couple of months ago. With the way everyone is, we had no choice. Your mother knows, but not your old man or my mother."

Joe's face grew bright red. Jake could almost hear the clenched teeth grinding; his eyes were flashing, his face was hard and unforgiving, his eyes narrow and fierce. "You sonofabitch," Joe said softly. "You had to do it, didn't you? Jesus, Jake, you really fucked things up." He tapped a cigarette from his pack, turned back, and leaned on the boardwalk railing.

"No, Joe, I didn't fuck anything up. I did something great. Just wait; the day you fall for somebody, I mean really fall, you'll understand. Your sister said it right, 'This is America, not Sicily.' Barb and I don't have a helluva lot of time."

"Now that's a really stupid statement," Joe said, wheeling around. "What happens if you get knocked off and maybe you've had a kid? Where does that leave Barb?"

"We had it all out, Joe. It may sound romantic, but Barbara said she'd rather have whatever time we could married than regret not having been together for the rest of her life." Jake stood next to Joe, both leaning on the railing, staring unseeing at the fishing trawler plying the waters a mile or two offshore.

After a long minute, Joe turned to Jake and put his hand on Jake's shoulder. "All right, you clown. So it's done. And I know Barb loves you, though God knows why." He paused. "The least you coulda done was take me along for a witness. . . . O Jesus, Pop'll have a hemohrrage." He stuck out his hand, then clasped Jake in a bear hug. "You crazy sonofabitch! Now I gotta have you as my brother-in-law!"

A broad grin covered Jake's face. "I never thought of that," he said. "I mean, a partner, okay, but to have you as my brother-in-law! I told Barb you'd go along with us. I got to tell you, it's not been easy, married but not being able to live together."

"Hey, kiddo, that's your problem!" Joe chuckled. "Ten years from now, we'll all laugh about it. Even Pop, I hope. Now that I know, I'll try to work on him, too. Hey, cumpar, you owe me big!" He slugged Jake hard on the arm, then looked down at his hand. "Jesus," he said, "what kind of training they giving you down at the armory?" He flexed his fingers. "Now, let's get back to that building before our guys fuck up something. Beers on you later, Martin. Lots of them."

"Mom," Jake said to his mother one evening over dinner. "The Sabatinis are really nice. Nothing phony or pretentious. Old world values. And Barbara —"

"Jacob, she's not of our faith. That's part of the old values, too." She gazed at him imploringly. "So many nice Jewish girls just looking to get married. The Isaacs' girl. She's very pretty, and a college girl, too. And what about that other one, whose family owns those newspapers? Now that would be a match!"

Jake breathed in deeply, cleared his throat, and said, "Mom, of course marrying a Jewish girl would be easier, but I have to tell you, so many of them are princesses. Sure, some Protestant and Catholic girls, too. Material things. How much I make, what kind of home I expect to live in."

His mother screwed up her face but didn't reply. "Barbara Sabatini has it all balanced right," Jake continued. "Mom, we fit together. Same ideas. Same values. Same hopes." He rose and kissed her on the forehead. "She reminds me of you. She really does."

"It's got to lead to heartaches, Jake," Helen Martin said with a shake of her head. She gazed for a long time at him. Her boy. Her fine young man. Everything his father wasn't. "But it doesn't look like you're going to change your mind." She sighed, clasped her hands. "Maybe soon I could phone Mrs. Sabatini. Ask her over for tea."

After weeks of his wife, son, and daughter all badgering him, constantly militating to gain his consent, Sal began to soften his stance. Jake was a nice man. And to break up these two might be the end of Martin-Sabatini. This boy was becoming someone. Jake — if only he weren't Jewish.

"All right," Sal said one day, when Joe was berating him for being so pig-headed.

"All right what, Poppa?" Joe asked.

"All right, Barbara can bring-a the boy here if she wants."

"You're great, Poppa," Joe said, pumping his father's hand furiously.

"But only when I'm-a here," he added, holding up a waving finger. "Only when I or your momma are here."

And so it was, finally, that Salvatore Sabatini accepted the American way, exactly four months, three weeks, and two days after the American president, Franklin D. Roosevelt, had spoken his somber words to all the Sabatinis huddled around their radio, and to Jake and his mother a mile across town, about "the day that shall live in infamy."

Sal had consented, but he had never expected to lose the battle of the wedding itself. To his great chagrin, he learned that the ceremony would not be performed as he had planned, before the altar of St. Ignatius Holy Roman

Catholic Church, but in the Sabatini living room in Elmont, New York. On Saturday, June 16, 1942. The intended chose the father of a classmate of Jake's, a judge, to do the honors.

Joe, who had dropped out of Hofstra College after one semester several years earlier, was drafted a few weeks after Jake reported to Fort Hollins, the advanced base for the U.S. Army Second Engineers. Joe elected the infantry and was shipped off to Fort Benning, Georgia, for basic training. He finished at the top of his class, rose quickly to the rank of private first class, then corporal, then sergeant.

Joe had received a weekend pass to attend the wedding. On Friday, Jake drove into Manhattan to pick up Joe at Penn Station. Joe saw Jake first, ducked behind a column, and grabbed him from the rear in a bear hug, knocking off Jake's officer's hat. Joe was resplendent in his uniform, new staff sergeant stripes on his sleeve, his body fit and toned by months of intensive physical training. Joe laughed, relaxed his grip, and hugged his brother-in-law.

"Hey lootenant, sir, you sonofabitch! Great to see 'ya. All I've been looking at is guns and rucksacks. Khaki, khaki every-fucking-where. GIs from all over the goddamn country. Can you believe it, half of 'em never saw an Italian in their whole fucking life! A few insults, a couple of free-for-alls in the barracks. Now we get along good. Had to explain to a few of them fuckheads they can't pull that shit."

"Swing first, think later, that's Joe Sabatini, all right," Jake said. "Anyway, looks like the Army agrees with you. By the way, Sergeant, didn't they teach you enlisted men that you don't hug officers? Section 8, it's called."

"Sorry, lootenant," he said, saluting smartly. "Now, cumpar, as your brother-in-law, a piece of basic advice — after tomorrow, with Barbara, all you got to do from now on is say 'yes' to everything she tells you." He laughed. "That's how you learn to live with Italian broads." He hoisted his duffel bag onto his shoulder. "We walkin' home, lootenant, or did you remember to bring the car?"

"Car? Oh, shit! I knew I forgot something." Jake grinned. "It's two blocks away, on Thirty-fifth Street off Ninth," Jake said. They started toward the escalator.

"Well, at least I got me a girl. What've you been doing for sex, Joe, jumping on some fat, dumpy little private?"

"No, birdbrain. They got some great chicks in the South. Babes who

flutter and faint over us handsome guys in uniform. Fact is, I met a really nice girl. Brigitte. Different from anyone I ever met."

"You should see your house," Jake said, as they were driving over the Queensborough Bridge. "Bedlam. I mean, real bedlam. Your mother's fussing. Everything gotta be perfect. Your old man doesn't know what the hell to do with himself. And Barb's acting as if nothing special was happening."

"Sounds like a good time to keep my head down," Joe said. "Practice for when we get overseas. Hey, what's the scoop?" he asked. "Think you'll be going over soon?"

"The Krauts are moving through Europe like shit through a tin horn," Jake said. "Any idea when your outfit will be shipping out? And which theater?"

"Hear all kinds of rumors. My guess is Africa. What about you, Jake?"

"Military secret," Jake said, pulling his eyes up into a double slant.

The next afternoon, at 4:10, almost on schedule, Barbara's Aunt Catherine played "Here Comes the Bride" on the upright piano while Sal Sabatini walked his daughter from her bedroom down the stairs, past the dining room to the end of the living room. She looked absolutely radiant; her bridal gown of white satin had been originally created in Sicily for her mother's wedding. Judge Thomas Hartman performed the short ceremony as the wedding party stood in front of the fireplace. Predictably, both mothers sniffed and dabbed their eyes. Jake kissed the bride considerably longer than tradition required. The guests snickered; Jake pulled away only when Joe yelled "Time!" and popped open a bottle of champagne.

Everyone hugged and kissed the bride and groom and one another. It was hard to say whether the heavy embraces were Italian or Jewish.

"All right," Sal announced with pride, banging the side of a half-filled glass with a spoon. "Over to the hall for the reception." The "hall" was the Sons of Italy, on Hempstead Turnpike in Springfield Gardens. It was time to spice this ceremony up with something Italian. The families and their guests began moving toward the door. "Hey, isn't this great, honey?" Jake whispered in Barbara's ear. "Believe it or not, everybody's getting along great. And, by the way, I love you. More than ever."

At the hall, after everyone had been seated, Joe stood on his chair, a glass of champagne in his hand. Jake tugged on his khaki tunic. "Hey, cumpar, *don't make too much of a fool of yourself," he warned. "You're lousy at speeches." Joe pushed his hand away.*

"I can talk as good as anyone," Joe said. "Even if I do get some words wrong." He tapped his glass with a spoon and addressed the crowd. "Ladies, gentlemen, family, cousins, and assorted citizens of the world," he began. "As the best man, I want to tell you, c'é n'cosa maraviliosa. Mia sorrelina si marìta a mio compagno di lavoro e megliore amico." *Then: "This is a wonderful occasion, my fabulous little sister marrying my terrific partner and best friend. Our two great families joined together." He gestured to his parents and then to Jake's mother. "As you know, it ain't been easy for these two kids, but, with God's will and our blessings, hey, let's toast them for long life! And lots of* bambini! *Barbara and Jake. Jake and Barbara Martin!"*

The combo — a trumpet, accordion, violin, and drums — broke into a tarantella. Sal stood up, took Barbara's hand, and started to bring her out on the dance floor. "No, Pop, wait!" Joe yelled. "The first dance is always the bride and groom. Pop, you gotta wait. You gotta wait."

There on the couch in the loft, I felt wetness on the fabric and lifted my face, burying it in my hands. My mind drifted to thoughts of Clancy, then Vietnam. Those guys in the second squad, in that village, surprised and butchered by the gooks. And that little girl walking in tight circles until she dropped alongside her mother. Watching the medics work on her until she stopped breathing.

I felt as if I were suspended, as if floating between layers of stratus clouds, darkness above and below. I got up and opened the window, peering out into the night sky. Heavy rain was falling, a tattoo of drops hit my face, mingling with my tears. The lights of the city blurred. I wanted to be absorbed into the night, into the blur, until I became nothing; nothing to think or feel or do. I felt myself being swept away, no longer in control. I shook my head, trying to clear my mind.

9

I TOOK a cab up to the Sixtieth Street Heliport. The weather had turned lousy, the rain scarring the windows; it went with my mood. Inside the small operations building, the young dispatcher greeted me: "You flying tonight, Mr. Martin?" He was wearing a yellow rain suit and hat, his glasses dripping.

"No," I said. "I just wanted to watch her through the large window. Just sit here a minute. Alone, if you don't mind." The dispatcher nodded and went to the rear of the building. I observed the water streaking down in jagged lines over the sleek metal body. The two long blades sagged from the top, drooping, like some huge, flightless, prehistoric bird. As I studied the helicopter, I decided it was indeed a clumsy, gawky machine. But it does fly. Does the job and doesn't ask for help, offers no advice, and expects no thanks.

After some time, I stepped out into the drenching rain. I felt as if I were carrying an enormous weight on my shoulders and back. Sisyphus . . . no, at least I could walk on flat ground — that poor bastard had to keep climbing the same hill. Christ, Henry, stop being so melodramatic.

The rain was pouring out of the sky the way it did in Vietnam. Except for an occasional person out walking a dog, the sidewalks were deserted. I began to run the ten blocks to my house, looking up to cross the streets. At one corner — was it Seventieth Street? — yes Seventieth — there was the grocery store on the corner — I banged into a wire trash can and fell. On my bad knee. Drenched, all of me. I should have been watching.

Inside my townhouse, I peeled off my hat and raincoat, shed my clothes, put on a robe, and poured myself a double brandy, which I took into the small breakfast area off the kitchen. I wanted to watch the planes break through the bottom of the overcast, their landing lights tracking preassigned paths before being turned over to the tower. Something reassuring about the way each one tracked the prescribed instrument landing system.

Important to meet with Steve and Ari quickly. Examine how not closing the Standard General lease will affect our sources of income. Without the lease, no $65 million permanent mortgage to replace the building loan, which was personally guaranteed. Banks have really tightened up. Can't be sure how Federated will deal with our expiring building loan. When I meet with MacDougall, must have a number of options, make him comfortable. Otherwise, he could call the loan.

Federated could foreclose, but it would take them at least a year or more. Banks are notoriously bad building owners. And worse managers. They get caught up in extensive bureaucracy. They either end up leasing only a portion of the empty space or leasing below market rents. Of course, they don't have to pay interest and amortization. But when they act that way, they tie up capital that could be better invested elsewhere, like in bonds, commercial paper, or loans of a different sort. You'd think stockholders and bank examiners would pressure them not to get into real estate. Actually, there haven't been that many foreclosures yet. The last thing banks want is to be strung out with a developer for umpteen years.

The phone rang. I don't want to talk to anyone. Except . . . maybe it's Karen, wanting to see me.

I picked up the phone, and in a heavy accent: "Hull-o. Ladies' Uptown Steam Baths, Mahmoud, proprietor speaking." I wanted to show Karen I was in a better mood.

"Henry? What's this 'steam bath and Mahmoud' business?" It was my father, his voice a little raspy.

"Hi, Dad. Just popped into my head. Good to hear you. I miss you." He must have talked to Steve. I didn't feel like a lecture or advice. "How's your wife?" I asked.

"Don't be funny. She's fine. I called you earlier. Twice." It wasn't difficult to tell when he was annoyed.

"Just came home. Haven't checked my machine yet. You sound upset."

"I am. Very. Steven just called. Told me the Standard General deal is down the drain." He waited for me to respond, but I knew there was more coming. "Well, doesn't that create problems? Major problems? Steve said there was no backup deal." Another pause, but I let him go on. "Remember my warning you that a building the size of 355 was too damn big to spec? That you'd better get tenants first?"

"Dad, I was dead sure they would take the building. And if they didn't, we had other good prospects. The market was strong when we began and looked even better going forward. You taught me about risk-reward."

"Yes," he said, "but I always made sure we never overstepped ourselves. A forty-thousand-square-foot industrial building on Long Island in 1953 is one thing. That fifty-story Taj Mahal you put up is another." My father had a pleasant way of challenging me. It was one of the things I always appreciated about him. His criticisms were direct but not offensive. We could talk them out without either one of us getting really angry. When I was fifteen I began to grasp what his business was all about. Sometime later he told me he had involved me as a way of getting me interested. Also to make me recognize, analyze, and solve problems. When he retired he gave his remaining one-third stake in the company to my mother as nonvoting stock. Steve and I owned the other two-thirds, as well as all of the class-A voting stock.

"Yeah, it is a big building, but we can handle it. And remember those first office buildings in Jericho on the expressway? I was at Middlebury then. I seem to recollect your sweating bullets until they were rented up."

"Henry, that was 1964. We grabbed the best piece of land in Nassau, at Exit 40, Jericho Turnpike. Real estate had yet to catch up with the economy. Low-cost labor on Long Island attracted New York companies. Secretaries would work for less to be closer to home. And, Henry, you seem to forget I had that first building over forty percent leased before I put a shovel in the ground. A little different, don't you think?"

I knew he wasn't being smug. Simply reminding me how rational and thorough he had always been. Still, I had been sure I was right with 355 Park Avenue. It set up like a huge winner, and we had clout with the banks. For Chrissake, half a dozen knocked themselves out trying to get our account. Who could have anticipated that the market would go so quickly from bullish to bearish, everyone hell-bent for the hills?

"I'll work something out, Dad. MacDougall's an old friend. We've got a good statement. Outside of Three-Fifty-Five, all our other buildings have solid cash flows." I could hear myself sighing, as if I didn't believe my own brave pronouncements.

"Supporting all that vacant land. Didn't you acquire more than you needed?"

"You taught me that buying a parcel early creates a low land cost. May be the difference between mortgaging out or having to leave money in the deal."

"Land and horses eat, son. Too much land, you starve." He paused. "This time it doesn't look like the standard recession, Henry. More like a three-headed monster. Call me after you meet with the bank."

He didn't usually make that request. He had stopped doing it years ago. Not that I didn't value his opinion or respect his experience, but the real estate industry had changed.

"You're thinking times are different," he added, as if reading my mind. "That I've been out of it and wouldn't understand. Well, there are still many parallels. Banks, vacancies, cash flows, liquidity. Henry, if you want I can jump on the first plane."

"No thanks, Dad. But I appreciate your support. As always. How are you keeping busy out there in the land of eternal youth?"

"Same stuff. Golf, a little tennis, some bridge, friends. Just came back with your mother from Fort Huachuca, Hereford, and Bisbee. Went up Ramsey Canyon to the beautiful Nature Conservancy preserve. We also booked a cruise to Australia and the Orient in December. Everything's fine except . . ."

"Except what?" I asked.

"Oh, don't tell your mother or Steve. I've been having some dizzy spells lately. Nothing serious, I'm sure. Better stay out of the sun. Some of my friends out here have gotten skin cancer."

I didn't like what I was hearing. Joyce's father had experienced dizziness. Turned out his arteries were clogged. Next thing you knew, triple bypass. Joyce's father was considerably younger. Dad was seventy-five. "Move up the date of your annual. Promise me, Dad."

"Sounds just like your mother. All right. I'll call tomorrow. And stay cool, Henry. That's always been one of your great strengths. Good night, son. I love you. Your steam bath business sounds pretty good. I'll take off thirty pounds, be the towel boy, or become a eunuch if I have to."

I laughed. "Call me after the doctor gives you the once-over." I said good night, then added: "Talking with you is always helpful, Dad. And by the way, I love you, too."

The pizza had given me indigestion. Or maybe the cognac. A nice, long hot shower. Oscar Hijuelos's new novel. Damn good. Just hit the *New York Times Book Review* best-seller list. Shit, I miss Karen. Wish she'd call. I was a real jerk tonight.

It took me a while to fall asleep, which was unusual. By the end of a day, whether it was business or sports, indoor or out, I usually have no trouble sleeping. Finally, I drifted off. Troubled dreams. In one, I was in a race, but the rule was that the one who came in first lost. I wanted to question the rule, but no one would listen. All of us were plowing through knee-deep, gravylike gruel, a smelly greenish mess. At first everyone was nondescript, but then I began to recognize some of my buddies. I was back in Vietnam, leading my company through the swamps toward some village we had to take. My buddy and XO Rich — First Lieutenant Rich Giannotti — was on recon. I knew he was in danger; he had gotten too far ahead of us. He was yelling for everyone to hurry up, he was about to enter the village and wanted more fire support. "Henry, for Chrissake, get your ass up here. I'm going in."

"Wait for the gunships and mortars," I yelled back. They'd blow those gook-ridden shacks to smithereens. "Wait, Rich, we're coming up!" But either he didn't hear me or couldn't. He looked back at me one last time, then dashed into the open, his automatic blazing. The dumb bastard always had a cigar stuck in his mouth, in a face that looked as though it hadn't seen soap and water for six months. He got no farther than ten yards when a sniper nailed him. Twice.

When I arrived, Rich was writhing on the ground. I turned him over. He was holding his stomach. His guts were spilling through his hands, blood and bile. I tried to push them back inside, but the more I pushed the more they kept coming out. He looked up and smiled. "Dumb sonofabitch," I said, holding his head in my lap.

"Yeah, but I won. I was here first. That's the game, you jerkoff. I won. I won." He bit the side of his mouth from the pain, then his body began to twitch and he ground his teeth. "Light my butt, you asshole. It went out in the rain. I mean it, do what I say!"

"Good God, Rich, you totally screwed up. The first one in loses! Didn't they tell you that?"

As I lit his cigar, everything changed to smoke. When it cleared, Rich was gone except for his second finger, which kept wagging. Then it pointed. I can't do that, I thought. Go where it's pointing. Then I was alone and it was pitch black. The sky had three moons in it. One was bare, the second laughing, the third crying.

There was a sign on a tree, a lone tree that had the bark of a sycamore but the needles of an evergreen. The bas-relief letters were in bronze in different sizes. Each letter was moving as if it were part of some tribal dance. I held the board firmly, but the words continued to dance. Then the sign sang to me: HENRY. HENRY. HENRY SABATINI. HENRY SABATINI MARTIN. IF YOU DON'T WANT TO COME IN FIRST, GO TO THE BEGINNING OF THE AIRPORT RUNWAY, AND WALK BACKWARD. IF YOU STOP, YOU WON'T BE ABLE TO START AGAIN. WALK BACKWARD REGARDLESS OF WHAT ANY OF THE OTHER SIGNS TELL YOU. YOU WILL NOT BE ABLE TO SEE, AND YOU MUST HOLD YOUR BREATH FOR TWO MINUTES.

I closed my eyes, gasping. Suddenly I was on a huge stage. The same greenish gruel seeped in, curling around the furniture and trees. A single lamp stood like a traffic light. Pastel-colored bulbs were flashing under the shade. I put my hand underneath and something grabbed it. As I withdrew my hand, it held a note, which read,

"Henry, think for yourself. Don't follow the leader." It was signed, "Jim Jones' Kool-Aid Bottling Company."

The lamp turned into a moray eel, its mouth gaping with huge razor-sharp teeth. It smiled at me and said, "Kiss me, kiss me." I turned to run, but remembered what the sign had said about walking backward. I wasn't sure whether to trust the sign or not. As I began to walk backward, the moray eel came closer. "We're in a race, but I'm faster," it hissed. "I want to kiss you hard." I tried to scream, but no sound came out. I kept trying and finally screamed myself awake. My pillow and sheets were soaked.

It was 4:30 A.M. The rain had stopped, and outside a thick fog had settled in, obliterating the buildings with milky gauze. I dozed on the couch, but woke when the automatic coffee machine began to grind the beans. At least it wasn't Rich grinding his teeth. Or the moray eel.

10

WHEN I arrived at our Garden City office park, a complex of
three four-story buildings we had erected eight years earlier, Steve's
and Ari's cars were parked in their assigned spots. I brought a cup of
black coffee with me into the executive conference room. They were
deep in conversation. I would have liked to have been that proverbial
fly on the wall, overhear what they had been saying. As a kid, I used
to fantasize I had that power.

Various cash flow sheets were spread out on the table. It looked
as if Steve and Ari could have been piecing together wallpaper before
hanging it. The summary page they were concentrating on was titled
"COMBINED CASH FLOWS, ALL ENTITIES." Steve looked up. "Glad
you could finally make it," he said.

"And a good morning to you, too, Steve," I said. He grumbled
something about having to pee and walked out of the room. I sat
down in his place and concentrated on the bottom lines, "SUR-
PLUS/DEFICIT, TOTAL INCOMES AND EXPENDITURES."

"How bad, Ari?" I asked. We would examine together how we
could handle the deficits that would now surely occur.

Ari Miller was solid as a rock and utterly meticulous. I liked
and respected him, though he was somewhat introverted and would
have had a tough time if he had to make his living as a salesman. He was born in Vienna in 1937. His parents had waited
too long to escape the Nazis, but bribed whoever they had to so

their infant son could. An older daughter remained with them. Papers were forged, and the underground placed Ari with a Spanish businessman whose next stop was Italy. From there, his guardian took him to Barcelona, where he was smuggled onto a ship to Alexandria in the care of a woman with six children, including Ari. Then finally to Palestine. When he was old enough, Ari made an exhaustive search for his sister and parents; he finally learned that they died in 1944 in a gas chamber in Bergen-Belsen. All he could find out about his sister was that she probably ended up in Sweden. That was all. He married an American Jew he met on a kibbutz, who bore him three sons. Ari spent six years at the accounting firm of Ernst and Young. After those six years, he decided to switch to a smaller company where he would have more impact.

I admired and respected my CFO, senior vice president for finance. Ari didn't hesitate to raise the red flag when he detected problems, and often proposed solid solutions. Armed with his analyses, I would determine our best courses of action, especially for new projects and acquisitions. Ari tried to make Steve feel involved, so he always made sure to send reports and memos to both of us.

"I'll know exactly how bad it is when I run a new combined cash flow," he answered. He looked up, his forehead furrowed, his lips squeezed together. "But we have big problems, Henry. Real big. Steve and I have already taken a preliminary look."

"All right," I said, "let's start wrestling with them."

Steve returned and leaned against the whiteboard on the wall. "Maybe it's not that bad, Henry," he said softly. "A bite into the pie, but there's plenty left."

I turned to him with astonishment. "Is this really you, my brother, talking?" I asked. Something else had to be going on.

"At first, I was against building Three-Fifty-Five. But if you remember, I finally agreed we should go ahead." He smiled as he said that. "Your perception of me is distorted. As usual."

"Yeah, well . . ." I began. Sometimes I just couldn't figure Steve out.

Ari pointed to the chart labeled "CASH REQUIREMENTS, NET."

"What doesn't help the situation," he began, "is our federal and state taxes. I've been working them over and over. Carry-forward losses have been used up, especially those donations you guys made some years back. And the capital gains on sales of your stocks and bonds drive the taxes even higher."

"The revisions for calculating depreciation are killing us," Steve said. He was referring to the diminution of deductions for tenant work, partitions, and other improvements we used to be able to take. He stood up. "This business is beginning to suck!" Ari glanced at me. "Plus, hundreds of thousands of dollars down the drain carrying those vacant parcels of land," Steve griped. "Sell them, and it would take some pressure off."

"No market," I responded. "If we did, we'd take a real bath."

Steve stared at me contemptuously.

"Okay," I said, "I'll do what I can to sell Montvale, East Fishkill, and the others."

"What really concerns me is the drain our vacancies generate," Steve said. "Very big. Two hundred thousand a month without Three-Fifty-Five. More if some tenants don't renew. Add in the building loan on Three-Fifty-Five. Megabucks every month."

"We must renew leases," I said. "At whatever price." Ari nodded, but Steve put up his hand.

"That would be a double hit," he said, shaking his head. "I mean, you lower rents too much, we can't service the mortgages. And we'd be short capital even if we could refinance. Plus much lower income for us."

"I'll run a new cash flow," Ari said quickly. "Stick around a couple of hours, it should be ready." He glanced up at me.

No matter what Ari came up with, the revised cash flow would most certainly indicate disastrous monthly deficits. "Look guys," I said a little solemnly. "I need some exercise. Helps me tackle problems better. Be back by noon, okay?"

"Earlier, damn it," Steve sniped. "I'm trying to get away with Joyce, remember? She's waiting."

"Sure. Two hours, Ari?" He nodded.

"What else you doing this weekend, Henry?" Steve asked. Why was he so interested, I wondered.

"Flying to Martha's Vineyard. A friend invited me up. Be better prepared for Monday with MacDougall."

Steve didn't respond. I thought of how it would be up in the Vineyard with Karen. I needed a break, and bright and early tomorrow morning I'd be out of here. Some old R & R would be exactly right.

"CLEARANCE, good morning, Chancellor Three-five-five Hotel Mike, with ATIS Delta, instruments to Martha's Vineyard." I had played lousy tennis at the club yesterday. I needed to leave my problems behind on Long Island. I wanted a lost weekend with Karen Viscomi. Spending time at her family's house on the Vineyard was much better than endless hours poring over numbers and thinking about the meeting with the bank on Monday.

I had filed an instrument flight plan with Flight Service Station at Islip, where I keep my twin-engine Cessna. The day was typical for late May, hazy with limited visibility. In the summer on Long Island early morning ground fog often results from overnight advection cooling, when cooler temperatures created over the Atlantic move in over the land. It arrives as thick fog that invariably burns off by mid-to-late morning. At best, the flying conditions today were marginal; it was smarter and certainly safer to file under instrument flight rules, known as IFR. I calculated the flight would take forty minutes, based on my average airspeed of 192 knots with winds aloft coming from the southwest at 20 knots.

"Chancellor Three-five-five Hotel Mike, you are cleared to Martha's Vineyard. Long Island Three departure, radar vectors Calverton, Victor four fifty-one Groton, Victor three seventy-four, direct. Runway heading, altitude three thousand, expect seven thousand ten minutes after departure. Departure frequency one-twenty-point-zero-five. Squawk four three four six."

"Roger, Clearance." I repeated the clearance, then asked, "Clearance, can you work out, Hampton, Victor two sixty-eight Sandy Point, direct?"

"Stand by one, Five Hotel Mike."

My routing was shorter, and I knew from *Notices to Airmen* that Calverton was *hot*, that jets were being test-flown at the Grumman facility there. A week ago, a Cessna 152 piloted by a student had almost collided with an F-16. Student pilots can be more dangerous than thunderstorms, ice, or fog.

"Five Hotel Mike, ready to copy?" I answered that I was. "You are cleared Hampton, Victor two sixty-eight Sandy Point, direct," he said.

I acknowledged by repeating his revised instructions. The tower operator released me for takeoff. I pushed the six levers on the yoke forward, surged down the runway, the power of 650 horses behind me, and rotated at 93 knots. When there was no more ground below to land on in the unlikely event I lost an engine, I pulled up the landing gear knob and the three wheels retracted into the fuselage and wings.

At 500 feet I was absorbed inside a layer of fog and concentrated on holding a heading of 240 degrees while climbing at 120 knots. The man in the tower came back on. "Five Hotel Mike, departure one-twenty-point-zero-five, have a nice flight."

I reduced manifold pressure to thirty-five inches and props to 2500 rpm, adjusted the fuel flows, and responded, "Roger, tower, one-twenty-point-zero-five, talk to you on the way back."

Flying alone into the blurred unknowns inside clouds is both demanding and exhilarating, and requires total concentration. Confined within the cabin — no place for a claustrophobic — you are entirely dependent on the instruments and your ability to use them properly. When flying blind, you have the disturbing feeling of not being able to tell whether you're right-side up or not. No visual frame of reference. Normal aerodynamic effects cannot be felt by your body. It's imperative that tasks such as changing radio frequencies or copying down instructions from an air traffic controller do not take more than a few seconds away from the pilot's constant need to scan the instrument panel.

Despite all my flying experience, I always feel a twinge of fear when I can't see outside the aircraft. Add to that the occasional thunderstorm cells, turbulence, or ice on the wings, stabilizers, and props. But, after you shoot an instrument approach, break out of the clouds, and see the lights of the runway, you feel a rush, an exhilaration.

The weather improved and the fog dissipated by the time I crossed over Brookhaven Airport. Numerous small planes, Cessna 152s and 172s, were practicing touch-and-go landings and takeoffs. They reminded me of a Second World War movie. The Battle of the Coral Sea. Swarms of dive-bombers like hornets attacking a Japanese aircraft carrier, a sitting duck. ATC gave me a change of frequency, to 132.25. I reported in: "New York Approach, good afternoon, Chancellor Three-five-five Hotel Mike on board. 5000."

"Roger, Five Hotel Mike. Maintain 5000, numerous targets circling near Spadero at three and eight o'clock, altitudes unknown. Monitor the frequency for deplaning jumpers."

"Wilco. No joy on the targets." A year before, on my way back from the annual 15,000-plane fly-in at Oshkosh with two friends and fellow pilots, Kim Sparks and Jackie Tulumello, some idiot near Binghamton, New York, discharged his jumpers at 10,000 feet right in front of us. I don't know how we missed those bastards. We were goddamned lucky. So were they. If we had hit one, he or she would undoubtedly have been killed on the spot. We would probably have crashed.

And a few weeks prior, near the Middlebury Airport in Vermont, an experienced woman pilot was flying her acrobatic Pitts in an air show. She was told there would be two jumpers. There were actually three. She didn't see the third until she hit him. The parachutist severed the wing struts and was cut into pieces. The impact probably knocked her unconscious as her tiny aircraft broke apart. It was surmised she had died instantly from a broken neck.

"Jumpers away," I heard through my headset. No, no, you dumb bastard! Where? Where the hell are they? Why hadn't ATC instructed the pilot to give the standard warning, "Three minutes to jump?" Change heading? Those jumpers were somewhere above me, falling through the sky at 176 feet per second.

"Five Hotel Mike. Where are those jumpers?" I tried to sound calm.

"About, ah, two miles and twenty degrees to your right," the controller responded excitedly. "Turn thirty degrees left, Five Hotel Mike! Left!"

"Wilco." A few minutes later, after I was clear of the immediate vicinity, "Look, you report that guy, or I will," I said with barely concealed anger. "If you don't, he's going to kill someone."

"Five Hotel Mike, are you willing to file a report?" was the controller's question. I knew the pilot of the plane carrying the jumpers was listening on the frequency.

"Affirmative! I expect contact will be made with me through Mid-Island at Islip. What's his tail number?" I damned well planned to follow this up.

The controller hesitated, then said, "Five Hotel Mike, it will appear in the report. You'll hear from us. Resume own navigation to Hampton. Correct heading to 110 degrees." The radar vector put me back on course.

Karen Viscomi was especially seductive when she shared some of her sexual fantasies with me. Her openness was surprising just after we had gone to bed for the first time. "We find a place," Karen said. "Yours, mine, some place where no one can bother us. I want candles, a Kenny G. tape playing. It's dark. You're standing up. You're not wearing a shirt or shoes or socks. Then you're going to watch me remove my clothes, not all of them, I'll keep just a little on. You can't touch me. Then . . ."

What I had learned worked best during the first several dates was to avoid touching, kissing, or anything that would give a woman the idea that having sex was uppermost in my mind. Actually, it wasn't always. Friendship was also important. Sharing things with a woman like Karen: sports, theater, maybe flying, conversations about anything and everything from deconstruction to the politics of race and gender, to the latest research into the expanding universe; what we believe in, what we want out of life.

The women I've known generally respond to that approach. When I keep my distance, it confuses them. Either consciously or unconsciously, they begin to wonder why I'm not making moves, whether something is wrong with *them*. When eventually I "accidentally" brush up against them, they almost always respond by gently taking my hand or offering a shy smile.

Karen was a lot of fun and very bright. I had taken her to lunch at the Four Seasons, where mega-deals are negotiated over some of the finest food and drink on that restaurant-laden island.

It had been over two years since Nancy died. From time to time I thought about what I wanted and needed in my relationships with women. I was aware that the first woman in my life, my mother, had made me feel I wasn't worth a tinker's damn. My father and brother were important to her, but for me she could only try to make a show of mothering. I sensed she had no heart in it. The result of that for me was not being willing to take the chance of becoming intimate.

I remember being with the as-yet-unmarried Joyce one wintry Saturday afternoon, nestled in my Greenwich Village loft. She had woken up from a nap and was sitting on the futon, a glass of wine in her hands. "Henry, try not to hold anything back. It costs you, and —"

"I don't hold back, I always give you everything I've got," I said. She calmly leaned over the bed and poured the wine all over my face. I leapt up.

"What the hell was that for?"

"To show you how much I love you." She wiped my face, then: "I'm not your mother, Henry. Once you accept the fact that your mother will never really love you, you'll be available. You'll never, *never* have the intimacy you say you want until you're willing to take the risk of getting involved. And giving up some of the control." She pulled me down on the futon.

I had heard what she said. Unfortunately, it didn't go any further than my ears.

I descended toward Martha's Vineyard, a stunning island of ponds and beaches and undulating moors, an enchanted playland. I couldn't see many people, but I knew they were there, fulfilling themselves with the summer's activities. I approached from the west over Gay Head, then over Long Beach and Menemsha Pond, toward the main airport in the center of the island. Oak Bluffs and Edgartown were ensconced to the east. The tower gave me permission to land. I entered a left downwind, turned the base leg and then into the final for Runway 24. I taxied to the parking area, waiting the 3.5 minutes for the supercharged engines to cool down. I thought I could hear something a little different in the sound of the left one. Probably my imagination. I'd check it when I did the engine runups before flying again, as I always did.

Karen, who had flown in a little earlier from LaGuardia, was standing at the gate outside the terminal, wearing white sharkskin shorts that clung to her as if wet. A bright blue and white striped tank top and blue topsiders, no socks. She looked great.

"Hi, Captain Marvel," she said, smiling. "The radio says the weather will be gorgeous the rest of the weekend. And the moon's still doing its job." We walked hand in hand to her car. "Oh, I forgot to tell you. My parents have dropped in for a surprise visit. We're always doing that in our family. Dad flew fighters in the Second World War and again in Korea. I'm sure you two will have a lot to talk about."

I must have looked like a kid in a candy store where the last Milky Way had just been sold. "Ah, that's great, Karen," I managed. "I'm sure we will."

"You'll love my mother, too," Karen said, with another disarming smile. "I bought a whole bunch of fresh veggies and scallops. Also fresh striped bass we can cook on the grill." She leaned over and kissed me on the cheek. "Several great restaurants on the Vineyard, but I prefer eating at home. Tomorrow, corn and steamed lobsters. Dad says they taste better boiled, not broiled. Big two-and-a-half-pounders."

The drive to the Viscomi home took us west to Chilmark. On the main road we passed traditional Cape Cod houses neatly separated by white picket fences, small lawns, and gardens. Lots of kids on bikes, some with fishing poles. Up and down small hills, past views of little inlets bordered by reeds and moors that reminded me of Scotland. Some who lived in these charming houses were retirees, former professors, and doctors plus a number of summer renters who had finally decided that year-round island living was what they wanted. One couple were my cousins Sid and June Schneider. Maybe I'd give them a call. . . . Hell, no.

Nancy had preferred the heated atmosphere of the Hamptons, the excitement of parties given by the rich and famous, the movers and shakers in the arts and business. I had found most of them pretentious and boring. We did that whole bit for a few years, spent weekends socializing and playing tennis. It was fun for a while, but a few weekends back in Middlebury, Vermont, convinced us that long-range, low-keyed time up there was far preferable to the frenzied nonsense of eastern Long Island.

"You look great," I said, edging closer. "I must say, I was hoping it would be just the two of us. How long are your folks staying?"

"Hard to say," she said. "They're like gypsies." Then she began to laugh.

"What's so funny? Have I missed something?"

She pulled the car over to the side of the road, stopped, and turned to face me. "Henry, I can't keep this up any longer. In fact, they were planning to come, but I talked them into putting it off until Monday afternoon."

I smiled and kissed her warmly on the mouth. "You really had me going," I said. Could I stay till Monday? There was that crucial meeting first thing with MacDougall. "Karen, in the next day or so, I'm going to make us both forget the rest of the world. That's a promise." I put my arms around her and kissed her gently, tenderly behind her ear.

"I'm surprised," I said after we made love that afternoon, "that you're not involved with someone." She remained silent. "Or is that none of my business?"

She walked to the window and gazed out onto the blue-green of Vineyard Bay Sound. "No," she said, "of course it's your business. After my marriage began to fall apart, there was someone I was in love with. From the office." She sighed. "Same old story. He said he was getting a divorce and would marry me. But then the pull was just too great for him. Two terrific kids, the standard guilt. Plus a wife who did everything she could to get him back. I met her once at a party. She blamed me for the fact that her marriage was failing, or had failed. Which was simply not so."

Karen sat down on the chair next to the bed. She reached for a piece of cheese and glass of white wine, and then handed them to me. "The eternal question is, how can anyone make marriage work? I know maybe two couples I can call successful. I may never tie the knot again."

"I'm the wrong one to ask," I said. "Nancy and I were never able to share enough. Anger never went away. We also had different ideas about kids. Now I regret we never had any."

Karen lay next to me and stroked my face. "Tomorrow," she said, "we'll share the magnificence of a sparkling Vineyard dawn." She nestled her face against mine. "Henry Martin, to tell you the truth, you'd be impossible to be married to, but you're nice to spend weekends with. Now close your eyes, and we'll nap."

That night I fell off peacefully into a deep sleep. If I dreamed, I didn't remember. The next morning was crisp and inviting. We rose early, just as the light was peeking up from the horizon. I rolled over, pushed her hair aside, and kissed her lightly on her neck. She smiled and nodded. "Yes," she whispered, "absolutely yes." Afterward, we ran down to the beach and found a secluded area. We took off our bathing suits, and dashed into the surf.

"What a wonderful way to start the day," I said.

"I have one problem with you this morning, Henry," Karen said as we dried ourselves with large beach towels. "Your beard is hurting my baby skin. I'll fix us up with Canadian bacon, lots of eggs, and English muffins while you shave. Then we'll drive into Edgartown and browse."

12

YOU can count with five fingers, maybe ten, those summer mornings on Martha's Vineyard when the ceilings and visibilities are un-
limited — the expression pilots use is "CAVU." That Monday I
lucked out.

Karen drove me to the airport at 6:30.

"This is without a doubt the only way to start out the week," I
said. "You were . . . oh, I've told you. I particularly appreciate your
parents' non-visit."

She nodded and patted me on my leg.

"How about dinner one night soon?" I asked.

"Call me tomorrow," Karen said. "No, I'll be in Albany. I'll call
you."

I grabbed her hand, kissed it, then kissed her on the mouth.
I turned, unlocked the door of my plane, removed the chocks, and
untied the two wing ropes and the one holding down the tail. I
stowed my gear in the back, ran through the pre-flight checklists,
and climbed in.

As I settled into the pilot's seat, Karen motioned that she wanted
to tell me something. I waved her over, and opened the small pilot's
window.

"I would deny this in court, Henry Martin, but I could get to like sleeping with you," she said, a big grin on her face.

"Thank you. But then it's obvious I was your first man. Talk to you soon."

She strolled to her car, sat on the hood, and waved.

I completed the routine for starting the engines and called Ground for departure instructions, which were simpler than they were for the instrument flight from Islip. I didn't need any reminders to check thoroughly the oil temperature and pressure on the left engine.

If one or both your engines quit and you're high enough, you may be able to reach an airport. Or pick the best spot to land. If it happens immediately after takeoff and there is no more runway left, you may have to execute a controlled crash. You are likely to walk away from one of those when you fly the plane straight ahead, but if you lose directional control because both engines are not operating, it can result in the aircraft hitting the ground in an unpleasant and unbecoming manner.

I taxied out to the active runway. The warm-up and pre-takeoff procedures indicated no evidence of any problems. "Tower, Three-five-five Hotel Mike ready Runway 24." The wind was from the northwest, coming in from behind the cold front that had cleared out the humidity. The morning was dazzling, the kind that makes you feel you can do absolutely anything.

"Five Hotel Mike, cleared for takeoff. Departure frequency one-two-four point seven. Come see us again some time. We like your Chancellor," the tower operator said, his comments almost a whisper. Air controllers don't usually say things like that, because transmissions are recorded. All conversations are supposed to be strictly business.

"I copy, Tower. She is pretty, isn't she?"

I swung the plane into the wind, rechecked the instruments and engine pressures and temperatures, shoved the throttles, mixtures, and propeller handles forward, my left hand firmly on the yoke. At rotation speed I eased back on the control wheel and the plane lifted off the runway. Shortly after takeoff I lifted the landing gear knob to raise the three wheels.

Then, at about three hundred feet past the point where I could bring the plane down on the runway, one engine lost power. "Okay, okay," I whispered, "airspeed, *airspeed*. Don't panic. You know what to do." My mind raced to the memorized procedure for "Engine Failure, No Runway Remaining."

I pitched down to blue line, the airspeed at which the plane will fly on one engine without stalling or loss of directional control. I shouted, "Mixture, Props, Throttle!" They were already fully forward. I didn't need to lift the gear because it was already up. Next, fuel: selector on main tanks and auxiliary boost pumps on. All were where they should be. Then, identify which engine failed. Verify it, fix or feather the propeller. My left leg had no effect on controlling the rudder, the confirmation that the left engine was the one without power. I feathered it by bringing the left throttle to idle, the propeller to feather, and mixture to idle cutoff. I managed to climb slowly to pattern altitude, which was one thousand feet over the airport.

"Tower, Five Hotel Mike. I'm having a bit of a problem with my left engine," I said trying to sound nonchalant. "Appreciate an immediate."

"Roger, Five Hotel Mike. Can you fly the pattern or do you want to land downwind? Any fire?" I knew someone was focusing their binoculars.

"No, the right engine's fine," I answered.

"Five Hotel Mike. Cleared for twenty-four. Don't be concerned when you see the fire truck. It's required." The tower instructed two other planes to fly clear of the airport.

I didn't respond, too busy making sure I maintained the necessary airspeed, altitude, and heading. I had to exert pressure on the right rudder to offset the yaw. I dropped the gear and held a higher airspeed and altitude than I would for a normal landing. I turned left 90 degrees onto the runway, verbally checked off items for landing, my eyes moving up and back between the end of the runway and the airspeed indicator. At the appropriate moment, I increased the rate of descent with the use of partial flaps. Training and instinct and feel — another way of saying experience plus common sense.

It was going well. I was feeling confident. About a half-mile from touchdown the right engine quit. "Goddamn it!" All right,

Henry, you're almost there, I thought. Watch your airspeed! And heading. Drop the nose farther.

It had been a long time since I had practiced landing without power, a dead-stick landing. A little like the training I had in Marine Air in a simulator, only that was for flying single-engine jets.

The landing wasn't nearly as smooth as I usually make, but at least I didn't bust the gear. More important, I was able to walk away.

When the plane came to a halt, I dropped my head for a moment. "Thanks, Up There." What if I had lost the right engine earlier and couldn't make the runway? "Thanks again." I felt perspiration on my face. An official car raced out behind the fire truck. I saw Karen jump out of the passenger side as I opened the pilot's window.

"Henry, what happened? I knew something was wrong when you turned around. And then silence." She looked shaken. I went to the rear and stepped down the stairs.

"I don't *know* what happened. Plane's designed to fly on one engine, but with none it gets a little more difficult," I said as we hugged. "I practice this stuff." I must have sounded like some hero shrugging off death one more time. "I have no idea why both quit. It's almost impossible." Then I thought, if I were paranoid I'd say someone had fooled around with both motors. Jesus! Nobody could hate me that much.

I turned to the official. "Can you guys tow me to a place on the field where there's a mechanic?"

"We have to clear the runway as quickly as possible," he said. "We'll bring you to a spot on the side not far from the terminal. There are no facilities. You'll have to bring in someone."

That would take days, maybe weeks. I'd have Sampson pick me up. He can bring one of the guys from Mid-Island. Then call MacDougall and tell him.

We drove to the airport manager's office. "Henry, my flight leaves at eleven, but it goes into LaGuardia," Karen offered. "Does that help you?"

"Thanks, but it'll be faster if Craig comes for me," I said, shaking my head.

After saying good-bye to Karen again, I made my call to

Sampson, then tried MacDougall at home. He had just left for his Melville office. I reached him on his cellular phone.

"Glad nothing happened to you, Henry." Whether he was telling a joke or a story or a business anecdote, John MacDougall always spoke in the same monotone and measured cadences. I asked him if he could change our appointment to early in the afternoon. "Sorry, I've got to be in the city for a board meeting," he responded. "Look, as long as we're talking, I heard a disturbing rumor about that lease with Standard General. I hope I heard it wrong."

Probably one of his golf partners had said something over the weekend. Bad news travels at roughly the speed of light.

"It was one of those political things, John. When I see you I'll explain what Jack Phelan told me. It had nothing at all to do with our deal."

"That's most unfortunate, Henry," he said. "The board is planning to scrutinize our portfolio of loans. Particularly the ones to developers. I'll know more after this afternoon's meeting." I listened carefully to the intonations in his voice. It began to sound like my "friend" John MacDougall might not be willing to exercise the power I thought he had in order to help me. Or perhaps he no longer wanted control.

"John, please explain to the board that we have other good prospects and that our cash flows are very positive. I'm sure they'll understand."

He was silent for a moment. Then he said, "The bank's examiners have been after us to place all questionable loans into the non-performing category." I knew that meant the bank would probably not extend and might demand that the loan be satisfied. If it were a smaller amount they might work with me, but not when it was $51 million. Bank examiners would press them. "Will you be in your office this afternoon?" he continued. "I'll need to talk to you."

I said I expected to be, but if not, Dianne knew where to find me. After I hung up, I went outside and meandered among old Second World War training buildings. I had to come up with a solution. Fast.

13

*J*OHN MacDougall called that afternoon. "Meet me in New York tomorrow. There's been a change. I have to have my attorney with me," he said in a tight, flat tone.

"Wouldn't it be better, John," I said rapidly, "to assess the situation first? We'll accomplish more without lawyers. We're certainly not at an adversarial stage."

"I thought you might say that, Henry. All right, no attorneys. But I want to impress on you that I've received very clear instructions from the board." Terrific, I thought. "My office at ten?" he asked.

"We could talk about it over lunch at the Players or Lotos," I suggested.

"No, not this time," he said. "My office. Ten."

"I'll cancel whatever I have." Then I added, "Look, I have some ideas that I think will work."

He didn't respond. "Ten o'clock. See you then, Henry."

I called Steve and Ari on the intercom and asked them to meet me in the small conference room. "Dianne, see if Jack Phelan is in." My mind was moving as rapidly as runway lights on a takeoff. The bank would demand a plan that would satisfy the examiners because they were calling the shots these days, not boards.

"Henry, Mike Allen called while you were on the phone, and Karen Viscomi is holding," she reported.

"I'll take her call, then get back to Allen. After that, try Phelan." She acknowledged my request. "Hi, Karen, have you left yet?" I asked, trying to sound chipper. Which was not the way I was feeling.

"I'm at LaGuardia, on my way. I was concerned about your situation with Federated." Karen understood how inflexible and demanding examiners and banks were becoming.

"Meeting with MacDougall tomorrow," I said. "He was right out of a loan committee meeting and sounded all nails." I had lost the positive edge in my voice so I said, trying to regain it, "I told him I'd repay him with a certified check for the entire amount." I hesitated, "Confederate currency, of course. MacDougall is from Charleston. I thought he'd appreciate that."

"You didn't really say that, did you, Henry?"

"No, Karen."

"I'll be back tomorrow," Karen said. "If you want to have dinner, a kosher Japanese place just opened. Fabulous reviews. I want us to appear in the *Times* with all the other movers and shakers."

"Let me call you as soon as I see how things are unfolding," I said. She told me I could reach her at her hotel after ten, after her dinner with some colleagues.

Dianne had Allen on the line. Perhaps between us, Mike and I could come up with a final plan for the partnership we had discussed. There was still enough income from buildings to interest investors. And if I developed an alliance with Allen's group, it could provide the capital to cope with the building loan.

"Good morning, Henry. No, afternoon, isn't it?" he corrected himself. "Have a nice time on Martha's Vineyard?" I must have been noticed in town or at the airport. "I'm told you handled that emergency exceptionally well, which doesn't surprise me." Then he added, "It's impressive to see how people behave under pressure."

"Thanks. I keep up my training." Undoubtedly Mike knew about the lease, too. "I suppose you heard the Standard General deal is not going to close," I said.

"Strange the way these things go sometimes," he said. "Nothing to do with intrinsic values. You offered them an innovative and competitive package."

"There are plenty of tenants out there," I said, trying to sound reassuring. "Ending up with better leases happens all the time."

"I hope so," he countered. "But too much space has come on-line at a time when companies are cutting back." He waited for me, but when I didn't comment he added, "There's bound to be a rough period ahead. The marginal developers are overleveraged and probably won't make it."

He was leading up to something. "Mike," I said, "Three-Fifty-Five is an excellent building. We can be very competitive if we have to. What about our conversation?"

"The Japanese and Germans have pulled out, but I do have investors from Hong Kong who are still interested in income properties," he said. "However, they've become very discerning and expect me to be very conservative."

"Maybe it could be explored with them?" I asked.

"Maybe, but don't assume anything will come of it. Prepare a package, and I'll have some of my people come over and review it." He paused. "I also wanted you to know that my partners and I have decided we don't want to pursue what you and I discussed the other evening." Allen had a style of presenting negative news diplomatically. "We consider you the best all-around developer in the East. There may be possibilities for the future," he said. "I'm sure you understand."

"Of course. Look, Mike, my situation is anything but critical. We've got depth and can handle any current problems."

"Henry, I also wanted to warn you. Federated's board has decided that an example must be made of your loan in order to impress the examiners. Federated went too far. They've got to counter that or have themselves placed in a special watch category. Their operating ratios are bad, and capital reserves will have to be beefed up. They're a candidate for a takeover."

God, the man was privy to everything. Lazard Frères' intelligence is better than most countries' during wartime — one of the reasons they're so successful. Also having the brightest people on their team.

"Thanks for the information, Mike." He wished me good luck and hung up.

"Mr. Phelan is in his jet, on his way to San Francisco," Dianne advised. "Oh, just a moment, he's on now. I'll put him through."

"Henry, this is Jack Phelan, the poor Irish lad from the Bronx returning your call from forty-one thousand feet. How are you, my boy?" He didn't wait for my answer. "First let me tell you that I had lunch on Friday with several of my friends. We discussed the current banking situation and real estate loans. Most of us are on one bank board or another. The operations people have gotten the banks in trouble. Developers are looking for some loan forgiveness or reductions in their payments."

He sounded like Allen, I thought. It was like listening to a judge passing sentence on my future. "Just as long as the banks don't go overboard," I said. "It would only exacerbate whatever problems the industry is experiencing."

"Hold on a moment, Henry." He got off the phone, then came back. "I've got to go back to a meeting. Even though I've done this many times, it still impresses the hell out of me to be able to fly across the country in my own plane, conduct meetings, eat, sleep, and make calls to all parts of the world. I never believed that the good Lord would provide me with a style fit for a king.

"Anyway, Henry, what you say may be correct, but remember history is filled with overcorrections. In any event, the men and women who have been responsible for excessive lending try to protect their jobs and pensions by taking actions that will rectify — or appear to rectify — their bad practices." Phelan sounded like an economics professor, but I knew he was right. I also knew that for bankers in positions of high visibility, like MacDougall, it was doubly true.

"By the way, Henry, why did you call?" he asked.

"Remember you said you might know of a company that needed space?" I said. "Anything turn up?"

"Actually I was going to call you, but not until something had been finalized." He paused and then said, "I might have something for you. Not the whole building, but half. Will that help?"

"God, it sure will," I said. "I've been called into a meeting with Federated tomorrow. It would be wonderful if I could announce a new deal."

"Now hold your horses, Henry. There's no commitment here,

just a possibility. It looks like the acquisition we were working on will go through. That's why I'm on my way to Los Angeles, after a stop in San Francisco to pick up a few of my people —"

"When will you know?" I interrupted.

"This whole thing has a great deal to do with our internal situation. I won't go into it now. But you remember our earlier conversation, I'm sure." I certainly did. His power struggle with Jordan. "I've called a board meeting for next week. It will be settled then."

"I understand," I said.

"Look, I have to run. Good luck, my boy."

"I can't tell you how much I appreciate your trying to help me," I said as we closed the conversation. So maybe things were not as bad as all that. I began to think about other options.

I met with Steve and Ari after my conversation with Phelan. Despite their concerns, I wanted to reassure them that we were not in any serious danger. "Look, guys, don't forget we have a bunch of leases with rent increases. And we keep amortizing the mortgages. Both those factors enhance our strength."

"And what else, kid?" Steve shot back. I was happy that his usual repugnant tone had returned. "We *also* have leases that are terminating and may *not* be renewed. As far as mortgages — Ari, give me the list, will you, please? We may not be able to refinance those buildings." I frowned. "Henry, you talk like some Harvard Business School kid. Wet behind the ears."

Good old Steve, I thought. Glass half empty. "Did you have a nice weekend?" I asked.

He gave me a dirty look. "As a matter of fact, no. It was a lousy weekend. But I'm sure yours was great."

I didn't answer, controlled a smile, and tried to sound sympathetic. "Sorry, Steve," I lied, "not every weekend with family can be good. Anyway, let me tell you what I plan to do with MacDougall tomorrow."

"Maybe Ari and I should be there," Steve said. I shook my head. Absolutely not, I thought, but I refrained from being so emphatic.

"I told you he talked about having attorneys present, but I got him to change his mind. Better just one-on-one. After he lowers the boom, I'll inform him about the new deal that's pending. And to reduce the building loan, pledge any proceeds left over from future remortgaging. That'll give him the ammunition to deal with his people — and the examiners." I liked my strategy. Reasonable and clever.

"What if he isn't satisfied with the 'what-ifs'?" Steve said somberly. "They could kill us."

I glanced at Ari. "For Christ's sake, Steve, there are plenty of solutions. This is only round one." I looked hard at him. He shrugged and glanced at Ari, who had apparently decided to remain silent.

We ended the meeting. A few minutes later Ari came by my office. "I wasn't going to say anything in there, Henry, but many of the leases mature in two or three years. Mortgagees won't finance against such short leases. Not unless you want to go on personally."

I told him I understood, but that the institutions we had been doing business with had not been demanding longer rental terms.

"It's changed, Henry," he said. "Especially with older buildings. The mortgage bankers' convention I went to last month — everyone was talking about tightening up. Especially the insurance companies and pension funds. Money has dried up."

"Israelis are supposed to be great optimists," I kidded him. "Where's your chutzpah?"

"Just want to caution you, boss." He turned and started out.

"Thanks, Ari," I said as he opened the door. "Oh, ask Dianne to step in, please."

"Your pregnancy becomes you," I said when she appeared. "How's it doing in there? Nice to be sheltered from this harsh world for a while." I stood up and watched the traffic moving on Franklin Avenue. The weather forecast was typical for this time of year: hot, humid, and a chance of thunderstorms.

"Dianne, what do I have to do this afternoon that can't wait?"

"A few letters to dictate." Her tone of voice was solemn and deeper than usual. Something was wrong. "I've drafted others that only require routine answers. No calls that can't wait, except Craig wants to review the problems with your plane. Major engine overhauls, or something like that. Want to talk with him?"

"Are you concerned about my bank problems?" I asked. "Don't be. I think I have things under control."

"No, I'm sure you do," she answered. Then, "It's something else." I sat down at my desk and waited for her to continue. "My husband. George."

"Have a seat, Dianne. What about George?"

She sniffled and seemed to be deciding whether or not to continue. "He's talking about separating. We haven't been getting along since I became pregnant. He didn't want another child after the two from his first marriage. He knows how important children are to me." She was close to tears.

"I'm sure you're worrying for nothing," I said. "He's just getting adjusted to it — your having a baby, I mean." I thought for a moment, and then said, "Make sure you find time to have fun together. Do things he likes."

She began to cry. "He's been spending a lot of time away." I handed her a tissue. She nodded thank you and excused herself. I told her to use my private bathroom.

Everyone has problems, I thought. Dad used to say, "If you aren't aware of problems, you're brain-damaged." Have to keep my head. There's always a way out. Sometimes just refusing to go down. Look at the weekend. Could have solved all my problems there and then, but managed to land okay. Both engines out. Hell, Henry, if you can do that, you'll work out Park Avenue, too. Keep remembering that. When the shit flies.

14

*A*FTER dinner at Primavera, I went home and settled down in my study to analyze the mountain of information I had gathered from Ari before leaving the office. I planned to offer MacDougall various possibilities.

Then I remembered I was supposed to call Karen. As I was about to pick up the phone, it rang. I grabbed the cordless receiver. I didn't look to see if the call had come in on my private line. Only a very few had that number.

"Henry, it's your father. I want to talk with you."

"That's funny, you don't sound like my father. He has this deep, Wagnerian voice, a heavy German accent, and yours is . . ."

"I'm glad you've retained your sense of humor," he said. "Now listen to me. Steven's filled me in on everything." I heard him sigh. "I've got three million in Treasuries. You can have them if it'll help."

His offer caught me unprepared. I couldn't talk for a few seconds. Then I responded, "Dad, that's exactly like you. But I wouldn't touch your security for anything. Look, everything will work out. I've got a zillion solutions to offer Federated." His T-notes certainly would help, but I wouldn't ask him for them unless I was at the end.

"I'm the one who got us into this," I said. "I'll find a way out."

"Sounds very noble," he said, "but fathers ought to be there for their sons. Mind you, Henry, you've become greedy and weren't watching the signs. But at this point, that's academic."

"I'm glad you're with me. It makes all the difference. Good night, Dad."

It was well after ten. Karen. "How did your dinner go?" I asked. I didn't wait for a response. "I can just picture you. That spectacular body in some very fetching nightgown. A shorty, with ruffles on the bottom . . . *woof.*"

"You have the body right, Henry," she said, "but the nightgown's all wrong. On trips, I take one of Grandma's muslin numbers. Anyway, I'd suggest phone sex, except I think it'll leave us more frustrated. But I'm thinking of all kinds of new moves."

I wanted to climb into the phone and be beamed all the way to Albany. "We'll practice when I see you," I said.

"When you called just now," she continued, "I was sitting here in bed, reading briefs. It's quite interesting. The dinner was elegant, it really was. Albany has some great spots. . . . Henry, are you okay?" she asked, suddenly.

"I'll know after my meeting in the morning. I'm deep into reviewing. Oh, did I tell you? Phelan is acquiring a company and said they might take half of Three-Fifty-Five. That would save my ass."

"You're going to find mortgaging extremely difficult," she said. "But you already know that, don't you? Anyway, I've got a couple of hours of work on these briefs. Dinner tomorrow?"

"Fine. But no kosher Japanese. Too gastronomically confusing. My place. About seven?"

"Don't expect me to be bright-eyed and bushy-tailed."

"I'll take you any way you come."

"I didn't know you were into puns, Henry. Anyway, give them hell tomorrow."

I slept fitfully. In a dream, everyone was trying to escape. The others all made it, but I couldn't find my passport. When I did, it was too heavy to carry. Time ran out. Those of us who got stuck — only me at the end — would be tortured. No matter how hard I tried, I couldn't lift my passport. I woke in a cold sweat.

15

*F*EDERATED'S executive offices at 180 Water Street in downtown Manhattan were dignified and refined. The top two floors were connected by a graceful interior stairway. Paintings of the original Dutch Colonial settlement at its address were positioned on the walls. The bank prided itself on conservatism, yet Federated's lending practices were anything but conservative. Even before the problems in real estate began growing. Federal and state banking authorities had begun to focus on the high percentage of speculative loans in Federated's portfolio.

I had utilized the fact that I had been a Marine infantry captain in Vietnam to help establish a relationship with MacDougall, paying homage to his having been a career naval officer with the highly respectable rank of a three-stripe commander.

I waited a full twenty minutes in the reception area before MacDougall's Manhattan secretary emerged to greet me. She looked trim, her tone a cross between matronly and motherly. "I'm terribly sorry, Mr. Martin, that you've been kept waiting." I looked at her, displeasure on my face. "Mr. MacDougall has been in the president's office for several hours. Even before I came in," she said with a warm smile. "He asked me to have you wait for him in conference room B. Coffee? Can I get you a nice cup of tea?" I shook my head.

A few minutes later, John MacDougall walked in, stopped to

size me up with his stare, said good morning, shook hands in a per-
functory manner, and sat down. I had decided it would be better
to place myself at the head of the table, a strategy I used when I
wanted to establish an atmosphere in which I would be perceived as
dominant. It would have been smarter if I could have arranged for
MacDougall to sit opposite me as equals, but I did not want him
sitting at the end of the table and me on one side.

"Sorry to keep you waiting," he started out pleasantly.
"Shawn — President Riley — and I had a number of matters to review." He cleared his throat and measured me again with his eyes,
reminding me of one of my old commanding officers. "Now let's examine our situation. I must tell you, Henry, your loan has received a
great deal of attention recently. From the boardroom all through the
administrative branch. And by the examiners."

All of which meant, I thought, that he'd been catching hell
from both the president and the board. A year earlier, the loan had
been processed by MacDougall's staff, with all the accompanying
data, then presented to the loan committee, which had approved
the amount and terms. The interest rate was negotiated at .75 percent over prime, floating. It had been challenged by the board, but
MacDougall and Riley made the argument that Henry Martin could
place the loan elsewhere at the same rate, perhaps even at a lower
one. The normal one-point fee was cut to one-half, with the same
argument proffered. Now, MacDougall's judgment and competence
were being brought into question. I knew that two critical concerns
for most bank officers were their jobs and their pensions, in that order. And certainly it would be MacDougall's ass before Riley's. Undoubtedly, he was in danger of getting the boot if the Martin loan
went into default.

I didn't wait for him to continue; I had to take the initiative. "I
fully understand the problem, John, I really do. Losing the Standard
General lease changes the equation. It was strictly political, why the
deal went elsewhere. I can get Jack Phelan to go into it if you want."

"That won't be necessary." He leaned forward. "The fact is,
there's no executed lease, is there?" he asked in a flat, deliberate tone.

"No, there isn't," I said. "But let me lay out some thinking, because it's not the problem it may seem right now." I played that

statement out slowly, hoping to dictate the way the conversation developed.

"I've been instructed to tell you that unless you can pay off the loan or reduce the face amount significantly, it will have to be called," MacDougall said flatly.

I was shocked, and it must have shown on my face because he said, "I'm sorry, but it's out of my hands." He waited for me to speak, then continued: "For whatever it's worth, my situation here could well be in jeopardy. Parallel to yours, in a way."

That's fine, I thought. You'll get your wrist slapped, maybe a golden parachute. But it could be the demise of a family company I had made into a commercial real estate investment power. "Look, John, I'd like nothing better than to replace your building loan with a permanent mortgage; obviously that can't happen overnight. But it looks likely that someone is about to lease half the building." I watched his face and saw a hint of a smile and a change in his attitude.

I was wrong. "With the loss of Standard General, surely you don't want me to believe you could come up with another tenant so quickly. For half the building? What do you take me for, Henry, some kid straight out of business school?"

I had never seen this side of MacDougall. I almost expected him to hiss.

I held my own anger in check. "For your information, John," I said firmly, hitting him with backup proof, "I was on the phone with Jack Phelan yesterday. He was in his plane on his way to California to conclude the acquisition. If it goes through, Phelan told me that Standard General would take half the space. I can get him to confirm that, but it would be a little awkward since he told me in confidence." I let my resentment register. Although that wasn't very smart of me.

"You were in Vietnam, Henry. You can't transport your men without boats, trucks, or helicopters. It's this simple — your loan cannot be paid off. A lease would obviously make some difference, but you're certainly not in control of whether that's going to happen."

He was pushing me into a corner, but I was not ready to capitulate. "You must have something in mind," I replied calmly. I wanted to find out what he and the others had apparently decided. Then I could counter. Always let the other guy show his cards first. Often he is not thinking what you assume he is.

"You and your brother are on this personally," he began. "I don't have to spell out what that means. We all know we can get a deficiency judgment, and —"

"Not easy to obtain," I interrupted. "It can take years."

"Yes, you're right," MacDougall said. "The point is, you clearly understand action must be taken."

"How and by whom?"

"Let's stop fencing," he replied. "There has to be a plan, not hopes and pipe dreams. Something that the bank and the examiners can accept." He rose and walked to the other side of the room. "You're quite resourceful. But let me warn you, the entire real estate industry is undergoing major change. We're not your enemy, Henry, but our posture is very different than it was even six months ago."

It was my turn at bat. I opened my folder. The summary page was on top. "The Martin Companies have many sources of income," I began. "Buildings all over the place. Leases with automatic increases in them. Mortgages that can be refinanced. Our gross income goes up every year, and our net cash income increases as well. Those leases can produce refinancings that can be utilized to reduce your loan." My language sounded canned. "Also outside, non-real-estate investments."

Again, his reaction was not at all what I expected. "First of all," he said, "yearly increases are out. Tenants are renegotiating their leases. Demanding and getting *reductions*. And tenant improvements like painting, new carpeting, and repartitioning even though the leases don't include them. Otherwise, they threaten to move out. Correct?"

He was. Some of our tenants were warning us that brokers and other landlords were offering to pick up the obligations of their leases with us as an inducement for them to move into their buildings.

"And," MacDougall went on, "forget about refinancing your mortgages. You'll be lucky if the institutions are willing to extend. Most want out. And you can bet it's going to get worse. That puts owners in a very bad position."

The conversation was going badly. Not the way I had planned.

I would have liked to slug him in the mouth, just to get him to shut up.

Time for a tactical retreat. "But developers have done well during recessions, even during the Depression," I said. "My company can weather any storm. I intend to pick up first-class buildings at distressed prices."

"Time will tell, Henry. By the way, your brother's and your personal balance sheets include various liquid assets, cash, stocks, bonds. We may have to talk about them."

I let that statement go unanswered. "John, I'll know about Standard General in the next few days. In the meantime, I'm going to see what else I can do. We own some excellent, well-located parcels of vacant land that can be sold." I watched his expression. Still deadpan.

"You and I will meet again next Thursday or Friday," he said. "Today's meeting was to make it clear where we stand and what we expect. Let me stress that we can be flexible, but only if it results in an elimination of the outstanding debt. Or a significant reduction." MacDougall sounded like an attorney trained to deal with defaults.

MacDougall sat back and waited for me to respond, but I didn't. "One more thing," he said. "Let me remind you we reserve the option to bring an action for foreclosure or maybe one personally against you and Steven as guarantors." He rose. "I hope that's not necessary." He reached out to shake my hand. "Call me if you wish. In any event I'll see you the end of the week. Same time."

I reached forward and grabbed his hand. "I'll confirm the day with your secretary." We said good-bye, and I left, drained and exhausted.

16

THURSDAY evening, over drinks at the Lotos, Cushing Trout III told me all about the board meeting. Trout was on the board at Standard General, though better known for his storytelling flair than his business acumen. He never forgot to tell people that he'd majored in English at Yale, and sometimes hinted that he had the Great American Novel in him. "Boardroom drama is great drama," he once told me. His version of what went on earlier that afternoon led me to think he might be right.

Cushing was Phelan's man, so I knew his story was not exactly objective, but he was, I also knew, a stickler for accuracy — except, of course, when the would-be novelist in him prevailed.

Thursday. Four in the afternoon. The forty-eighth floor of the sheer, sculptured, metal-sheathed Standard General building. The shuffling sounds of papers, the swishing of folders being withdrawn from briefcases, chairs being pulled away from the long, curved, red oak conference table, the muffled noise of men and a few women shifting in leather chairs, a few nervous coughs.

John Calbraith Phelan, Jr., presiding, as he had for eight years. The consummate tactician, strategic planner, seasoned politician.

"To all of you, a very good afternoon," he began. "This is indeed an important meeting. We must remember that whatever happens will be in the best interests of our fine company and its stockholders." He gazed along the

length of the table, stopping at the eyes of his directors, fixing on each for a moment. He had spent considerable time discussing his ideas and plans with many of them separately; some he saw in person, either for dinner, lunch, or breakfast, a few in his or their offices. Those who were not in town were reached by phone.

Jack Phelan, sounding very much the sovereign, was confident that he would, by the resounding repudiation of his primary detractor, Timothy Jordan, arrange for his elimination. Phelan had pulled Jordan from a middle-management position into the senior ranks. When a few board members pushed his candidacy, Phelan went along and selected Jordan to be president. Jordan was imposing. A quarterback at West Point, four years of military service ending with a place on a general's staff, near the top of his class at Columbia Business School, where Phelan had originally met him, and before Standard General, a stint as assistant to Justin Diamond, Jr., chairman of R. Jackson Publishing Corp. Personable, blond, and tall, he had a handsome wife and three delightful young children.

But Jordan had become something of a pest and would now be summarily swatted away. Oh, not by an embarrassing vote by the board. It wasn't done that way. Jordan would tender his resignation, recognizing he had nowhere else to go but out. Phelan had already picked a successor. He had even lined up a few opportunities for Jordan — not in their industry but with companies where Jordan might be effective. Opportunities that would let him exercise his talents as chief executive officer, and make himself a bundle of money.

"This special meeting was called because we must vote on the G & E acquisition. You received your informational package several days ago. For the record, I will reiterate what appears on the summary page. Grayling and Elon is a distinguished old-line firm whose products fit nicely with ours. Their volume is quite respectable, $650 million, their profits attractive, five percent net after taxes." He hesitated, staring at the faces turned toward him. He stopped at Jordan's.

"I'm aware President Jordan opposes this and has talked separately with some of you. He and I have a major difference over this." He paused, adjusted his glasses, and ran his thumb slowly across his lower lip. "I shall entertain a motion. Some preliminary discussion may be in order to help clarify why we should seize upon this opportunity. Yes, Conrad, you first." Phelan remained standing.

Conrad Greenberg, something of a dandy and gadfly, headed a voracious management consulting firm and was Jordan's nomination to the board, a trade-off for the two new directors designated by Phelan. "Mr. Chairman, while I believe in making acquisitions that help expand us vertically, I do hold some serious reservations. I'm not suggesting that I will vote against the motion, simply that I don't believe it has been demonstrated — with all due deference to the chairman — that acquiring G & E is in our total best interests. . . ."

Damn you, Greenberg, Cushing thought, why didn't you share your so-called concerns with Phelan before the meeting? With all the advice and help he's given you, including consulting business from his friends, you owe him, damn you.

". . . Fellow board members, it seems to me the kind of cash we'd have to segregate could jeopardize our liquidity. You will notice that in the last three quarters we've experienced a frontal erosion. These are difficult times, I believe our banks have set a limit on borrowing. Isn't that correct, Jack?"

"No, that is not the case. Now really, Conrad," Phelan responded, "I should think you'd understand that the increased line I've established with our banks was just one of several choices available to create the capital necessary for this acquisition. There are others. We could put out a debenture, float one of several types of stock issues, like a convertible, for example."

"Yes, but —" Greenberg complained.

Phelan cut him off. "I've already had several conversations with our lead underwriters, Morgan Stanley." He let that remark sink in. "And Goldman Sachs has been trying for years to get our account. I've talked with them, too. They've lined up major funds with their overseas sources. As much as we would need."

Greenberg leaned back in his chair and folded his hands.

You're such a jerk, Cushing thought.

"Anyone else wish to comment?" Phelan asked in a stern tone. "Please, don't hesitate." A hand went up from the far end of the table. It was Jordan's.

"Of course, Tom. I was sure you would want to say something," Phelan said with a smile. "The fact that we differ on this is healthy. Discourse provides the directors with various opinions. Please, Tom. The floor is yours."

Let the weasel have his say, Cushing thought. *It'll be his last. Jack made you president, and he'll cut you down. You, Jordan, are one of his mistakes.*

"Ladies and gentlemen," Jordan said in a tone that Phelan recognized had been rehearsed for this occasion. His inflection was deeper, his pace more measured than normal. "Undoubtedly Chairman Phelan has been one of the best leaders in corporate America. Standard General has grown from a middle-sized company into a sophisticated giant. We offer a wide variety of consumer and industrial products, from metals to chemicals, from housing to lumber, from newsprint to computers. Few if any companies are so widely diversified, and we have to thank our chairman for his astute and brilliant leadership for all these years."

Jordan cleared his throat and looked around. "However, even great leaders are prone to mistakes. It's my judgment that we'd be putting ourselves at great exposure and risk were we to acquire Grayling and Elon." He motioned to one of the secretaries who had been taking minutes. She quickly went to the end of the room and pressed a button that caused a screen to drop. Another secretary turned down the lights and hit a button that turned on a projector. Jordan moved to its side and grabbed a pointer.

"This first chart conveys a historical analysis of the profitability Grayling and Elon has experienced over the last five years. As you can quickly see, a definite decline appears. It's true, and Jack is correct, they did enjoy five percent net, but it looks very much like in a year or two, their profits will decline to one or two percent. Is that what we want? I don't think so, fellow directors. As it turns out, they've done some acquiring of their own, as indicated in this next chart. Unfortunately for them, modernization of plants and particularly computerization wasn't high on their list of priorities. They're paying the price." He surveyed the room, pleased with what he had said. "Let me repeat, I don't believe they are for us. However, I am prepared to offer two other companies, either one of which would make for superior acquisitions."

What an ass! Cushing thought, looking around the boardroom at the sea of pale, grim faces. *Give 'em hell, Jack. I'm sure you still have a majority here. After all you've done for Standard General.* He looked at Phelan. *If Jack was angry, he sure wasn't showing it.*

"Please raise the light a little higher, Jennifer Anne," Phelan requested. "Thank you. All Tom has said is accurate, and I was completely aware of it. Buying a good company that has made a mistake, as they have, is exactly why we should acquire them. What you left out, Tom, is that the price we're paying contemplated years of lower profitability. It's a steal, say five times earnings. The point is that when they are absorbed, our managers replacing most of theirs, we will turn them around. Grayling and Elon is a household name in consumer products. The buy is both timely and quite a bargain." Phelan smiled, as if he were dismissing an overzealous child.

"Now, if there are no more statements," he continued, "I think we can get on with the vote." Another hand went up. Robert Ellington Prince's. He was wearing an elegant three-piece suit and ornate gray cowboy boots that made him appear taller than his five foot seven. His hair was thick, wavy, and dyed black. Parker enjoyed considerable prestige and had recently given a series of seminars at the Harvard Business School, his alma mater. Phelan had confided to Cushing that Parker had had lunch with Jordan that day, together with two other vacillating board members.

"When we were at the business school," Parker started in an officious tone, "I remember my professors going over case after case in courses that dealt with mergers and acquisitions, about the histories of companies that did well and those whose appetites made them sick. But it was when James Fallberg, who at that time was CEO of General Production, came in for a seminar that a point was made that has stayed with me to this day. Unless a company's profits are growing, their products and manufacturing at the leading edge, their viability will not be efficacious."

That language, Cushing thought. What a pompous ass. Even more than Jordan.

"Such is the case, my friends, with Grayling and Elon," Parker continued. "I'm afraid President Jordan is correct. We should not proceed with an acquisition. We don't need them, and I for one am against it because being able to turn them around is anything but a foregone conclusion. They are very sick." He sat down. Phelan observed a few of the others nodding in agreement, but the vast majority did not.

"Any other comments?" Phelan asked. A silent shaking of heads. "All right, ladies and gentlemen, it's time to vote. Let me say that what's at issue here is more than this acquisition. I believe it's a referendum on the management of our company."

Conrad Greenberg raised his hand. "Mr. Chairman, I wish you wouldn't state it that way. I'm sure the board feels that although you and the president differ on this matter, it doesn't require that kind of vote, ah, and the implications that go with it. Perhaps it would be better if this were tabled, and we met in a week." He looked at Phelan as if he were pleading.

"I appreciate your suggestion, Conrad, but we gain nothing by waiting. Everyone understands the issue. The vote will be closed, without signatures. That way, no one need be embarrassed." Phelan sounded like the venerable sage, the leader who would obtain the result necessary with a minimum of fallout. He had recently given a lecture at his own alma mater, Columbia Business School, on key choices a CEO makes when he possesses power. How it's used, Phelan had said, requires vision together with a certain objectivity, coupled with a degree of maturity — but without vindictiveness.

"Jennifer Anne, pass out the envelopes, please. The closed ballot is preferable, everyone." He sat down at the end of the table. "After the meeting, I'd like to invite you all for cocktails. And dinner afterward for any of you who can stay." Phelan smiled affably and said something quietly to the director sitting at his right. He nodded when the person whispered something back. Phelan gazed around the room and smiled, the expression of a leader who had handled a difficult challenge in exactly the manner he had anticipated.

Allison Lee, secretary of the board, opened the envelopes as if she were handling eggs, unfolded the contents, and lay each of the ballots on top of the previous one until she was ready to tabulate the count. She noted in two precise columns votes in favor of the motion and those against. When she had finished, she rechecked her numbers. Then she looked up, her brow furrowed.

"I don't know what to say," she said slowly, trying to control the alarm in her voice. "The vote is against the motion!" She avoided looking at Phelan.

"What is the count?" Phelan asked calmly. When she didn't respond. "Allison, what is the count?"

"Ten in favor, twelve against."

In the silence that ensued, several mouths gaped, but on the majority of faces were smiles, some only a flicker, but smiles nonetheless. But the broadest smile was on Phelan's face. He stifled a laugh. What those bastards won't get from me, he said to himself, is any satisfaction.

"Well, now it seems that the majority has determined that my recommendation for the acquisition does not meet with your approval. Oh well, I'm sure you know what you're doing." He glanced around, but only a few of the directors returned his gaze. *"As I said earlier, cocktails are being served."* He stopped for a minute and added, *"I have to admit I am a bit surprised."*

Somehow, Jordan and Greenberg had reached enough of the others to bring Phelan down. They probably had offered Parker something he couldn't refuse. Phelan could have accepted the defeat and continued, but his authority and power had been so seriously damaged as to emasculate his leadership.

The following day, Phelan advised the board that he was submitting his resignation, effective immediately. At sixty-one, Phelan ended his career in a far different way than he had ever imagined. The Wall Street Journal *and the* New York Times *carried the story on their front pages. His termination was a huge shock to the international business world.*

I called Phelan from the Lotos Club. He answered and, without talking about his resignation, invited me to meet him early the next morning in front of his residence. He lived in a magnificent apartment building on the corner of Fifth Avenue and Sixty-eighth Street, overlooking the Central Park Zoo. From his penthouse duplex, one could see most of midtown Manhattan.

That morning a low, gray ceiling of clouds cut off the tops of the buildings. I had slept intermittently. Phelan smiled and shook hands with me. "No, not your car, we'll go in mine." We walked over to his limousine. I wondered where he was taking me. I wouldn't have minded if we were going to his jet for a flight to Ireland.

"It's most appropriate this morning to have some breakfast at O'Hallahan's Diner," Phelan said when we were seated in his limo. He disconnected his phone. "It's been in the same family for generations. In the Bronx, of course. When I first went there, the only thing I could afford was coffee." He laughed. "What amuses me, Henry, is remembering how I talked old man O'Hallahan into meals. I simply promised him a large increase in his business if he would do two things — give me twenty bucks a week for promotion and one good meal a day. 'What, are you daft, lad?' I remember him saying. 'We

Irish are not prone to pissing away hard-earned dollars on the likes of harebrained schemes like yours. And not to be duped by charmers the likes of you.' "

I wondered to myself how Phelan could handle his crushing defeat, as if today was just another day. Maybe he was simply trying to erase it from his mind. That or, more probably, he possessed tremendous inner strength.

"But I convinced O'Hallahan, because I wouldn't give up," Phelan continued. "It took me weeks of hard work. What I did was get some of the folks in our neighborhood — oh, the Irish, to be sure — to take more of their meals at O'Hallahan's. I told them that his food was the best in all of New York, and priced far below any others. I exaggerated a bit, but there was also truth to it. And I told them that if they were not totally satisfied, I would refund them each a dollar.

"Now about what happened yesterday. To be sure, it hurts. I wasn't prepared but should have been. Anyway, it's over, it's done. One day we're all finished. We move out or they throw us out. I forgot some of my own cardinal rules. If you're in a fight, my boy, you'd better be damn sure of your support and your weapons. I never dreamed a majority would vote against me. I put them on the board. They were my people.

"Look," he continued, "my mistake was assuming there was no way I would lose. I drew the line. Jordan won. I do give him credit for working hard and pulling it off. I plan to call him tomorrow."

We were traveling up the East River Drive, just before the entrance to the Triboro Bridge. Phelan's attention seemed to be taken with a heavily loaded barge being pulled on a long cable by a tugboat. After a few moments, he said, "I'm glad you called. It was very nice of you." He smiled. "I'm afraid I can't help you with that lease." He searched my face, then said, "But, may I say to you, don't give up. Fight like hell. Keep trying to create solutions with your bank. They're better off working with you."

"MacDougall laid it out at our meeting," I responded, trying not to sound dejected. "They want my head. The only thing I can think of is to try to convert some of our assets into cash." Then I added, "It's like asking a bunch of hyenas to wait, even though they haven't eaten for a week. Banks are also in trouble, as you doubtless know."

Phelan nodded. He did know. He sat on Citicorp's board. "Returning to the Bronx this morning is very important to me," he said. "Keeps things in view. Reminds me where I came from." I thought I saw tears welling up in his eyes. "It'll be difficult to adjust, I've no illusions about that. But I'm a healthy and vigorous sixty-one. Too many things I've not had time for. Family, fishing, trips to distant lands with my wife, those grandchildren. God, they're absolutely precious.

"You, Henry, have many years before they turn you out to pasture." We were entering the Cross-Bronx Expressway heading west. "My last piece of advice is, don't take yourself too seriously. A man's ego can do him in when he loses perspective and believes his own PR. Your enemies want you to fail, sometimes even your friends and relatives. Now, I don't want you to become a cynic. Failure is simpler than success," Phelan said. Then slowly, with a wry smile, "We'll see if *I* can handle it."

"You're one helluva model, Jack," I said. "If the time comes, I hope I do half as well."

Phelan laid his hand paternally on mine. "I tell you, Henry, having humble beginnings doesn't hurt." He laughed. "Maybe I can get O'Hallahan to restore my twenty bucks a week."

17

I SPOKE with Hollick the following Monday morning. "Can't help you, Henry. I know you want to sell those parcels, but I'm just too busy to take them on. Maybe another time. Have to go," Hollick said, abruptly ending the conversation. Since when does a first-rate broker not have the time to try to sell something? Not even curious to find out what my asking prices were.

Something's very rotten. Why the hell would Jerry Hollick, whom I've paid over a million bucks in commissions for past deals, be so cold? So snide? Then I remembered how angry he had been a few years earlier when the commission we negotiated was far lower than he wanted. As a matter of fact, he had been rip-roaring mad.

And what Ari had said about losing those renewals that we assumed would be signed. We should have been able to keep those tenants. We had good relationships with them. If the rents were the problem, they would have made us counteroffers. Steve was handling those leases. Not the best negotiator, granted, but even a rank amateur couldn't lose those deals. He never discussed them with me. Not that he had to, but in the past he always did at our weekly review meetings.

Lunch with Joyce in Greenwich Village. Wonder why she suggested it. Just a friendly get-together? Perhaps. I've missed her.

I was waiting for her. As she stepped from the cab, I took her hand and said firmly, "Come with me." A few doors down, I pulled her inside an entrance. "I've missed you." We kissed. We looked at each other and smiled. The spark was still there. "A much nicer way to say hello than as casual acquaintances," I said.

"Yes, Henry." She looked away, her eyes a little sad. "But we're no longer . . ." She turned and walked to the restaurant.

After we were seated, Joyce excused herself to go to the ladies' room. I thought about our years together, those special moments, how close we'd been. I did love her. Never was willing to acknowledge it. My mistake was taking her for granted.

"Joyce, this is supposed to be the new in place. What's-her-name said so in the *Times* last week. Had a little trouble getting a reservation, but . . ."

The waiter flew over, smiling and cordial. We gave him our orders. I ordered two glasses of white wine, the Montrachet, the best in the house.

After the waiter left, she locked her eyes on mine. God, they were pretty! She waited for a moment, then: "Henry, I'm pregnant." She sat back and waited for me to respond. When I didn't, she added, "Aren't you happy for me?" She paused. "It doesn't matter if you're not happy for me," she said firmly. "Most of all" — her voice broke — "*I'm* happy for *me* because I'm pregnant. And I'm happy for my child."

I must have looked astonished. I also managed to knock over my water glass. People at nearby tables looked over, but my eyes were focused on Joyce's.

"I can't believe it!"

She stared at me, then rose, turned, and walked rapidly across the room. I looked for the waiter, didn't see him, threw two twenties on the table, and raced outside. She was standing in the same place where I had kissed her, facing the building, her hands over her face. Sobbing.

She noticed me next to her, wiped her tears, and said, "You never understand, do you? Your reaction is typical Henry. I had hoped you'd be happy for me. I should have known better."

"You married Steve on the rebound," I said. "That was obvious. The baby should have been mine. Maybe you can get an abortion."

Her face turned crimson. "Goddamn you, Henry! Steve's my husband, not you!" She looked desperately toward the street.

"Steve has something that was always lacking in you. You know what that is? *Commitment.*" Joyce was in high gear. "And he loves me. Guess what? I found that I'm beginning to love him, too."

"I did the best for you I knew how. It's just that . . . your being pregnant surprises the hell out of me, that's all," I said almost in a whisper. "Let me give you a lift," I added. "Please. I am happy for you."

She glared at me and moved forward. For a moment I began to think she might accept my offer. She stepped into a cab, slammed the door, and motioned the cabbie to drive away.

I stood there and watched the car until it turned the corner. The doorman asked me if I wanted a cab. I shook my head and walked east toward the Bowery. I was oblivious to where I was heading. Oblivious to everything else for that matter.

Sometime around 4:30 the next morning, I gave up the notion of sleeping. Tired, yet restless. It was important to focus on what to say to MacDougall, to keep Federated from commencing foreclosure proceedings. I had had a few discussions with Steve and our primary attorney, Calvin Howard Ostreicher, who was unusually talented and very adept at strategic and tactical planning.

I was drawn to Cal for several reasons. He was personable, strong-minded, soft in manner, and knew how to compromise to get results. But he could be tough when necessary and fiercely loyal to his clients. He possessed a rare ability to cut through the nonsense, focus on the essence of an issue. At sixty-six, Cal was a cross between a rabbi and a judge. He was extremely trustworthy and a real mensch. He was anything but attractive physically, balding and wore thick glasses. He had been an excellent left-handed first baseman in his younger days, but broke his hand during the Second World War, when he was a Ranger and paratrooper. Most of all, I admired his capacity to enjoy himself and turn what most people find difficult or tedious into fun and pleasure.

Cal had considerable experience negotiating bank workouts.

His skill could make it difficult for a bank; I knew that we could at least impede or delay their actions.

I phoned him at seven. I remembered Cal was an early riser from the weekend Nancy and I had spent some years ago at his country home in Hawley, Pennsylvania. Cal and Eva loved fishing and had a house on a fifty-acre lake in a 1,600-acre compound owned by twelve families. Their combined properties encompassed the hills, streams, and dams around the lake. It reminded me a little of the Adirondack League Club near Old Forge in upstate New York, both because of the setting and the owner's rules. No powerboats on the lake; tight, self-imposed laws restricted hunting for both members and their guests. It was a nature preserve, containing an abundance of fish and game. The lake brimmed with large pickerel, pike, and bass. The fields and woods seemed to be teeming with deer and bear, muskrat, fox, rabbit, and even a few mink and weasel.

"Sorry to call you so early, Cal, but I'm getting close to the moment of truth with Federated. When I see MacDougall Thursday, I'll have to have my act together. I need to anticipate what to expect."

"Okay," he said, laughing. "Just a minute, Henry. Have to go to the bathroom." He came back on the phone several moments later. "I've reviewed our options. *Your* options, Henry. What I'm going to tell you we've discussed, but I want to make sure you fully understand the dynamics.

"Banks will try to do anything they can to avoid a mess, such as a long, drawn-out foreclosure proceeding. Except, of course, if the examiners force them to bring a formal action. They'd much prefer not to take title to a problem property, because it makes them responsible for it. Tenants can always be difficult, plus all the environmental issues that accrue to ownership. I mean, owning can be like the bloody plague."

"So?"

"So," Cal went on, "you get into this game with them. Sure, they've got you personally on the note for the building loan and theoretically can attack all your other assets. First we either say or intimate that the partnership is considering filing a Chapter Eleven bankruptcy. We might threaten that because we believe with a cramdown of their mortgage to a lower amount or a reduction in the rate of both, we'll be in a better position to rent the vacant space at competitive numbers. And we're better at it than they are. They know that. We'd present that in the bankruptcy plan we offer the court. Of course, they'll have one, too. Defensively they have to.

"That's all for show, Henry. What they're really concerned about is appearance and responsibility. All aspects. They just can't end up looking like total schmucks. The guys on this, MacDougall and the others, don't want to and can't take the responsibility to cram down the mortgage. They'd really prefer their superiors to order them to do so. Or some judge, if it went to court."

It was enormously helpful to hear Cal laying this out for me step by step.

"What the court really wants in this type of action," he went on, "is for plaintiff and defendant to come to a settlement. Now, let's assume both of you — eventually — want an agreement, although in this situation that may not happen. So the court is like a facilitator. A broker. Everything you and the bank do, it's a kind of dance. Pirouettes in a Stravinsky ballet."

"Don't start getting artistic, Cal," I said. "As you were talking, I was thinking what the legal fees could amount to. I want a flat fee. No endless hours at $325, plus juniors at $225."

"You know I can't do that," he replied. "Brennan, Dolman never does that. But remember, if we accomplish what you need, our fees are dirt cheap," he said. I could hear some smugness in his voice. But unfortunately he was right.

"Something I can't figure out," he said. "I've got good friends at Federated. House counsel was a classmate of mine at Cornell. They won't represent themselves in this action. Never do. Anyway, I had lunch the other day with my friend. Concerning other matters I have with the bank. The conversation turned to you and your loan.

"My friend Gilbert looks up from his mushroom omelette and says, 'Cal, this client of yours, Henry Martin. I've never seen the bank acting like this.' I asked Gilbert what he meant. 'Well,' Gilbert says, 'and this is not something you can ever attribute to me, they're pissed off, as if they feel they've been duped in some way. MacDougall has been told not to give any ground at all. No compromises. They're out for Martin's scalp.'"

Why? I thought to myself. Why? "Great, Cal, that's sure to help matters. I really don't understand. I've always been straight with them. A year ago I was their wunderkind. They were kissing my ass all over the place."

"Henry, should I be there when you meet with MacDougall?"

"I was hoping to work something out with them without a blowup," I replied. "I hope we are not at the point of attorneys. Then they'll bring in their top gunslinger. Most of those guys get their jollies by kicking ass. Real bastards."

"We can handle whatever they come up with," Cal said. "That's why you use me. Jesus, I didn't realize how late it was. I've got to get to the office."

"It's scheduled for Thursday morning," I answered.

"I have a meeting scheduled, but I'll be there," Cal said.

Thanks, Cal. Talk to you later."

I turned off the speakerphone, got dressed, had a quick breakfast, and walked the two flights down to East End. My limo was waiting in front of my house, looking more and more like a hearse. "I'll walk to the heliport," I said to Charles. "Drive out to the Garden City office and wait for me there. I'm not sure yet what my plans are. Oh, first please pick up my dry cleaning. And when Charmagne comes in, see what she needs in the way of food." He tipped his hat, his face a mask. I wondered. Did chauffeurs ever smile?

It was just before eight. The temperature–dew point spread was close, making air difficult to see through. A cold front was due later, along with a dip in the jetstream. But for now, York Avenue appeared tired even before the heat would bake the street.

It was only a five-minute walk. Sampson would have the helicopter pre-flighted and ready for the trip to Long Island.

When we landed, I telephoned MacDougall from the waiting room. He always arrived in his office early, and I wanted to catch him before he became involved. "Good morning, John. Henry Martin. Look, I'd like to change tomorrow's meeting. I plan to bring my attorney along. He believes he can help the situation."

"If you bring him, I'll have to bring mine," John said harshly. "This could get out of hand very quickly, Henry. I was going to try to settle this with just you and me." He sounded angry. "You might as well know that we learned quite a bit about some of your liquid assets. Exactly what you have and where. Apparently there are assets you didn't put on your statement. As far as we're concerned, they're the best source of reducing this loan."

I didn't respond, but wondered to myself how the hell he had gathered that kind of information. What assets was he referring to? I had a sinking feeling in the pit of my stomach. Like being on a flight in a winter storm with fuel leaking rapidly from the tanks and my hands paralyzed by the cold.

"I don't know what you're talking about, John, I really don't," I said finally. "You know I don't play games. But please understand that we don't use cash and equivalents to replace mortgages. We can't do that. They're needed as a basis for overall credit. With Federated, for example. Besides, nobody can develop and build for all cash. Yes, there's a real problem with the building loan mortgage. But the bank will have to be patient. I plan to liquidate other properties to provide monies to reduce the loan." Don't be so goddamn intransigent, I thought.

"I'll call you later about the meeting," MacDougall said. "If you change your mind about having attorneys, let me know before ten. In any event, I will speak to you later." He hung up without even so much as a good-bye.

Where have all the good old-fashioned amenities gone? I thought.

18

GOING to the meeting with MacDougall two days later was a little like being dragged handcuffed into court by a sadistic sheriff and hearing the judge hand down a sentence of ten years at hard labor. Maybe I exaggerate a whit. Let's say it was no fun.

Steve wanted to join Cal Ostreicher and me. I couldn't think of any reason why not. Cal met us in Garden City, and we drove together to Federated's Long Island office in Melville. I wore my bank outfit, a double-breasted, midnight blue pinstriped suit, an azure blue monogrammed shirt with pure white French cuffs and collar, a crimson solid silk tie, and a white *H.S.M.* handkerchief in my breast pocket. Charles held the doors of the limousine as we stepped in. Steve and I sat in the backseat, with Cal facing us.

"I would strongly suggest," Cal began, "that you listen to what they have to say first. Then, let me do the talking." He glanced at me for a reaction.

"Fine with me," I said. "Keep me from losing my temper and saying something I'll regret."

"Won't be the first time, little brother," Steve threw in. "I remember several times when you —"

"All right, Steve," I shook my head. "Not now. I *said* I was going to keep quiet."

"I've heard that one before," Steve mumbled.

"Knock it off," I said. "We're trying to deal with the bank, save your 'get Henry' tirade for some other time."

"Remember," Cal said, "what their gunslinger, as you called him, Henry, is there for. He's their workout person. His role is to create the perception that you're the bad guys and have to pay the penalty for all the evil you've done."

"Wait just a minute," I said. "We haven't defaulted on the building loan. Not yet, anyway. Even if they don't extend it, they're better off working it out with us."

"True," Cal said. "But they'll press for collateral and a big reduction. They know from your statements you have other assets."

"I'm not letting them get their little hands on those," I swore. "We set up our real estate so a loss there wouldn't domino the rest. Plus we need whatever liquid assets we have to protect our other properties."

"I can see you getting into one big fight with them, Henry," Steve whined. "Our whole portfolio could be endangered." He was beginning to go into high gear. "You had to stick your spire up onto the New York skyline for the whole world to see. Henry Martin, the biggest dick of them all."

"Steve! I've had about enough of your fucking sniping."

"Look, you two," Cal cut in. "Play sibling rivalry when I'm not around. Okay?"

We managed to remain silent until we arrived at the Federated building. We had been told the meeting was scheduled in their largest conference room, on the third floor. We cooled our heels in the entrance foyer for twenty minutes.

When we were finally ushered in, MacDougall was seated. He rose to greet us. He was cordial but formal. "This is J. Robert Malenti, the bank's chief asset manager. Ah, no," he corrected himself, "he heads the workout section. And this is Mr. Cunningham, our counsel." Their attorney was tall, thin, and had bad skin.

We shook hands perfunctorily before sitting down. Malenti took off his jacket, revealing red suspenders over a pink shirt. He was squarely built, about five ten, and looked as if he spent two hours a day lifting weights. Maybe three. He remained at one end of the table, with MacDougall on his right and Cunningham on his left, yellow pad in front of him, prepared to take notes. Cal sat at the other end, Steve on one side, me on the other. I tried to size up their gunslinger. Probably runs four times a week, jumps out of airplanes, scuba-dives, and thinks Outward Bound is child's play. Otherwise an absolute pussycat.

"Well, gentlemen, shall we start?" Malenti began. "The loan comes due very shortly. I'm sending you the official notice today. All the stipulations described in the note and mortgage will be invoked. Penalties, recourse, that sort of thing. I understand you advised Mr. MacDougall you would not be in a position to pay off the loan?" He stopped and glanced at us one by one. "My position is that if you do not we will file an action for foreclosure, and go after you personally for every penny you owe us."

The sonofabitch was grinning. I wanted to vault from my seat and slug the bastard. But I clenched my fist, holding it beneath the table as I glanced over at Cal.

"Okay," Cal began, "you *could* do that, I suppose." He hesitated, then said, "Of course, Mr. Malenti, we would serve you with discovery demands, immediately put in a defense that would slow you down, file a Chapter Eleven right before the gavel goes down, submit a plan of reorganization, and let the court determine whether or not we as the debtor-in-possession can continue to operate the property. That'll take a year, probably more. And who knows what we would find in discovery proceedings, examining bank personnel.

"I don't have to tell you, Mr. Malenti," Cal went on, "that the loan's interest rate is no longer commensurate with market conditions, which is a major factor. And before you respond to what I've said, let me remind you that a lender must show that the reasonable value of a property is lower than the mortgage in order for that lender to be granted a deficiency judgment. That'll be quite difficult to prove. I'm sure you're aware of that." I had always liked Cal, but he had just gone up another notch in my esteem.

"I've heard of you, Ostreicher. Obviously you're quite knowledgeable in these matters. But so am I. We've both been down this road before." Malenti's face became more chiseled, his jaw muscles hardening. Easy to tell this guy was paid to be tough.

He waited for Cal to say something, but when he didn't Malenti continued: "Yes, you can hold things up for a time, but you know we'll eventually get the building and a good chunk of your clients' liquid assets as well. They did personally guarantee." No response from our side. "Now," Malenti added, "there might be other things we would consider. And what I'm going to say next is not an offer, just thinking out loud. As it now stands, the loan aggregates about $60 million. Interest is plus or minus $500,000. Each and *every* month. We might be willing to accept a paydown of the balance due by at least $15 million, which they could take from their other assets. Stocks and bonds. Plus additional collateral security."

"And what might that be?" Cal asked.

"Second mortgages on all your income properties, enough to cover our loan by 125 percent of the outstanding balance."

I stood up, but Cal waved me down. "And their personal guarantees?"

"They stay on, of course. You're not trying to be cute with me, are you, Mr. Ostreicher?"

Cal let a good half-minute go by before he responded. "There is not one chance in ten thousand we would be willing to even *consider* what you suggest," he said, his words carefully measured. He picked up a pencil and placed it between his two index fingers and said, almost in a whisper, "I don't want my clients to have to go through a protracted fight, but if we have to we will. You're not offering them much. If anything. You realize, of course, that while that would be going on they could probably rent the building. Wouldn't it be far better to cooperate and work with them? Reduce the interest and give them time to get it rented? They'd also try to sell the building." Cal raised his hand. "The Martins have been at this leasing business for a long time. Even if the bank were to get the building, whoever handles it would never do as good a job. Motivation's not the same."

"And how, Mr. Ostreicher, will they pay for the tenant improvement funds?" Malenti asked. "We're certainly not releasing the reserves for that. As long as you brought that up, we've concluded they've done a bad job. *I* will do considerably better." He got to his feet, probably to display the muscles rippling ominously beneath his impeccably starched shirt, and stood behind his chair, his hands on the back. "There's something else. I'm not accusing these gentlemen of being playboys, but too many hotshot developers got fat during the go-go years. Bought expensive playthings, became too arrogant to recognize that the market had drastically changed."

Now both my fists were clenched. I glared at Malenti. "We've been through recessions before, *Mr.* Malenti. Maybe you haven't. We wouldn't be where we are — and the bank wouldn't have knocked themselves out as much as they did to get our business — unless The Martin Companies were the best."

"Were," Malenti emphasized. "The problem is not ours but yours. We demand what we are entitled to — repayment of the loan when it's due. Nothing less. It's your performance — or lack of it! That's why we're here today, Mr. Martin."

"Mr. Malenti," Cal interjected, "wouldn't it be more accurate to say that both sides have a problem? Perhaps there may be something that can be done, like some monies to reduce the loan in return for an extension or a moratorium on interest payments."

"Not on your life," Malenti shot back. "The bank's in no mood to do that kind of compromising. Especially since certain liberties were taken with the financial statements." He finished with a certain cynicism in his voice.

What the hell was he referring to?

"You'd better explain that," Cal said. "We don't know what you're talking about."

Now it was MacDougall who spoke. And with obvious bitterness. "It appears that some documents did not contain the proper signatures. And the numbers for income and expenses for a number of the buildings were grossly inaccurate. We also have a suspicion that specific assets that should have been listed on your financial statements may not have been. If they were omitted, that would not be a legal breach, but we would take a very dim view of it. Destroys whatever credibility your clients had with us." He switched his gaze from Cal to me.

I stood, incredulous and furious. "I simply don't know what in hell you're talking about."

"Don't you, Henry?" MacDougall said. "We have it on good authority."

"You're nuts!" I clenched and unclenched my hands. Cal put his hand on my arm and tugged me down.

MacDougall stared at me. "And how do we know you haven't transferred company funds into your own account? Or Switzerland? No, we can't prove it, but we have our suspicions."

"I'd like to know why you think so, Mr. MacDougall!" I knew my face was probably as red as the proverbial beet. "Where'd you get that crazy idea?"

"That information is, as they say, privileged," MacDougall responded in a steady voice.

Then Cal came to the rescue. "Gentlemen, I think we've gone as far as we can today. My clients and I will study carefully everything you've said. We'll get back to you."

"When?" was the curt question from Malenti.

"Very quickly. A few days. I'll call your attorney, Mr. Malenti."

"Here's my card," Cunningham said. "No more than three business days. Have a nice day, gentlemen."

"Let's talk this over at lunch at my club, Glen Pointe," I said when we were outside. "That ridiculous statement about Swiss bank accounts — where the hell did that come from?" Cal and Steve both shrugged.

Over lunch, we dissected the meeting. Cal emphasized the seriousness of defaulting. "What makes it more difficult is their accusation of falsified reports and illegal signatures. Normally they'd end up doing some compromising, but they're not going to budge on anything. Not with their current attitude."

I shook my head. "It's completely crazy, that nonsense about our having money stashed overseas! I can prove our reports weren't exaggerated."

"Very difficult when they want to believe the worst." He hesitated, then added, "you don't have any Swiss bank accounts, do you? I hear people bragging about them at cocktail parties."

"Jesus Christ, Cal, no!"

As we were finishing our meal, Cal said, "Look, I've got to run.

What I want you two to do is to search through all your assets and compile a list of how much you can convert into cash. We give them that, and it may delay legal action." He sighed, as if stymied. "I can't tell how much will be enough. And if we need to, we'll file for Chapter Eleven. But there are problems with that I won't go into right now."

"Okay," I said. "But we have a whole bunch of other real estate that requires infusions of cash. And renewals like the office buildings in Montvale and several here on Long Island. Cal, tell Charles to drop you at the Westbury station and then come back for us. The Long Island Railroad runs to Penn Station about every half hour or so." He nodded. "But if it's imperative you get in faster, I can have Craig run you back in the helicopter."

"No, thanks. Those little whirlybirds make me nervous. I've got things to read on the train." We shook hands and he departed.

I turned to Steve, who was pouring himself some tea. "Who the hell would be trying to give us the business? That crap about phony reports. Oh, maybe once or twice I signed your name."

He shrugged. "You usually have answers," he said matter-of-factly. "You figure it out."

"I don't know. I really don't know," I said, shaking my head. Then, changing the subject, "Let's jump on the cash flows with Ari. Delay some of the accounts payable; also negotiate lower numbers for new tenant work. Pay down some of those land mortgages at a discount, except that'd mean using cash now. That won't solve it. Let's hold on to our reserves."

As we were walking out of the dining room, Norman Schefer, a golf friend, rose from a table. "Hi, Henry. We're a threesome. Tee-off time is in about half an hour. Want to join us? Chance to bring your handicap down."

"I'd love to, Norm. Of course you'd lose money, but sorry, I can't. Meetings back at the office. You fellows enjoy your game."

Charles hadn't returned yet from the station so I said to Steve, "Let's walk a little. The weather's nice. I need some fresh air."

"Me too," he said. "Joyce is into walking and wants me to keep in shape. She's really changed. I guess you should know. She's pregnant."

"I knew I had better register surprise. "Oh, ah, congratulations! Changed how? Maternity clothes, layettes, that kind of thing?" I asked.

"No, deeper than that. It's like she's sort of preparing a nest. Talks a lot about family. Everything else comes second."

A deep sense of sadness suddenly overwhelmed me. Steve kept blabbering as we walked, but I was thinking how nice it would have been if that baby were mine.

Back home, alone with my thoughts, it was difficult not to acknowledge the depth of my desperation. In a flying fantasy, I was on instruments. I didn't have the knowledge I needed to survive. I was rolling over, out of control, fighting panic. Had to get down safely, and yet for almost the first time in my life I was helpless, incapable of putting together what I had to do.

I sunk down on my couch, feeling empty. I reached for the telephone to call Karen. No. I couldn't bear her to see me this way. Beaten and bewildered. Was that a refrain from some song? If not, it should have been.

Nowhere to hide. Nowhere to get out of the way. Maybe run away. Chuck the whole mess. Big brother, you run the business. Okay, *Stevo*, you can have it all. I'll check out, maybe Alaska or Canada. Become a bush pilot. Find a wife. Keep it simple. Maybe fly myself into some nice ice storm. Very romantic. Totally unrealistic. Still, better than what's going on down here. And sure as hell it's only going to get worse.

19

A FEW weeks later, on my way to the office, my car phone rang. "Good morning, Mr. Martin. Sorry to catch you in your car, but it seemed important." It was Dianne. "Mr. Ostreicher said to contact him. Immediately." Nothing good to report from Cal, I thought.

"I'll call Cal and be there in ten minutes." I noticed that Charles's head seemed slightly cocked, as if trying to overhear my conversation. Yeah, he's really been too nosy lately. Have to talk to him about that. Oh, for God's sake, Henry, you're turning paranoid.

"They're going for the jugular, Henry," Cal said, his usually controlled voice a notch too excited. "I don't understand it. They have nothing to lose by continuing to negotiate. I talked to their attorney, and he said they weren't serious about Swiss bank accounts. Mostly the reports and signatures." Frustration and anger seeped through his words.

"What the hell's the matter with those clowns?" I asked.

"They'll cover themselves legally." He continued. "Nothing we offered in the meeting was agreed to by them. So we can't contest their actions."

"You make it sound like Three-Fifty-Five is gone already," I said. Now I was getting really angry. "Cal Ostreicher didn't get his reputation by succumbing to a bunch of stiffs."

"Who's talking about succumbing?" he said. "There's something called 'lender liability.' And other defenses. I'm starting to get pissed, but I can't afford to lose my perspective. Have to take another call. Talk to you later."

In the office, I had just begun to read some faxes when Ari Miller called me on the intercom. Needed to see me pronto, he said. "Problems, Henry, big ones. Now First Republic wants all new cash flows and updated balance sheets. Bank examiners coming down on them. Apparently they too have loaned more to us than they should have." He let out a deep sigh. "They insist on major reductions."

"Better check with some other lenders," I said. "European American and Citibank. Maybe State Bank of Long Island or Dime Savings Bank." I could feel my jaw muscles tightening. "Just a minute. Don't our loan agreements give us a full year?"

Ari slumped down in his chair. "Commercial bank agreements always contain the right to call a loan. Remember? I'll make those calls."

"Comb our accounts. I know your rainy-day excess balances routine." I smiled. "C'mon, we've dealt with bankers before. Always want somebody else to take the responsibility."

"New mood, Henry. The '80s are finished. Time to get real conservative."

My eyes locked on his. "You're beginning to sound like Steve. If I listened to him, we'd still be putzing around with little industrial buildings, like my father did. Look, I'm no fucking genius, but The Martin Companies succeeded because we took calculated risks."

"I'm fully aware how you've elevated TMC to where it is today," he said. "But, I repeat, it's time for circumspection. Steve's conservatism does have its place." He was almost pleading.

"That's not you, Ari. Steve's been whispering bearish nothings in your ear, right?"

"No," he replied, a trifle annoyed. "But I've read those lectures you gave at Stanford. You traced the cycles of real estate investment, how some owners and developers lost their properties during severe declines."

"I'm flattered, but you didn't read on. I also said that fortunes are made during recessions. Even in the depths of the Depression. Bernard Baruch said something like, 'When everyone else is dumping, that's the time to buy.' TMC is powerful, has good depth. Our holdings are diversified, not like most developers."

"True," he said, "but we simply can't stand a concerted assault by our lenders. They're all revising their loan formulas."

I knew what he meant: coverages based on loan-to-value ratios. They liked shorter leases if rents were rising. Now they want ten-year leases. Amortizations cut way down, maxed at twenty years. No hangovers — loans longer than the length of leases.

"What I'm trying to tell you, Henry, is that we don't want to be stuck out there on some goddamn limb. I mean, how much can we carry?"

I hadn't heard him this forceful in a long time. I leaned back in my chair. "I hear you, Ari. We'll be all right. As long as we keep renewing leases and keep our vacancy rates low. Land, well, that's always harder to move, but I'll get cracking."

He stood up to leave. "The big question mark, of course, is Three-Fifty-Five. If we don't work out something with Federated —"

"Don't be so pessimistic," I broke in. "Steve's pessimism is enough for this company. Keep your cool, Ari. We have to carry a sense of history — remember to stay calm. Only a very few can become leaders; all the others want to follow. Just like in the animal kingdom."

After Ari left I made a call. "Karen? Henry. You free this weekend? How about blasting off for a few days? It's a perfect time for Martha's Vineyard."

"Can't," she said. "Mom's sixty-fifth birthday is Sunday. I'd invite you up to the Vineyard, except I know she wants only family."

Her tone did not indicate an absolute no. Or maybe I was fantasizing. "Hey, Karen, what about this? We'll fly to Nantucket or Block Island this Friday as early as possible after work. I'll get you to the Vineyard early Sunday." I hoped that masterful plan might do it.

"Let me see what I can work out, Henry. If I have to be there by late Saturday afternoon, would you still want to give it a shot?"

"Absolutely! Maybe I'll talk you into forgetting your obligations."

"You're the most persistent man in all Manhattan." Karen

laughed. "No, I take that back; in the entire metropolitan area. Try to keep it in your pants until the weekend, all right?"

"I promise," I said.

"I'll call you tomorrow," she said. "As soon as I work out logistics."

I received a fax from MacDougall, and it contained precisely what Cal had predicted. In addition to disclaimers, their attorney demanded full payment within ten days or else they would commence foreclosure proceedings. The tone was what I guess is called "from your friendly banker." I faxed a copy to Cal.

He called immediately. "Bullshit, Henry. Pure bullshit. These proceedings can take a year or more. Everyone knows how very difficult it is in New York State to obtain a deficiency judgment. Sit tight, my boy. We're about to engage them in a fight that'll make them regret they refused to negotiate."

"That's what I like to hear, Cal. The bastards. Except it's not helping me with my other lenders . . . and with my tenants."

"Hey," he said. "Upbeat! For God's sake don't you go depressive on me."

Cal was right. And his words were tonic. "Don't worry, Cal, a negative thought rears its ugly head from time to time, but I smite it with my bare hands."

"Some metaphor!" Cal said.

"I'm impressed," I said, thinking of Cal with new respect.

20

SEVERAL demoralizing weeks followed, each worse than the one before. Discouraging news from almost all of our properties. On Wednesday, Dianne asked to see me privately, unusual for her. "May I close the door?" she asked. I nodded and waited. "May I talk with you candidly?" she asked again.

"Yes, of course."

"Mr. Martin, ah, Henry," she began, "I know that things are very strained right now, and that there are great pressures, but . . ."

"But . . ."

". . . you're being insensitive to your staff. I mean, you're snapping at me and everyone else. No matter what we're doing, you constantly interrupt to ask for something else. Practically screaming sometimes. Look, we all care, we really do. I know what's happening is recondite. And —"

"*Recondite?*" I asked. I hadn't heard this from Dianne before. Maybe she'd been talking to Cal about metaphors.

"I do have a degree in English," she said, slightly miffed. "You're taking it out on us, and frankly we don't deserve it. Things might go better if you lightened up a little."

"Has it occurred to you, Dianne, that I'm the only one around here who can deal with the kind of problems we're facing? Problems of a magnitude I'm sure you can't even imagine." She looked down, and I realized I was sounding like the type of guy employees resent.

They work for him, but only because they have to. "All right," I admitted, "I didn't mean to show the strain. Look, I really need your help, and everyone else's, too. I do things my way but I will do my best to keep my tongue under control." I looked squarely at her. I could see her lip quivering.

"Will that be all, Mr. Martin?"

"Yes, thank you, Dianne." I paused. "Do you have any idea where Steve is? We're in a firefight here." I pulled a folder out of my briefcase and, without looking up, said, "Let me know right away when you've located him, *please*," I made sure to add.

Several minutes later, she tapped on the door. "Steven told his secretary that he was away with Mrs. Martin and cannot be reached."

"Thanks," I said. After she had closed the door, I said, mimicking her voice, "Away with Mrs. Martin and *cannot* be reached!' Goddamn it!"

"Hello, Cal. You sound upset. What's wrong?"

"I *am* upset. I'm quite disturbed about something. I need to see you. In person. Shall I come over to your office?"

"No, I'll come to yours. First thing tomorrow."

After a week of muggy summer days, it was one of those flushed, perky mornings, the sky sharp, the air crisp, people striding along vigorously as if they were enjoying their walks to their destinations. Even Charles was chipper. "Top of the morning to you, sir. Did you rest well?" he asked.

"Yes, thank you, Charles. Very well." I hated fawning, although I've done enough of it myself. No one really gives a damn how anybody else actually feels. I had to focus on my meeting with Cal. For the life of me, I couldn't figure out why he was so disturbed.

"Charles, first to Mr. Ostreicher's office, then to Jerry Hollick's, then my office. You know who Hollick is?"

"Yes, sir, your lead broker. Will you be going to your racquetball club this afternoon, sir?"

"I'm not sure, but I want you to pick up a package in Manhasset.

Here's the receipt. By the way, would you happen to know where my brother might be?"

"Ah, no sir, I really don't. He didn't talk to me about that."

Steve used my car once in a while. I didn't mind except when I needed it at the same time. He could have had his own, but he said it would only lead him into bad habits. Holier-than-thou Steve. "Living high on the hog can get you into *big* trouble, kid," he would say, with that smart-ass grin of his.

Think small, Steve baby, and small you'll always be.

The elevator in Cal's building whisked me up to the forty-third floor. The lobby and waiting room were decorated with rich wood paneling and thick Persian rugs. Paid for by clients like me. Not to mention the fancy rent. I was told Cal was waiting for me in conference room A.

"Good morning, Henry," Cal said as I walked in. He looked grim. Worse, he didn't get up to shake hands. "Shall we get right to it?" he asked.

"You look more like my hangman than my lawyer," I said.

"I want you to be careful, Henry. I have to ask you certain questions, and I expect accurate answers. The entire truth."

"There's no other with you, counselor," I answered, trying to mask my sarcasm.

"Did you ever sign anyone's name on any company documents?" he asked slowly.

"Once, maybe twice, as I said. Out of hundreds of papers. Meaningless ones. Probably because they had to be executed immediately and Steve wasn't available."

"That's wrong, you know," he said. "And in the reports that you submitted to me, which I forwarded to Federated Bank, was any of the lease information . . . Let me rephrase that. Did the total of rents include leases that were not actually signed by the tenants?"

"What? Are you asking me if I doctored any reports?"

"That's exactly what I'm asking. Some developers have been known to take such liberties. Anticipating lease finalizations."

"Absolutely *not!* Ari provides a separate column for those situations. We've always done it that way. Look, I don't check all the arithmetic, but I do scan them. And I can tell you, Ari's meticulous."

"All right, Henry." Cal stood up, walked around the table, and put out his hand. "I accept what you're telling me. I'm sorry, but you have to understand that in my position as an attorney . . ." His voice trailed off. Then, noticing the expression on my face, he said, "Obviously something doesn't add up here. I was told that you lied about the rental reports and company statements."

I couldn't believe what I was hearing. "What sonofabitch loaded your ears with that bullshit? Jesus!"

"I can't disclose that. I'm sorry. But it's doing — it's obviously resulted in — a lot of damage. Now I can begin to understand why Federated has its back up."

"Haven't I got enough on my hands without somebody bushwhacking me? We go back a long way, you and I, Cal. You know I'd never do such a thing. Never!"

"I know," he said, his voice steady. "At this point my hands are tied, confidentially. But I can go to Federated's attorney with an affidavit from you that what they've heard is *not* the truth."

"The truth!" I bellowed. "The fucking truth is, I'm in deep shit, and *someone* . . ." I tried to read his face, but his expression was deadpan. Attorneys become very practiced at not revealing their feelings, and Cal was among the best. "All right," I said, calming down slightly. "If we're going to survive, you understand I have to know."

"I'll get through to Federated one way or another," Cal said. "In fact, I'll try them now. Be back in a few minutes."

I sat back in the chair and let out a deep sigh. My knee was bothering me. I'd torn the ligaments playing football at Middlebury. A few weeks ago I had run into a wall playing squash and smacked it again. And my damn stomach was giving me trouble, too. Probably too much coffee and spicy food.

"They're going to call me back," Cal said as he reentered the room. "I'll phone you the minute they do." Then, he put his hand on my shoulder. "Hang in there, Henry."

"Someone's trying to sabotage us." Ari Miller and I were having lunch in Hunan House, off Franklin Avenue, a few blocks from the office. Our favorite Chinese restaurant. Jackson Wang, the owner, had just served us his special house soup. He'd seen us come in, pointed to his own table, went into the kitchen, and prepared it himself.

Ari looked at me incredulously. "Did I hear you right?"

"I was with Cal earlier," I said. "Bad blood with Federated. Real bad. They've been told two things — one, that we've falsified our reports and statements, and two, that I've forged Steve's signature when I shouldn't have. They even toyed with the idea of Swiss bank accounts."

I cleared my throat and stared hard at him, looking for a reaction. "You aware of anything? Even what may not have seemed significant at the time?"

"No, absolutely nothing. Whatever I've prepared for banks has always been the *emmis*. The truth. Oh, I don't wear any haloes. I have been aggressive about tax deductions. But if we were ever examined, most if not everything would stand up." As Jackson brought in the soup, he shook his head, as if delving deep into his memory.

"There is something," Ari said, wiping his mouth.

I was about to ask what when Jackson appeared and stood over our table. "You want fresh vegetables with seafood today?" he asked. "Make it with oyster sauce, the way you like?"

"Sure." Two cute secretaries walked in. They worked for the insurance company in the space next to ours. One gave me a big smile. I nodded back.

"Henry, I did find a scrap of paper in your car yesterday, when you asked me to put those reports on your seat." He leaned forward. "Slipped to the floor, I guess."

"What'd it say?"

Ari reached for his wallet and carefully unfolded a slip of paper, which he studied for several seconds.

"When're you going to give it to me?" I asked. "After New Year's?"

He handed it to me. I began to read: "Been listening real careful. Near as I can tell he's not said anything special on his car phone yet. Nothing in his briefcase or from his place. But, I'll keep my eyes open."

No signature, but I didn't need one. I recognized the handwriting immediately from other notes I'd received.

"C'mon, Ari, I've just lost my appetite." I dropped a twenty on the table, waved to Jackson, and practically raced out.

Late that afternoon, Charles picked me up at the office and drove me back to the city. At my townhouse, I asked him to come inside. We were on the first floor, in the butler's pantry behind the garage.

"Let's see, Charles, it's been just about three years, hasn't it? Yes, next month." He gazed at me, a smile forming on his face. I turned to one side, as if searching for something, maybe for my wallet, to give him a fat thank-you tip for all his good service. "Well, I have a special present for you, to thank you for all your loyal and dedicated service." And with that I belted him in the stomach with as hard a left as I could summon. When he doubled forward, I slammed a right squarely on his mouth. My hand stung.

He crumpled into a sitting position and looked up at me, his eyes wide, blood pouring from his lip. "If I ever see or hear from you again, so help me, I'll really beat the shit out of you!" He seemed stunned, mesmerized, didn't even try to get up. "Who'd you write the note to? Yeah, I have it. And I've got major connections with the police."

Now he struggled to get up. I grabbed him by the collar and swung him around, my other hand forming into a fist. "Who, goddamn it?"

"I can't tell you, sir." He tried to look away.

"You goddamn well better," I said, my face contorted, my fist poised for another strike.

"Please, sir, don't. Please . . ."

"*Who*, Charles?" My fist was in his face, an inch from his bloodied mouth, my other hand grabbing him by his collar.

"Your . . . your brother," he said in a near whisper.

"If you're lying to me, you'll be in even deeper shit."

"No," he said, "your brother." He shambled toward the door, his handkerchief to his mouth.

"Just a minute! Where'd you place the goddamned bug?"

He looked away. "Behind the picture in your library by your phone." Then, almost pitifully, "I didn't think it would hurt you if your brother knew things maybe he should as your partner."

I still held him. "How much?" I demanded. "How much did he pay you?"

"A thousand dollars."

"Jesus! A tightwad even when he's breaking the law! Your idea or his?"

"Mine, sir. I didn't think it —"

"You don't know how to think, you turd brain. What else did my brother put you up to?

"Nothing," Charles mumbled, averting his eyes.

"What else!" I insisted, grabbing him by the collar. I could see fear in his eyes. I *knew* he'd done more mischief than the bugging. Then it came to me. "You were an Air Force mechanic, weren't you, Charles?" I shook him again, like a rag doll. "You fucked around with my helicopter, didn't you? The clamps on the oil lines. And the day *both* my engines died on Martha's Vineyard? That was you too, wasn't it?" I kicked him hard in the groin, and he crumpled, grabbing his nuts. I hauled him to his feet. "If that's true, you and my brother are both going to spend a lot of time behind bars."

"You can't prove a thing," Charles said, cringing as he spoke.

"Maybe yes, maybe no. Now, listen to me carefully. I'm going to have your place checked tomorrow by some friends of mine on the force. Better not try to take off. Now get the hell out of here!" I kicked him literally out the front door.

Steve, my brother, hates me that much? I kept shaking my head. After I calmed down, I called Steve at home. "Anita, this is Mr. Martin. It's very important I speak with my brother. I know he's in the city someplace. Can you tell me where? It's important."

"Yes, Mr. Henry. They'll be back in a few hours. Mrs. Martin called earlier."

"All right, Anita. I don't care how late it is. Please tell him to call me."

Steve didn't. About seven the next morning, I called him. "Didn't you get my message?" I made sure my voice sounded normal.

"I'll take it in the next room. Your sister-in-law's sleeping." He put me on hold. After what seemed like a long time, he picked up. "I didn't call you back because it was late, and I was tired."

Bullshit, I thought. "We have a big crisis on our hands," I said calmly. "A new one. We have to talk right away. Cal said we have to make some important decisions. Today."

"Since when do you want my opinion? I thought that you were handling things, solving all the problems."

"Get off it, will you? We don't have time for that petty bullshit. Besides, Dad called. You didn't have to tell him everything. That wasn't right, Steve. Dad doesn't need to know all the gory details."

"*Right?* You're saying that wasn't right? I wasn't aware you were in a position to make judgments, Henry. Okay. I'll come by your place. About an hour."

"Sooner if you can. We should be in the office by nine." Steve said he'd be there in forty-five minutes. I wondered what thoughts were going through his mind. Did he know I had found out? Probably Charles told him. Of course. Charles had told him.

I took my breakfast out on the terrace. Overnight the weather had changed. The sky had become slate-gray, and the wind had shifted to the southeast, the sky and the wind harbingers of the rain to come. The ceiling was broken, I guessed, at about five thousand feet.

21

WE went into the kitchen. I poured myself a cup of coffee.

"Want some?" I asked Steve.

"No," he said, "not for me."

Symbolic, I thought, not accepting anything from me.

I suddenly turned to face him.

"Why, Steve? Why?" I had planned to confront him when we were in the library, but it just came out, like blood from a wound.

I examined his face. His expression was as languid as ever. I walked into the dining room; he followed. We sat down at the long French Provincial walnut table, Steve directly across from me. "You must hate me," I said, "really hate me. More than I had ever imagined."

He stared at me for what seemed an endless time.

"I don't have a thing to say to you." His voice was a combination of coldness and satisfaction.

I pushed my chair back and stood up. "Why, Steve? It makes no sense!"

"You want to know why? I'll tell you why," he said, his voice almost metallic. "Twenty-something goddamn years, Henry, you making all the fucking decisions without me. *You* went ahead with Three-Fifty-Five, completely bypassing me. Made deals for land and financing. Important meetings with our banks and tenants. Even signing my name, didn't you? Never looking for my input. Oh, yeah, you go through the motions now and again. What do you take me for, some kind of idiot?

"You've made me look like a horse's ass long enough, Henry. I watch the way Joyce reacts when we're all together, when you brag about some deal *we've* made. She lights up like a Christmas tree. You think I like seeing that? Do you?"

"Have you completely flipped out, Steve? Do you hate me *that much?* Your jealousy about Joyce and me — if that's what I'm hearing — is ridiculous. There's nothing between us. Just old history."

"I have to live with that 'old history,'" Steve said evenly. "Always had your way with Dad, too. His wunderkind. Fooling himself it was the same for you and me as it was for him and Uncle Joe. Dad never really had any use for me. Oh, he may have cared, sure, but his Henry — wow, look at him walk on water!"

"You had Mom. Don't you think it hurt knowing she always favored you? What did you expect me to do? Not try to be the best I could? And maybe your wife did love me once, but no longer. She loves you, you jerk."

We sat there stiffly for several seconds. Then I asked quietly, "Is this why you sabotaged me with Federated? You hated me so much you'd do in your own company?"

"*Our* company," Steven said.

"Okay, but the result's the same." I paused. "But Jesus! You wanted to kill me. Not just ruin me. *Kill* me! Yeah, I got it out of Charles. I thought the problem with the helicopter was one of those freak happenings. But when I lost both engines in Martha's Vineyard, I got suspicious. I thought somebody . . . but not my own brother."

"I may hate you, Henry, but I had no idea about Charles tampering with your aircraft. Honest!"

"Okay. That would have been unbelievable. You could have sold me your interests several years ago, Steve. Why did you stay so long with a guy you loathe? It makes no sense. And it makes less sense what you've done with Federated. You're destroying me, but you're destroying yourself as well. It's crazy!"

"No, little brother, I guess it wouldn't make sense to you," Steve said contemptuously. "Except for one thing. See, Henry, I've finally figured you out. Control. You couldn't share anything even if your life depended on it. I thought you might change as we got older, but with you it's a dead end." He stared at me. "Maybe that why you've never been able to make any permanent relationships."

That stung. I pushed back my chair. "All right," I said. "So you're getting your revenge, stupid as it is. But by taking the company down you're hurting Dad, too. For God's sake, retract those things you told Federated. That whole pack of lies."

"I have no intention of retracting anything," he said evenly. "Frankly, I don't care if it does go down! I'm starting my own business. Software. Nowhere as big a company as TMC. Like TMC *was*. But I won't have you to contend with, will I?"

"C'mon, Steve, we're brothers. We've shared things all our lives, despite everything you just said. Stop hating me. Think of Dad. His vision." Steve had gotten up as I was talking and headed toward the front door.

"I finally won one, Henry," he said. "A big one. I'm going to enjoy watching you go down. I hope you go through just half the hell you've put me through all these years!" He slammed the door behind him.

I stood there, stunned. Then, in a trance, I turned and walked out on the terrace. It wasn't chilly, but I found myself shivering.

I sank down on one of the lounge chairs and dropped my head into my hands. It was dark, as dark as the time when Clancy's parents came to Beaufort to take his body home. They told me they didn't blame me. His father wept and hugged me. When we separated he'd said, "It's not your fault. Kevin made the decision for himself." I wept, too. "I'm sorry," I said, "I'm so sorry. If only he hadn't tried it."

I rose and stared at the landing lights of the planes landing at LaGuardia. I suppose I did push Steve aside. I had never truly realized how he felt. I wonder what else he'd wrecked.

Young Henry captivated the whole neighborhood. His smile was spirited, streams of morning sunlight; he loved being the object of attention and before he could talk seemed instinctively to know how to charm his father. Jake tried to pay equal attention to both of his sons; he loved Steven too, but doted on Henry, perhaps because he was with Henry from the start, whereas he'd missed Steven's first two years.

Henry inherited high cheekbones, heavy eyebrows, long eyelashes, and fair complexion from his father, the pronounced jawline, wavy hair, and dimpled chin from his mother. His blue eyes sparkled like a pristine lake, dancing from object to object. Passersby and family members alike would remark how alert he was, how handsome. Despite increasing evidence to the contrary, his grandfather Sal insisted Henry was the spitting image of Joe. He produced a picture of Joe as a baby to prove it.

Barbara Martin also tried to love her sons equally, but she clearly favored her firstborn, perhaps trying to compensate for Jake's subtle but undeniable preference. Unfortunately for Steven, his father couldn't grasp the complexities of parenthood. The special attention and affection that Barbara lavished on Steven seemed illogical to Jake, since Steven was never as cute and appealing as Henry. Steven seemed an introvert, whereas Henry hated nothing more than being alone. During their sons' formative years, Barbara rarely complained to Jake about any aspect of their family life. She adopted the pattern she observed in the patriarchal Old World home of her parents: the papà supra tutto *deference her mother had accorded her father.*

After the war, Jake and Barbara settled into a garden apartment on Tulip Avenue in Floral Park, Long Island. The old Martin-Sabatini Construction Company had been dissolved when Jake and Joe went into the armed forces, so Jake formed the Martin Construction Company with savings and money borrowed from both families. He seemed so intent on becoming successful that Barbara began to worry. Jake worked day and night, as if obsessed. And he was. Whether for himself, his family, the memory of Joe, or because his genes demanded it, he wasn't sure. But he worked, ceaselessly, seven days a week, fifty-one weeks a year.

Barbara finally put her foot down. She told Jake that unless he paid more attention to her, to the family, he'd be in big trouble with her. Sal also gave a him a talking to; reluctantly, Jake promoted three of his men and slowed down his mad pace. Much to his surprise, the business didn't seem to suffer.

"Listen, honey," Jake said, taking her in his arms, one Sunday into his new schedule. "It's not that I want to work seven days a week. But I have to stay on top of every detail. When Joe was here we split the load. Now . . ."

His voice trailed off. "Anyway, you're right, Barb. Today I'm all yours. I'll call Sal and ask him to run by the new job before we come over. Okay? We'll have a picnic at that park in Roslyn."

Screaming came from the next room. "Boys!" Barbara admonished. "Please play nicely." Both parents headed into the living room, where Steven was glaring at Henry, who was trying to hold back tears.

"He broke my, my truck," Henry blurted. "And then he hit me!"

"He wouldn't move it out of the way!" Steven retorted. "Anyway, he pushed my truck out of the way first!"

Jake picked up Henry, now six years old. "Boys, I want you to play together. Like brothers should. Now hug and make up." Tentatively, they both stuck out a hand and, not very convincingly, touched each other.

Barbara stroked Steven's face. "Honey, you're the older brother. You must help teach him to do things the right way."

"But he never listens to me!"

"He will," she said. "He will." She stood up. "Daddy isn't working today, and in a little while we're all going to that pretty park in Roslyn for a picnic. You remember, the ducks and geese."

"Yay!" they both cried, suddenly united. "The ducks and the geese!"

"Then later we'll go over to Grandma Angela's," Jake chimed in. "Grandpa always has great toys for both of you."

"Cal," I said into the phone, "Steve was just here. He admitted lying to Federated. Must have sent them an anonymous letter. No, he didn't actually say it, but it's clear he did. We had a helluva row. He quit." Cal didn't respond. "The question is, what else did he do?"

"Meet me in thirty minutes, on the front steps of the Metropolitan Museum," Cal said.

"Why there?"

"I don't want to talk in the office. We'll walk in the park." I detected a slight waver in his voice.

"Driver, let me out on the next corner." I needed to breathe some fresh air. I crossed Park Avenue, heading west to Fifth. Then I turned south for the ten or so blocks to the Met. I waited for the light to change on Madison. As I stepped onto the street a delivery bike slammed into me. I went down, but instinctively rolled as I hit the street, which helped break the fall. Fortunately he had been moving slowly.

"Dumb jerk!" I yelled, picking myself up. "Don't you watch the lights?" He was a kid and frightened, fearing retribution from this well-dressed, probably well-heeled man standing in his face. I should have been looking. Bikes are a major menace in New York. Too absorbed in my thoughts. "All right, all right," I growled. "Just don't go through red lights." I brushed myself off, checking to make sure all the pieces were intact.

Cal walked down the long steps of the Met and met me on the wide sidewalk in front of the huge Beaux Arts structure that spanned the four blocks between Eightieth and Eighty-fourth Streets. It was one of those summer days when the weather is balmy and moist. We walked without saying anything until we reached an area where there were a few benches and some open grass. Joggers were running along the path next to Central Park's East Drive.

"Let's sit here, Henry," Cal began. "Here's the deal. You and Steve will have to waive your right to retain separate counsel." He gave a deep sigh, then, "Steve came to my office yesterday. He agreed to release me from my confidentiality limitation and signed away his ownership in return for you waiving any claim you have against him. Although he's done everything he could to ruin you, it's my feeling there's a part of him that is not happy about it."

I stood up and looked straight ahead at a pair of runners, a couple with identical sweat suits. "How bad is it, Cal?"

"I'm not making any judgments. What Steve's done is a classic case of revenge. He spewed stuff about the two of you since you were kids."

"That isn't any of your business," I exclaimed. I looked at him. "I'm sorry, Cal. I mean, that you have to know such private things."

"Anyway, Henry, you have a choice. Steve's willing to give up all of his stock — no, you're a partnership — all of his interests — providing you give him a general release from any and all claims, suits, whatever."

"I'd like to sue the shit out of him," I said. "Cal, I don't think

I told you that Charles tried to sabotage my planes. Both the copter and the twin. I'm satisfied Steve wasn't aware of it. Charles was going to try to get more money out of him. But if my parents knew about all these details, it would devastate them even more." I paused. "At least get Steve to talk to Federated."

Cal shook his head. "I asked him. He won't."

"He's made his point, Cal. I'm on the brink." I had visions of forcing Steve to confess to Federated. Maybe knocking him around until he did.

"You're not forgetting why he's done this, are you?" Cal said. "There's more, Henry. I think you're going to find that Steve's gotten to some of the brokers, many of your tenants, and even some prospects. He didn't go into chapter and verse with me. But I had the impression he told them that you got the company in big financial trouble."

Good God, I thought, how do I undo this? Where do I even start?

We walked back toward the Met and stood on Fifth Avenue waiting for a taxi. "Look, Cal," I said, "I'll call MacDougall and you call Cunningham. Make Federated understand what Steve did."

"It's not going to make any difference," he said. "You still face a foreclosure proceeding unless you obtain financing to take them out. Or an acceptable tenant." A cab pulled up next to the curb. He opened the door. "And we've tried that, haven't we?" I nodded. "Call me later," Cal said. "Let me know if you want me to draw up the papers for you and Steve."

I took a cab home and picked up my red BMW convertible, then drove up the East River Drive toward the Triborough Bridge, trying to sort out the various elements in my mind. Now Steve, my partner, was the enemy, and he'd made Federated Bank an even bigger one. What were my choices? First, damage control.

I picked up my cellular phone and called the office. After Dianne gave me my messages, I asked for Ari.

"I'm on my way in," I said. "A whole new ball game. I'll clue you in when I get there. Pull the roster of tenants. And, do you know where Steve keeps his files on prospects? And the one for the brokers?"

"I think so," Ari said. "I don't have a key to his file . . . actually, I do. Anything else? You don't sound too hot."

"I've been better. Switch me over to Dianne." I waited. "Dianne, ask Ken Grubin to meet me about twelve, twelve-thirty. Get some sandwiches, all right? Tell Ari I want him to join us."

I walked into Ari's office. He stood up as I closed the door. "My brother, blessed be his ass, has sabotaged us. We've got to find out how badly." I looked out my window. "Steve is out of here. Left lots of wreckage in his wake. He more or less admitted to Cal and me that he lied to Federated."

"Good God, Henry! I mean, Steve is your *brother*."

"Incredible, isn't it? But now the question is, how badly are we hurt?"

"You're not going to like this, Henry," Ari said. "He's cleaned out all his files."

"I should have suspected him." I walked over to the window. A woman with her two young children were entering the party store across Franklin Avenue. "Well, see what you can reconstruct with his secretary."

"She called in sick. The word is they don't think she's coming back," Ari said, a hangdog expression on his face.

"Why the hell didn't someone tell me? Or you?" I shouted. "Look, get hold of her. I don't care if you have to go to her house. Offer her a nice bonus. We've got to get information, okay?"

"I'll try, Henry. But don't be surprised if I don't get anywhere. Are we meeting with Ken?"

"Yeah. I'll visit Hollick. Call or see the other brokers." I walked him to my door. "I'm counting on you. You're going to be one busy guy. When we get a handle on things, there'll be an increase for you. A big one." I wondered if he believed me, given the situation. "Monday at noon I'm calling a company meeting. What I'll tell people is what I'm saying to you now — that The Martin Companies are still viable. Still powerful. And that no one is going to take us down."

Dianne caught my eye and said my father was on the phone. I wondered what my dear brother might have told him.

"Good morning, Dad," I said. "How's it going in the land of perpetual sunshine?"

There was a long silence. "I'm devastated by Steve's phone call, Henry. I can't believe you two have split up. I gather the company is in deep trouble. Steve didn't go into details. I tell you, Henry, nothing could be worse news than this. Bad blood between my two sons. I asked Steve several times what caused it, but he wouldn't say. He said it would have happened eventually anyway. . . ."

"Dad, I'm as shocked as you are. I had no idea he harbored that kind of resentment. Steve is gone. Quit. There's no way I could change that." I knew how this was hurting my father and decided not to say anything about what was done to my aircraft. I tried to soften the blow. "Dad, maybe it's for the better. He's always detested me. It's partly my fault. I didn't defer to him enough. Now he'll be free to do something on his own. Dad, please don't feel bad. Just two brothers cut from very different cloth."

"I haven't told your mother. She's going to take it very hard."

"She'll blame me. Want me to talk to her?" I asked.

"No. I'll find the right time. Look, I can come to New York and help you. Get a plane out of here tomorrow. I used to be a damned good negotiator. You know that."

"Thanks, but it would take too long for you to catch up on all the details. I'll keep you informed. Your opinions will be very helpful." I hesitated, then added, "Dad, we'll get through this. The company's strong, and you've got a son who won't let the bastards get to us."

"Yes, Henry, I know that. But it breaks my heart about you and Steven."

I didn't know how to make him feel better. We chatted for a few more minutes, then he said good-bye. I thought I heard his voice break.

My father couldn't help me, but Jack Phelan could. I called his home number, and his wife, Margaret, answered.

"Hello, Henry. Yes, he's here, but he's a little busy right now. Can he call you back shortly?"

I called Hollick, but his secretary said he was out at a closing. You never knew if it was the truth or not. To be fair, Dianne often did the same when I didn't want to speak to someone.

I tried a few potential tenants and tried to reassure those I spoke to that we were as strong as ever. Then Cal called.

"Federated is intransigent," he said. "We could delay them on foreclosure. But — and they weren't specific — I think they may want to go for some other kind of action. In any case, none of this is going to help your reputation. Your other bankers, and God knows who else, will take a different look at their relationships with you."

"That's a nice way of saying I'm a dead man."

Cal hesitated, "As long as we're facing facts, you can assume Steve has gotten to almost everyone."

"But they all know Steve's my partner," I countered. "It shouldn't take a genius to understand how jealous he was of me."

"Henry," Cal said, "Steve has told them he's left the company because you've done all these terrible things. Convincing, if they want to believe the worst."

"So, there's a majority out there who would like to see me strung up and baked slowly over the coals. All right, counselor, what do we do next?"

"I can't tell until you give me a full damage report. Review your exact status, and we'll take it from there. . . . I have to take an overseas call. Talk to you later."

When we hung up, Dianne gave me several messages. One of them was from Old Stone, a bank in Providence we did some business with. I told her to hold my calls.

I went into my bathroom, let the water run until it was cold, and stuck my head under the faucet. I stood looking at myself in the mirror. There's strength in that face, I said to myself. They are not going to take you down. They haven't before, and they won't now.

I walked into the outer office and heard Dianne talking to Jack Phelan. She covered the speaker end of her phone and whispered his name. I nodded to her that I would take it in my office.

"Well, Henry," he began, "I'm hearing all kinds of things about you."

Good Christ, it's true that bad news travels faster than shock waves from an earthquake. "They're attacking me from almost every direction, Jack."

"Based on some distortion, I would think," Phelan answered. "What can I do for you?"

"I thought you could give me some advice. I want to make sure, after I put this whole thing into perspective, the necessity to make important decisions." I could hear my syntax falling all over itself.

"Yes, but that won't change the facts, whatever they are. Perception is reality, Henry."

"Do you have any time soon to discuss the situation with me?"

"Margaret and I are leaving this afternoon, flying to Florida, and then boarding a cruise ship for the Caribbean with two of our grandchildren. For about ten days. However, they do have ship-to-shore phones."

That's no help, I thought.

"You'd be surprised what can be accomplished on the phone when it's necessary," Phelan said. "Henry, I know this sounds trite, but make sure you don't lose your objectivity."

"I'll do my best."

"Oh, Henry, one more thing. Remember those lunches, and some of the things we talked about? Ego and arrogance. The two kinds of ego? One is the healthy kind, the kind that permits us to believe in ourselves. If we didn't have that kind of ego, you and I would be followers. What I was trying to make you understand is the other kind of ego, the destructive one that we too often ignore or suppress."

"You want me to see a psychiatrist, Jack?" I immediately regretted saying it.

"I don't have to continue with this, Henry," he bristled. "*I'm* just not sure you understand the differences. You've still got a thing or two to learn."

"I'm sorry, Jack. I'm sure I do. Just my frustration."

"Just a minute." I could hear him telling his wife he'd be off the phone in a moment. "I have to finish packing. Quickly then, the destructive ego can become pervasive when we fail to observe its presence in ourselves." There was a pause. "Often they alternate. It's very difficult to detect which one is operative. History is replete with the lives of men and women whose downfalls resulted from an excess of destructive ego. In your situation, Henry, you achieved what you have by utilizing both. But you've got some serious straightening out to do. God, I must sound like a preacher."

He did.

"One last remark, and listen to me carefully. It's important you continue to believe in yourself, because you're going to be tested as you never have been before. Have to go. I hope you retain a little of this."

"I've taken mental notes. I'll work on it. And thanks, Jack, for taking the time. Have a great holiday."

"My secretary can tell you how to reach me, Henry, if there's an emergency."

I never did go for all that psychological mumbo-jumbo, especially when the enemy is charging down the hill. Or was it up? Jack had lots of time on his hands these days. Lectures and seminars at business schools all over the country. A little different when you're up to your ass in crocodiles.

22

"*W*HAT'S your assessment?" I asked Ken Grubin. "We're being besieged from every quarter. Steve has effectively blown up our munitions. Do we still have enough reserves to withstand the onslaught?"

Ken, my accountant, was born and raised in Brooklyn and was very savvy. About fifty, tall, full-faced, he was a big man but not fat. He sported a beard, probably because he was balding. He combed his thinning strands across his pate, but the outcome of the battle was no longer in serious doubt. He had an unconscious habit of sticking his tongue in one cheek when he was concentrating. He gestured a lot, and his long arms made his movements all the more fluid and eloquent.

Ken was not your typical accountant. That's why I chose him way back when he was working for Morris Ginsberg, my original accountant. I helped him get started with a loan, but told him my one condition was that his firm always remain in the same building as mine. Quick access was mandatory. I liked Ken, as much for his professionalism as for his easygoing personality. But most of all, because he never hesitated to disagree with me.

"Federated has to be our major concern. Also, the other loans and mortgages, your cash situation. Ari and I have some serious analyzing to do."

"But what's your gut feeling, Ken?"

He eyed Miller, then me. "Maybe not enough cash or bank credit to cover all our needs. We'll know in a few days."

"Not a few days," I said firmly. "Tomorrow."

"We'll try. I've assigned a couple of juniors together with some of your people. They'll run analyses. Ari and I will study them, and —"

Dianne burst into the room. She had the look of someone in shock.

"Your mother is calling. Something about your father. I couldn't make her out, but I think your father's had a stroke. Or a heart attack. She's on line six."

I grabbed the phone. "Mom? Mom?" No response. I waited several seconds, then hung up and called back. Four rings and the answering machine came on, so I dialed their second number. Jesus Christ, I thought, why wasn't she picking up? I called the first number again. The machine again.

"Dianne, book me on the next flight to Phoenix. It'll probably be difficult at short notice. If it leaves in more than two hours, make arrangements for a private jet." I turned to Ken and Ari. "Look, put it together. Nights if you need to. You understand why." Ken waved.

"Dianne, get hold of a Phoenix operator. Ask her for the phone numbers of the hospitals closest to my parents' house. I'll call the emergency rooms." I paused. "No, you book the flight. I'll check the hospitals. And Dianne, you'll have to drive me to the airport."

She nodded, started toward the door, then turned back. "What about Steve?" She asked. I stood there, my mind racing.

"Steve . . . Steve. Yes, I'll call him. Probably my mother already has."

The news wasn't good, but at least my father was alive. Not a heart attack, a series of strokes — debilitating, but not massive. Too soon to know the full extent. It took about twenty minutes to locate him in St. Joseph's Hospital, and then to ascertain his condition from the attending doctor.

I had not really given much thought to my father's slow but inevitable decline. The shock of his sudden strokes hit me like a blow to my gut. Hell, he's seventy-five, but in top physical condition. No reason not to assume he didn't have many good years left. Mother, too.

I talked to Steve from my car. He said he was making his own arrangements to fly out.

"Look, the important thing now is what we can do for him," I said.

"All right. When we get there, I'm going to act like we've made up. But have no illusions, Henry, you're one hundred percent *out of my life.*"

"I don't need you, either. I never did."

He hung up. I don't know why I thought of it at that moment, but I was wondering how Joyce could think of spending the rest of her life with Steve. Then I remembered what she told me over our last non-lunch. About my not being able to make a commitment to her.

Except for the maternity section, hospitals always give me the feeling of finality; they exude grimness. I also hate the notion that when you step over the hospital threshold you relinquish all control over your destiny, your life. Entrust it completely to the competence of the medical professionals. Or the incompetence.

Maybe I was influenced by what I saw in Vietnam, the crazed field medics trying desperately to cope, the panic at the base hospitals. I decided they'd have to put me in a straitjacket to bring me into one of those places.

I found Mother in the waiting room, pale and distraught. She seemed to be shorter and heavier than I remembered. She reminded me of my two Sabatini aunts, and several of the cousins. If she had been dressed in black, I could have been greeting a Sicilian peasant woman.

We hugged. "My Jake, my wonderful Jake." She collapsed against me, as if seeking strength. "I've been praying to God, Henry. You must pray, too. Where's Steven? He should be here."

"He'll be here any minute, Mom." Her face was an image of emptiness. Her eyes darted, birdlike, nervously back and forth. "We're here with you."

"Why didn't you come together? You should have." Her expression was one of clear reproach.

"Steve and I will work things out, Mom. How's Dad doing?"

"I saw him a half hour ago. He couldn't talk, but he smiled. They said in a day or so they'll do a battery of tests." She began to sob. "I love him so much, Henry. So much. Tell me he'll be all right." I tried to console her, but I knew Steve would do a better job as soon as he arrived.

In Mother's presence, Steve and I put on a convincing act of brotherly affection. Away from her, we had nothing to do with each other, not even traveling to and from the hospital. The chief neurologist, Lawrence Scharfman, a man who'd been in his specialty for many years, told us that he was generally optimistic.

My mother was shaking visibly, and I suspected Scharfman was offering her the reassuring words she so much wanted to hear. But, when I got him alone, his story was less optimistic.

"It's still too early to say for sure the degree of recovery," he said. "What I said just now was more for your mother, since I can see how upset she is. Understandably, I might add."

"We appreciate that," I said. "What's your honest opinion?"

"The good news is none of the strokes was major," he said. "But the man is seventy-five —"

"A *vigorous* seventy-five," I countered.

"I'm afraid strokes don't always depend on physical condition."

I stayed in Phoenix three more days, most of which was spent in my father's room, sometimes alone, sometimes with Steve and my mother. It was painful to see him this way, all tubed up, so white and impassive, but I joked with him, as I always had, and sensed I was making him feel better. It was apparent that Steve resented my little routine. I didn't care.

The day I left Phoenix, I went to my father's room. There was a sharp crispness to the early morning Arizona air. The sun hadn't worked its way higher and pushed heat down through the atmosphere. "Heading back to the sweatshop in the Big Apple, Dad. Get things straightened out." I went over and kissed him. His eyes kissed me back.

"I'll call every morning, about this time. I expect you to be out there for a round of golf by Christmas. When I call, Mom can hold the phone if you need her to. We can settle all the national and international political and economic situations. And then we'll advise Congress." I turned to my mother and planted a kiss on her cheek. "Be back in about a week. Maybe sooner." I smiled at them both. "I'm as near as the phone."

Several weeks later, on a Sunday, at 2:30 in the morning, a call came from St. Joseph's.

"Dr. Scharfman here. I'm afraid I have bad news." My heart fell. I knew now, for the first time, what that trite expression really means. "Your father had a massive stroke a few hours ago. We put him in intensive care, but his breathing was affected. The device helped for a few hours, but the shock to his system was just too great. I'm truly sorry, Mr. Martin. There was nothing we could do."

I made arrangements for a private jet and called Steve. I wanted to get to Phoenix to be with my mother as quickly as possible.

I was in a state of shock, operating mechanically. Steve and I made the funeral arrangements, selected an oak coffin with an engraved Star of David on top, called family and friends, and ministered to my mother, who was inconsolable. I left most of that last chore to Steve, who rarely left her side for the next three days. And she, literally and figuratively leaning on him, seemed to find at least intermittent solace in his physical presence. The funeral and burial were something of a blur; I shook dozens of hands, embraced dozens of cousins and aunts and uncles, and children of all the above, most of whom I barely knew. I gave a short eulogy, but broke down toward the end and couldn't finish.

Tears streamed down my cheeks. Macho Henry, ego-man, dissolved in a pool of water. But then I remembered Dad's story about the time he broke down at the Courville cemetery in France near the end of the war.

Joe Sabatini fought all through Africa and the Italian campaign without a scratch, from Algeria to Palermo to Anzio. He was awarded a battlefield commission when his lieutenant was blown to pieces by a land mine. He had taken over his platoon, quickly establishing himself as their competent but demanding leader.

D–Day found Joe on the beaches of Normandy, leading his troops through heavy German fire, winning a Silver Star, a second Bronze Star, and a Battalion Citation. Casualties were staggeringly high, but again Joe escaped serious injury. He received shrapnel wounds, for which he was awarded a Purple Heart.

One afternoon, during a lull, Joe sat down to write Jake, his first letter in four weeks.

France, late summer, 1944

Dear Jake,

I hope this gets to you. We've been moving so goddamn fast I don't even have time to look around. As for sleep, forget it. Maybe an hour here and there, not like you boys having it soft in the Engineers. But we got the fucking Krauts on the run. Ike's invasion surprised the fucking Germans. We ended up hitting the beach at St. Vaast-la-Hougue (hoo, hoo — get my French!) on the Cherbourg peninsula. We passed St. Lo a week ago. These towns and cities are real quaint — or were. Right now they don't look so good.

I lost a lot of my boys. (The censor won't mind my saying this, because it's common knowledge both sides took tremendous losses.) Kids, a lot of them, fresh from the States. I feel so much older than my men. It's no fun leading, but at least I got me a couple of real sharp platoon leaders. What a laugh. One of them is from West Point. They never taught him this kind of fighting in his classes. I like him because he's willing to learn. The other is a tough Jewish kid from the Chicago streets. Good guy. Knows the drill. I told him about us and our family.

So write me, knucklehead. Especially now that they promoted me to Captain. Yeah, I got two silver bars, like you, buddy. Imagine us, a pair of captains, clowns from Brooklyn. I gotta tell you, I miss you, cumpar. Hell, all the family. And Brigitte, my girl in Georgia. You're the first to know we're engaged. When we get back, we'll start again, okay? I want us to build our company into something terrific. Only thing first you knock out those Nips, and I'll beat the shit out of the fucking Krauts.

Watch your ass, Jake. We didn't get this far to screw up now.

Your hero and brother-in-law,

Joe

In the far Pacific, Jake and his company of combat engineers had battled from island to island, often along with the airborne infantry who were parachuted into the interior, behind the fighting on the beaches. The Japanese defended themselves ferociously against the troops coming ashore in waves of landing craft and by air at the airfields.

Jake's orders were to repair the landing strips that had been heavily bombed by the Air Force even as invasions by the infantry and armored cavalry were taking place. Jake seemed to possess a rare degree of leadership that motivated his men long after they had decided they couldn't take another step or dig another foxhole. He also insisted they be as good with weapons as they were with bulldozers.

Some engagements were surprisingly easy, others endless nightmares. When they were dislodged from an airstrip, the Japanese often faked leaving, but hid nearby. After the Americans had established themselves, they would infiltrate and mount counterattacks. On Okinawa, in one of the worst campaigns of the war, U.S. casualties were devastatingly high. The heavily entrenched Japanese fought from the beaches, from the hills, from caves in the mountains. G–2 intelligence had reported heavy concentrations of the enemy defending the strategically important airstrips.

For Jake and his men on Okinawa, the combat was brutal. In one mission, they captured the airstrip only to lose it again. The next day they regained it. Two days later, an infantry headquarters commander advised him that the area was finally secure and that he could begin the cleanup and prepare it for U.S. fighter planes.

Perhaps it was instinct, perhaps caution, but Jake didn't like what he sensed. Independently, he stationed guards at strategic points around the airstrip, and ordered them to remain alert for possible attacks. Nothing happened the first two days, but during the second night, under cover of a heavy overcast, the Japanese infiltrated and killed the guards with knives. Jake had established a communications system; reports were to be sent every hour. Shortly after midnight, his sergeant woke him to inform him that the reports had stopped coming.

Before the alarm could be sounded, heavy mortar fire rained down on Jake's headquarters, destroying his communications tent, which prevented him from contacting his platoon leaders at the perimeters to assess their situation and from contacting battalion HQ some miles away for desperately needed infantry and artillery support. Rounds and rounds of mortar and machine-gun fire poured in on them. He screamed an order to his company sergeant, one of the few career soldiers in his unit. Just as he did, the sergeant was hit by shrapnel from a mortar round, literally blowing half his head off. Several other soldiers were hit; the unit was close to panic.

"Listen up, men!" Jake yelled, climbing onto a rickety folding chair. "Grab whatever you can! Get what's left of the radios. And don't forget your weapons! Follow me to those trees. I mean, now!" They scampered, a few lugging equipment, 60mm and 81mm mortars and machine guns, trying like hell to keep their heads down. When they reached the clump of trees, Jake looked around and saw one of his men on the ground, writhing in pain, about halfway between the trees and the destroyed headquarters tent. Without thinking, Jake raced back to him, bursts of mortar fire on all sides. But he wasn't thinking: he was on automatic. He lifted the soldier, both of whose legs had been hit, and carried him back to the cluster of trees. Later he wondered how he ever could have carried the soldier, who weighed twenty pounds more than he did, and still move that fast.

But Jake didn't escape scot-free. Just as he reached the front line of trees, he felt a sudden whack, as if someone had struck him. He couldn't believe it was a bullet. But reaching down to his thigh, he felt the blood and could feel the metal in his flesh. He had a medic wrap his leg, and went on as if his wound didn't exist.

They huddled there, the trees affording a degree of protection. Jake positioned his team at the periphery, setting up machine guns and bazookas just behind. He utilized a zigzag defense in a general configuration of a triangle. The Japanese who had escaped fire from established points were caught in crossfire as they advanced. Jake's troops had to repel several attacks. As dawn approached, P-38 Lightnings and F6F Hellcats made several strafing runs on the Japanese positions, which were followed by a sweep of the area by fresh U.S. infantry units. By afternoon, Jake gave the order for his men to commence the task of repairing the airstrip for incoming planes.

In a ceremony several weeks later, Jake was awarded the Silver Star and Distinguished Service Cross for leadership and gallantry in action, plus a Purple Heart for his wounds, and a Presidential Unit Citation *for his unit. The following month he was promoted to Major and given command of his battalion.*

A freak Jeep accident near Chartres several months later, in September 1944, a month after the joyous liberation of Paris, pinned Joe underneath his vehicle. Despite all the doctors' efforts, Giuseppe Xavier Sabatini, who had survived twenty-four months of grueling combat, died three days later in a Seventh Army field hospital from multiple fractures and extensive internal injuries. He was twenty-nine years old.

In November 1944, Jake was relieved of his command and sent back for duty in the States. Jake, learning that Joe had been buried in the military cemetery in Courville, received permission to return home by way of Europe. As he drove in a Jeep through the devastated countryside, he felt as if he were viewing the aftermath of an apocalypse. Troop carriers and trucks lay on the edges of the roads, on their sides or tires up; tanks sat like so many squat or squashed toads, scorched or scarred. Jake wondered about the agony of the men who had been caught inside. He was impressed that the Germans had also used horses and carts. At one point, he saw a German Messerschmitt fighter plane that had crash-landed in a meadow. Had the pilot escaped? Or had he died in the crash, or in the ensuing inferno?

Following the directions of the military police, Jake found the well-maintained cemetery three miles west of Courville. A dirt road led into a pasture through an entrance marked by a simple sign. Tidy row upon row of crosses, with an occasional Star of David. The land looked like an undulating sea, several large oaks interrupting the flow of the terrain. After checking the map, Jake finally located the grave.

A silky breeze wafted scented air across the pasture. The fall afternoon was balmy and peaceful, and Jake found it difficult to imagine what this same field must have looked like only a year before. He stood ashen-faced at the foot of the grave, his cap in his hands. Two lines of tears ran down his cheeks. He remained quiet, trying to accept the reality that Joe was gone forever, that they would never again be able to be together, work together, laugh together.

"Joe," he whispered, "you dumb sonofabitch. You were always the one telling me to watch my ass. What a stupid way to do yourself in. After all you went through, a fucking Jeep accident! C'mon, you could drive. There were no broads to look at." He fell to his knees, edged his body forward onto

the grave, arms extended as if he were trying to embrace the small mound. He wept uncontrollably, unashamedly. For several minutes, he struggled to regain his composure. Then, remembering a Jewish custom, he searched the area, found a number of small stones, and placed them in a neat row next to the small wooden cross.

"Okay, Joe," he said. "I hear you. 'Go back to the States and start the business again.' You'll see, I'll make it into something, bring your dad in with me. And I'll stay close to your family. Yes, and get Brigitte's address and write her. Maybe see her. Okay, okay, I'll see her."

Jake began to walk back to his Jeep but then turned back. "Joe . . . I . . . good-bye, pal." Again, tears streamed down his face. "I love you, buddy. Never knew just how much, cumpar. Wherever you are, take care of yourself." Jake held himself rigid in a salute for a very long time, then marched stiffly to his Jeep and sat in it, his arms and head on the steering wheel. Then he drove to the nearest airbase and hitched a ride on the first flight back to the United States.

Jake had a three-week leave. It was bittersweet, clouded by Joe's death. The porch window of the Sabatini home displayed a gold star, as did those of several other neighborhood families whose sons had also given their lives for their country.

Jake was then ordered to report to artillery command headquarters at a base in the Midwest. He and Barbara decided it would be best for her to remain in their apartment near her parents while she awaited the birth of their second child.

Jake was discharged from military service in September 1945, and returned home just in time for the birth of his second son, Henry. Every day for weeks, Jake, Barbara, and the boys made a point of visiting Sal and Angela. On a certain visit Sal drew Jake aside. "Jake," he said awkwardly, "I know you love-a Joe as much as Angela and me. We family. Always family, you know that. You give us two fine boys, due belli bambini." He embraced Jake in an Italian bear hug. "And the little one," he said, "do you know? I swear he look just-a like Joe."

Jake reestablished himself in the construction business and brought in Sal. He made him head foreman, which greatly pleased the old man and brought him even closer to his son-in-law. "Build them good," Sal would tell Jake as they rode around inspecting their jobs. "Build them good and build them cheap. People will come. We'll get plenty of work."

"During the war, you and Joey away," Sal said, "it was real tough, tough-a gettin' materials. Except when we got the government jobs."

"You did your part, Sal," Jake said. "All those letters and packages from home. Of course, Barbara really kept me going." Jake laughed.

"What is so funny?" Sal frowned.

"I was thinking about the time I got a package from Barbara. All my men knew I was Jewish. So I opened this package: Genoa salami, crackers, olives in a can, and the smelliest cheese ever. The guys all looked at me like I'd been putting them on. 'What the hell's all this, Captain? No Jewish mother would ever send her son this stuff. You're not Jewish, Captain! You're fucking Italian! . . . Sir!' "

23

*A*FTER the funeral and three days of the Jewish mourning period, which my Italian mother respectfully observed, I returned to Long Island. The onslaught began the moment I arrived and didn't stop. My enemies and detractors seemed to be multiplying exponentially. Federated was cinching its grip tighter and tighter. Around my throat. The foreclosure of 355 Park Avenue seemed more and more imminent.

My nights were bad, sleep erratic, my dreams tormented. I socialized very little, ate alone, usually at home, read, watched a tape, or some inane TV show, fell asleep in the chair, woke up later, went to bed for what remained of the night. Maybe I'd sleep two hours at a time. Getting up to jog, which I had always enjoyed, was becoming a more and more unpleasant chore.

I tried other banks and lenders: G.E. Credit Corporation, Bankers Trust, and the Commercial Credit Corporation. An exercise that led nowhere. No institution was willing to replace the mortgage without leases in place. The loan, including a month of interest that was in arrears, aggregated to over $65 million. And the harsh reality was that I had guaranteed it personally. Building loan lenders require this because permanent, or takeout, mortgages are rarely available until there are tenants. Even if I wanted to drop the building, and lose the $10 million of our own funds I had invested in the venture, I couldn't. I was, as they say, on the hook. A meat hook. I was beginning to doubt there was a way out. I was also wondering about myself.

"Not much more you can do, Henry," Cal said at a meeting in my office. Grubin and Miller were there, too. "At least you've stopped servicing the loan. That'll reduce the drain. You've tried selling the building?"

"Yeah, of course. No one's interested. The market's scared. If I had discretionary capital — one of those big vulture funds — I could keep Three-Fifty-Five and also pick up some other prime real estate at a fraction of its replacement costs."

My private phone rang. Very few people had that number. It was Karen, returning my call from earlier that morning. I told her I'd call back as soon as the meeting was over.

"Overbuilding," Ken said. "Very simple. Values tumble. A classic recession, this one severe. You lose your building and equity, but perhaps you could effectuate a tax swap — a 1031." He was referring to trading 355 for another property. The capital gains tax is postponed, because with a trade a taxable event has not taken place. It will, sometime in the future when you sell the second property. "But remember," he added, "Federated may try to prevent you from doing that on Three-Fifty-Five because you've guaranteed the building loan personally, but you will want to create a swap."

"I was going to suggest that possibility, Ken," Cal said, "but I don't think there's sufficient time for a 1031. Federated's moving too fast. However, the partnership could file a Chapter Eleven, which would delay them."

He looked at me. I had no response.

"Yes," Ken agreed, "but remember, if you default on the Federated loan, the capital gains tax has to be paid. Federal, New York State, and New York City. And don't forget about depreciation. A wonderful invention, except whatever you've deducted from your taxes in past years must be recaptured when you sell — in this case default. A defaulted mortgage is deemed a sale. Those boys in Congress figured that out. 'Play the game all you want, fellas,' they decided, 'but *we* eventually get *ours*.'"

I had spent the previous few weeks frantically searching for either a buyer or a tax swap. Time, and Federated, were beating down the door.

"If I sold the building or defaulted on the mortgage, what would the capital gains be?" I asked Ken.

"I'd have to figure it out," he said.

"Guess. Roughly. To the nearest hundred trillion."

He looked hard at me. "Well, you've had the building about two years or so. Interest, depreciation, and other deductions we've taken. Let's see." He borrowed my calculator and did some fast figuring. He scratched his head, looked up, and said, "Oh, three to four million dollars. And due April fifteenth."

"We always extend our returns," Ari joined in. "To October fifteenth."

"No, this is different. All of it has to be paid on April fifteenth," Ken repeated.

"There's no way in God's heaven I have, or can raise, that kind of cash," I said. I searched their faces for an answer, any kind of answer.

"Well," Ken said slowly, "it would be possible to work out a payment schedule with the IRS, but you have too many other assets they would grab. After we finish, you, Ari, and I should review your cash position and every other aspect."

"Henry," Cal said, "listen to me carefully. Except for the tax consequences, it may be the wisest thing for me to talk to Federated about our giving them the deed in lieu of foreclosure. There's no point in protracting the inevitable. What do you think?"

"I suppose that makes the most sense, but first I need to assess the entire picture, see what we have left. See if we can revamp and get some other extensions. At least lower some of the carrying costs. Renegotiate other mortgages I haven't guaranteed. Tell Federated — Cal, tell them we want to work with them. Also, please, reiterate strongly that whatever they've been told by Steve is absolutely not true — I did *not* falsify numbers." I felt out of breath. Maybe out of energy. And clearly out of ideas.

"Yes, I will, Henry. There's a good chance they may be willing to effect a trade-off: withdraw the action for foreclosure plus any other actions. All they want, when they've gotten over their anger, is the building and what they can get out of it. They've written *you* off,

Henry, but that's neither here nor there." He got up to leave. "I'll be back in my office later. Call me if you need me."

Written me off? 'Neither here nor there,' my ass! It may take a while, but so help me I'll be back. Ring the fucking gongs and clang the goddamn bells. Mauled, maybe, but not crushed. Not this boy.

The three of us went to work assessing every detail of our liquidity and cash needs: accounts payable, payroll, mortgage payments for the vacant land and for tenant vacancies. Then, line by line, everything we could think of to reduce total expenditures. The bottom line was: we had to cut expenses, drastically, wholesale. That meant selling land at virtually any price, just to get rid of it, reducing staff, and finding dozens of ways to spend less.

"Henry," Ken said, "you'll have to, uh, reduce your personal expenses as well. Steve's out, so eliminating his draw will help, but with the way things appear, you're going to have to cut down. You know what I mean."

"No, what *do* you mean?"

"Well, for starters, your helicopter and your pilot. Maybe your plane, too. What is it, a twin Baron?"

I stared hard at him and said, "A Cessna 414 Chancellor."

"You asked for my help," Ken said, angry and defensive. "I didn't insist, remember? I have a number of other things I can be doing right now."

"Oh, don't get so pissed. I just don't like to hear you spell it out." I glanced over at Ari, who was sporting a worried expression. "Okay, okay. I'll start slimming down, given all our problems."

"*Your* problems, Henry," Ken shot back.

"What's bothering you, Ken, getting too hot in the kitchen?"

"No, I'm used to problems. That's what an accountant is for. But I'm a little distressed by your attitude. The last thing you want to do is alienate your colleagues."

With that, Ken got up. "I'll end with this, Martin — you can make it but not without doing what I said. Maybe not even then. And definitely not with that attitude."

"Hold on a minute," I said. "I show the stress by lashing out and being sarcastic." I looked at Ken. "I'm sorry. You're the last guys I want to offend."

Ken came over, stuck out his hand, and we shook. "With that kind of thinking, you'll be better able to deal with our problems," he said, lingering on the word *our*. He headed toward the door. "I've admired what you've accomplished, Henry. But frankly, you're not the easiest of clients. I'm glad you said what you finally did." He smiled. "See you later."

I reviewed the figures again with Ari. Ken was right. No question about it: I would have to get rid of some of my favorite possessions.

"No, Henry. Labor Day weekend isn't good for me," Karen said. "I'm sorry. Other plans."

"Maybe you could 'unmake' them. We can fly down to Hilton Head or to the Greenbriar. I've missed you. And I really want to be with you."

"Henry, you should understand you're not the only guy I date. Call me Tuesday afternoon. Maybe we can have dinner Wednesday. I have to go to Boston early on Thursday."

"Why not Tuesday morning? Won't you be around?"

"Just a minute," she said. "First, I don't like answering that question. And second, I don't like to feel I'm somebody's instant gratification."

"I'm sorry, Karen. I withdraw the question."

She laughed, a kind of musical flutter that was both charming and enticing.

"What's new on the disaster front?" she asked, thankfully changing the subject.

"Worse. Liquidity problems. Federated's pushing my magnificent Three-Fifty-Five over the brink. I told you how my brother sabotaged me." I hesitated. "I'll be all right. It's just that for the first time I have to swim upstream. And avoid the crocodiles."

"With your drive," she said, "you'll figure out a way."

"Thanks," I said. "Have a nice weekend. Talk to you Tuesday."

Have a lousy weekend, I thought. As for my drive, a bit reined in these days.

*

Karen and I did have dinner Wednesday, at Petrossian, the best place in New York for caviar. Karen devoured the Malassol with obvious relish, accompanied by shots of Russian vodka. I bought an orchid for her before I picked her up.

After dinner, we took a cab back to my place. I tried to be upbeat, but the atmosphere somehow didn't seem right.

"Have I done something wrong?" I asked her. "You seem a little withdrawn."

"No, nothing. You've been your usual Prince Charming self." She smiled. "It's just that being involved with more than one man makes things a bit difficult."

"Ah," I said — I hoped calmly. "Well, whoever he is, he couldn't appreciate you as much as I do."

I lightly touched the back of her neck, ran my other hand down her back, and gently kissed her ear. "I want you, Karen, I want to make love to *you*."

Karen shivered slightly as I ran my fingers across her face, lightly from under her ear, across her cheek, between the bottom of her nose and her lips, and then very lightly across her lips.

She was against me. I pressed her closer, gently crushed her breasts to my chest, spread both hands firmly on her rear. Our kisses were deep and prolonged.

When her breathing became jagged, I said, "Karen, it's not just the lovemaking. It's how good just being with you makes me feel."

"Yes, Henry. *Molto bene*," she responded.

I remember carrying her through whatever room we were in to my bed, which was king-sized and very comfortable. I began by making love to her, touching, kissing. Karen was more than ready and came first. In fact, second, third, and fourth — a kind of consecutive abandonment.

But something happened. I suddenly lost my erection.

Karen looked at me, surprised. I can't recall our position, but after we had disentangled, she said, "It's all right, Henry. Really. It happens. Could it be you're angry I'm seeing someone else?"

Yes, but it wasn't only that. I couldn't get my mind off my

freefall. Off the collapse of TMC. When I tried to invoke various sexual fantasies, my mind kept drifting back to business. And, yes, I was also thinking about Karen and her other boyfriend.

I sat up. "The vultures were just waiting for this opportunity. Now they have it. In spades. And I suppose I'm also beginning to wonder about my so-called powers. It's really a laugh, I talk you into having sex, then I can't perform."

"Henry, I told you not to worry. Stop thinking in terms of performance."

"Plus your seeing someone else. That really does bother me, I have to admit. How come I'm not enough for you?" I jumped out of bed and walked over to the window.

Karen sat up in bed, the sheet tucked under her arms. "You've got it slightly screwed up," she began. "You're the one who's a bit of a hypocrite. It's okay for you, but not me. Let me ask you a question. Are you really committed to me? No one else you haven't or *wouldn't* sleep with?"

"Look, Karen, I —"

"Look, nothing," she said. "We both live by the same standard. I care about you, Henry. Very much. I'd like to help you, but I don't think I can."

"Why not?" I said.

"Do you really want to know?" I nodded. "Because we're too much alike. I'm as driven as you are. Well, almost. And we're not that involved in each other's interests, or lives. To help you, I'd have to wait around a lot," she said. "Not my style, Henry. Do you understand?"

I suppose I did. I doubted we could change, or that we wanted to.

"It's late," Karen said, "I have an early flight." She dashed into the bathroom. Before closing the door she said, "I'm not saying I don't want to see you anymore, Henry. But you need time to work things out."

I walked her downstairs. As we waited for a cab, she said, "A man doesn't have to be powerful all the time, but a woman does want her man to need her. In a very particular way." She kissed me as a cab pulled over to the curb. "That doesn't fit you, Henry. Not now, anyway."

I watched until the cab turned the corner, then looked up and down East End Avenue. It was a rain-infested night. A shitty night. What the hell: What did I expect, sunshine and roses?

24

*I*N the months after my father died, my mother came to New York more frequently, and always stayed with Steve and Joyce. The closer Joyce's due date, the more my mother fawned over her. My mother told me that if the baby was a boy she wanted him to be named Joseph, after my uncle.

Seeing my mother again made me think about how screwed up our family relationships were. I don't know why it had taken me so long to figure it out. All the women I'd encountered in my life — was taking them to bed all I wanted? I seemed to need to keep proving that women wanted me. Because my mother didn't?

The simple truth was that I was not going to let any woman ever hurt me again. I kept control, but it cost me plenty. Intimacy, for example. Acknowledging this truth was one thing; making permanent changes was quite another matter.

I viewed women as physical objects, never as individuals. Splendid qualities and values, or not, they were objects nonetheless. I had never permitted myself to get emotionally involved. Never permitted myself to make the kind of commitment that would result in the full bloom of what can exist between a man and a woman.

My manner of relating to women was entirely different from Steve's. Talk about hypocrisy! My brother basically clung to my mother's religion, Catholicism, but when it suited him, he could be Jewish, or Lutheran, Joyce's religion. Or agnostic or atheist. A master chameleon. Well, at least Brother Chameleon had made a commitment to get married.

The weather inside my office was like a tropical depression, gathering force and heading straight for me. Cal telephoned one morning later that week. "I can't wait to hear what you have to say," I said. "Every call I get these days is a real bummer."

"I'm sorry, Henry. It's been a long couple of months. Any progress with your banks or mortgagees?"

"Couldn't get even *one* to recast terms and payments. It's as if they've all been huddling together."

"I don't know if this helps, Henry, but you have to keep in mind you've also had some terrific years." I heard the cliché; at least he sounded as if he cared. "The Federated situation hasn't been resolved," he continued. "According to Cunningham the bank is willing to take the deed in lieu of the foreclosure, but they haven't given up the possibility of an action."

I cleared my throat, a nervous gesture when I was tense and under pressure. "Won't they have a tough time proving it? We could subpoena Steve. He couldn't lie under oath."

"The bank understands they don't have a real case," Cal said.

"Then why, Cal?"

"Because they're still angry. They convinced themselves you are a bad guy. Malenti likes nothing more than to be on the attack when right seems to be on his side. Makes him into a white knight." He paused for a minute, to have a word with someone in his office, then came back on. "I'm sure in their discussions they included the 'Cain and Abel' stuff, you and your brother. Steve the good guy; Henry the villain. Revenge. A morality play. Except they have it backward. Anyway, all they have is a large building loan on which nobody is paying interest. We know that sits badly with bank examiners."

I cleared my throat again. "Cal, they have an appraisal. It should make their loan look quite comfortable."

"That's one of the reasons they're so willing to take the deed," Cal replied. "In a protracted case, delays build up months and months of lost interest, which reduces their comfort level."

"Cal, the bottom line is that if I dump money from assets outside my real estate holdings, there's a small chance of surviving. But TMC would be smaller. Much smaller." I heard a deep sigh. It wasn't Cal's.

"How much could you raise?"

"Ken and Ari are working up three different scenarios. This may surprise you, but there's always been a part of me that has viewed real estate development as very volatile. I pulled some money out from remortgages and sales of some of the old industrials. Dad and Steve liked that idea. I didn't decide it alone. I also plan to sell stocks and bonds. And my helicopter. Put a mortgage on my townhouse. Or better, sell it. Whatever has to be done." I didn't like having to enumerate further. What I said should convince him I was serious. "The market did seem ready for another classy office building. We had the Standard General lease fully negotiated. And other prospects in the wings." I needed to hear my rationalizations.

"Yes, I know," Cal said. "We get the Federated situation behind us, pick up the pieces, and go on from there. As you said, there's plenty of money to be made in recessions."

"Except," I interjected, "it takes capital. Who the hell will want to be involved with me after this?"

"Hey, you were always Mr. Positive. So, you're getting kicked around, Henry, but that old ego of yours, the old ambitious streak will definitely rear its beautiful head again."

"Now look who's mixing metaphors. Anyway, Cal, let me know what develops from your end. By the way, I need to talk to you about several of the other mortgages."

"Tell Ari to send me a synopsis on each so I can do some planning."

Dianne waddled in and gave me my messages. I reviewed the mail, and gave her dictation. I must have tuned out at one point, my mind several million miles away.

"Are you all right?" she asked.

"Yes. Thanks," I said, coming back to earth with a resounding thud. "After we hit the important calls and letters, please set up a meeting with Ken and Ari. For eleven A.M. Here in my office. No, make it eleven-thirty."

The three of us sat down at the coffee table in my office. "All right," I opened, "what have we got?"

Ari nodded to Ken. "Our studies," Ken said, "whether they follow A, B, or C, all point to the same conclusion. In a nutshell, Henry, significantly downsizing of TMC is a given. Taking the worst case, C, you'll be about a quarter of the size we are now. Here, have a look at the 'Assumptions.' You'll notice we've projected the loss of two-thirds of both the industrial and office buildings, either through defaults or sales. Any sales will in most cases be used to eliminate the mortgages and pay the capital gains taxes. No liquidity from any of them."

"That bad?" I asked.

He reminded me "C" was the worst case, but that "A" and "B" were only slightly better. We spent an hour going through the other — better — scenarios, and I saw they were right. If C was the rock, A and B were still pretty hard places.

I got up and went over to the whiteboard. We had listed the properties by number, their size, and degree of solvency. I stood in front of it for a long time, figuring in my head what it all meant, then turned and said, "Do you think you can manage things without me for a while?" Their eyes widened. "I don't think I can be of any further help right now. I'll give you power-of-attorney, whatever you need. Give it to Cal as well. The point is, I really have to get away."

Ari spoke first. "Doesn't sound like you, Henry. Frankly, it's always been you in control." Ken nodded.

"But you're probably right," Ken said. "We *could* manage things from this point on. You're aware that the decisions we would make will not necessarily be the ones you would have made." I nodded. "I assume you'll want Cal, Ari, and I to consult, and then proceed with whatever course of action we think appropriate?"

"Yes," I responded. "I trust you guys implicitly. I'm not sure where I'll go, but it won't resemble Manhattan or Garden City, Long

Island. I'd like to leave as soon as possible. I'll advise Cal. Let me know exactly what you'll need from me before I go." I walked over to them and shook hands. After they left, I sat down and turned off the light, as if darkness would help me see more clearly. About why my life was falling apart. About who I really was. I needed to find out.

25

*T*HE entire spectacle, the whole glorious pageant, gone. Poof. My creation destroyed. Well, almost. Between my banks, their gunslingers, and vengeful wardens — plus assorted creditors — I felt like some fat dude forced into the Pritikin Center for three months of drastic weight reduction. Or better, that my flesh was being stripped by those grotesque vultures out on the African plains. My pride was being cut out of me.

They all grabbed a piece over that fall and winter. What I was left with was a fragile shell of my former empire, a few properties. The bulk had to be sold at fire sale prices and the deeds simply given back to the mortgage lenders. A few offered to accrue the payments of interest and amortization for the vacant buildings, but I decided that holding on under those circumstances would only increase the total debt, especially since I didn't have enough tenants left to pay sufficient rents. It was a huge burden to stay afloat, and unrealistic that I would be able to cope with even more vacancies later on.

I met Cal and Ari at Glen Pointe for lunch toward the end of that week for a last round of talks. "Ken, you and Ari tell those bloodsuckers what they're offering isn't any help. If they want to reduce the size of the mortgages, yes, that would make a difference." I glanced at one and then back to the other. "Otherwise, tell them to shove it."

"What about the vacant land? We might —"

"What do I want to struggle with land for? No way in hell anyone's going to want me to build them a building."

"Henry, don't you think you're going a little overboard?" Ari added. "The baby with the bathwater?"

"God, I hate that cliché," I said, shaking my head. But it made me reflect for a moment about the last scene at Steve's house, when I watched Joyce with her infant son. For reasons I couldn't figure out he had a *bris* for his son. I went because my mother asked me to take her. She knew nothing about the reasons Steve and I were not getting along. And as far as she was concerned, ignorance was indeed bliss.

I was transfixed by Joyce's devotion, her complete absorption with the creature she had made. She was hardly aware of my presence. I was overcome by sadness. That kicking, giggling child could have been mine. If I regretted anything, it was not being a father. No. Something else, too: not having someone to really love.

"And, guys, the closing on the sale of the helicopter should take place on April ninth. I've put my townhouse up with Meredith and Leslie. Take what you can get for the other assets. We're not dumping, but don't hold out if you get decent offers."

"What about a place to live?" Ari asked.

"I have a place down in the Village. From a long time ago. Nancy used it as a studio." Not true, I thought, but what difference did it make?

After the waiter cleared the dishes, Ken said, "How do you want us to handle the brokers and all the others?" He was trying to cover all the contingencies. "Do what we think we need to?"

I nodded. "Yeah. Look, you're a great team."

"Do you know how long you'll be away?" Ari asked hesitantly. "In case we need you?"

I turned slightly to observe the two women rising from a table in front of where I was sitting. One, Joan Fingold, was unusually attractive. She was aware I found her interesting. I think she also understood the way she looked in her tennis outfits drove me a little crazy. Short, pleated skirts. A polo shirt revealing just enough. Joan was married to an immature jerk who worked for his father, a member of the club because his father paid for it. In her late thirties, she had two cute daughters whom I played with once in a while.

I had vaguely courted her, but lately it didn't seem worth the effort. She had been careful not to encourage anything, but when the occasion permitted, we did tease each other. Persiflage. I wasn't sure whether she was available or not. With a husband like hers, life couldn't have been very exciting.

Joan gave me a half smile as she passed our table. That was all I needed. After she had left the dining room, I got to my feet. "Be back in a minute," I said to Ken and Ari. "Have to powder my nose." I saw her walking out into the parking lot, and I caught up with her.

"Hi, there." She smiled and waited. "You know, Joan, I was thinking. I know this may sound bold" — I know from experience that anticipation can often be a turn-on — "but I was wondering if you'd like to have lunch one day. Maybe go to a museum or concert in the city. Or just get together. Maybe add a little color to our lives?"

She opened the door to her car, then looked back at me, "I suppose it might," she said. "But, then again, it might *not* be such a good idea. I *am* married, you know, even if you're not."

"Look," I said, "did anyone ever tell you that we regret the sins of omission, not the ones of commission"?

"I've heard that." Her eyes narrowed. "You are an attractive man, Henry, and if I didn't know any better I'd be very tempted. Too bad, because my life does leave something to be desired."

"Well," I said, "it so happens mine does too. So . . ."

"So," she said slowly, "I'll be okay, thanks." She sat down, closed the door, and without a gaze or a gesture, started her convertible, drove rapidly through the parking lot and down the driveway. I took a deep breath and returned to the dining room, feeling worse than when I had left on my mission.

"Look, Henry, we were talking while you were gone," Ken began. "I think Cal shares this with us — it's the wrong time for you to be away. It says something to the market. You still do have properties. You're not *bankrupt*." I examined his face. "It's not fun duking it out, but the industry will respect you for it."

"He's right, Henry." Ari chimed in. "If you're away for an extended period, there'll be rumors you're gone for good. It'll be hard for us to counteract that. Perhaps you should stay here for a few months, help us try to reestablish ourselves. Then after the winter, take off if you want to." His look was almost imploring.

They were right, of course, but my mind was made up. "Let me think about it. I appreciate your suggestion. I know those bastards would love to start rumors of my premature demise."

As I drove out to the airport in Islip, I mused about getting out of business altogether. Like those guys from Goldman Sachs, a few of whom I knew, who had left for different lives. More time with families. Giving something back to society. An end to their ratraces. For them, maybe, but not for me. I wasn't ready for that. Probably never would be. Not to mention that I had no family to spend more time with. And I'll bet most of those guys were miserable because they probably couldn't go back again. Like former top-ranked tennis pros who try to make a comeback. Kerplunk!

A year earlier I had traded in my twin Baron for the much larger twin-engine Cessna Chancellor. I bought it from RAM Aviation down in Waco, Texas. They offered a new package, and for promotional purposes, made me a terrific deal. Not only would they completely overhaul the engines on the 1978 plane, but they would repaint the outside, provide a completely new interior as well as a new panel of instruments and avionics. The finished aircraft was gorgeous, with winglets and vortex generators for lift and faster speed; also color radar, a stormscope, a GPS that was the ultimate in navigational equipment, and many other amenities, including de-icing equipment. The engines were turbo-charged, which meant the plane had a service ceiling of 30,000 feet. Its airspeed averaged about 200 knots; it was pressurized and air-conditioned. Everyone said it was one of a kind.

I checked it out down in Texas on a test flight. I had flown aircraft like this one before. In some ways, because of the turbochargers, there was more to do flying this one than a jet. Most large twins had two pilots up front. This one could be flown by a single pilot, and most of the time I liked it that way.

I requested and received a special number for her, 355 HM. She was like a mistress to me. Making love with her was nice. We roamed around in the sky, our playground, floating, swaying gently to music only we would hear. When I was with her I could turn off the world out over the Atlantic or over the north and south forks of Long Island, past Montauk to Block Island, around Martha's Vineyard, Nantucket, and Cape Cod. Most of all I loved flying over Vermont, where the fall and winter can be — and usually are — so tranquil and pristine, when the Green and Adirondack Mountains and Lake Champlain offer their wound-healing balm.

That afternoon, after leaving Ken and Ari at the club, I turned off my car phone. I just wanted to be alone. I preflighted the plane carefully, punched out with Clearance/Delivery at Islip and flew to the deserted airport at Montauk. I parked 355 HM and walked down the runway to the east, over the dunes to the shallow freshwater lakes just before the point and the lighthouse.

I sat quietly as scaups and buffleheads swept in from the sky, alighting on the lakes to begin earnest conferences with their colleagues. The day was calm, the wind busy somewhere else. The late winter sun did not have to contend with clouds and shone with clarity and friendliness. The tall grasses had turned brown, offering tufts and seed pods. Short, wild choke cherry, beach plums, dwarf oaks, and hollys of several kinds mingled in small patches of sand. The peace I felt was, I suppose, my version of what people feel in churches or synagogues. That afternoon, away from the howling storm into which I had been thrust, or, as Steve would have said, the storm of my own making — I began to find some of the direction I needed.

After what seemed like a long time, I stood up, ambled to the dunes that protected the flats where the two ponds resided, stood on the highest dune, and faced east. My thoughts seemed to turn me around and around, as if I had lost control. I had to struggle not to fall down.

These words came back to me: "Oh, Lord, God, please help me for I know not what to do nor where to go in my affliction." I said them, I thought them, I kept saying it again and again.

Finally I seemed to hear this in the wind: "Help comes from within."

I cranked up 355 HM, flew back to Islip, drove into Manhattan, went to Smith and Wolensky for Caesar salad, a thick Delmonico steak, and a half-bottle of their best Montrachet.

The next morning, I told Ken, Ari, and Cal that I'd stick around through sometime in April, and that we would fight it out together.

Part 2

Lay upon the sinner his sin,
Lay upon the transgressor his transgression,
Punish him a little when he breaks loose,
Do not drive him too hard or he perishes.

The Epic of Gilgamesh

*I*T was, as I had feared, the most ignominious winter I had ever experienced. When things at last stabilized, and the sun remembered to climb again from its low December path, I began to think more and more about getting away.

But though the sun lifted itself higher and higher, it did not manage to cure the depression that stuck to me like the tentacles of some giant octopus. Once it became known that I had lost 355, my centerpiece, as well as so many other properties, the brokers, bankers, and other developers rapidly lost interest in me. Daniel Spear seemed particularly to revel in my downfall. I could sense it when we played squash. He was more cocky than ever, and more condescending every time he whipped my ass.

"Whatsamatter, Henry, losing your grip?" he said one day after he'd wiped me out, 21–6.

"Maybe you ought to take some lessons, Henry," he said on another occasion, then added, "though I'm not sure what difference it would make. Where's that old *spark,* kid?"

Normally I would have responded to his taunts by lifting my game, but now his tasteless digs only drained my confidence. So had the smirks and whispers in the locker room.

I saw Karen Viscomi several times, but it just wasn't the same. I didn't feel like mounting a campaign; my head wasn't in it. And I didn't like it when she talked about her other dates. Her fantasies had been one thing, but having other lovers irritated the hell out of me. She reminded me again and again that I was a hypocrite, and she was of course right. But when a woman tries to change me, I turn into a Missouri mule.

The advent of April. I needed to put an end to the dark, enveloping thoughts of winter. I needed to hear grass grow, see plants break through the soil, revel in flights of geese migrating north against the steely sky. I badly needed the resurgence of juices everywhere. I needed to feel alive. I had not gone bankrupt, but with the business situation as sour as it was, I was mired in depression.

The recession would eventually bottom out, and it would obviously take several more years for the excess amount of space to be absorbed. In any event, I'd had enough. It was time to go. But go where?

Iceland? England? Norway? Too early in the year. And long distances over water are best flown with two pilots to share the navigation and possible emergencies. Mexico and Central America? A friend had moved to Costa Rica. Maybe too hot. Maybe head west. Canadian Rockies, Alaska. That sounded good. Wildlife galore: wolves, Kodiak bears, moose. Salmon. Yes, probably the best fishing anywhere. Get the maps and landing approach plates from Jeppesen.

No plan, no reservations, no time frame. Away! Gone! I'm ready to sniff the spring winds for new, moist, full, fat, rich smells.

I lifted off Islip Runway 33 with full fuel, after having filed an instrument flight plan to Canada. The Canadians require you to take a rifle when you fly over remote areas, not to protect you from wild animals — although that's what you might think — but rather to be able to shoot game if you went down. I liked the idea anyway. Who the hell knows what I'd run into?

I took complete camping gear: small propane cook-stove, foldup saw, waterproof matches, sleeping bag (my whole senior year at Middlebury I slept in one; I hated to make my bed), freeze-dried food, a couple of those silver survival blankets, a bottle of scotch. And personal stuff.

I had decided to make my first fuel stop in Wisconsin. Not in a big city, but in a town with a seaplane base as well as standard facilities for landplanes. I wanted to renew my seaplane rating. Why seaplanes? I was going to Alaska; more seaplanes there than anywhere else.

Wausau. That fit. Wausau of the insurance company ads: the train station in the background: stability and continuity. Okay, Wausau.

Because the weather was CAVU and the forecast good all the way to Wausau, I chose to fly direct, utilizing GPS — Global Positioning System — navigation.

"I'd appreciate flight following," I requested from Clearance, "GPS direct Wausau, Wisconsin. Identifier, WSA. Altitude ten thousand, five hundred." I chose that altitude because the headwinds would be increasingly stronger the higher I flew. However, the higher the altitude, the lower the fuel consumption. I balanced the two criteria, and selected 10,500.

"Roger, three-five-five Hotel Mike, have a good trip."

The climbout was routine, engine temperatures normal. I leveled off at my final altitude and talked to other controllers I had been switched to as I passed through at LaGuardia and the thickness of aircraft around New York. The GPS indicated approximately four hours to Wausau. This length of flight lent itself to utilizing the autopilot.

There are times when I feel as though I've been invited into the halls of the gods, to share the magnificence of the ethereal, ever-changing skies, and to disconnect from my fellow human creatures. I felt at peace, as I often do when I've lifted myself through the gravities that hold me so tightly to earth's realities.

After western Pennsylvania, the ridges of the Piedmonts curled in parallels, pushed together as if by some giant kicking up from under the land. The flattening terrain between the ridges was filled with farms stretched into green squares and rectangles. En route, charts provided specifics for navigation and visual references like highways and railroads, rivers and lakes, airports, cities and towns. I watched the land passing underneath, as if on a magic carpet.

The cold front had devoured the moisture-laden clouds, and I could see strips of spring land showing lush, verdant colors; fields that had hibernated and were now awake. They were the farmer's children that he had nourished and cultivated. He had fed and cared for them over the long winter, and now they were delighted to do his bidding. I could also see his barns and homes tucked snugly between the clusters of oak and elm, and his driveway where his wife's car was parked. I wondered if she was content, or perhaps bored and lonely, the sweetness and excitement of their courtship and early years together replaced by work, her husband's and children's needs, the endless chores, the food, the canning and sewing, the books and accounts, the housekeeping.

Farther, over Ohio, Indiana, western Illinois, and lower Wisconsin I looked down on corn and grain towers in the towns, the gleaming railroad tracks that in times past had carried freight trains, cargos from autumn harvests. Now largely replaced by ten-wheelers that rolled down roads, highways, and superhighways, trailers that followed dutifully behind smoke-spouting diesel engines heading off to distant mills.

And the towns themselves, venerable and wise from years of wind-filled winters and scorching summers, one-streeters usually, the bank and post office, the 4-H clubs over the hardware or general store. And often a river running right through the town, or next to it, winding toward the Mississippi, Missouri, or Ohio rivers, cottonwood and willow trees lining its shores.

I flew through two time zones, the winter of my losses channeled further and further back into memory.

"Five Hotel Mike, you are twelve miles from Wausau. Report airport in sight, or switch to their frequency, one twenty-two point eight."

"Roger, Minneapolis. Unicom frequency one twenty-two point eight. Thanks a lot for your help. Hotel Mike."

Wausau Unicom reported a Piper J-3 Cub in the landing pattern and also an Ultralight nearby. Terrific. These guys had no radios. I slowed down from 190 knots to 120. Where the hell were they, especially the Cub that was somewhere in the traffic pattern?

"Wausau traffic, I'm a Cessna 414 Chancellor. I'll slow down as much as I can and also enter a wide left downwind."

"Yeah, that should help, Mister," was the reply from the ground.

"The pilot flying the Cub doesn't bother much with other planes."
I could just imagine some rachety old coot they had to lift into the
plane, get his feet on either side of the stick and on the rudders, then
scream out "Contact!" when they pulled the prop. Old planes didn't
have starters.

I made the proper announcement: "Twin Cessna, left downwind, Runway three-three." Where were those little putt-putts?

"Hurrah for you," came a snappy voice from the Cub. "Try to
land that thing without busting up a gear, okay? We don't like having
to fix up those fancy machines."

"No worries, friend," I replied. "I suppose she lands the same as
my jet fighter used to. Maybe a touch slower. You sure you got five
miles of runway?" I teased. "Looks a wee bit smaller from out here."

"Well, hotshot, if you fly as good as you talk, we'll see you on
the ground. Otherwise, we notify your next of kin."

"All right, Admiral," I said. "You're on. Twin Cessna on final."
I greased in the landing, knowing I was being observed by the locals. As I taxied to the FBO, the fixed base operator, I saw the Cub
come straight in, no downwind or base, just straight on in. In a non-
controlled airport such as Wausau's, it was not illegal. Just a little
worrisome.

I waited the three and a half minutes after landing for my engine
turbochargers to cool, then secured the controls, noted the Hobbs
time, opened the split door, watched the ladder fall, and the steps
open up. That pilot flying the Cub, should I give them a hand lifting
him out?

The Cub's split panels opened. I saw someone in a flying suit
swing out in one liquid motion. So, it wasn't an old pappy. In fact,
it wasn't a he at all, but a tall, lithe she. She strode over as I was putting on the pitot tube covers, then shook her long dark hair as she
removed her cap and headset. It fell into straight lengths about her
shoulders.

"Pretty swanky machine you have there," she said for openers.
"I bet she goes a mite faster than my Cubbie." She stood an erect
five six, plus or minus, and despite the bulk of her one-piece flight suit,
I divined a lovely figure. My guess was she was in her mid- to late
thirties.

"I watched that soft three-point landing of yours. A real beauty. How long you been punching holes in the sky?"

Her skin was light, but her features contained hints of more than one culture. As I knew when her almond-shaped eyes met mine.

"Since my mother flew me here from Alaska. She was a WAF in the Second World War. Ferried every kind of plane under creation. She also instructed any number of wet-eared cadets who almost always insisted on ground-looping their Stearmans. Did you know the Russians used women fighter pilots extensively? They flew those old 1930s biplanes and knocked out plenty of Nazi fighters in combat and bombers on the ground. Gutsy women, wouldn't you say?" There was a challenge in the way she framed her question.

"Uh, huh," was my eloquent response.

She hesitated, as if unsure whether or not to continue. "That plane, is it yours or do you work for some corporation? I run this place. Together with my brother."

She stuck out her hand. I took it. Her grip was strong and firm.

"Martin," I said. "Henry Martin." By then, a beat-up, eight-cylinder Olds had arrived. The man who stepped out looked about ten years younger than she, and a little taller. Solidly built, he had curly blond hair and sported a Pancho Villa mustache. His smile was broad and warm. A natural smile.

"Moving on or staying over? We'll give you a good deal on fuel," the woman asked. I liked her open, friendly style. "I'm Julie. Julie Roppel. This is Lenny Dale. He likes to be called Len. My brother."

"Well, heading west and north, but not on any schedule. The plane's my company's. I'm the company. With my brother, but I basically run it." I realized my explanation was beginning to sound complicated, so I changed the subject. "Flying in your family?"

Len's eyes lowered as he spoke. "Both our folks were pilots. They started the flight service here. The school, too." He looked at Julie. "Dad was killed climbing, Mom didn't last much after."

"I'm sorry." I didn't know what else to say. I remembered so many people saying that to me when Nancy died. I suppose there's not much else to say. If this young man had been my friend, I might have said that I knew how it felt, but I really didn't.

"Where you staying tonight, Martin?" Julie asked.

"The nearest decent motel, I guess." It sounded as if she might be thinking of offering me a room in her house. The last thing I wanted. The reason for the trip was to be alone, find myself. Find what was slipping away. Unless it was already gone.

She must have sensed my thoughts. "Best Western," she said. "Big indoor pool. You can borrow our car if you like."

It was not unusual for FBOs to give pilots a courtesy car to use even if he didn't buy fuel. But customarily I would gas it up if I drove more than a few miles. I liked these people. And also what she said next.

"And you're invited for dinner. We'll cook you a thick Midwestern steak you'll remember, plus some solid vegetables and pasta. You're not a recluse, are you?"

"No," I said with a laugh. "But I promised myself I'd stay solitary this time. That's the purpose of this trip." I was immediately sorry I had said that, and looked quickly over at her brother. "Do you have any WAC charts? I'm missing a few sectionals, too."

He nodded. "WAC charts no, but we have sectionals. C'mon into the office."

I put 355 HM to bed, tied her down, and put the control locks in place. Then I walked into their office.

Old photos had been tacked on the walls, together with newspaper articles and other memorabilia from the '30s, '40s, and '50s. Models of planes from those eras hung from the ceilings. A blackboard at the far end of the room was filled with names of student pilots on it and their schedules. "You've got an active flight school here," I said, glancing around the room.

"We sure do," Julie said. "And we're proud of it, too. Well, Martin, are you coming to dinner? We eat about six-thirty. Drinks first."

I wasn't sure whether I wanted to get to know everything about their family, so I stalled and asked if I could use the phone to call the Flight Service Station, to check the next day's weather. The forecast was for dense morning fog and low IFR conditions on and off indefinitely. Certainly not the kind of weather I would choose to fly in if I didn't have to. And I didn't. So it looked as if I might be in Wausau for another day at least.

I relayed the weather forecast to Julie and Len. "Yes, I'd like to have dinner with you," I said. "You'll have to tell me how to get there." Then, turning to Len: "Tomorrow, or maybe even later today, I'd like to rent one of your seaplanes. I'm rated, but it's been a while."

"Can't. We have a two-oh-six on floats, but it's in for its annual. Getting it ready for the season."

"Too bad. Mind if I take a few of these airplane magazines with me to the motel? I'll return them."

"Not at all," Len nodded.

"One of us will pick you up," Julie said. "About six-fifteen? Don't dress up. And remember to take a shower."

"Julie!" Len shook his head. "Sorry, Mr. Martin. She has absolutely no savoir faire," he said, mutilating the pronunciation.

Julie pointed at her brother. "Give them a little education and see what you get, Martin?"

"Henry," I said, "please call me Henry. Martin was what they called me when I was in the service."

"Sorry," Julie said. "No offense, but you strike me as Martin."

I decided not to argue. If the lady wanted to call me Martin, what the hell. "Six-fifteen," I said. "On the button."

The Best Western was exactly as Julie described: both levels of rooms opened up on a huge interior pool, at least a hundred feet long. Tables and chaise lounges were placed around it, as well as Ping-Pong and pool tables, and various other games. The manager told me that Wisconsin winters are long and that his customers came for weekends, fantasizing that they were in Florida.

I brought a scotch on the rocks up to my room and luxuriated in a long, hot shower, thinking of it as a kind of ritual purification.

My business problems receding, I began to feel better. I knew they were still there, as New York was still there. But I was here, fifteen hundred miles away. And I was going off to a good home-cooked meal. I had been too wrapped up in myself to recognize that there were other worlds besides mine. It was time to take a look at them, even though I would eventually have to get back to mine.

2

*T*HE telephone rang. It was the clerk at the front desk. "There's a lady here to see you, Mr. Martin," he reported. "What shall I tell her?" His smug tone told me that he had seen more "him-and-hers" in one week than most of us see in a lifetime.

"Tell her I'll be right down." I put on a new crimson-colored Lord & Taylor shirt, tucked it into my chinos, donned a pair of tasseled loafers, no socks, and slung a cashmere sweater over my shoulders, tying the sleeves loosely around my neck, European style. I descended the stairs to the pool area, was engulfed by the thick humidity, and quickly walked into the air-conditioned lobby.

Gone the shapeless pilot garb. Julie was wearing a pair of tight-fitting jeans and a jersey polo shirt that left little question about her measurements.

"Hello," I managed.

She waited, then said in a throaty voice, "Hi." She looked at me looking at her. After a couple of eons, she said, "Martin, your mouth is hanging open. Shall we go and have dinner?"

"Follow me, Martin," she said after a minute. As she swung around, I followed her every curve and how they moved. Outside was a red Alfa Romeo convertible, on the front seat of which was a large, standard poodle. "Sirius, in the back!" She started the motor and zipped away.

Her hair was jet black. I guessed one of her parents was native

Alaskan or Canadian. She was sexy, spunky, combative, and blunt to the point of being offensive.

She roared down the road, over Interstate 51, then pulled over sharply, screaming to a stop.

"Showing me how you can bring this mad machine to a halt in three seconds flat?" I gasped.

Julie turned and stared straight into my eyes. "I forgot to tell you, Sirius back there is my bodyguard."

I gave her a look that loosely translated meant: "What does that have to do with me?"

"I'll tell you what it means to you, Martin. I wouldn't want Sirius to hurt you."

"Look, we met an hour ago," I countered. "I'll be out of here in a day or two." I turned around and confronted a friendly dog who had been nudging the back of my neck. "You have nothing to worry about from me."

"Do you believe that, Sirius?" She turned to me. "Let's begin by getting rid of any questions you've been thinking up." She roared away from the side of the road without any warning or signals.

"All right. Was your mother here your real mother?"

Julie reached her version of cruising speed — roughly a hundred, I calculated. "No, not my biological mother, if that's what you mean, but without question my 'real mother.' Len is my adopted brother.

"I'm Native American," she said. "In case you hadn't guessed. Part Inuit, part Tlingit. Born and raised in Lake Minchumina. Nearest road is . . . there aren't any. It's a little place about a hundred miles northwest of Denali. Mount McKinley to you. When my French-Canadian father became a permanent drunk, he also became a wife beater and a child abuser, so we left him. First to Whitehorse in British Columbia, then to Fairbanks. I never heard anything from him until we learned he had drowned in late winter. He ran a trapline up there for furs. Went through the ice.

"At least he had the decency to cut the dogs loose when he figured they wouldn't be able to pull him out and that they'd only go down with him. After that my mother did her best. We moved to

Ketchikan, farther down on the Alaskan panhandle, between Juneau and Vancouver. I was sixteen when she died.

"Mom — Randi — had flown up to Alaska to retrieve her husband's body. He was killed climbing on Mount Elias. It's nineteen thousand feet, and damned unfriendly. So, Randi and I both needed someone. We met in Ketchikan. I was a mess. Wild. She took me back here to Wausau with her. It was her strength and love that turned me around. That was some years ago. When I lapsed, Mom pushed and pulled me. She made me work hard at school, after I had caught up. A scholarship to the university, a master's in education, but here I am flying. That's enough of the story for now, Martin."

We were traveling in an established residential area of Wausau. The streets were uniformly laid out, houses set on small, neat, rectangular lots. Julie didn't stop at the stop signs. "Got another question, as long as you've offered," I said. She nodded. "Been married?"

"I will answer that," Julie said, "but some other time. We're almost home."

We pulled up to a small, pre–Second World War, canary yellow, one-and-a-half story Tudor house on a street named Waukesha. Green shutters and flower boxes hung below multipaned, double-hung wood windows. An orange wind sock had been placed on the peak of the roof and a smaller one on the lawn next to a driveway that led to a separate two-car garage in the rear. In the small parking area, a basketball hoop had been attached to the side of the house.

"Welcome to Wausau Flight Services' Downtown Operations," Julie announced as we came through the front door. "Meet my Aunt Nadine. She and Mom used to fly all over the place in Alaska back in the '50s, when you had to fly by the seat of your pants. But then, you wouldn't know about that kind of flying, would you Martin? Aunt Nadine, meet our guest Henry Martin, a hotshot pilot from *New York*!"

I greeted Julie's aunt, who was serene by comparison and seemed amused by our badinage. She was in her late fifties, not unattractive. I assumed she and her dead sister, Randi, had always lived together. Her neatly combed gray hair was held in place by a tight barrette.

She was obviously not Julie's blood relative. You could see that she had been a handsome woman in her prime. She taught high school English and history.

"Can I make you a drink?" Julie asked. "I'll even open a new bottle of Stolichnaya." She smiled at me, then glanced at her aunt, who shook her head.

"I'll have a very light scotch and water, if you have any. Without ice. Really light."

The two women disappeared into the kitchen. The living room was cluttered with knickknacks and mementos, doubtless collected by Randi and her husband over the years. The rug was frayed at the edges. A pair of plain couches faced each other, with a homemade coffee table between them. A small TV stood in the corner. The furniture in the dining room and hallway was also simple. Not a frill in sight, but everything was spotless. I did notice several scrapbooks and assumed they contained photos and articles about Randi and her husband's flying exploits.

Len came down the stairs. In such a small house I had heard him taking a shower. Julie came back with drinks, together with some pretzels and potato chips.

"Well," I said after we were all seated and began to eat, "you folks are very nice to have me over. Frankly, it's a kind of hospitality I'm not used to."

"We figured you're used to eating rich food in those fancy New York restaurants. Out here in the provinces it's pretty simple. We're not big on finance and fashion," Julie said, a grin across her face.

"I suppose," I responded, "you have to depend on traveling salesmen and minstrels for news. I'll fill you in best as I can."

When Julie got up to get herself a second vodka, her aunt scolded, "Honey, don't you think you ought to hold off on another? There'll be beer with dinner you know."

Julie ignored her and poured herself a drink.

"I'm not worried, you understand," Nadine said when Julie was in the kitchen. "Not about our Julie. She can take care of herself." Her voice trailed off. "It's just that too much liquor is bad for you." Nadine looked around and shrugged. Len gazed the other way.

At one point during dinner, Len turned to Nadine and said reproachfully, "No Hammerschlanger's, Aunt Nadine? What's wrong, out again?"

"Aunt Nadine," Julie said. "Didn't you pick up a case? You promised you would."

"I tried, I really did," Nadine said, looking thoroughly admonished. "But they were plumb out. Again. I love that beer. Peter Bauer, at the deli, took down my request and said he'd see what he could do. Especially since we're such old customers."

I glanced around at them. "What's so special about that beer? You have lots of wonderful local brews. This is Wisconsin, isn't it?"

They looked at one another and shook their heads, as if I hadn't a clue. "Tell him, Julie," Len said.

"Hammerschlanger beer is without any question the best there is. Like love in a canoe," she replied.

"Is that their ad line?" I said. "If the beer's half as good . . ."

Instead of responding, all three suddenly broke into song: "Hammerschlanger's beer is like love in a canoe — fucking close to water!" They all roared.

Back home, I would have doubtless reacted badly if I'd been the butt of a joke, but here, I laughed. "Can I put in my order, too? Make it ten cases. I'll try to get a distributor for it back east."

It occurred to me that Julie might be a bit nervous in spite of her bluster, and perhaps that's why she was drinking. In any event, the evening was relaxed and fun. I was feeling good. Wausau was turning out to be exactly the right beginning for my odyssey.

Coffee laced with Drambuie was served after homemade walnut ice cream over homemade apple pie. Julie drove me back to the Best Western. I asked her if she wanted me to drive, but she shook her head.

She pulled in to the side of the motel next to the outside stairs that led up to my room. A few lacy clouds crossed over an almost-full moon, the air was scented and very much alive. It was quiet and so was she.

"Thanks for dinner," I said. "I really enjoyed it."

"What's up for tomorrow?" she asked. "Are you moving on?"

"No," I said. "Not with that weather."

"I'm glad," she said. "Why don't you call me in the morning? I'll show you our town." She leaned over and kissed me on the cheek, then once quickly on the lips. I dwelled on her eyes, deep set and very brown, now almost black. I kissed her tenderly on each eye, and then lightly crossed her lips with mine.

"I'd better go," she whispered.

I was on the verge of inviting her up for a nightcap, then remembered Aunt Nadine had said something about expecting her right back. Anyway, it had been a long day, I rationalized.

"See you tomorrow," I said, and kissed her again lightly on the cheek.

After she left, I went up to my room. In some ways, I was glad Julie had gone. I had just fallen asleep when the phone rang.

"Can't sleep. Want me to come by?"

"I'll meet you downstairs right where you let me off. Uh . . . where's Sirius?"

"At home where he belongs." She laughed. "He is very jealous."

I greeted her, we kissed, and ran up the stairs like two kids. I started toward her, but Julie pushed me gently back, pulled my sweater over my head, moved behind me, and let her fingertips wander across my back, from the spine outward, over my shoulders and neck, through my hair and across my eyes, then she pressed herself against me. She began to trace the muscles and curves on my back with her lips. Then, slowly, she touched the back of my body with hers, until I could feel all of her against me.

She moved around to face me. "I don't have anything to be concerned about, do I? You know . . ."

"Not a damn thing if you mean what I think you mean."

She took off her polo shirt, then let her jeans slip to her feet. Everything seemed in slow motion. She took my hands, reached around to the back of her bra, and together we unhooked it. Then she held my hands and pulled my palms from her hips slowly over her nipples, which became harder and harder. I heard the unevenness of my breathing. Hers too. She took my right hand and brought it down across the flat of her stomach, over her panties to the area between her legs. She trembled. I could feel her moistness as I moved my fingers under her panties and slipped into her.

We tumbled onto the bed, she under me at first until she said breathlessly, "No, wait." She removed her panties and pushed me down on my back, placed my hands above my head, and laid her body over mine, her legs closed until my erection was pressed down. She raised herself slightly, separated her legs, closing them around it. "Shh," she ordered. "Wait."

I was out of it, lost in pleasure and anticipation. Finally she spread her thighs wider. When I was fully inside, she moved in a circular motion until she became rigid and climaxed, emitting a long, animal-like moan, one I had never heard before. I quickly reached the point of no return and shuddered.

I fell into a doze and awoke when Julie pulled away, laughing. "Beats sleeping."

"Any day," I agreed.

"Or night," she added.

"I'm not sure I've had enough of you," I whispered.

"So what are you going to do about it, Martin?" she said.

"Henry," I corrected.

"So what are you going to do about it, Henry?" she said, moving her fingers artfully across my mouth, then her tongue across my chest. We made love again, and then fell into a deep sleep. I awoke some hours later when she bent over me and planted a full kiss on my mouth.

"I want to get home before the rooster crows. Aunt Nadine's liberal, but she doesn't have to know I spent the entire night with you. She'd say it was too soon. She'd be right."

"No, she wouldn't." I held her hands in mine. "We could have waited, but that would have been wasting valuable time. See you tomorrow. No, today. Sleep well."

"I will." Julie closed the door. I went to the window and looked out into the Wisconsin sky. The night bathed in contentment, the world completely at peace. I looked at Orion's Belt, then the Pleiades and Big Dipper. I tried to find Jupiter and Mars. Maybe I did, maybe I didn't. It made no difference.

3

*H*ALCYON days enveloped in saturnalia. The next two were simply fantastic. Julie and I played like kids. Everything was fun. Games of all kinds, new ones we invented. Dashing around in her Alfa Romeo with the top down, regardless of the rawness, mist, fog, and the cool temperatures. Her family seemed to accept me completely. Nadine kept an eye on us, but because Julie was happy she kept any comments to herself.

Sex taking showers, sex in the car, sex on the floor, sex on the edge of the bed, and any other novel idea either one of us had. We even did it in the corner of a furniture showroom. "Henry, I've always had a fantasy of doing it here."

"C'mon, Julie, you're nuts. Someone's sure to see us. Think of Aunt Nadine!"

"Quiet. Sit in that big armchair over there in the corner, and I'll get on your lap. If anyone comes along, we'll read newspapers and tell them we always try out furniture before we buy." And, by God, we did it, just like that.

The weather cleared. Two days became four. Aunt Nadine and Len were undoubtedly wondering when I would leave. More curiosity than a suggestion I leave.

"Henry," Julie said one afternoon as we were dressing, "this has been great fun, but I'm neglecting our operations. I'm shooting over for a few hours to relieve Len."

"Oh," I said to her, my disappointment obvious. She stopped tying her shoes and searched my face. I didn't want her to leave.

Even though we were so different, Julie and I seemed to belong together. I had never felt this way with Joyce, with Nancy or Karen.

"Would you consider coming with me?" Her face remained impassive, ancestral. "I've never felt anything like I do with you." I took a deep breath. "I need you, Julie Roppel. I want you."

Finally, she spoke. "I've had more fun with you — in and out of bed — than I can remember, Henry Martin. But it's all been play. We have to get back to our lives." She was candid. And maybe correct.

"Don't be so sure," I said. "We don't know how things might unfold. They could even get better."

She came over and folded her arms around me. "Nothing could be better, Henry. Nothing." She pulled away. "But if we're meant to be, it'll happen. Even with you battling it out back there in the trenches of New York, and me teaching flying here in Wausau."

I didn't want to plead, to pressure her. In the long run, I knew it would never work.

At dinner that night the spark was missing, as Aunt Nadine was quick to note. "What's the matter with you two?" Nadine asked. "Have a squabble?"

I shook my head. "No," I said, "Julie has to get back to work, and I have to leave tomorrow." Under the table, I squeezed Julie's hand.

"So you'll be separated," Nadine said matter-of-factly. "It's not the end of the world." She looked over at Julie, then back at me. "Henry, some more steak?" she asked.

"A small piece. I'll share it with my friend here." I turned to Julie, who nodded. "I have to say, at the risk of sounding corny, these last several days have been just wonderful. I was a complete stranger. You've made me feel like family. It's your cooking and the Hammerschlanger's!"

"You're still an eastern dude," Julie said, "but when you made that wide pattern the day you landed, we decided you couldn't be all bad. Very considerate of you."

"I was just trying to save my ass from a crazy."

The rest of the meal was filled with the same banter, but I felt a tug somewhere in my heart. "Henry," I told myself, "remember who you are. You don't fit in here."

That night, Julie and I didn't sleep very much. Too busy talking and playing. I made sure not to make any unrealistic promises, but I did say I would fly back to see her, whether in Wisconsin or in Timbuktu. I didn't know exactly when, but it would be as certain as the ice breaking up every spring.

I ate a solid breakfast in the motel, checked out, and drove to the airport. I filed a flight plan to Calgary, because the following day I wanted to fly to Banff and Lake Louise, then up the rift valley along the Fraser River, to Watson Lake, and then to Dawson in the Northwest Territories. I had been told the scenery was spectacular, the Canadian Rockies rising sharply into the skyscape.

Len topped off both wing tanks and together we preflighted. "She doesn't use much oil, does she?" he asked. I told him to sit in the left seat — the PIC's, the pilot-in-command.

"Wow. Look at all this stuff. As much as an airliner."

"Yeah, makes you feel comfortable. Stable in turbulence, too. Well, better be going." Outside on the ramp we shook hands warmly. "Say good-bye to everyone, and give that sister of yours a kiss for me."

He smiled. "Why don't you tell her yourself?" he said, looking over my shoulder. I turned around. Julie was walking in our direction, grinning.

"See you later," Len said, and headed to the office.

Julie and I stared at each other. I couldn't understand why she was wearing that happy smile.

"Well," she said, "aren't you going to help me with my luggage? I brought sandwiches. Where's our first stop? And, by the way, I'm about to demonstrate my flying skills in your fancy twin-engined bird."

"Julie! You're coming with me? This is fantastic!" I picked her up and whirled her around a full 360 degrees.

"Blame it on Len. He told me to go. An opportunity not to be missed."

She looked at me seriously. "Just so you understand, Henry Sabatini Martin, I get my butt back here by Sunday. No matter what."

"Why all this luggage? All you need is a frilly nightgown. Will Sirius survive without Mommy?" I asked as I tugged her suitcase from the seat of the Alfa Romeo.

"Aunt Nadine will spoil him silly," she said.

As an experienced pilot and instructor, Julie asked me if I had done a complete preflight inspection on the plane.

"Of course, just now. And before I left Islip, I had one of the other pilots do one with me, from stern to stem." Then I told her about the sabotage. She looked shocked.

"Anyway, I got here safe and sound. So if something was going to happen, it would have already." Julie nodded, and we climbed into the plane, but not before she checked the oil levels on the dipstick for each engine.

"Hope you don't mind," she said. "It's your life I care about, too. Both engines indicate over eleven quarts. Okay?" I nodded.

Suddenly I thought of New York. A mile-high skyscraper soared from nowhere out the Wisconsin fields. The Martin Companies. Big Business. Big Banks. Big Trouble. I burst out laughing.

"What's so funny, Henry Martin?"

"I just had a vision," I said.

4

"*W*ILL you get that silly grin off your face, Henry?"

I had swung 355 HM into the wind on Runway 15, after announcing that I was "taking the active."

"Julie, read the airspeed indicator and tell me when we accelerate to eighty-nine knots. That's rotation speed for this plane."

Julie leaned over to kiss me, couldn't reach, so she unbuckled her seat belt. "Julie," I chided, "we're about to take off! Put that thing on, will you?" Apparently I said that with the mike open.

"Hey," Len responded over the unicom, "you've got a stuck mike. I can hear you."

We both laughed. I wagged my finger at her, turned my attention back to the controls, held the brakes, watched the manifold pressure spool up, glanced over at the temperatures and the inverted Y's on the gauges. When Julie called out that airspeed had reached rotation speed, I pulled back on the yoke and the plane rotated.

"Three-five-five Hotel Mike departing northwest," I announced. "Thanks again for everything, Len. Especially for having a sister. Except I may have to dump her out at twenty thousand feet." I had tried to give him a hundred dollar bill, but he wouldn't accept it. I made a note to send him something special from Alaska. The thought had crossed my mind to send the family a moose — not a stuffed one — and name him Hammerschlanger, the First.

Because the weather was marginal, I had filed an instrument

flight plan. I contacted Minneapolis Center after changing from the Wausau frequency. "Radar contact established, one zero miles northwest of Wausau." Our flight path would take us through North Dakota and then Montana. Hang a right at Cut Bank, north 328 degrees heading into Canada, pick up Victor 21 to the Lethbridge VOR, then Victor 301 to Calgary. I estimated the time en route.

We flew between thick, pancake layers of clouds, on top of one soft gunmetal gray blanket and under another. I requested an altitude based on the winds aloft. When we reached 12,000 feet, I engaged the autopilot and concentrated on the navigation, glancing over every minute or so to observe the engine instruments and measure their temperatures.

"There's coffee back there, Julie, behind the last seat on your side. Just a couple of inches for me. Cups are next to the thermos." She nodded, licked my ear as she rose, a twinkle in her eye.

She returned with a cup of coffee in each hand. Stark naked. She put her cup in the copilot's holder and handed me mine, which I had trouble grabbing. I placed it in my holder, after taking a quick sip so it wouldn't spill. Then she moved her left breast gently against the right side of my face.

"Henry, let's do it up here. We can become authentic members of the Mile-High Club." She twisted so both firm breasts were pushed against my face, knocking my headset off.

"Are you crazy? We could be upside down, and I wouldn't know it." She licked the grooves of my ear, the end of her tongue teasing.

"Oh, Henry, you're a killjoy. What's autopilot for, anyway?"

I heard Minneapolis Center calling, a bit annoyed: "Five Hotel Mike, do you read? We've been trying to reach you. Switch to one thirty-two point two-five." I responded, my voice a little unsteady, checked in on the new frequency, and settled down.

"Tell you what, Julie. When we get to Calgary, I'm going to find the largest bed in town."

She held my hand and kissed it. "I'm going back to get us some junk food we can gorge ourselves on." She returned fully clothed and sat down in her seat. I turned off the autopilot and offered her the controls. She flew well, holding the heading and not climbing or descending more than 100 feet.

"Julie, can I talk about something?" I was feeding her a chocolate glazed donut. She gazed over at me. Her face was not only beautiful, it was beatific — which worried me.

"Julie, that expression on your face . . . I really care about you, but I'm all over the place emotionally. This past year has been a horror show for me. Know what I'm trying to say?"

She peered out of her window as if she hadn't heard. "Will you just let me fly this plane?" she asked quietly. "You're the one who's on his own." That sounded harsh.

I had warned her; now she was warning me.

"Ketchikan and farther up, Atlin on the Canadian side," she resumed, "I want to show them to you. Maybe Lake Minchumina, too. Near the Yukon River, at the base of the Kuskokwims." She squeezed my arm. "But I think Minchumina may be too far."

"Sounds great," I said. "Maybe Atlin first. I had planned Banff and Jasper, but the weather guys are forecasting a low that'll hang in for several days."

Within minutes, the weather did begin to deteriorate. "Minneapolis Center, three-five-five Hotel Mike, I'd like to go over to Flight Watch and come on back with you." They approved the change of frequency. Flight Watch advised that the weather would not be clearing in Calgary as originally forecast, that the warm front had developed into a stationary front. Calgary reported 600-foot ceilings with visibility two miles in light rain and fog.

The conditions, though marginal, were acceptable because the minimum altitude for an ILS approach is 200 feet over the runway threshold, plus a half-mile visibility. Still, I was concerned about the temperatures at the various altitudes. Pilots were reporting moderate to severe rime ice down to 4,000 feet. We did pick up an inconsequential amount of ice as we descended, through layers from 11,000 feet.

Julie called out the altitudes. We worked so easily together, sharing flying, something we both loved passionately. Once we were finally established on the Localizer for the ILS, I dropped the gear at the Final Approach Fix, broke out, and picked up the REILS — the runway end identifier lights. I put in the third ten degrees of flaps and rounded out, touching the runway on the three wheels.

"Not bad for a beginner," Julie commented.

We taxied to one of the FBOs on the field.

They recommended a nearby motel with rooms overlooking the airport. They also suggested the Calgary Air Museum, which we decided to visit later that afternoon. After lunch and after checking out the king-size bed in our suite. It wasn't a mile high, but we felt miles above the floor.

Next morning, before departing, I studied the radar in the weather office. It indicated thunderstorms moving from the southwest across our flight path. I didn't want to alarm Julie, but with the rain heavy and ceilings low, I sensed she knew the score. I set up the navigational aids, the VORs and GPS, checked the radios, the other instruments, and the de-icing equipment.

"Tell you what," I said, while we were taxiing to the departure runway. "You keep your eye on the radar for echoes and the Strike Finder for lightning. I'll watch the flight instruments. You do the radios." She put the end of her tongue into the corner of her lips. "We'll get up to twenty-four thousand feet, then we'll see the monsters," I said. "Only a hundred miles to get past them."

I didn't disclose that from a point north of Calgary to Atlin, we would not have radar coverage, and at some point north of St. John, we would lose all radio contact. That would mean relying on the GPS and pilotage, the dead-reckoning method used before modern-day equipment. You place a map on your lap to identify mountains, lakes, streams, and an occasional road or settlement. And you don't move your finger from your present position on that map.

The climbout proceeded normally, but at about 12,000 feet ice began to form rapidly on the wings and tail feathers. We both saw it. "Henry, the wings!"

With ice, it's a question of how thick and how quickly, whether it is rime or clear ice. Of the two, clear ice is more dangerous. You get the hell out of that situation fast, very fast. I had neglected to check temperatures aloft. The information would have indicated any inversions. Sometimes a high layer can actually be warmer than a lower one. What I wasn't sure of was at what altitude we would break out of the clouds and into the sunlight. When that occurred, sublimation would normally dispel whatever ice has accumulated. The critical element for flight is lift, based on the flow of air over the top of the wings. The weight of too much ice results in an uncontrolled descent.

"It's either up or down to get out of this," I said as calmly as I could. I glued my eyes on the airspeed indicator and concentrated on the feel of the controls. If the speed dropped off or additional weight of ice prevented maintaining our attitude or climb, I'd have to descend. The problem with that was, we would pick up additional ice before we got down to warmer temperatures. That can be typical of a cold front riding under a warm front, flying from warmer air into colder air.

The controls began to feel sluggish. I was getting concerned — a slight understatement — but didn't want Julie to be concerned. "Okay, let's see," I stated slowly, "if we . . ." I noticed the clouds beginning to thin just above us. "Hey, Julie, look up there." A few minutes later, we broke out and found ourselves bathed in the warmth and light of our wonderful star, the sun.

"All right!" I shouted. "Goodness is its own reward."

"Henry, you almost had me peeing in my pants. I've always dreaded ice. You're not very amusing." I looked over and was rewarded with a very broad smile. I reported the conditions to Calgary.

We flew to Fort St. John for a fuel stop after crossing over the VORs at Rocky Mountain House and Whitecourt, and finally the one at Grand Prairie. It was unfortunate we couldn't fly northwest from Banff, via the rift valley. This geological phenomenon had been created by the glaciered, precipitous Canadian Rockies, through the Purcell and Caribou Mountains, past Jasper to Williston Lake, a thin, fish-shaped, 150-mile body of water. Someone told me the scenery was spectacular: the way the Fraser River carves through the Monashee Mountains to Prince George and Lake Williston north of Mackenzie, its length seemingly endless.

The clouds at Fort St. John dissipated, and after a pleasant lunch downtown, we departed. We were rewarded with limitless vistas of the knife-edged, glacier-saturated Rockies. They were as rugged as I've ever seen mountains not smoothed by erosion: one empty valley after another, sheer walls and craggy protuberances pushed up sharply from the land, a few flat areas stocked deep in fields of snow, countless fractured glaciers, small but determined in their permanency. Flying over these pristine areas gave me the feeling we were intruding into places we didn't belong.

My thoughts turned quickly to my aircraft. There was no more reason for engine failure here than anywhere else, but going down here would be a wee bit different from landing at an airport in the East. Or anywhere.

I took photos with my wide-angle Panasonic and zoom shots with the Canon. At one point I noticed twin peaks with a U-shaped ridge between them, its edge pointed. I wondered why it hadn't yet been rounded by eons of erosion. I decided to check it out and headed down.

"Henry, you wouldn't. You're not going to fly *between* those peaks. Please! I don't have to be convinced about your skills."

"Just having a little closer look," I said matter-of-factly. But I knew I was showing off.

"For God's sake, Henry!"

We slid nicely between them, past and immediately over yet another deeply carved valley. I heard her sigh. An old friend once taught me to listen to sighs. Usually we're not aware when we make them. They provide a quick idea how someone really feels.

The clouds billowed up, forming gigantic cream puffs that tower tens of thousands of feet. We didn't want to mess with them and scooted around or between. Our little craft could be torn apart by severe updrafts and turbulence.

"If you don't mind, Henry Martin, I'd appreciate it if you didn't take my life in your hands without my permission."

"A deal," I said. "But your life was never in danger back there."

"Says you."

"Okay," I said. "From now on I'll ask permission."

As we continued, no longer in radio contact, I glanced between the GPS course deviation indicator and the magnetic compass. In these higher latitudes, the mag compass tends to be erratic, controlled by the proximity to major iron deposits, also by being closer to the magnetic north pole. So we only had the GPS.

After crossing the Rockies, we flew over the Stikine Range and Cassiar Mountains, between Dome Mountain and the Three Sisters Range, past the settlement at Dease Lake, its paved runway and seaplane base appearing like an oasis in a green desert. Such a different world here. I wondered if I could ever adjust to it.

5

*A*TLIN was an outpost, almost an illusion. Fed by one long, rugged dirt road from Whitehorse, the capital of the Canadian Yukon Territories, 120 miles away. You don't drive unless you have no other choice. You can also reach it by a gravel airstrip using a nondirectional beacon. Of all the instrument approaches, the NDBs are the most demanding to fly. But in the Midwest of the United States and remote places in the world, NDBs are the least expensive to maintain and therefore used almost exclusively. They operate on the low-frequency radio band, the same as for AM radio. For years, radio stations served as locator beacons.

I found Atlin both by watching the NDB needle point to the station and also by locating Atlin Lake: 100 miles north to south and shaped a little like a cormorant standing with its head raised. We descended to about 3,000 feet above the runway situated to the east, flew over the village, then up the lake, and turned back.

"Atlin traffic, Three-five-five Hotel Mike, six to the southwest, will enter a left downwind for two-six." I spotted a plane taking off, but heard no response. I learned quickly that any resemblance between methods and procedures in the Lower 48 and the bush is virtually coincidental. Perhaps this is because FAA is headquartered in Washington, D.C., thousands of miles away. But more likely it's due to the difference between the pragmatic needs and routines required up there versus those in populated areas. Bush pilots, more often than not, dispense with traffic patterns, wind direction, and radio calls. But there are no better pilots anywhere. Flying in the world's most difficult conditions demands superb skills. Also the determination to survive. Planes go down in bad weather. Comrades make incredible landings in implausible places, fly out downed pilots, or fly in the parts necessary to repair the damaged aircraft.

Atlin and its magnificent lake were cradled in a valley between two staunch mountain ranges. The village spills down a decline to Atlin Lake, its edge dotted with homes, docks, a few boat ramps, a single church, plus the Atlin Inn and cottages. Of particular interest to me and those who utilized their services was Jerry and Susan's Summit Air Charters. Fifty-five-gallon gasoline drums lined their dock, plus paraphernalia used by their seaplanes to transport people and equipment. Several streets ran from the top of the knoll straight to the water. The false fronts on gable-roofed buildings were reminiscent of Gold Rush days. Log cabins and clapboard houses were painted a multitude of bright colors.

Flowering grasses with fluffed, wheat-type tassels in empty lots. Spring and summer flowers like phlox and Queen Anne's lace like ossified snowflakes. Moose racks over front doors, dogs sleeping or wandering, and deep piles of stacked wood, always a reminder of the deep winters. Men who worked twelve to fifteen hours during long-lit summer days. Trucks with all their lights on, the four-wheel drive workhorses, and the Atlin Trading Post, run by congenial Native Canadians who all knew one another, and knew that most would never live anywhere else.

A man in a large pickup truck stopped near the fuel tanks and observed the plane as we taxied off the runway. I waited to cool down the engines before shutdown. He continued to watch us as we opened the door and stepped down the ladder onto the gravel.

He drove closer, and from his window said, "Helluva flying machine you got there. Beautiful paint job. Pretty as anything. You, ah, need anything?" He left his truck, came over, put out his hand, and offered a smile. "Tate. Jerry Tate. I run the flying operation here. Summit Air Charters, with my wife Susan. And a seaplane base on the lake."

I liked him immediately and got the feeling that he knew exactly what he was doing, knew this country and how to fly in it; also that he genuinely wanted to help us. Jerry was medium height, in his early forties, probably slightly heavier and thinner on top than he had once been, and physical in the sense that he appeared to be up to whatever he undertook. The smile on his face seemed a harbinger of outright laughter.

"Thanks," I said. "We're up from the States, hoping to spend a little time here. How's the fishing?"

"If you promise not to tell, fantastic. Our lake trout cooperate nicely. Average ten to fifteen pounds. And salmon all through the rivers during their runs. I fly hunters around who try to take mountain sheep and goats; we also do a big operation hauling salmon off the Taku River. Even have two Shorts for heavy shipments."

"You really have a Short?" Julie asked. "And I know you, Tate. Some years ago my mother and I flew in here. On our way down from Fairbanks. You helped us with a bad magneto. We were heading down to Wisconsin."

"Yeah, now that you remind me. The Short sure is a funny-looking bird, but does a whole bloody lot of work. Quite a pilot, your mother. Yeah, I remember her clearly now. Didn't she ferry planes during the war? You're just as pretty now as you were then, ah . . ."

"Roppel. Julie Roppel. My mother's name was Randi."

"I wasn't sure if you were here before, even though you said you wanted to show me Atlin," I said.

"Got to leave a few surprises for you . . . Jerry, this is Martin. Henry Martin. Back east he's a big shot. But that stops at the border. Right, Henry?"

Jerry and I laughed. "Right you are," I said.

"I can give you a ride into town and set you up at the hotel," Jerry said. "The only place we have. But I'd suggest one of the cottages near it on the lake. Hotel's pretty grungy. But the only place to eat dinner. There's also the Pine Tree Cafe for breakfast and lunch.

"I'll set you up with Ian, Ian McGregor, our best fishing guide," he went on. "Oh, the bar at the hotel's where everybody goes. Won't take you long to meet folks."

This was exactly what I had been hoping for. Days and nights in this magnificent place at the end of the world. I probably should have been in touch with the office, but I didn't want to spoil my time in Shangri-La. I felt freer than I had since . . . since I was that cocky kid blasting around in Marine jets. How much of it, I wondered, was Julie's effect on me?

We settled into a rustic cottage right on the lakefront. Rustic is a polite way of saying run-down. But so what if the bathroom door didn't close all the way, or the water in the sink kept running, or the shower was an old rusted enclosure, or the floor wasn't level? Who cared? The view from our porch was spectacular. We saw Cathedral Mountain directly across the lake, and other glacier-frosted mountains, their peaks and ridges encompassing most of the lake. There were pine- and spruce-covered islands near us and a lovely log-built house on one of them. It reminded me of sections in the Swiss Alps.

It was mesmerizing to watch the pontoons on Jerry's Beaver break the water as he took off parallel to the shoreline: first the roar of the powerful engine as he put the plane up on the step — the lifting of the plane's weight onto the top of the water — then the buildup of speed and smooth liftoff, the lake's surface filling in the grooves created by the indentations of the pontoons. The plane climbed higher and higher to cross the mountains. I imagined what Jerry saw as he flew through the splendor stretching across the Sloko and Florence Ranges, the tongue-like Llewllyn and Tulsequah Glaciers, toward the Tulsequah and Taku Rivers. And the incredible Devil's Paw thrusting its knife-edged triple peaks sharply into the sky at 8,500 feet.

I stepped outside to give Julie time alone, but when she was in the shower that first afternoon, I slipped out of my clothes and joined her. "Henry, how did you know this turns me on?"

"Doesn't everything?"

"Stand behind me and soap me up. And even if I beg you to go faster, don't listen to me."

"You talk too much," I said.

I began with her neck and the back of her shoulders, then had her raise her arms straight up, slowly bringing my soapy fingers over the front of her shoulders, even more slowly sliding them near and then onto her breasts, circling her nipples in ever smaller circles, then once, twice over them, scooping my hands until my fingers found her now-hardened nipples.

"Oh, Henry."

Down across her flat stomach, hesitating, around her belly button, across her hips, bending down to reach her thighs. In deliberate motions, down her calves to her ankles, my body pressed against her back and rear, my arms around her lower hips, my fingers moving up her inner thighs to the beginnings of her pubic hair, slowly, ever so slowly, feeling her body gyrating, her hands reaching back behind my head.

I made her stand like that, even though she wanted to face me and put her arms around me. Then I moved in front of her, water splashing my face. She moved her body against mine and held my penis, lifted one leg and guided it in. She strongly pulled my buttocks to her. We both came at the same time, screaming into the cascading shower, laughing, holding each other up.

Still entwined, we struggled onto the bed, dropped, and slept for several hours. I woke up first and looked at Julie. The landscape of her face, her high cheekbones, black eyebrows and eyelashes, her completely contented look. And with her arms thrown around me, her head turned inside my left arm, her mouth slightly ajar against my shoulder — had I ever felt this way before?

Julie purred as she woke. She kissed me softly.

"Julie," I whispered after a moment. "I want to be your lover. And not just for one week."

Her eyes opened fully. "You don't need to say that. Henry Sabatini Martin is not the type to make rash statements. Think of your reputation."

I didn't enjoy the teasing. I put two fingers on her lips, and pulled her close. I peered into her eyes, wanting to see every thing that had happened in her lifetime. "Julie, the simple fact is . . . I'm afraid I've fallen in love with you. It's terrific and illogical, but true."

"Be careful." She reached over and took my hand. "I'm different from anyone you've known, besides we're up here in Shangri-La."

"You *are* different," I said. "We're opposites. That's probably what makes it great."

I hesitated, then said slowly, "I never really loved anyone before. In my own way, I loved Nancy. For a while anyway. And one or two others, but oh so briefly. But my ego always got in the way. Kept me from losing myself, letting go. *I* was the problem. Whatever was happening between the other person and me. I guess I was only focused on me." I held both of her hands.

Julie pulled one hand away and laid it gently on my face. "We've only known each other for, what, a week?"

"Julie, I said what I did because it's the *emmis*. That means the truth. Remember I'm the one who tried to warn you."

Julie got up, put on my shirt, which bottomed out below her buttocks, and walked out onto the porch. We both turned to see Jerry taxi the seaplane to his dock across the small bay. It was seven in the evening. This far north, in late spring, it would be many hours before the sun settled down for the night.

All of a sudden, she turned and looked straight into my eyes.

"I don't love you, Henry. Not yet, anyway." She leaned against me. "You're exciting and fun. But Henry, there's something else."

"You mean, there's *someone* else? If you've got someone else, then how can you be sleeping with me?"

"Hold on, Martin! I know *you* have women waiting for you back in *New* York." She laid stress on "New" and tried to mimic an eastern twang. "No one owns me. And no one owns you. We do what we want, with whom we want, when we want, right? We don't answer to anyone but ourselves. Isn't that how we both want it?"

I put on a pair of khaki shorts, opened the screen door, and jumped down on the grass. A breeze crossed my face, touched with the scent of spruce. I ambled toward the beach, my hands deep in my pockets.

"Henry, wait a minute," Julie yelled from the porch. She dashed barefoot to catch up with me.

"Julie, you're not dressed," I said.

"Oh, I don't give a shit." She put her arms around my neck and pressed herself against me. "We came up north to have fun. Don't spoil it."

She pulled away and pulled me by the hand. "Hey, let's put

our tootsies in the lake." We meandered to the small beach and sat peacefully on a large rock. Julie draped an arm over my back.

"I've been serious with several guys and married two of them," she said. "I promised myself I wouldn't get emotionally involved again until I had become a whole person. As far as Bill is concerned, he's out on ships most of the time. We've had this — I don't know — affair, I guess. The last five years. I'll never marry him. He knows that. I don't love him, but we have had great times."

She scrutinized my face, which I was trying to keep tough and square-jawed. "You *seem* to be listening, Henry. But are you? Do you know what Amelia Earhart told George Putnam fifty years ago on their wedding day? 'I shall not hold you to any medieval code of behavior, nor shall I so be similarly bound. I must be free to pursue flying.' "

She sat on my lap and leaned back against me. "I find you more interesting than any man I've ever met. And that's not a load of Hammerschlanger's, either." She slapped both her feet on the water, beaver-style.

I must have had a hangdog look on my face. She got up, leaned down, and planted a soft kiss on my mouth. I could feel her warmth on my thighs.

Normally I would have become aroused, but I was too busy absorbing her words. I knew my feelings for her wouldn't last indefinitely unless they were reciprocated.

"Mom tried to get me to see how I kept repeating the same mistake," Julie continued. She pointed to a bald eagle cruising near one of the islands, then looked back at me and laughed.

"What's so funny?"

"Just thinking." Julie cleared her throat. "You wouldn't want to be another one of my mistakes, would you?"

"I don't plan to be," I said. "I want to know everything about you I don't already know."

"I'm not ready."

I grabbed a stick, began to break off small pieces, and tossed them one by one into the water. "Women responded to me in New York because I was the king of the pile. Except, I came out pretty empty."

"Look, I don't want to hurt you, Henry, but that doesn't change things." She turned and faced the cottage. "I'm getting chilly. Let's get dressed and go to the lounge for a drink." She pushed me. "You've made me ravenous. I mean, for food."

I could feel anger mounting, but vowed to keep it in check. But first, I needed to know why I felt angry.

Jerry was right about the bar. It was obvious who was local and who was not. Except for a few tables where men talked intently with one another the people were extremely friendly. Julie and I were greeted with hellos and nods. A few we had been introduced to by Jerry earlier in the day stood up as we passed their tables to shake hands and to introduce us to others.

Jerry walked in with Sue, waved us over to a long table already occupied by a number of locals. All were talking. I went up to the bar to fetch drinks. Julie wanted a vodka. The bartender, a good-looking blonde, also doubled as the cocktail waitress. In the photo on the wall behind the bar, three men were mooning at the camera.

"This half-wit pilot we hired didn't check a high oil temperature reading he was getting," Jerry began after I asked him during the second round of beers about unplanned landings and takeoffs from glaciers.

"We didn't hear from him when he was supposed to call in from Juneau," Susan chimed in. "So late in the afternoon — this was October and the lake was frozen over — Jerry tracks this guy's route."

"Yeah," Jerry said, "there he was, sitting on his fat ass up on this fractured ice slope. At least he hadn't completely wrecked my plane. I checked it out from what I could see." He took a huge gulp of beer. "I wouldn't say there was a decent place for me to land, but what the hell, we had to get the bugger out of there. My insurance doesn't cover dumbness.

"The kid never had the right feel for mountain flying. I had to let him go. Hear from him now and then. He made captain with Air Alaska. Nice and easy. Those guys steer their planes, punch numbers into their computers. I think I'll take me one of those jobs. Make a whole lot more. And all those gorgeous stewardesses!"

Sue punched him hard. "Flight *attendants,* you sexist bum."

We were halfway through the second round. Julie, I noted, was on her third vodka. "Well, when I was a kid, probably a little like the one you described, I flew Marine Air." I glanced over at Julie. I had already told her about that part of my life. But not much about the rest. Perhaps I was getting tired of hearing myself brag.

"Made this bet, another jet pilot and myself. A guy named Clancy." I didn't need to embellish. "A stupid, dumb challenge — to fly under a bridge. I made it, but a shrimp boat got in Clancy's way. He veered, hit the end of his wing, cartwheeled, and went down in flames, as they say. They threw me straight into the infantry and over to Vietnam."

I looked at the faces of my listeners. Julie shook her head.

"Male macho shit," she slurred. "You guys give me one swift pain in the ass. Why is it you men" — her eyes settled on me — "are convinced that bravado bullshit impresses us?"

No one said a word, staring hard into their mugs and glasses, hoping Julie would stop. No luck.

"I've seen the way men treat women. Firsthand. Spent the first sixteen years of my life in places like this. I'm a half-breed. My father, the bastard, kicked my mother and me around. Other stuff, too, but I won't go into the shitty details." No one moved, but I put my hand on her arm. She gave me a dirty look and took another sip of her drink.

"You seem to have all the goddamned answers, Julie," I said, testily. "I'd love to be as wise and mature as you. Maybe we males do that stuff because you women encourage us to perform."

I stood up, but she pulled me down. "Henry, I talk too much. Forgive my bad manners." She threw back her head and slugged down the rest of vodka number three.

"Hey, Jerry," I said, trying to change the mood, "how about some chow? Does the meat have hair on it, or is that just a rumor?"

"Wrong," he said. "Hair is the appetizer. You get through one of our meals, we make you an honorary citizen."

"What else do I get for being such a cooperative tourist?"

"A ride in my seaplane and maybe an opportunity to use a busted parachute." He put out his hand, which I grabbed and shook with both hands.

Later, back in the cottage, I reflected on Julie's scene, and also how I handled it. I shouldn't have come down so hard on her, especially in front of the others. She does drink too much, I thought. She also has a problem trusting.

6

THE next few days were an exquisite blur. As addictive as the weather. We fished almost as obsessively as we made love. Ian McGregor, a young man in his early twenties, half white and half Native Canadian, whizzed us thirty miles down the lake one morning to a narrow strait between a small island and a bouldered shoreline. We wagered five bucks for the first lake trout and another five for the largest. I nailed a twelve-pounder, Julie caught two, and Ian two. Several more insisted on trying to scrunch my hook. Ian landed the largest.

On our return to Atlin, Ian pointed to movement in the water about two hundred yards in front of us. Two bears, one black and one brown — unusual that they were together — were swimming between two islands. We circled widely to take photos, but that made them reverse direction. Since they were probably exhausted, we scooted out of their way. They scrambled up on shore, walked, then ran to the other side of the small island, swam again the short distance to the mainland. They disappeared quickly into the woods.

A few intimate picnics on secluded, pristine beaches, soft walks on deserted dirt roads in and near town, huge breakfasts at the Pine Tree, conversations with people only too willing to chat, afternoon naps, a cocktail for Julie on our porch or down by the lake, delicious trout steaks at a cookout with Jerry and Susan and their three kids, beer and dinners at the "exclusive" Atlin Inn. And sex at unpredictable moments during the day and in the middle of the night.

Everything was perfect — except, though I found Julie as loving as ever, she was somehow remote. Or was it I who was remote, angry that she wouldn't commit herself? I had fantasies of thrashing her ancient mariner on some fog-enveloped pier in San Francisco.

That evening Jerry and I replaced the broken wires on one of the blades of the propeller on the left engine, so that ice wouldn't form on the prop. One thing less to worry about. Jerry dropped me at the cottage to pick up Julie; we were having dinner at the Inn. I noticed a candle burning on the porch table, wildflowers in the center, dishes and glasses set next to a bottle of white wine. I stepped through the door to find Julie standing by the stove. Fresh trout steaks were being pan fried, the smell of butter filling the cool evening air.

"Well, *Mum*," I said with a mock British accent, "glad it's not the same old fishcakes again." I pulled her to me. "Now here, *Mum*. I got you some nice, fat bear meat. Had to hand-wrestle the sonofabitch for three hours."

"*Mum*, is it? Eat this here grub, because it's all I could steal. Spuds in the oven and veggies from Susan." We kissed. "Eat heartily, old boy. I have big plans for you later."

I resisted the frequent temptation to call the office, though I couldn't help wondering whether Cal, Ken, and Ari were making the right moves. They probably needed my input. I had hoped to escape all that, but never imagined I would succeed so well. Thanks to Julie. I was smitten, like some schoolboy. Even if I was talking to someone else, I would find myself trying to overhear what she was saying.

We discussed moving on, talked about our choices, and realized we'd never get as far as Minchumina. The week was rapidly winding down.

"Okay," Julie said, "stop overnight in Juneau, then down to Ketchikan. Things I want to show you. I can fly to Minneapolis from there. Len will pick me up."

"I'll drop you off. Unless I can convince you to come back to New York with me."

"New York? Not for me, Henry. Sounds exciting, but it's not fair being away any longer."

"C'mon, Julie. It's not as if you're going to get fired," I said, annoyed. She stared at me, without comment.

We packed, I paid our bill, and walked over to Summit Air to settle up for the sightseeing flights and say good-bye. Jerry was about to make a flight to Skagway, pick up hunters in Juneau, then drop them off at Ben-My-Chree, a village near Mount Swizer. He told us they were a group of attorneys and doctors, some from Atlanta, the others from Chicago. "They always talk trophies," he said. "Here more to compete than to learn."

"Look, Henry," he counseled, pulling me over to the map on his wall. "In that jet of yours, you could bomb over to Juneau in probably thirty minutes, but I promise you terrific sights if you fly this other way. Now, pay attention. I don't care how many instrument approaches you've shot. More experienced pilots have bought it in Juneau than most anywhere. It's all off NDBs. You make damn sure you don't mix them up — Elephant, Coughlan, and the last one at Mendenhall. You got that? That plane of yours is too pretty to crunch up. And I have too much to do here to come and bail you out.

"Julie," he said, turning to her, "you keep swatting him to make sure he stays awake. Altitude! You'd better have enough." Jerry put his hand on my shoulder. Sue came over and kissed us both.

We climbed into Jerry's pickup truck, with instructions to leave it at the airstrip. After a thorough pre-flight and the other mandatory inspections, we took off, dipped low over the seaplane base, wiggling our wings in farewell.

Jerry was right. I flew down the channel at about 200 feet, next to the beautiful glacier we had seen from Ian's boat, its melting waters cascading over boulders to pour into the lake. Then up the vast, unfolding Llewllyn Glacier, its gigantic tongue of fissured ice, the peacock blue and turquoise in the paralleled gashes so bright it was distracting. Wide brown bands, speckled with dirt and rocks, continued down the frozen flow as far as we could see. Jerry had told us that glaciers pick up debris as they move on their inexorable journey down from the heights where they are formed.

We turned past Lake No-Lake, a small body of water. In August, when the temperature rises to a particular number, the lake drops as much as 800 feet in just a few days. Enormous amounts of water bottom into the Taku River, leaving towers of ice several stories high on the lake's bottom. We followed it and dropped down quickly to that roaring river, browned with mud and silt. The Taku is one of the largest salmon rivers anywhere. Chinook, Cohos, Sockeye, and Pinks all take their turns swimming back upstream to spawn in small tributaries. It's almost incomprehensible how a salmon leaves that precise location, travels thousands of miles in the Pacific or Atlantic for years, and then miraculously returns to the exact spot where it was born. Provided, of course, that there are no dams in its way, no men or bears to terminate its run.

We passed into Alaska from Canada. Fortunately the weather had improved over the forecast, the ceiling nice and high, around four to five thousand feet. I called the tower, observed several seaplanes flying in the same direction I was. Juneau has a long, single runway for landplanes and a water runway adjacent to it for seaplanes. Strange for flatlanders like me, but a common arrangement in Alaska.

I followed an Alaska Airlines 737 over the hill that rises sharply a short distance from the end of the runway. An amazing setup for an airport; there wasn't any other area flat enough. Jerry hadn't mentioned it, but it was clearly marked on my instrument approach plate.

We parked, grabbed a cab, and headed into town. Julie had been touting the Alaskan Hotel, a former brothel from the early days, replete with small rooms for men and their favorite prostitutes. The current owners, who were from New York, had refurbished it, and each room had a sink and toilet. The nineteenth-century lobby was restored, social rooms, bar, and halls looking exactly as they had during the Gold Rush days.

We checked in, walked on Franklin Street through town, past the dock where seaplanes were resting alongside. At this time of year there weren't many people. Later, cruise boats would unload tourists who would crowd the shops. I had seen a documentary once, not a very flattering one — squat, short-haired women in slacks, pot-bellied men in shorts, cameras slung around their necks, throwing away money on mementos of their trip to the rugged north. Early the following morning, after a night during which we had heard every groan and grunt, every squeak of the bedsprings from the other rooms, I said, "Let's get the hell out of here. Unless you don't want to get any sleep." Julie readily agreed.

"Sorry, Henry. I remember it as better. Maybe because I was young and impressionable."

The previous afternoon we had passed the Barinhof, a first-class hotel. After a sumptuous breakfast, we checked in. We signed up for a rafting trip, plummeted down the Mendenhall River over a short but exciting series of rapids. Drinks at the bar, a cozy dinner, and luxuriant sleep. But in the middle of the night I woke up in a sweat. Only three more days.

We packed after a full breakfast in our room. "What about a pop over to Sitka on our way down?" I asked Julie. "See all that Russian architecture. Wasn't Sitka Alaska's first capital?"

"The Kiksadi, a branch of the Tlingits, occupied the area first. My people, my mother's, around Ketchikan are Haida and Tlingit. Gets a little complicated. You interested?" she asked.

"I really am. Sometime I'll tell you all about my screwy Italian-Jewish amalgamation."

"You mean you're not purebred either?"

"An affiliation of disparate tribes," I said. "What about your mother's?"

She ran her hand through her long black hair. "It would be easier to take you into the museum in Ketchikan. After that we'll go to Saxman, the Tlingit village. Quite an array of totem poles, each with its own tale." She kissed the tip of my nose.

We left Juneau, heading south down Stephens Passage. The tree line was at about 3,000 feet. Fishing boats dotted the channel like toys in a bathtub. We turned west at Frederick Sound, and near Point Gardiner I spotted what I had hoped to see: a whale. "Look at that!" A huge slap of a tail on the water, its splash impressive even at our altitude. "He dove!"

"Circle the spot. He'll surface." And surface he did, for another impressive and graphic display. "He could be playing," she said.

The Sitka weather was going down, so we turned south. We crossed Kuiu Island, Sumner Strait, Point Baker, and Prince of Wales Island, the third largest island in the United States, after Hawaii and Kodiak. Large swatches were cut into the deep green forests on the hills, not quite clear-cutting, but enough to become concerned about excessive timbering. Farther down, in Clarence Strait, near Thorne Bay and Kasaan, tugboats were towing endless rafts of logs.

Eventually, we caught sight of Ketchikan. At Julie's suggestion, we did a fly-by, with permission from the tower at the airport. What a beehive! Everything comes and goes through the Tongass Narrows: cargo barges, floatplanes, ferries, fishing and logging ships. Houses hung off steep slopes, interspersed with splotches of evergreens. The airport, I quickly learned, consisted of a single runway that was higher than the terminal, requiring a taxiway up the hill from the terminal below. We landed, and I asked the FBO to top off the gas tanks.

After we passed through the terminal to get transportation into town, I was struck by the unusual set-up. "What's this, Julie? You have to take a ferry to get over to Ketchikan from the airport? Is that the way they make money around here? Get you by the ferry?"

"No, by the souvenirs. And in the old days, our sporting women. Creek Street. Really quaint.

"We'll stay at Cape Fox Lodge," she continued. "A short tram goes up to it. You overlook the harbor, and the food's excellent."

Two more nights and days, I thought. I felt a rock in my stomach.

"What's the big sigh for, Henry?" Julie asked.

"Not looking forward to Sunday." I squeezed her hand. No response.

I registered us as "Mr. and Mrs. Martin" and made a point of saying "my wife and I" to the clerk at the desk. We had a quick bite, then checked out the Five Star Cafe bookstore. At the museum, Julie explained how the southern Alaskan Indians differed in custom and development from Alaskan Indians from other areas in the state. Some thrived on salmon and goods they made, others did less well.

At dinner, over a second order of succulent oysters, Julie said, "I want to say something to you, Henry. Despite myself, I'm beginning to see *us* as a possibility." She paused. "But deep down, I believe that marriage is just plain wrong. Or any kind of permanent commitment. At least for certain people. It can destroy a good relationship.

"Tell me I'm wrong, Henry," she went on. "Tell me how you and

I would make it, for God's sake. We're so different. Different values. Different goals. Different backgrounds. That's the truth regardless how we might rationalize it."

"I think you may be confused," I said gently. "About freedom. Unless you've convinced yourself that freedom means not making a commitment. From making that flying business of yours a lot better."

"You mean *bigger,* don't you?" she replied. "You easterners always think bigger is better." I flagged the waitress down and ordered another ale. "What else are you thinking?" Julie asked. "I mean, aside from the business."

"How about a contract, renewable every five years?"

"How about annually?" she said.

She was right. We were so different, I thought. I knew that Julie didn't care about money and power. New York would be the last place she'd want to live. And I knew that when I returned to New York I would be fighting for my life. So I wasn't quite sure how to answer her.

"Well?" she asked. "My go-getter, my problem-solving Henry Sabatini Martin is stumped?"

"Not stumped. Pondering."

She sighed. "Henry, we're shadow-boxing. You lunge — I back off. I lunge — you back off. That's not good."

"Okay, I do have something on my mind." She was looking directly into my eyes. "This is a little sensitive, but I have to mention it."

"Now's the time."

"Julie, you described some of your close calls up there in your flying machine. Could it be your reactions were too slow? You know what I mean. Your drinking. Every pilot is taught in ground school that liquor does not make you quicker. Anything but."

"Martin, I can cut it out right now if I wanted. I may drink, but I fly sober. Okay? Why don't you get off my back?" She got to her feet. "I've lost my appetite."

"Sit down," I said quietly. "Please!" Julie turned and walked out.

I ordered a scotch, picked at my dinner, and walked back to the Cape Fox Lodge an hour later. The rain was coming down horizontally, but only a fraction of the average of 300 inches a year. I walked to the window and watched it. Julie was fast asleep. After several minutes, I undressed and slipped quietly into bed.

When we awoke, neither of us brought up our exchange at dinner. Better that way, I decided. It was our next-to-last day.

Julie took me to the Tlingit village, just south of Ketchikan.

"Big time totem poles, Henry. Originals collected from abandoned villages and cemeteries on Tongass, Cat, and Pennock islands. And from Cape Fox. Plus reproductions made from cedar logs in that building over there."

The poles stood like sentinels, their dignity and bearing commanding reverence. Each was expressive in its striking detail. And each carried its precise message. I didn't have the faintest idea what they symbolized.

We sat on a bench in the center of a dozen of the denizens, each thirty to forty feet high. "Displays of spirit power and wealth were critical to my people," she began. "I won't take you though all the history, about tools, food and diet, and hunting methods. Their winter dwellings were very significant. Four to six families, twenty to thirty people. A single hearth and smoke hole plus low-rising platforms used for living quarters. You get pretty friendly with your cousins.

"Only the Tlingit and Haidas carved totem poles. Now get this — totems were *not* images of deities, as those self-centered missionaries wanted to believe. They generally memorialized a man's personal history and also signified his wealth. The Raven was central to Tlingit and Haida beliefs. The raven was supernatural, a trickster in their myths and legends.

"You see other animals and bears. Also the Thunderbird. The Tlingits were divided into thirteen units, not 'tribes,' because there was no political unity. Their shamans were powerful communicators with the spirits. They could foretell future events and had healing powers. I'm going to be one in my next life.

"That's the essentials," she said. "I could go on for hours, but class is over for today. Now can we get smashed in our room, make love, and eat if we get hungry?"

"Roppel, you continue to amaze me. I suddenly realized how

little I know about either of my parents' cultural histories." I stopped abruptly.

"What's the matter?" she asked. "So you'll learn about them."

"No, that's not it. It just made me think, here I am forty-five and I don't have any children." I hesitated, then moved my face closer to hers. She gave me the hint of a smile but didn't say anything.

We followed her plan point by point. Several hours later we decided we were at last hungry. Over a candlelit corner table in the Cape Fox restaurant we ordered several appetizers instead of entrees, capping them with a bottle of champagne. I raised my glass, she matched me, and we touched.

"A spectacular week, Henry. One I can't expect to have ever again."

"Just a taste," I said.

She looked out through the large window. The rain had slowed to drizzle. She turned to me and leaned across the table.

"While you were showering, Henry," she said. "I was sorting out our week together. Analyzing. It's what I've taught myself. First, you should know that I'd never try to change you. Maybe have some influence, that's all." She took a sip of her champagne. "But, if you were to ask me what it is about you that concerns me most, I'd have to say it's your priorities. They're all backward."

"Oh," I said, "if that's all. . . ."

"I'm not sure you understand how this relates to us," she continued. "But it does. I don't think you've ever learned, when you come right down to it, to put anyone ahead of yourself."

"If that's what you think, nothing I say is going to convince you otherwise. But for whatever it's worth, I remember doing a lot of things this week with you first in mind."

She took another sip, then laid her hand on mine. "Yes, you did. I'm sorry. I went too far."

"Maybe things went too far too fast," I said. "I don't think so, but clearly you do. I'd like you to come to New York, but you're not ready. Not to stay; just to see if your prejudices against me, against us easterners, stand up to the light of reality."

"Sounds like a good idea," she replied. "But we need some time off. From each other."

"So you can forget me and pick up your other relationship with the ancient mariner?"

"I didn't think you were the jealous type. I misjudged you."

Just as I felt I had finally made an inch of progress, she finished her sentence.

"He may be a mariner, Martin, but he ain't ancient."

7

*O*UR last day.

"You're not talking," Julie said. We were level at 22,000 feet, winging down from Ketchikan high above a solid but variegated deck of gray clouds. The GPS indicated three and a half hours to Seattle. Refueling. Julie flew from the right seat. I had been quiet, but not because I needed to concentrate on the weather or navigation. We had passed over Prince Rupert, tracking an invisible path that followed the inland waterway toward Vancouver Island. The plane was doing fine. I wasn't.

"I feel like shit, if you must know."

"I do too," she said. "All this week, there was always more time, more days to look forward to, and now . . ." I glanced over and noticed a few tears creeping into her eyes. "I *will* miss you," she said. "You know I will." She ran her fingers gently over my lips. "Call me when you arrive back in New York, Henry. That you made it all right."

"I was hoping to stay over in Wausau."

"Can you? I'd love it." She reached over and took my hand. I wanted her to put the plane on autopilot, but reason prevailed.

Julie made a smooth landing on one of Seattle's parallel runways. Planes continued to land and take off, scattering in every direction. The mammoth airliners seemed to be tolerant of our Lilliputian aircraft. I knew the pilots would be talking to each other about how gorgeous the plane looked, its sleek design, winglets, unique paint scheme.

We taxied over to the FBO, parked, and requested fuel. As I finished filling out the form, Julie threw her arms around my waist and hugged me from the rear. I expected her to say something, but she didn't. We strolled hand in hand a short distance past the office. The whine of jet turbines filled our ears.

I turned her to me. "I've never felt as close to anyone in my life."

She stepped back and locked her eyes on mine. "You've never met anyone like me before, Henry. And you never will again. But I worry what will happen to you once you get back to New York," she said. "They beat you up pretty bad. Even an ego like yours can take only so much."

"Julie, I *could* stay a few more days."

Her face brightened for a moment, then clouded, "I must get back to teaching my little fledglings." She impressed her sweetness on my lips. "Henry, send me a letter from time to time. If the spirit moves you. I'll try to decipher what you're trying to say."

I shook my head. "I can't take any more compliments. My ego's getting too big to fit into the plane."

"Turn around," she commanded the line boy when we had walked back to the plane. "This is not for you . . ." She drew her lips across mine, placed her hands on my rear, and pulled herself ever so tightly to me. "Remember me when you're back with all those city women," she said.

"Come to New York," I pleaded. "Then you won't have to worry."

Before we departed Ketchikan, a fax had arrived from the office. It said to call in Sunday, that Ari and Ken would be in the office. Now I slipped into a phone booth while Julie talked to a weather briefer in the pilot's lounge.

Ken answered and put me on the speakerphone. "What a loyal bunch. Working on Sunday," I said. "I guess it takes extra time to count all the rent money."

"Sounds like you're feeling good, Henry," Ken said, a certain tightness in his voice. "Climb any big mountains?"

I ignored the sarcasm. "Right now New York seems like a bad

dream. The Canadian Northwest and Alaska are incredible. Should I stay?"

"Only if you can find a decent job," Ken said. "This operation is not what it was, Henry. When a company shrinks the way we've had to —"

"What exactly are you saying?"

"Cash flow. Sludge. Plus tax problems. The sales of those buildings. The recapture of the depreciation we took over the years. Understand?"

"Ari, I don't want to talk to him anymore. How are you holding up? And what messages did I get?"

"I'll tell you this, boss," he answered. "I've been spending so much time here, Edith pulled out my old sleeping bag and dropped it next to the front door." His voice was firm. "I'm just telling you. Maybe I have to think about another position. She's worried about our future."

"Hang on," I said. "Look, you've been on the firing line too long without a break. Plan to take a week off, okay?" I had to think fast. "I've got some new ideas I want to share with all of you." My VP of finance didn't respond. "Things will work out."

I glanced around to see Julie smiling, her thumbs up — the weather ahead was forecast to be good.

"How bad is our cash situation?"

"Don't ask," Ari said. "Your messages — your mother, and your women, of course. That's plural. One I think I recognized. She said she'd call again. You want the others?"

"I'll call my mother from here. The others I'll take care of when I get back. Did Steve call?"

"No. Cal has additional termination papers for you to sign. Oh, about the cash situation. Our lead banks are demanding the balance of our loans be paid off, or at least they insist on a firm reduction schedule. I put them off, saying you'd be back this week."

"Good. I'm in Seattle. We'll meet the minute I return."

With the normal west-to-east tailwinds, I selected 26,000 feet for the leg from Seattle to Missoula, Montana. Once again I was able to fly above the weather. Our flight path took us across the Cascade Mountains on a line over most of Washington State, across a piece of Idaho, and over Montana. Through breaks in the clouds, we were afforded extraordinary views of rugged ranges, rolling hills sown with wheat, cattle ranches that stretched for miles, and small towns.

At one point I turned to Julie. "How come you and Len never thought of beefing up your business by acquiring a big twin or a jet? There must be companies that need to fly places from Wausau." She glanced at me. "I realize," I continued, "that it would be an expensive operation, but planes can be leased, you know. Or get a partner who wants some use of the plane plus the benefits of depreciation and write-offs."

She nodded. "Once upon a time, we were thinking seriously about doing just that. I decided against it. I don't know, I had this long conversation with myself, and . . ." she trailed off.

"And?"

"It would have meant a very heavy commitment of time. All our resources would have been on the line. Yes, it would have been terrific to have a jet. It wasn't so much the risk, but the loss of what I decided was more important to me."

"Which is?"

"This may be difficult for a man like you to understand. I treasure my freedom *above* making money and having, in this case, a jet. I cherish having time *not* to have to attend to too many things. Call it lazy."

"But think of the opportunity," I said, ignoring her reasons. "You could build up your operation, hire people. Better, *lease* a second jet *after* you lined up enough business. A whole bunch of ways to expand *and* have more free time."

"Henry, this little Indian maiden is comfortable with where she is. I've come a long way, thanks to Mom, Len, and Aunt Nadine. Not having to chase rainbows. No, wrong. Maybe chasing rainbows, but not material ones."

She tugged on my arm. "You and I *are* very different."

I shook my head, as if admitting defeat. "Maybe we are. Maybe we are."

The next day, when we were in range, Julie called Wausau Unicom. Len sounded elated. "Hey, I'll get Aunt Nadine. She'll want to be here when you guys land. We received our ration of Hammer-schlanger's. Some dude from Chicago bought the deli. Wanted to get started on the right foot."

It was a joyous welcome; we had gifts for Len and Nadine. Julie suggested I stay at the Best Western. "Don't be upset about not staying in my room. I'll be with you, of course, at the motel. You know, Aunt Nadine."

Julie and Sirius drove me to the motel. I checked in, stowed my bags in the room, then walked the one flight down to the lobby, where Julie and Sirius were waiting under the NO PETS ALLOWED sign.

"I was thinking about something," Julie said as we pulled out of the motel parking lot.

"Shoot."

"I don't know much about the kind of real estate you do, but I'm not short on common sense," she said. "So you built that big monument in Manhattan, you and your brother. You overreached, didn't you? And so you lost it." She put her hand on mine. "Perhaps in future deals, you'd be better off having someone else put in the dough. Better to own a smaller portion than bet the entire spread, no?" she asked.

I ran my hand over my chin, and shook my head.

"Listen to me before you discard my suggestion."

"It just wouldn't work."

"Why not? You don't always have to take such enormous risks, do you?"

"If I did what you suggest," I said, "I wouldn't be able to keep control."

"But it seems to me you should protect yourself a lot better when you set up your deals." She patted my head gently — much the way she patted Sirius, I noted.

"Julie, I appreciate your concern, I really do. Maybe I just don't want to think of all that right now. God knows, I'll have to face it soon enough."

When we were almost to her house, I turned to her. "Do me a favor tonight, will you Julie?"

"What?"

"Please don't have more than two drinks —"

"Why not?"

"Damn it, you know what I mean. When you have too much to drink you lose control."

"I know what you really want, Martin. You want to control me."

I looked over at her. "Now who's blocking out what she doesn't want to hear?"

"Mind your own goddamn business, Martin. Okay?" Suddenly I wasn't looking forward to tonight's dinner.

But dinner turned out to be delightful. Everyone was in a good mood. Aunt Nadine and Len were pleased to have us back. And we found ourselves going on and on about the exotic highlights of the week.

"Grizzlies don't work. Seems they have a union," Julie said. "Anyway, we saw these two grizzlies out ambling around. No worries. No hurry. Just out ambling."

"Henry said you saw whales," Len said.

"One whale," Julie said, laughing. "Sometimes Henry sees double. Or quadruple."

"But what a whale," I countered. "Ninety tons of grace and beauty."

I had been watching Julie, afraid she might overreact to my admonition about her drinking, but she had only two drinks all evening.

On our way back to the motel, I thanked her for a great dinner.

"I didn't do a thing, except drink."

"Sparingly," I said.

"I'm not an alcoholic, Henry."

"I know you're not an alcoholic," I said softly. "It's the combination of flying and alcohol that worries me. Not the alcohol itself." But I know I only half believed that.

"Henry," she said, "do you trust me?"

"Of course I do."

"Then stop worrying," she said. "Save your worries for New York."

Part 3

But if the wicked turn from all his sins that he hath committed . . . and do that which is lawful and right, he shall surely live . . .

Ezekiel xviii

I

*W*HEN I arrived in New York, spring was producing a glittering display of bud and bloom.

Ken, Ari, and Cal had done a good job. Addressing the financial realities, they had sold buildings and land, negotiated workouts with subcontractors and other trade merchants, and worked out settlements with the banks.

We weren't flat broke. My team had downsized the staff, renegotiated our office space lease, moved into smaller quarters. They had even cut their own salaries and fees.

"Coffee, anyone?" I asked them in the new conference room. They shook their collective heads. "Let me begin by saying that I'm very grateful for your efforts and performance. Even though we've been reduced to a shell of what we were. Let me lay out where we go from here." I took a few sips of coffee, and fixed them with my gaze, one by one. "We *will* resurrect this company of ours. We'll restore it to its full potential and power — the two big P's. Re-create ourselves. Bigger. Smarter."

They glanced at one other, then at me. Ken broke the silence. "How will we manage that, Henry? Where's the fresh equity capital coming from? You're not forgetting we're just about wiped out? And, if you haven't already heard, Federated sold Three-Fifty-Five in a package to a group composed of Amalgamated and two partners."

"I'm not really surprised, Ken. That's what lenders are doing with buildings they have to take back. As for our company, we're leaner and a lot sharper. Phoenix from the ashes. My timing was off, that's all."

"No, Henry, that isn't all," Cal said. He waited a moment, and then said carefully, "I realize that what I'm going to say you're not going to like." He cleared his throat, then took a deep breath. "You got into trouble because you refused to recognize certain basic realities, Henry. You thought you were clever enough to overcome anything put in your way. If you still think that way, you'll just do it all over again."

"You talking about ego, Cal?" I asked.

"To be blunt, yes."

I stood up, walked around to where Cal was sitting, and put my hands on his shoulders. "I'm *not* getting into a discussion about my ego. But let me remind you that without that ego, we'd be where most of the world is — nowhere."

"We know that," Ken said. "What Cal is saying is we got into deep shit because we — you — went too far."

"All right. I recognize the buck stops with me. But I also believe we can resurrect this company. And I do see things differently." I circled the room. Something symbolic about that. "I told you what's on the table. If you want to be part of the future with me, this is the time to declare."

I didn't wait for answers. "Here's my offer — fifteen percent, without any investment on your part. Five percent each. What do you say?"

All three nodded. But then, almost as a chorus: "But where do we find the capital, Henry? Can't rebuild out of hope and thin air. Where, Henry?"

Where?

I made calls to several out-of-town banks, all of which at one time had solicited business from us. None would give me the time of day. Almost all of my personal wealth was tied to the values of my properties. My hideaway pad in the Village had been sold, as had my helicopter. I had reluctantly let Craig Sampson go. I retained the plane and my townhouse, deciding I could keep them, at least for the moment. My father had left my mother enough to live on comfortably. I quickly dismissed any thought of asking her for a loan. But "Where, Henry, where?" kept echoing in my mind.

A few competitors had raised money on Wall Street through a real estate investment trust, selling portions of their companies to the public, thereby eliminating financing from banks and paying off their mortgages. A REIT also provided money for acquisitions. But the current net assets of The Martin Companies precluded that possibility. Conventional mortgages? Conventional mortgage lenders were getting scorched and were uninterested in refinancings or making new loans. The idea of spec developing was about as unattractive as shaking hands with an angry water buffalo. That kind of real estate wasn't possible anymore. What kind of real estate was?

I kept telling myself that at least we were still in business, but that was increasingly becoming cold comfort. And I needed a little warmth sometime soon.

Julie and I talked at length almost every morning or night. She missed me, she said, was enjoying her students, was back to jogging. The late spring weather was magnificent, flowers blanketing the pastures and hills, and the animals were busy acting out their spring rituals.

"When are you coming to New York?" I asked.

"When are you coming to Wausau?"

Stalemate.

Joyce telephoned. I almost didn't want to take the call. Family stuff? About Steve?

"Hi, Joyce. Good hearing from you." Searching. "Ah, how's the baby?"

Her voice was warm and embracing. I remembered how it could sound when she wanted it that way. "He's a real handful, but great."

"And Steve?"

"He's fine. Getting settled in his new business."

"And you?"

"It's been a long time, Henry. I heard you were away. I've been concerned."

"About the company or about me?"

She didn't answer. Then, "Would you like to have lunch? Bleecker Street, off Spring."

"I remember the place."

"Thursday, if that's okay. Will I still recognize you?" I told her I'd be wearing a chartreuse bowler and a violet carnation in my lapel. She laughed and said good-bye.

"Where, Henry, where?" I asked myself. Left, right, and center, looking for investors.

Mike Allen couldn't help, although he really would have liked to. I met with a Delta Upsilon fraternity brother from Middlebury, Willard Jackson, a successful investment banker, and another classmate, Bruce Hiland, who was with Goldman Sachs. Both said bluntly neither domestic nor foreign investors were interested in real estate ventures. Some groups had put together vulture funds to buy distressed properties from banks that had taken back properties in foreclosures. And from the RTC, which had to take over troubled assets from defaulting banks. Most of the nation's largest developers were shedding whatever they could, simply to remain afloat. Many didn't make it.

Some parties suggested I contribute a pool of my buildings and become *part* of a REIT. I would be trading my properties for stock in a publicly owned company, thereby relinquishing control. The price would be based on a multiple of the net rents. Under certain circumstances, I might be required to personally guarantee the mortgages. In other words, end up with very little cash, especially after paying high transactional costs, legal and accounting, as well as other fees and commissions. Plus, at some point in time, have to pay huge capital gains taxes. No thanks.

More calls to Julie. I even wrote letters.

"Well, the real estate tycoon really *can* write an intelligible letter," she teased. "Who would have guessed?"

"I did attend one of the better colleges," I said.

"Did you learn anything?"

"Enough to tutor the coeds."

"In human biology, right?"

"It wasn't in math."

"I thought you were good at figures."

"Was," I said. "Was." I paused. "Do you miss me enough for me to fly there for a long weekend?"

"Maybe in a week or two," she said after a moment's silence. "I have a stomach virus. Seeing my doctor next week."

"Sorry to hear that. You're probably working too hard."

"Flying's not work. Work is what *you* do. Speaking of which, how's business in the large tomato?"

"Big Apple."

"Whatever."

"It's terrible, thank you. People with money don't return my phone calls."

"Is that why you call me?"

She added that the weekend I came out we could fly up to northern Michigan and stay at a nice place near the Straits of Mackinaw. Fun things to do and see, lots of art and culture. I told her we'd never make it out of our room.

I met Joyce as planned. She wore a big smile and a beige spring suit with a flowered print blouse. Having a baby hadn't reshaped her one bit. If anything, her face reflected a new maturity. I had dressed carefully and applied my best aftershave lotion. As I helped her get seated, I placed my hands on her shoulders.

"Please, Henry, you're making me uncomfortable."

"Sorry, I didn't mean to." I sat down and looked at her.

"I'm hungry," she said. "Let's order."

"You're still lovely, Joyce."

"No new lines in your face, I see. Or bags under your eyes. I noticed your walk, Henry. Shoulders back. Head up. I'm glad you're all right. From all I'd heard, I was afraid you might be depressed. I see you're not, and I'm glad."

We spent the next hour in small talk. Ex-lovers can end up in a long-term friendship. I hoped Joyce wanted more than that, probably because I didn't want her feelings for me to change. But they clearly had. What I said or did no longer had the same effect on her. Somehow, we both managed to avoid mentioning Steve's name, even once.

We finished lunch, stepped outside, and strolled to the corner. It was a bright, sparkling spring afternoon, sun pouring down from a cloudless sky. "Say hello once in a while," she said, and gave me a peck on the cheek. I watched her get into a cab and head uptown.

I called Dianne from my car as I emerged from the Midtown Tunnel on the Queens side. She ran down the list of calls. "Oh, there's one coming in on the other line. Want to see who it is?"

"No, I'll return it when I'm back in the office. Did Leo Singer confirm our tennis game?"

"I'll fax Dr. Singer again." She called back a few minutes later. "It was Mr. Phelan returning your call. No rush to get back to him, he said, but if you want to reach him, he left a number." She gave it to me.

No rush? I'd been trying to reach Phelan for a week.

"Henry, my boy," Phelan said, "nice to hear from you. I trust you had a good vacation. Killing all the appropriate dragons back here?"

"Every time I slay one, six more jump out from behind a bush — no, a building."

"Well, I'm glad to hear your sense of humor is intact. What can I do for you?"

"I'd like to explore something with you, Jack. Any chance of meeting?"

"I'm off this Saturday with my wife on a holiday to Ireland and Scandinavia. Not much time before I leave. But I could have dinner with you tonight."

"You're on. Lotos Club at seven-thirty?"

"Fine."

I called Dianne, and told her to reschedule my tennis date. And to tell Leo that I'd spot him three games each set.

A receptionist at the Lotos Club directed me to one of the libraries.

Phelan rose to greet me. "So, my young friend," he said, smiling and shaking my hand. "None the worse, I suspect." We sat in plush red leather chairs. "I remember telling you that certain men rise up from defeat and come back to achieve the highest positions of leadership. Take Herbert Hoover. Or Harry Truman." A waiter took our drink order.

"I appreciate your taking the time, Jack. Especially given your schedule."

I surveyed the room. Men and a few women engaged in conversation. Some were reading newspapers. A waiter brought a scotch for Jack, Campari on the rocks with a twist for me. I was on the edge of my chair, but decided it was best to sit back and sip my drink.

I cleared my throat. Jack's opening remark encouraged me to cut right to the chase. "History has proven that substantial monies can be made even in the depths of a recession," I said. "Even during the Depression, when it was at its worst." Jack seemed to be listening carefully. "An old adage," I went on, "buy when everyone is selling and sell when they're buying." He nodded and sipped his scotch.

"We've had a near collapse in income properties. Prices have dropped like a plane without wings. Now is the perfect time to pick up buildings at incredibly low prices. At values that reflect bottom rents. The theory is simple —"

"I know," he interrupted. "Eventually rents rise as demand increases and available space is limited. The return on investment starts out modestly but climbs over time. I agree with your premise. You're about to ask me if I'll furnish some capital. Am I right?"

I nodded.

"Actually," he said, "I wasn't surprised to hear from you." He laughed. "You sound like John Phelan as a kid in the Bronx, convincing old man O'Hallahan how to increase his volume."

He paused, a frown forming on his leonine brow. "This said, Henry, right now you're anything but an ideal candidate to invest with. You have some proving to do. And I'd better spell out the conditions I would require" — he paused — "*if* I were to decide to involve myself. Based on certain standards — which would have built-in controls and others we would have to agree on in advance — I may be willing to invest. Even become your partner. Limited and silent, mind you. Let me emphasize, *limited*, not general.

You would be responsible for everything, guarantees and so forth. I would also require that you put in a small part of the investment."

"I'll find whatever it takes."

"Understood," he said. "That's the easy part. Strictly mechanics. The difficult part will be proving to me your plan is sound. For each particular transaction. Also, the controls I'd require you might not agree to. Don't get me wrong. I'm not out to hamstring you. A man like you must be given his head, I recognize that. But enough small talk." He heaved himself from the armchair. "Let's get some dinner. The fish is excellent. So are the game birds. But, I forget. I'm *your* guest tonight."

The dining room in use that evening was the grill room, aesthetically tasteful, the decor and paintings representations of New York in the first decades of this century. We were seated at a secluded table. After ordering, Phelan picked up where he'd left off. "Henry, you've proven you're talented. But remember what I once told you — history is glutted with the sad tales of men who believed that they were invincible."

He leaned forward. "Let me be blunt, Henry. Are you suffering from an overdose of ego? If so, why would I invest with such a man? Or has your ego been moderated?" The maître d' led three men to a table near ours. They recognized Jack and came over.

He introduced them. One was a prominent banker. "Oh, yes, Mr. Martin," he said, "you're a developer, right?" I nodded. He smiled with a kind of smugness I have always detested, but I wouldn't give him the satisfaction of a response. They spent another minute in chitchat and then sat down at their table. I noticed them whispering. I smiled across at them. Go fuck yourselves, I thought.

"To continue, Henry. I believe that with counsel from me, close cooperation, and the monitoring of your actions, a partnership might work. However, my involvement would have to remain absolutely confidential. Of course, your close associates would know, but all funds would come from an attorney. For two reasons — if you blow it, I've lost money, but it wouldn't reflect on my reputation. Second, it's better for you that the world not be aware I'm involved."

I didn't agree. His name would be an enormous plus, especially in the present market.

"I'm flattered, Jack. No, more than flattered. Grateful. How do you envisage structuring such a deal?"

"Here's the way I see it," Phelan said. "I make the initial investment. We both get a ten percent return for our investments. After they're paid back, we split fifty-fifty. I think that's fair. And you must participate in the capital contribution to the tune of ten percent. Also, decisions, major ones, will require my approval."

I would have preferred a straight fifty-fifty with no investment, but I was willing to accept almost any offer. "May I ask what level of investment you had in mind?"

"At least ten million. Two million to start, with two additional tranches of four million each, spread out or not, depending on the deals. That amount can be increased. I might even get some of my friends to join in and create a larger capital pool. There's even the prospect of raising funds in the public market." The waiter whisked off our appetizer plates and deftly replaced them with new ones. "It all has to do with how you perform."

He buttered a biscuit. "I'm not supposed to have butter. Let's hope it's margarine." He patted my hand. "I want it crystal clear between us that the reports and monitoring I require are acceptable to you, not because you have to in order to get my funds, but because you believe I can be helpful."

"What are you afraid of, Jack? That I'll repeat the same mistakes? I think it's safe to say I've learned from them."

"I hope so. Frankly, it has everything to do with that damn ego of yours. I believe in strong egos, God knows, but I think yours may have gotten out of control. It needs to be tamed." He bent his impressive head over the main course and began to attack it with authority. Then he looked up. "I'll think all this over carefully and call you from Europe," he said. "I want you to understand I am not committing to anything yet."

I looked across at him. He was tough, but I knew he was sincere. He sounded like my father. Everybody, it seemed, was trying to tell me the same thing.

As we finished the meal, he said if he decided to proceed, we could sit down with our attorneys and work out an agreement quite quickly.

On the sidewalk outside the club, where a dozen sleek limousines lined up like so many obedient butlers, Phelan warmly shook my hand.

"I've always liked you, Henry. Maybe because I see a bit of myself in you. When I was younger I had an ego big as a house. Almost did me in a couple of times." He paused. "So I know it *can* be tamed."

He gave a hearty wave as his limo pulled away from the curb. No commitment, Henry. He could think it over and decide against it. Remember that, I told myself, before you get your hopes up too high.

Still, I felt more optimistic than I had in months.

Later, I called Julie. "How about this — spend a few days here with me in the Large Tomato. I promise, no parties, just tramping around in the wild woods of Manhattan. Terrific food, a show if you'd like, and plenty of me. I'd also like to introduce you to my guys. Can I tempt you?"

"A deal," she said. "But I want it in writing."

I laughed and said she'd have a fax in the morning.

2

WITH Phelan on holiday I was forced into limbo. But I had a gut feeling he would say yes, and so on that optimistic basic I did considerable strategic planning.

I took Ari to lunch and convinced him how it made sense for him to stay on. He really wanted to, he said. His concern was not whether we'd regain our past glory, but whether the company would or could remain viable. News of Phelan's possible infusion of capital settled it for him. It had the same salutary effect on Ken and Cal as well.

"It's not a certainty," I cautioned.

I called Julie to arrange her visit. "How will I remember who you are?" I asked.

"I'll be the one in the short skirt, cowboy boots, hat, and packing two six-guns," she warned.

I met her the following Friday at the Northwest Terminal at LaGuardia Airport. She looked terrific. She literally threw herself at me, coiling legs and arms around me. Several of the arriving passengers watched, some shocked, some amused. "I decided to dress more in keeping with the environment of the Big City. Where do I get my passport stamped?"

"Not to worry, sweetheart. You're with me. I'll get us through," I said in my best Clark Gable voice. We jumped into my car.

"What's the plan? First show me the sights? Then your etchings?"

I pulled out onto Grand Central Parkway. "If it's all right with you, I thought we'd grab a late lunch at my club, then head to the office. A few checks and papers to sign."

Julie curled up next to me. "I've missed you. Your body, not your mind."

"I'll be faster than lightning in the office, then to my place in Manhattan for, uh, whatever. Then I want to take you to Le Cirque for dinner. About the best French food in town. After that, if we're not too beat, jazz down in the Village."

"I think this country girl will just about make it through dinner."

Julie and I made a grand entrance into the grill room of my Glen Pointe club, where people turned to rubberneck.

After lunch, we strolled on the grounds, under magnificent huge red maples, white pines and hemlocks, dogwoods, mulberries, chestnuts, ginkgoes, beeches, and other specimen trees.

We put time aside to talk and hold hands. We stopped at intervals to hug and kiss. I felt both tender and tentative. Ready to pick up where we had left off.

From the club, we drove to Garden City. Eyes focused on Julie as she preceded me through the office. I had never brought a female friend there before. Dianne came in with folders that required my signature, and I introduced them. While I signed checks and letters, Julie scrutinized every photo, plaque, and framed letter on the walls. When I was finished I said, "I'd like you to meet Ken and Ari. Cal Ostreicher is in the city. You might meet him while you're here."

Ken and Ari were in the conference room. When we entered they rose and shook hands. From the look on their faces it was clear they found Julie to their liking. Ari and I reviewed a few business matters, while Ken engaged Julie in conversation.

The telephone rang. When I heard who it was, I told Dianne I'd take it in my office. "Be back in a minute," I said. Julie's face made it clear she was not pleased.

"I know this is late, but I was wondering if you were free this weekend?" It was Karen Viscomi. "I've got the house in Martha's Vineyard all for myself." She sounded like Mae West on a good day.

In that minisecond I thought about being together. Lord,

Temptation, thy name is Karen. "Oh, God, I'm sorry Karen. Normally, I'd love to, but I can't. Tied up this weekend. I'll call you for dinner."

"There's a tone in your voice," she said. "Not the same Henry!"

"Don't be silly. It's just that I came out of a meeting to take your call."

"I understand," she said. "Sorry it didn't work out. Take care of yourself, Henry. I miss you."

"If you don't mind my inquiring," Julie asked as we were driving toward Manhattan, "could that have been a call from an old friend?"

"The lady is insightful." I laughed. "Aren't you the same lady who declared that nobody could tell her what to do?"

"Absolutely. I was just curious."

"You know, Julie," I said, "despite our grand declarations, let's face it. We're both possessive." Julie was looking through her side window, apparently oblivious to my pregnant observation.

"There are more automobiles on the Long Island Expressway than in the entire state of Wisconsin," she said. "What a lousy commute! I'll take the sticks anytime."

"I told her I wasn't available this weekend," I said, then added, "and that I was very involved with someone." Half true.

"Thanks, Henry." She snuggled up next to me. "Especially for a guy who usually sees several women at a time, if my reports are correct."

"Me? Everyone knows I'm straight and pure." She made a face. "Besides," I added, "how good a lover could I be if I were thinking of you when I was with someone else?"

"By the time I'm through with you, you won't be able to *look* at another woman," she said.

We teased each other for a few minutes. Then Julie said, "I wasn't going to mention this, but . . ."

"But . . ."

"Well, in your conference room, after Ari went back to his office and you were talking to your schnitzel, your buddy, Ken, started to come on a little."

"Like how?"

"Oh, the typical bullshit. 'If I wasn't married, I wouldn't let a woman as incredibly good-looking as you out of my sight.' "

"Jesus Christ!" I exploded. "That —"

"Hold on, Henry. I'm sure he doesn't really mean to make a pass at your woman."

"Well, he shouldn't be that dumb. I'll straighten him out pretty goddamn quick!" I was quiet a few minutes and then asked, "Julie, are you trying to make me jealous?"

"I guess we can't take each other for granted, can we?" she said. "I suppose it all has a bearing on how much we're willing to commit, doesn't it?"

"Absolutely," I said. I grabbed her hand and squeezed it.

It was a weekend to remember. Julie loved every place I dragged her, every morsel of food, every jazz joint and show — two in three days — and her energy never seemed to flag. The second night I took her to Cellar in the Sky, the romantic enclave tucked inside the Windows on the World, and let her marvel at the luminous city below. I felt a little like Satan displaying his wares. I could tell she was impressed.

"New York's not such a bad place," she said as we strolled home after dinner. "If only there weren't all those people!"

"I can't talk you into staying on?" I asked toward the end of the weekend. We had just finished brunch at the Tacky Oyster, a new restaurant on Columbus Avenue. We were walking next to Central Park and then to Lincoln Center for a Mozart concert.

"I could get used to you being around, Julie. You know — to do my socks and underwear. And some of that old-fashioned Wisconsin cooking."

She wagged a finger at me. "You have it backward, pardner. With me, men do the cooking. And the sewing."

"Only kidding."

"I love you, Henry," she uttered softly.

"I love you too," I said.

"So where do we go from here?" I asked, more to myself than to Julie.

"I go to Wisconsin," Julie said. "And you go to, what's it called, Nassau?"

Julie departed from LaGuardia on Monday evening. I told her I would fly to Wausau in two weeks. Driving back into Manhattan, I missed Julie tremendously. If I didn't want to lose her, I had better well do something about it. The question was: What, exactly?

On Tuesday, Phelan called from Ireland. He wanted to explore time frames, how long I thought it would take before our investments would be returned. He also asked me for more specific overhead numbers, what I was estimating for tenant improvements, overhead and brokerage. I said I was putting all that together and would have it ready by the time he got back. "See you then, Jack."

But he called the following day. "The game is on, Henry. I'm in. Congratulations. I'm looking forward to winning big with you. Also to having fun in the process. See you back in New York."

"Jack, that's wonderful," I said. "And I guarantee —"

"No guarantees," Phelan said. "In life, there are only hopes and expectations."

"Well then, I give you my formal expectations," I said.

"That's better, Henry. See you next week."

After he hung up I let out a whoop and a holler that echoed throughout the office. Hell, through all of Nassau County!

3

*P*HELAN returned from Scandinavia a week later.

"So, Henry, are you still inclined to proceed as planned?" he said when he called.

For a moment my heart sank. Had he changed his mind?

"Of course, Jack, unless you've had second thoughts."

"On the contrary. The more I've thought about it, the more my elderly juices have started flowing again."

We met three days later at the Harrison House Conference Center in Glen Cove. Only the two of us, our lawyers, and our secretaries with their trusty word processors.

Jack and I saw eye to eye on virtually everything. It was the lawyers who sometimes got caught up in various points of order or substance. Have to prove their mettle, impress their clients, I thought. But before they went on too long, like two dogs fighting over a meatless bone, Jack would step in and end the argument with a: "I don't see that as a problem, gentlemen. Let's go to the next point."

Over lunch, which we shared alone, I thanked him for moving things along so quickly. And so fairly.

"Well, thank *you*, Henry. The point is, with the exception of something that *really* makes a difference, I want the basis of our new relationship to be as good for you as for me. I win that way, don't I? Most businesspeople don't understand that." He took a bite of his turkey sandwich, then looked hard at me. "You'll conduct yourself in the same manner, won't you?"

"Of course I will," I said.

"When I find that you don't, it's out to the woodshed." He laughed. "We Irish, in my generation anyway, haven't forgotten the importance of certain values, including ones applied to our rear ends. You Jewish boys are familiar with that too, I'm sure."

"Jewish-*Italian*," I reminded him. He laughed and apologized for not remembering. "At the risk of sounding obsequious," I said, "the truth is I'm very excited about this new partnership. You're going to see stunning results."

He stuck out his hand. "We'll close formally next week, Henry, but as far as I'm concerned, this is a done deal. After we sign, it's out for the best dinner in town."

At odd moments — driving, in the dead of night, shaving — my thoughts focused on where I was at that moment in my life. I missed my father, deeply missed our conversations. My so-called family, I realized, consisted entirely of my mother and Steve. Pretty thin. And then there was Julie.

The next day, I received a call from Phelan. "Well, my boy, I have a wild idea," he said.

"Not too wild, I hope," I said, half seriously. "You're supposed to be the one reining in this wild horse."

Phelan chuckled. "It *is* pretty crazy," he said, "but the more I ponder it the more I like the idea. Poetic justice has always appealed to me."

"I think I'm getting an inkling of what you're talking about."

"Your building," he said. "Yes, Three-Fifty-Five Park. What if we tried to re-acquire it?"

"Are you serious?"

"Very." He paused, as if pondering carefully his next thought. "As you probably know," he went on, "Federated sold the property in a package to Amalgamated and two partners. At a big discount, naturally. It could make an attractive buy, depending on the price we can negotiate. There's bound to be a number of other bidders."

"God, I'd love that, Jack. But there's a problem," I said. "Without tenants, we'd have to carry the building vacant. One that size? No thanks! I've been there."

"I know you have," he said. "But what if there was a tenant for two-thirds?"

"That of course would change the equation," I said. "Can I ask who?"

"Not yet. That's still completely confidential. The problem is, how to buy Three-Fifty-Five without the world finding out we have a tenant. These people can't sign a lease subject to our procuring the building. They're publicly owned; their attorneys won't let them. Henry, meet me for lunch at my club. We'll brainstorm." He paused. "I have to tell you something else."

"What?" I asked, still a bit fearful he would say he'd changed his mind.

"This is fun." He laughed. "Gets the old blood going."

The sellers of defaulted notes and mortgages generally make a good profit. Assume they purchase at a 50 percent discount off the fair market value and sell for a profit of 40 percent. Shopping centers, industrial and office buildings, garden apartment complexes, golf clubs, and so forth. Sometimes, they even sell a contract before having to take title. With regard to 355, they didn't care whether we had a tenant or not. Their chief asset manager was none other than my old friend Malenti, who had left Federated and was now with the fund that had acquired this property. If we had to have the building he would have pressed for a higher price. At one point, I told him, "Look, Mr. Malenti, this is not the only property we can purchase. Seventy-one million is our best and final offer, subject to a due diligence period of ninety days, which will include the finalization of financing arrangements."

I let Malenti stew for a few days. Now I had something he wanted — a bit different than when we originally met. Finally he called, but I let two days elapse.

"Henry," he said, in one of the conference rooms in Cal's law firm's offices. "May I call you Henry?" I didn't respond. "Look," he continued after a few moments of silence, "your offer of seventy-one million is significantly less than the building is worth. I can sell it for a higher amount."

"Then why haven't you?"

"Maybe I will," he said, "but the buyers are questionable. We're concerned they would go to contract, try to get the money, and if they didn't, walk. There are enough outs in any deal that would probably let them get their down payment back."

"Well, isn't that the situation, Mr. Malenti?"

"Yes," he said, "but I'll tell you what —"

"No, I'll tell *you*," I interrupted. "We like the building and think it's got good potential. You want us, our best price is . . . seventy-four million."

"How do I know you've got the funds?"

I paused. "There's a letter of credit sitting right now at Citicorp. It recites our ability to make this deal. That should be good enough." He studied my face for a few moments and agreed it was.

We settled for seventy-four million, five hundred thousand. The agreements to purchase the deed and assign the mortgage were executed. We expected to conclude the actual lease within the due diligence period, and Jack and I would have signed our partnership agreement within that time. The prospective tenant for the building was willing to sign a letter of intent. That was critical in the negotiations for gap financing and permanent financing.

What a turnaround! Calls came in from both brokers and developers. Daniel Spear congratulated me, then inquired how I had arranged for the capital. I was not about to tell him. He asked me to play squash. I promised him I'd whip his ass.

There were other ramifications. Owning 355 again would result in tax benefits. Taxable deductions for interest and depreciation. The Martin Companies would own only 25 percent because we had to bring in additional investors. I had Ari and Ken revise our overall cash flows. They indicated higher income, especially at the point when the re-acquired 355 was leased up.

I was feeling good, but I would never forget the recent scorching.

I swaggered less. And Phelan wasn't about to let me behave badly. His was respect I coveted.

About eleven o'clock on a warm September morning, I drove to the Engineers Hill Industrial Park in Plainview, to a building located on Commercial Drive, adjacent to the Long Island Expressway, the offices of a computer software company. I parked in the visitor's area, entered the attractive, two-story lobby, and walked over to the receptionist.

"Steven Martin, please," I said slowly.

"He's on the phone right now, sir. Who shall I say is here?"

"An old friend. I want to surprise him."

Shock registered on my brother's face when he appeared. I put out my hand, which he took only after a few moments. "Steve, I wanted to see you," I said. "Things to talk about. Let's go for a drive."

He hesitated, then told the young woman behind the window that he'd be back shortly. I suggested Cold Spring Harbor, where we could walk on the grounds of the Cold Spring Harbor Laboratories. I was a member of the board of directors.

"Hey, how's your little guy?" I asked as we drove. "Haven't seen him since the *bris*. He crawling yet?" Steve's face lit up. He bubbled as he expressed the joys of being a father. I couldn't help but feel envy.

We parked and began strolling. Yellow school buses were unloading hordes of youngsters. Their teachers had them in twos, holding hands without talking. We walked toward a bench under a large copper beech.

"I don't know where to begin," I said as we sat. "I see everything differently. I guess these past few months have left their mark."

Steve looked doubtful. "Really?" he said. "Do people really change? Underneath it all, I suspect Henry Sabatini Martin is still the same person."

I let that remark sink in. Sarcasm? Old resentment? Steve's feelings would probably never change. Then I remembered my promise to Dad that I would always include Steve in whatever I did in business. Impossible now, but foremost in my mind was his basic insistence we remain together as brothers.

"Look, Steve, we don't need each other. But we are family, as thin and as bad as it's been. And it hurts Mom. If Dad were here, he would make us reconcile." I glanced over to see his reaction, but his face was expressionless.

"Whatever I did to you over the years or whatever my effect on you was," I went on, "you gave me back in spades." He pulled his lips together tightly. "Still, it's stupid for us to bear anger and grudges. Life is too short."

"I suppose you're right, Henry." He stepped toward a pine cone and gave it a soccer kick. "But it's been a whole lifetime."

"I know. It can't get any worse, can it? All I'm suggesting is we make a new start."

We walked to his car and headed to his office. I was hoping he'd comment on what I had said. Though I was doing it more for Dad than for Steve, I still wanted a real reconciliation. "Henry, are you sure Joyce isn't part of the reason?" a voice within me said. No, I responded. Gone. Over. Done with. Joyce has a new life, a good life. And I'm not part of it. But throughout the drive back, Steve limited his conversation to minutiae.

All right, Henry, you tried, I said to myself as we drew up to Steve's office. Takes two to tango — I guess Steve's not the dancing type.

Steve let me off beside my car in the parking lot. I got out and went over to Steve's side. He rolled down the window.

"Mom's flying in on Monday," he said, "staying with us for a week or so. It would be great if you could come out for dinner. Any night. Just let Joyce know. . . ."

He trusted me to communicate directly with his wife.

I smiled.

"I'd really like that. I may be in Wisconsin, though. I'll let you know." We shook hands. This way, if I couldn't make it, he'd know why and not be offended.

I got in my car and drove away, feeling better about us than I had since we were kids. Life is *too* short, I kept repeating as I slipped onto the expressway.

4

OUR timing to acquire the 355 building was perfect. The recession was bottoming out. Firms were adopting a more aggressive attitude and beginning to think again in terms of expansion. Larger expenditures for plant and equipment. A reduction in downsizing, even some rehiring. The change was by no means universal, but if you studied the fundamentals you could detect a shift. Disinflation was dying a much desired death. Inflation did not have to be the alternative. Alan Greenspan and the other members of the Fed seemed more attentive to the lessons of the past, when the agency resorted to draconian measures without fully calculating the consequences. If the Fed had truly learned its lesson, the nation might be able to pursue a path of sustained growth without the devastating cycles of boom and bust.

The Martin Companies, too, began to experience slow but steadily rising gross income. Financial institutions slowly began to treat us as if we were no longer Typhoid Mary.

My greatest pleasure would be in taking the calls from all those bankers and financial gurus who had refused to take mine all those months. Careful, Henry, I told myself, don't let that ego get out of control. I could still hate their guts in my soul of souls.

Almost as pleasurable would be the prospect of proving the journalists wrong, the ones who had hovered like vultures when my company was collapsing. Now they would sniff around for stories about how I had gone from "riches to ruin and back again." Since perception is reality, let those who read about me draw whatever conclusions they liked. It still gave me a certain buzz to see my name in the papers, but it wasn't as important as it had been. No one cared as much as I had once believed.

I was glad Steve and I had reconciled. We would never become close, but at least we were developing something that resembled civility. During my mother's visit, I did go over for dinner — even went so far as to play with my nephew. Joyce showed me how to change his diaper. The kid squirted me in the face.

Joyce shrieked with laughter. "Welcome, Uncle Henry! Welcome to the wonderful, carefree world of Joseph Jacob Asmund Martin."

"Two middle names?" I asked. It was the first time I had known my nephew's full name.

" 'Asmund' for the Norwegian blood in him and 'Jacob' for his grandfather." She looked over at my mother, who smiled approvingly.

Steve brought in drinks. Uncle Henry carried Joseph to the outside patio, where he placed the baby in his crib. The four adults then proceeded to have another round while Steve grilled steaks. It was a pleasant evening.

5

A CALL came in on my cellular phone when I was returning to my office the following day. It was Len. Something in his voice made me tense up.

"I'm glad I found you. I've been trying to reach you for two hours."

"What's wrong, Len?"

"It's about Julie."

"What *about* Julie? Has something happened to her?"

"Yes, Henry" — his voice trailed off — "I'm afraid she's had an accident."

"Goddamn it, I told her she drives too fast," I said.

"Not a *car* accident, Henry. *Plane* crash."

"Is she . . . ?"

"She's alive, Henry. But busted up real bad. Any chance you can get out here? Like quickly?"

I felt faint.

"I'll charter a jet as soon as we get off the phone. Len — is she going to make it?"

"I don't know. They're not sure of the extent of —"

"How did it happen?" Alcohol, I was sure of it.

"A student. She was showing him how to do short field landings and takeoffs. He panicked, froze on the controls. They hit some trees at the end of the runway. He's in shock. Suffered deep cuts and bruises and a broken arm, but Julie . . ." His voice broke.

"I'm on my way. Len, go down to the hospital and whisper in Julie's ear that I'm coming. Will you do that for me, Len?"

"Sure. But I don't think —"

"Will you do that for me, Len?"

"Sure, Henry. Right away."

I called Mid-Island Air Service and had them arrange a plane for me at Islip. They called back and said it would take about six hours to arrange for a Citation.

"If you don't have one in two or less, I'll call someone else." I told them. They phoned back. A plane would be available in an hour and a half.

I didn't want to do any of the flying. Too long since I had checked out a jet. And my mind wouldn't have been on flying.

I sat alone in the rear, the swoosh of the jet at 41,000 feet in my ears. I began to think about Julie's crash. Was it really her student's fault? Or were her reactions too slow? Drinking can bite pilots. Some believe that a night's sleep will eliminate any effects. Maybe for some, but not for others.

Julie and me, I thought. We were so different. A commitment. Do I want it? Yes. With all the warts and wrinkles? All the weaknesses and funny bones? Yes. On some issues we're going to fight like hell. And what would I do when I ran into temptation? I'd run like hell, that's what!

Prior to takeoff, I had called Len and given him my estimated time of arrival. He met the plane. We embraced like long-lost brothers.

"I just came from the hospital," he said as we jumped into his car.

"The doctors think now she has a fifty-fifty chance."

"No better?"

"That's what they said."

"Give me the details."

"A broken rib punctured her lung. She's in surgery. They're not concerned about the lung, that'll heal. It's . . . her liver."

"That's not good. What about other injuries?"

"Busted leg and real bad gashes and bruises on and near her hip.

She went unconscious after they hit. They're hoping there were no head injuries."

We were silent for several minutes.

"They wanted to helicopter her to Minneapolis," Len said, "but they decided they couldn't wait."

We parked at the emergency entrance next to half a dozen ambulances that were poised to race off to the scene of some new accident. Time in the waiting room inched forward so slowly I had a feeling they'd stopped all the clocks. We tried to learn something from the nurses. Either the doctors didn't know or wouldn't divulge any information.

Two hours later one of the surgeons emerged. He removed his green cap as he approached. He was not tall, had a long face, and dark, thinning hair. I was stunned by how young he was. "Hi. I'm Ben Rosenberg." He slumped, exhausted, into a chair. "She's sustained extensive internal damage. We've removed her spleen, but that's not as serious as her lung. More damage than we thought." He shook his head. "She also lost a small piece of her liver. That liver of hers isn't the best one I've ever seen. We set her shoulder and left leg, the side where she took most of the impact. She's got a high fever, but that's to be expected."

"What's the overall prognosis?" I asked, unconsciously leaning against Len for support.

"She's incredibly strong," Rosenberg continued, "that's very much in her favor. But we really won't know for several hours." He sat down and then asked, "Either one of you type A Positive?"

"I am," I said.

He nodded. "We'll probably need some of your blood."

"She'll be in Recovery for quite a while," Rosenberg said. "Why don't you go home and get some sleep?" We stood up, shook hands, and thanked him. "I'll be here. People think we know exactly what will happen, but many times we really don't."

"Where's Aunt Nadine?" I asked as we were driving home. I was surprised not to see her at the hospital.

"Can't take waiting rooms. She's done enough of that. Believes in contacting Julie's spirit."

I asked to stay in Julie's room. I opened her closet. I smelled her clothes and smelled her. I looked in her drawers and touched her socks and underwear and sweaters and shorts. Every drawer.

Then back onto her bed, my head on her pillow. I began to sob, softly at first. I moaned and turned over, my face into her pillow. I sat up after a while, my face between my hands. "Oh, Lord, God, Maker of whatever we are. Please. Make it okay. Make her survive. She's good, and Lord, she's loved very much. Please help her." I dozed that night, but I did not sleep.

The next day, Rosenberg remained irritatingly noncommittal. He let us look in on her, but she was out of it. The endless tubes and the ghostly appearance of her face were devastating.

I knelt down beside her bed and whispered soft words, honeyed words, in her ear. No reaction. Promises I wasn't sure I could keep. Still not the slightest flutter of an eyelid. Silly things. Goofy things. Still nothing. I left feeling all the color in the world had drained away. Julie, more full of life than anyone I'd ever known, so deathly still.

The next day, Rosenberg, while still refusing to commit himself, was "cautiously optimistic."

"The odds?" I asked. "How much better than fifty-fifty?"

He remained silent, then shook his head.

"How much better?" I insisted.

"Fifty-two-forty-eight," he said at last.

"No better?" I importuned.

"No better."

"I'll take it," I said.

The following morning, Wednesday, Rosenberg greeted us almost cheerfully. "I'm very encouraged," he said.

"How encouraged?" I asked.

"Very," he answered. "In fact, I'm pretty sure she's going to make it."

"Odds?"

"Oh," he said shaking his head, "sixty-forty. No, that's my conservative side talking," he said. "She is definitely going to live. What I still can't answer is whether she's going to be the way she was."

"Julie's going to live!" I yelled, and hugged Rosenberg so tightly and so swiftly he must have thought he'd just hooked up with a grizzly. Then I let him go, and grabbed Len just as tightly. "That's all I wanted to know."

On Thursday, Len and I and Aunt Nadine — whom we had convinced hospitals were really fun places — tiptoed into her room, having endured the standard warning by the nurse: "Only a few minutes." Julie's eyes were open, unblinking, fixed on the ceiling.

"Well, Ms. Roppel, you seem to be getting a great deal of attention from strangers," I said. "We thought you might like to see a few familiar faces."

Julie turned her head slightly in our direction. "The three of you look worse than I must," she whispered. "What'd the FAA say?"

"The standard line so far," Len said. "They've pulled the plane out of the trees."

"That's no way to make a short field takeoff," I said, and immediately regretted it. "You've had a bad time, sweetheart, but the doctors say you're on your way to a full recovery." She frowned. "No, I'm telling you the truth. It may not seem like it now, but they say in a couple of months you'll be fit as a fiddle."

"Henry's right," Aunt Nadine said, bending over to plant a kiss gently on Julie's forehead. "That's exactly what Dr. Rosenberg told all of us."

"What about the school?" Julie whispered.

"Same as before," Len said. "Alfred panicked and froze. Everyone knows the crash had nothing to do with you."

"We'll lose students," Julie uttered faintly.

"Maybe a few," Len responded, trying to be upbeat.

The nurse came in to shoo us out. Julie asked for a moment alone with me.

"Henry," she began weakly, "even assuming I survive, I'm going to be a mess. Scarred. Disfigured. Maybe an invalid. I don't want you to wait for me. Understand?" A frail smile formed on her face.

"That, my friend, is not up to you. Do you remember? Up in Atlin you told me I'd never meet anyone like you. And do you know what? — I agree with you."

Julie motioned me over to the edge of her bed. I held her hand.

"You shouldn't wait for me," she whispered. She closed her eyes briefly. "I wish you could lie down next to me."

"Get better immediately," I commanded, "and I will. Only it won't be next to you."

"Oh, Henry," she said softly, "just when I'd come to the conclusion that just maybe you did love me, then this happens." She looked at the ceiling. "The body you loved is gone, Henry. What's left is a bloody mess." Then she looked back at me. "I know you — beauty's a necessary part of the equation for you. Not your fault, just the way it is. And whatever beauty this little half-breed might have possessed is gone, Henry. Gone."

"I don't give a damn," I said.

"*Yes* you do."

The nurse came in, furious. "Please," she said. "You *must* leave!"

I stood up and looked down at Julie. "I need you," I said. "And I love you, Julie."

She closed her eyes again, only this time her smile was not faint.

6

*B*ECAUSE of Julie's accident, the closing with Jack Phelan was put off for ten days. I wanted Ari and Ken present. Phelan was entering the relationship without having to guarantee anything personally, but he could lose his entire investment and also that of a group for which he had become the nominee. A courageous gamble on his part.

The offices of Jack's attorneys were located on Madison Avenue, a couple of blocks from 355 Park. The closing was scheduled for 9 A.M. A good hour earlier, I took a cab to the Seventy-second Street and Fifth Avenue entrance to Central Park. The air was filled with the smell of fallen leaves. Gray squirrels scurried everywhere, racing along the ground or dashing from branch to branch. I saw a few birds, and knew that soon robins and other migrants would pass through, tracking the sun to the south. I inhaled deeply, reveling in New York this time of year.

At 8:45, I walked — no, sauntered — back to Fifth Avenue. I wasn't concerned about the closing. It would occur, they would all be there. I thought about Julie, hoping she wasn't in too much pain.

"I see good color on your face," Phelan said, shaking my hand, as I walked in at one minute to nine. "Well, shall we get on with it?"

"Good morning, everyone. Nice to be with all of you." I poured myself a cup of hot coffee but resisted eating a *schnecken*.

The attorneys shuffled sets of papers, then laid them out on the conference table. The pattern was for one of us to sign first, the other to follow. Jack signed, looked up with a smile, and waited for me to sit down. I was standing at the large window, viewing Central Park, noticing the bustle on the streets down below. Light was filling the canyons like fresh water running down rows of parched corn. I felt captivated, and didn't move. It was as if the script called for the others to wait patiently for me.

Finally I turned and faced them. I looked at Phelan, then at Ken and Ari, then at Cal and Jack's attorneys. "Forgive me, I just wanted to savor this moment."

I walked over to the conference table, asked Phelan if I could use his pen, and signed all the documents. He sat next to me. When I finished, I handed him his pen and pushed back my chair. We both stood up.

"Jack, I . . ." We embraced in a bear hug. The others clapped.

"Well, Henry, it appears we've begun something special. I'm very pleased for you. Let me say that I have watched you change. I've been rough on you. For good reasons. You've grown and matured, even exhibited courage. But now you've added humility."

I nodded. "Thank you, Jack, from the bottom of my heart. For giving me this opportunity to come back. I promise you I'll give it everything I've got."

"I expect nothing less," he said, encircling my shoulder with his right arm.

"Except . . ." I said.

"Except what?"

"Well, I'm going to have to split my time between here and Wausau for the next few weeks. Oh, nothing will be neglected as far as the building. I guarantee you."

"Guarantee, Henry?"

"Sorry — you know what I mean. How about 'pledge'?"

"Much better, Henry. I've heard about your friend out there. Hope to meet her soon." He paused. "I understand she's quite special."

I hesitated a moment. "She's more than a friend, Jack."

We opened a bottle of Dom Perignon and toasted to our future success. I didn't actually drink any because I was going to fly. Then, after shaking hands all around, I left, drove directly to Islip and flew my plane low along the shores of the North Fork of Suffolk County. Flights of Canadian geese made their undulating V's southwesterly over Peconic Bay. I landed at Mattituck, walked to the pond a short distance from the airstrip, and sat quietly observing mallards and black ducks chattering in the lee of the wind.

The folks at Mattituck let me use their phone. I spoke to Julie, who congratulated me on the closing. She was still in the hospital but, as of today, she said she was able to sit in a wheelchair. She sounded better, her voice resonating with energy. I told her she'd better start practicing because, in case I'd forgotten to tell her, I was a professional wheelchair racer.

Several days later, I called her again at the hospital. They informed me she had been released. A full three weeks ahead of schedule. I called her at home, expecting Aunt Nadine to answer.

"Hello." It was Julie's voice.

"Julie. How're you doing? Congratulations on being home."

"Henry! Yes, I'm out. I didn't give them much choice. I told them I was going to blow up the joint if they didn't release me."

"I'm sure they took you seriously. Anyway, I'll be out in a week or two."

"Where are you?" she asked, and I heard disappointment in her voice. I knew she'd been hoping to see me sooner. "And what's happening with the deal of the century?"

"We have a few more things to finalize," I said. "I'm calling from the Getty building in Jericho. The Tip of the Tongue. Terrific food, great atmosphere. I'll take you here next time you come to New York." On the corner, I could see, lit by the streetlight: WAUSAU TRUST BANK.

"It's none of my business, Henry. But are you alone? It's all right if you aren't. Nobody likes to eat alone. I understand that."

"Catching up with an old flame, darling. Nothing to worry about, I assure you."

She didn't sound reassured. "Oh," she said. "Only an *old* flame. Well, enjoy your dinner. Talk to you soon."

I hung up and walked back to my car. Four minutes later I

parked, walked about two hundred feet, and noiselessly opened the front door to Julie's house. Sounds were coming from the living room. TV sounds.

I peered around the corner and saw the back of her wheelchair. "Don't you know too much TV is bad for the eyes?"

For several seconds, she didn't move, as if frozen. Then, "You shithead! I was just thinking of flying east with my tomahawk to scalp this blonde you were having dinner with — where was it? The Tip of the Tongue?"

"How did you know she was blond?"

"That's how I saw her."

"Oh, Julie." I kissed her gently on the lips.

"Henry, how long are you staying?"

"Not sure. How about forty years?"

"Henry, be serious. When do you have to return?" I shrugged and pretended I was about to sit on her lap. She pushed me off. "I don't like this. This is not you, Henry. How many scotches have you had?"

I pulled the ottoman over to her wheelchair and took a deep breath. I took her hand and said, "Forty years, Julie. You heard me the first time. Make it forever. For the rest of our lives. I know it wouldn't work for you in New York, but it's where I . . . Real estate's right for me, especially now that I can do it properly. When I'm not there, I'll be here. Say three days there, the rest of each week here. And, of course, weeks off and vacations."

Julie didn't say a thing, so I pressed on. "You'll still have the school with Len. We're dynamite together. And if you'll let me, we'll get a jet or two. What I'm trying to say is that I need you. You've made me understand so many things. About life. About me. About us."

She moved her face to mine, so close that all I could see was one oversized eye. "What happened to the ego maker?" she said. "The guy whose obsessive ambition constantly propels him to the top. Gone? Forgotten? On hold?"

"I'm not sure," I said. "All I know is I've found the woman of my life and I'm not about to let her go."

She gazed at me, dabbed the corners of my eyes, then shook her head ever so slightly. "Henry, do you really . . . believe . . . ?"

I was silent for a moment. "I do," I replied. "I won't pretend it'll be easy, Julie. If I worry, it's mostly about me."

I dropped to my knees and ran my hands gently over her bruised, bandaged face. "Julie," I said slowly, "what I want most of all is to be with you. Today, tomorrow, all the days of my life." I kissed her gently.

She tried to smile. "And how long do you think it'll be until you've bought up every decent building in Wausau?"

I shrugged. "I don't know. A year? Two? Never?"

Then she said, tears brimming, "Henry," kissing first one of my eyes, then the other, "if you still want me looking like this, it must be love."

"Is that a yes?"

Julie leaned forward, as far as the wheelchair allowed, and wrapped her good arm around me. After several moments, I leaned back, looked up, then back at her.

And for some reason I couldn't quite understand, I started clapping. Slowly at first, then faster and faster.